Seven Noble Knights

Seven Noble Knights

To Linda

J. K. Knauss

JKKnauss

Tempe, Arizona
2017

Published by Bagwyn Books, an imprint of the Arizona Center for Medieval and Renaissance Studies (ACMRS), Tempe, Arizona.

© 2017 Jessica Knauss.
All Rights Reserved.

Map © 2017 Jessica Knauss. Created by Nuno Alexandre Vieira.

Contents

The Characters in the Saga   1

Part One

Chapter I	5
Chapter II	9
Chapter III	27
Chapter IIII	33
Chapter V	47
Chapter VI	67
Chapter VII	89
Chapter VIII	105
Chapter VIIII	117
Chapter X	133
Chapter XI	143
Chapter XII	153
Chapter XIII	165

Part Two

Chapter I	181
Chapter II	203
Chapter III	219
Chapter IIII	233
Chapter V	243
Chapter VI	257
Chapter VII	267
Chapter VIII	277
Chapter VIIII	297
Chapter X	315

Historical Note	335
Sources and Further Reading	341
Acknowledgments	343
Reading Group Guide	345
About the Author	347

The Characters in the Saga

In Castile

García Fernández, Count of Castile

Doña Sancha, Lady of Lara, the most important region in Castile; Ruy Blásquez's sister
Gonzalo Gustioz, husband of Doña Sancha; the Lord of Lara
Their sons, the seven noble knights of Lara:
    Diego González
    Martín González
    Suero González
    Fernando González
    Rodrigo González
    Gustio González
    Gonzalo González
Muño Salido, the seven noble knights' tutor

Ruy Blásquez, a nobleman of Castile
Doña Lambra, his wife; Lady of Bureba, a region north of Burgos
Blanca Flor, their daughter
Álvar Sánchez, Lambra's beloved cousin

Justa, Lambra's maid
Little Page, Lambra's servant
Gotina, Lambra's maid
Adalberto, Lambra's servant
Luz, Sancha's maid
Ermenegildo Antolínez, Ruy Blásquez's vassal

A jongleur, a traveling musician
Fulgencio Benítez, Ruy Blásquez's vassal
Ramiro Mendoza, Ruy Blásquez's vassal

In Córdoba

Almanzor, chamberlain of the caliphs of Córdoba
Zaida, sister of Almanzor

Mudarra González ibn Zaida, son of Gonzalo Gustioz and Zaida
Yusuf ibn Iksandarani, Mudarra's guide

Hisham, Caliph of Córdoba
Ghalib, a general of Almanzor's army
Viara, a general of Almanzor's army
Isaac, Almanzor's physician
Fatima, Aysha, and other members of Almanzor's harem
Walid, Mudarra's chess master
The Governor of Segura, Mudarra's chess opponent

A Note on Spanish Names

The titles "Don" and "Doña" function about the same as "Sir" in English. They can only be used with first names. "Don Gonzalo" and "Don Gonzalo González" are correct, while "Don González" would never occur.

Medieval Spanish men frequently used patronymics for their surnames, ending in "-ez." Gonzalo González means "Gonzalo, son of Gonzalo," while that man's father is Gonzalo Gustioz, or "Gonzalo, son of Gustio."

Part One

974 A.D.

Chapter I

Gonzalo González peered between the wild grasses where once had grown someone's grain. He had lain in the dampness for so long that his boiled leather back plate and metal mail were weighing him down. He measured each fingerwidth of sunlight that revealed the golden stone walls of Zamora before him while the stars faded overhead. He had long since lost his sense of amazement at the Moors' audacity. Three hundred of them had set up their camp and war machines before the city's main gate, which remained barricaded.

He turned his face to see his uncle through the dewy stalks and whispered. "Why can't we charge the Moors now, while they're still asleep in their tents?"

"It's not the right time," Ruy Blásquez said through his teeth.

A groan escaped Gonzalo's mouth. It never seemed to be the right time for Ruy Blásquez. Gonzalo, his six brothers, and a hundred other knights had arrived at their vantage point in the dark, but they'd made no fire, set up no tents, done nothing to break the silence or the monotony for those hours. Even the birds that morning withheld their songs, waiting along with Gonzalo for something, anything, to happen.

Gonzalo pulled at the tufts of grass and wrapped leaves around his fingers, then plucked them out again, counting: it had been a summer, a winter, and most of a springtime since the city gates had opened. His stomach clenched to think of the innocent Christian people inside the walls. Had they roasted their dogs and horses or gnawed on their boot leather? Had the rain been enough to heal their parched lips?

"Why didn't the King of León ask for Count García's help earlier? We Castilians could've saved Zamora and gone home months ago."

"The King of León has concerns with Navarra and Barcelona and within León. He can't be concerned with Zamora and the Moors all the time. But I would've liked to be here months ago." Ruy Blásquez let out a snigger that caused a stir in the soldiers a few paces behind them with their swords, daggers, and bows. "This is your first foray for Count García. Months ago, you wouldn't have been here asking stupid questions."

"I've been into Andalusia with my brothers lots of times."

"Gonzalico, breaking a siege is not like your happy little raids, where your brothers protected you from Moorish sheep and chickens."

Gonzalo scowled. "Let me in there, uncle, and I'll show you how prepared I am."

"Hush!" Ruy Blásquez hissed.

Shifting his weight among the lumps in the earth, Gonzalo glimpsed a small figure creeping along the outside of the city wall. As the sky brightened, he estimated from his bare feet and the way his tunic fit that the blond boy had not completed ten years. He must have climbed through a hole in the barricades of a gate on the other side of the city. Gonzalo glanced at his uncle, whose older eyes hadn't caught the movement.

He smiled to see the boy reach inside one of the enemy tents and pull out a steel scimitar. The young Zamoran carried it to the foot of a wooden siege tower, where he pulled something out of his rope belt. When he struck it against the blade in a flurry of sparks, Gonzalo let out a chuckle. Apparently, the boy intended to free Zamora by setting the enemy camp ablaze. He would make a brave knight in a few more years.

A warrior emerged from the tent where the boy had taken the scimitar. A dagger glinted in the nascent sunlight behind the boy.

This was the time to attack, whether Ruy Blásquez willed it or not. Taking his first deep breath since sundown, Gonzalo rose up and covered the ground faster than his uncle could say "Wait," yet again. He thrust his sword into the infidel's unprotected back. The enemy fell, but it was too late. The boy lay contorted and blood flowed from his neck and seeped into the soil.

Gonzalo cursed and spat. Pausing to catch his breath, he turned in the direction of his battalion and channeled his rage. "Our patron, Santiago, is with us! Death to the Moorish devils!"

His uncle came howling toward the enemy camp, sword aloft, and Gonzalo's six brothers and the rest of the soldiers followed close behind, shouting "Santiago!"

When the murderer gurgled at his feet, Gonzalo hacked beneath his jawbone so that he bled as brutally as his last victim.

He picked up the boy and carried him, supporting his neck with care, to the cover of the siege tower while his cohort rushed past. The boy's eyes had already glazed over. Gonzalo cursed again. Why would God allow the Moors to take such a young soldier from the world? He shut the eyelids and folded the arms across the still chest. He made the sign of the cross on the boy's forehead. As soon as they had the Moors under control, he would make sure a priest blessed the boy.

"I will tell your mother how brave you were," he said. He unsheathed his sword again and leapt into the shouting, shoving mass of warriors. He would chase the enemy away for good.

Chapter II

Gonzalo felt a heavy hand on the back of his neck. He spun away from the bench and drew his sword to defend himself from the Moorish demon who was trying to claw Gonzalo's heart out of his chest.

"I see you *are* awake," said his eldest brother, Diego. He cupped the point of Gonzalo's sword and eased it downward. "We thought you'd dozed off."

Gonzalo's eyes adjusted to the mellow rays of afternoon light coming in the tavern windows. They caught the bronze highlights in Diego's hair, dark brown like his, like all the brothers. Martín, at the other end of the table, gathered up the black and white pieces of his chess set into their filigreed ark and slid the coins he must've won into the pouch in his belt. Suero stood near the door, fastening his stiff hawk glove to his left hand.

"Quickly, Gonzalico," said Fernando, his middle brother. "Father's outside waiting for us. The bride has arrived in Burgos at last!"

"Strange that the groom still hasn't," muttered Gustio, Gonzalo's nearest brother.

"That's exactly why we must meet the bride, to stand in for our uncle," said Rodrigo with characteristic attention to form.

The seven brothers stepped into the street, and the sunlight flooding between the eaves of the two-story buildings distressed Gonzalo's eyes. He embraced his father and his old tutor, squinting, then retreated into the shade behind the wooden columns. Their group wove in and out of the colonnades down the packed earth street, right, left, and right again, passing red and white flags draped from balconies and receiving effusive greetings from everyone they met.

No one knew what was keeping the groom, Ruy Blásquez. Burgos had been preparing for his wedding, a reward for saving Zamora, for five days, and Gonzalo hadn't slept more than a few hours in all that time.

There had already been music, chess games, backgammon, feasting, and friendly jousting matches in an area Count García had cleared out by the river. Gonzalo's family—his mother and father—had been sleeping in one of the red and white tents on the riverbank, and Gonzalo and his brothers had helped set up more of them for the bride, her servants, and their uncle.

When Gonzalo's father, the seven brothers, and their tutor passed through the gate in the grey stone walls of Burgos, the bride's tent came into view. Like the others, it was white with red seams, but twice as wide. At the top flew a purple flag, the only one of such a rich color among red, blue, green, and yellow ones. Gold foil castles, the emblem of their frontier county of Castile, decorated each section, and the door flaps shimmered with more gold foil. Two days before, Gonzalo had personally spread fresh straw on the floor. The tent contained a chest, a bed frame piled with silken pillows such as he had never seen before, and a table complete with a polished metal mirror in which any maiden should be thrilled to gaze upon herself. Gonzalo hadn't told his brothers, but it seemed as if the count were preparing for the arrival of a queen. Was this marriage a proportionate gift for Ruy Blásquez's service in Zamora? Gonzalo hadn't yet received any prize from Count García but a hearty handshake.

They stopped in front of the gilded tent. "Your mother must've gone inside," said their father.

"We'd best wait for them to come out. We don't want to crowd the bride," said their tutor, Muño Salido.

He proceeded to order the brothers according to their birth, creating a straight line with the pointed tips of their shoes and making sure no one's sword scraped against another's thigh. Gonzalo, always last, wondered about this mysterious bride, Doña Lambra de Bureba. All he knew was that she was only Gonzalo's age, but had already governed her own estate since her parents' death a few years before.

The tent flap lifted, and Gonzalo's mother looked out at them, beaming. Ducking back inside briefly, she reemerged holding a hand so white it almost wasn't there at all. Her maids had hardly had time to shake the dust of the road off a simple blue tunic, but Doña Lambra took the delicate steps of royalty. Her blonde braids shone with a light of their own past her slight waist. Though her mouth remained as straight as the line the brothers made, her red lips were round and inviting. Her clear blue eyes seemed to throw out sparks that sped Gonzalo's heart. The entire line of brothers, with their father and Muño Salido, held in their breath.

This was not meant to be the second wife of some undistinguished noble whose only recent claim to glory had truly been Gonzalo's doing. Gonzalo imagined riding a powerful brown horse to tour his own future estate, somewhere near Salas—no need to go far from home—with Doña Lambra astride the same horse, holding tight to his chest. Feeling the heat rise in his cheeks, he shook his head. She was going to be his aunt, no matter how much he might prefer her as his bride.

Gonzalo dimly took in that several people had followed Doña Lambra out of the tent. Aside from several servants, male and female, a blonde maid stood by Lambra, nearly as beautiful as her lady. Gonzalo grinned at her, and she demurely looked away. Count García surveyed the crowd with his gloved hands on his hips.

"Hey, Gonzalo, come and meet your future relative, and bring those sons of yours," the count said with a smile. "Ah, there they are! I would never have known, since they're so quiet."

The family, including young Gonzalo's mother, laughed. It was unusual, if not unheard of, for any of them to find themselves at a loss for words. Gonzalo's grin turned into a frown as the last person, a tall mass of muscle in an embroidered red tunic, left the tent. Álvar Sánchez's blond bulk was the only real threat to the González brothers' claim as the best knights at the wedding, or in all of Castile or León. Gonzalo had derived no greater pleasure than facing Álvar Sánchez in the daily jousts and knocking his proud posterior into the rocky soil of the riverbank. To Gonzalo's annoyance, there were also days like the one before, when Álvar had unhorsed Gonzalo and proceeded to deny him the right to finish the fight on foot.

He hadn't imagined Álvar Sánchez would be here now, but he was Doña Lambra's cousin, after all. Suddenly he noticed that not only did the cousins have the same shining hair, but also the same steely gaze. In Álvar, the sparks made Gonzalo want to prove him wrong, while in Lambra, they provoked more pleasant thoughts Gonzalo would have to will himself to ignore.

Doña Lambra stretched an arm toward Álvar Sánchez, and he stepped beside her to allow her to lean on his treelike strength. Gonzalo stopped himself from growling.

Álvar swept his arm to present the family to Lambra. "As you know, Doña Sancha is Ruy Blásquez's sister."

Gonzalo's mother looked dull and grey next to his new aunt. Around her neck hung an alabaster crucifix with rubies at the wrists and ankles. On anyone else, it might have gone unnoticed, but it overwhelmed his mother's tiny frame and distracted from her still youthful face. She clutched Doña Lambra's arm and breathed, "We're going to be sisters."

"Doña Sancha is also blessed to be the mother of the seven noble knights of Lara," Álvar Sánchez continued.

Sancha's face lit up again. "My pride and joy, all seven. This is my husband, Gonzalo Gustioz," she said. The rings on his fingers glimmered as he ran his hand over his tidy, greying beard, then took Lambra's hand to kiss it. Where his fingers weren't shining with amber, vermillion, and azure gems, they glinted with a golden sheen.

Young Gonzalo was sure Doña Lambra must be dazzled, but she gave no such sign.

She bowed her head. "My lord."

"Don Gonzalo is the most powerful man in the region of Lara," Count García informed Lambra, whose brow furrowed.

Gonzalo's father's hand modestly batted the count's words away. He showed Lambra to the head of the line, where he slapped the tall, bearded knight's shoulder. "This is my firstborn son, Diego González." Diego kissed Lambra's hand.

"Don Diego is my *alcaide mayor*, my highest representative in Castile," said the count.

Although she asked no questions, Lambra squinted at Diego, betraying her confusion. Young Gonzalo held in a guffaw while he imagined the things they must have told her about Ruy Blásquez, her husband-to-be: that he was the hero of Zamora and the most important knight in Castile. And yet her sudden nephews, older than Lambra, were nobler and held more titles than her husband. Gonzalo considered taking her aside to explain who the real hero of Zamora was, but knew he would look like a shameless braggart.

"Doña Lambra, this is my younger brother Martín," Diego said.

Martín grinned and kissed her hand while Diego continued, "He's the best chess player I know. Maybe he could teach you."

"Lady, your beauty reveals your nobility more than any title. You must already know how to play chess," Martín said.

"No, I don't."

"Then perhaps we will have a spare moment during the wedding celebrations when I can show you how. And my entire family would be honored if you come to visit us in Salas, the capital of the region of Lara. Once we're related by this marriage, we'll have feasts for you such as you have never seen."

Doña Lambra's cheeks reddened. Gonzalo thought she must be accustomed to flattery, but perhaps not from someone as handsome and as able to keep his promises as his brother.

Martín introduced his younger brother Suero, who kissed Doña Lambra's hand, making sure his hardened hawking glove stayed behind his back. High-ranking servants had been watching over Suero's goshawk in Count García's mews since their arrival, but Gonzalo knew he would seek it out soon. Suero didn't look right without a hawk on his arm. The first words he spoke were, "This is the middle brother, Fernando González."

Fernando gave a bow with military discipline. "Most honored, my lady." He gestured to the brother next to him, who had seven daggers of all shapes and sizes in his belt along with the sword. "This is my younger brother Rodrigo."

"An honor, my future aunt," Rodrigo said. "And here is my younger brother Gustio. If you dare, ask him a question. He'll never lie."

Doña Lambra raised her eyebrows. "Is that so, Don Gustio?"

"Never doubt it, my lady," he said as he made a sweeping bow.

"Then tell me, is your uncle, Ruy Blásquez...." Her voice started resonant, but tapered to a whisper while her eyes darted about, searching for a word.

Gustio didn't suffer from the same uncertainty. "We've known him forever. I love him as if he were one of us brothers. My brother Rodrigo is named for him. As to whether he's a good warrior, you have the siege of Zamora. As to whether he's honorable...."

"That will do, Gustio," cut in Doña Sancha. She took Doña Lambra's hand and patted it warmly. "And this is my youngest, Gonzalo. We call him Gonzalico."

Young Gonzalo grimaced at the pet name, but just as quickly flashed a smile at the pretty maid and at Doña Lambra next to her. He looked into those sparking eyes and detected a strong spirit. It was impossible to tell whether it was angel or demon.

Doña Lambra held out her hand for a kiss. Gonzalo grasped it and pulled her body toward his. He hadn't had time to imagine the thrill of her firmness underneath the tunic when the warm, grassy fragrance with a hint of sweet dampness floated off her hair and the wool. Perhaps it was the lack of sleep, or it might have been that Doña Lambra deserved a nobler, more vigorous husband, closer to her age. Before he knew what he was doing, he'd planted a kiss on the silken skin near that icy eye. He'd aimed for her lips and missed his target for the sole reason that she turned away and pushed against him with a firm "No."

His mother's "Gonzalico!" and Gustio's shocked stare reprimanded Gonzalo like a child, but it was Álvar Sánchez's raised fist that made him release Lambra's hand. To cover the protest he saw forming on her lips and his own pounding heart, he said, "Welcome to the family."

His brothers gathered around, so eager to tell Doña Lambra about their youngest brother that they jostled between her and Álvar Sánchez.

"Gonzalo's learning about law. I often consult him when cases come before me," said Diego, the eldest. Gonzalo smiled at him and mouthed a thank you. He never intended to test his family's ability to cover for him again.

"He's good at everything he tries," said Gustio.

Suero added, "He's even a decent hunter when I lend him my goshawk."

"Your goshawk?" young Gonzalo shrilled. "You're lucky I let you hold him sometimes."

"Now, boys," Muño Salido said over their boisterous teasing. "Let's act like the nobles we are." Scratching the chin under his grizzly beard, he stepped forward.

The crowd opened up and made a passageway between Doña Lambra and the older man, putting distance young Gonzalo did not think was coincidental between himself and his aunt-to-be. Young Gonzalo's father said, "This is Muño Salido, my sons' tutor. I entrusted him with every aspect of their education. They know nothing he doesn't know, and I've never been disappointed with the way he's raised them."

Muño Salido's cheeks turned pink under the white hairs at the compliment. He bowed toward Doña Lambra as deeply as his old bones could manage. "And now, my lady, I would like to teach them that we are imposing on you when you must be tired from your journey."

Count García chuckled. "Don't go yet. My final gift to my beautiful cousin is just arriving now."

Fifteen male pages dressed in bright blue tunics, hose, and suede shoes, marched toward the count. He opened his arms toward Doña Lambra, signaling their new mistress. Their brown hair fell to an identical length on their necks as they lined up and bowed before Doña Lambra's retinue until their caps grazed the ground.

"Oh, look at this darling little page!" the pretty maid next to Lambra said.

The page hadn't been noticeable when they were bowing, but now he stood a head shorter than the next shortest page in the row. His tunic swallowed him and his arms barely peeked out through the sleeves.

Lambra smiled. "How old are you?" she asked him.

"Twenty, my lady."

"Days, maybe, but certainly not years!"

Her ladies laughed. The page looked at his shoes, blushing.

The count stepped in. "If he doesn't please you, cousin, I can replace him."

"On the contrary, my lord, this is the most pleasing of all your gifts. I shall keep him with me always."

The pretty maid took his hand, "What's your name?"

"Teodemiro, miss," he stammered in reply.

"I'll never remember that," said Doña Lambra. "You'll have to answer to Little Page."

The maid whispered in his ear and he stood in surprised attention, but young Gonzalo noticed Doña Lambra was taking breaths as if to say something.

"Don't worry," said Count García, "I've provided your new servants their own tent next to yours."

Doña Lambra shook her head. She wrapped her arm around Álvar's as if she could no longer balance on her own. Finally, the pretty maid asked, "My lord, when will we have the pleasure of meeting the bridegroom?"

The count answered looking at his cousin. "He's not in Burgos yet, but I expect him soon. I'll let you know, and we'll have a formal betrothal that day."

A tear ran down Lambra's tense face. Álvar's hand looked like that of a giant as he tenderly brushed the tear away. Doña Lambra looked up at him in a way that made Gonzalo feel she would not dodge a kiss on the lips from him. Gonzalo felt sick. They were first cousins, practically brother and sister.

"We'll see you all at the wedding," Álvar Sánchez said. "And if nowhere else, at the tavern. I believe you know it." He stared at young Gonzalo, and although it was the last thing he wanted to do, Gonzalo looked away first. "Come, dear cousin, rest in this tent I prepared for you," said Álvar. He and Doña Lambra entered the tent and Gonzalo spat on the ground with rage.

"How dare that stupid beast take credit for the work we did on these accommodations?" he said to his brother Gustio, who shrugged.

"Did that give you the right to fondle our uncle's wife?" His laugh stung Gonzalo's ears.

"You can both look forward to a lesson with me later," said Gonzalo's father. He took Gonzalo's mother's hand and began to consult with the count. Doña Lambra's new pages headed to their tent and her maids filed into the bride's, but the pretty one remained speaking with the Little Page. Gustio winked at Gonzalo and by ancient, hallowed agreement, they eased toward the two servants.

"Hi, beautiful," Gustio said. Startled, the Little Page ducked inside his tent. Abandoned to the brothers, the maid eyed the tents around them.

"What's your name?" asked Gonzalo.

"Justa," she replied, "my lord."

"And are you as just and fair as your name?" said Gustio.

"Stop, you're scaring her," said Gonzalo to show her he could be trusted. She continued to tremble. "Look, in the clearing there's a jongleur tuning up his fiddle. Won't you come dancing with us?"

She backed away until she pressed against the bride's tent, but Gonzalo and Gustio followed. "I don't know the steps."

"That's all right, we'll teach you," said Gustio.

"I must return to my lady," whispered Justa. "She'll be very upset."

"So many maids and the most beautiful one can't leave the work to the others?" said Gustio.

A movement at the tent flap drew their attention. "Justa, our lady is asking for you," said a dark-haired maid with her belt cinched tight.

The blonde maid slid away and disappeared into the tent, but the dark one winked at Gonzalo. "My lady doesn't mind if I take my pleasure away from her."

"By all means, come with us," said Gustio, "whatever your name is."

"I'm Gotina," she said, taking Gustio's hand. She looped her arm through Gonzalo's. "Pleased to meet you."

Gotina must have had Moorish blood. Her curves and wriggling dances kept Gonzalo spellbound for hours. He had been prepared to let his brother have her, but memories of holding Doña Lambra drove him ever closer to Gotina's embrace.

The avid crowd, tossing small coins and cut pieces of bigger ones, made the jongleur saw away at his fiddle until all three strings broke. The crowd kept the beat clapping, and soon enough another musician stepped in with a double flute. With a look of horror, the fiddler ducked between dancing feet to gather his coins and ran inside the city walls, probably to find more strings. The double flute was louder than the fiddle and shrill in Gonzalo's ears. Somewhere beyond the swirl of skirts and tunics, he'd seen some bales of straw and was backing toward them even as Gotina grasped his hand tighter.

"Where are you going?" she shouted between the flute's shrieks. She wrenched Gonzalo's hand into the air and he realized they were doing a round dance, left and right, back and forth, arms up and down, pacing in a circle around and around the flutist, whose instrument could not break, who could keep playing until his lungs gave out. Gonzalo was no longer moving of his own will, carried by the other dancers and the illusion of Lambra in his arms. His body got heavier and heavier until his hands slipped out of the grasp of the dance and he stumbled atop one of the straw bales.

Gotina tried to sit in his lap. He stretched his back with weariness, and somehow her sleeve snagged on his belt. She pulled it out and shouted, "There's a hole. My lady will never let me attend at supper with a hole in my sleeve!"

"Shouldn't you go and darn it?" groaned Gonzalo, his head in his hands. "Or doesn't your lady have need of you?"

He heard no reproach or reply because Gustio had joined them. "Come here, my lovely," he told Gotina. "Gonzalo is too little to keep up with so much fun, but I'm bigger."

"All right," she said, sidling up to Gustio and putting her head on his shoulder. Gonzalo closed his eyes with relief.

"Tell me your worries," said Gustio.

"I can tell you think Doña Lambra is beautiful, and it's true, but the outside doesn't match the inside," Gotina told him.

"No?"

"It never has. She's always treated us like slaves, even though most of us are of noble birth. Justa was even raised alongside Lambra as a foster sister. Her parents were friends of the count, but Lambra beats her and starves her more than anybody else."

If that was true, it was no wonder the poor girl trembled when Gonzalo and Gustio talked to her. Gonzalo opened his eyes.

"And is Lambra pleased with this marriage?"

"No. She thought she would always rule Bureba without any interference. Count García came riding up to our front door with no warning. He didn't even write ahead, and Doña Lambra was chasing us around the hall to get a meal ready for him and his retinue. He announced that she was going to marry some knight we'd never heard of and she cried for hours, no, days. She flooded the table with tears and ruined our cooking efforts. What a disaster! She thought she could torment us forever, and now she's going to be some knight's plaything. How far the mighty fall."

"That knight is our uncle," said Gustio.

But something near the city gate seemed to have caught aflame. Gonzalo looked closer, and realized it was Doña Lambra. He couldn't tell what was golden brooch, what was shining silk, and what was smooth skin, almost too glorious to look upon. Her maids had crafted a sort of tunic, complete with headdress, out of the yellow silk Gonzalo had seen inside the chest in her tent. It was a gift from the count from among the Moorish spoils of war.

Justa and the Little Page accompanied the flamelike bride, who held Álvar Sánchez's arm close to her breast as they walked.

"Where are they going?" Gonzalo wondered.

"Who knows?" said Gotina.

"Look at the way she touches Álvar Sánchez," said Gustio.

"She's enjoying herself while she can. Before the count rode up, my lady used to say she would get a papal dispensation so she could marry Álvar Sánchez."

"What?" Gonzalo stared at the gate, although Doña Lambra had already passed through. Her longing for her cousin hadn't been a mystery, but Gonzalo would never have dreamed someone of such nobility would try to justify her base desires before God. Who was this prize bride? Gonzalo stood, and when Gustio and Gotina stood, too, they headed for the gate. Gonzalo's only intent was to follow Lambra and Álvar Sánchez, but his brother Rodrigo was inside the city wall, calling to him and pushing against the tide of people who also seemed to want to go where the cousins had gone.

"Where have you two been?" said Rodrigo. "We don't have much time. There's going to be bull baiting in the tavern plaza."

"Oh, I've always wanted to see that! Have you ever seen bull baiting, Gonzalo?" asked Gotina. She didn't wait for Gonzalo to ask if that was where his new aunt was going, but dragged her companions by the elbows, with Rodrigo close behind.

The plaza was a confusion of people trying to find safe vantage points on the second story. Three of the plaza's corners had already been sealed off with temporary timber walls, and the fourth wall was visible, ready to be wheeled into position. Gonzalo, Gustio, Gotina, and Rodrigo hurried up the stairs and made their way onto a balcony, where four more brothers and other men and women grasped spears and stones to throw at the bull that would appear below.

Gotina had ended up next to Gonzalo again. She was whispering, "When does it start?" when the last downstairs door was barred and the beast lumbered into the plaza ahead of a couple of boys waving sticks and shouting as they herded it. They dropped the sticks and helped several other men close off the fourth timber wall, and the bull was isolated. His black mass heaved mighty breaths and his horns looked sharp enough to cut the air while he tossed his head and pawed at the ground.

Gonzalo felt drawn to the balcony across the plaza, where Doña Lambra's stare sent an arrow into his heart. She was hanging onto Álvar Sánchez and once she unlocked her gaze from Gonzalo, she pointed at the bull and talked with Justa and the Little Page. Gonzalo couldn't look away so easily. Lambra's hands on Álvar Sánchez's tunic reminded Gonzalo of the grasping hands of the damned souls in the altarpiece in Salas. The demons in the picture stood placidly while the sinners flocked to them. The love between these two cousins must be stopped or this woman would bring nothing but sorrow and perdition to Gonzalo's family.

A man on the balcony opposite the bull lowered a red mantle and waved it vigorously. The bull darted across the plaza, the man pulled the mantle away, and, in the absence of the original target, the beast rammed its horns into the nearest door.

"My door!" exclaimed the shopkeeper above.

The bull wrenched out and turned this way and that until someone else on the opposite side waved a grey cape. This time, the citizens were ready, throwing homemade spears, lances, arrows, and rotten vegetables at the animal. Gonzalo stood back to observe while his brothers joined in the throwing. Diego's aim was true. A lance stuck straight out from the colossal muscle over the bull's neck. The animal stood still, heaving and eying the crowd from under the weakened muscle while objects continued to strike it from all sides. Blood ran from the wound down to the hard-packed earth. Forgetting to breathe, Gonzalo watched Lambra gesture as if she were forcing the lance into the bull's heart. She never flinched.

A cabbage knocked the lance loose. It fell to the earth with a dull thud. The bull snorted and lowed a long, mournful note that echoed eerily off the wooden fronts of the buildings.

A man on Doña Lambra's balcony flourished a red mantle, and when the bull finally decided to charge it, the man shot down a spear he had tied to a long cord so he could pull the weapon back up and throw again and again. Everyone in the balcony craned their necks to see the gore exposed under their noses as the bull's head sank lower and lower with every charge. Lambra gave no sign of wanting to look away, her eyes growing wider and wider. When the wound had opened, the man jerked up on the cord harder than he needed. The lance flew into the air, spattering an arc of blood across Doña Lambra's face and headdress.

Gonzalo's new aunt froze in place. The bull wasn't moving, either. The game was over.

Doña Lambra disappeared from the balcony, and the servants and Álvar followed. Gonzalo thought she must have gone downstairs to wash the blood off. He and his brothers pushed through the crowd on the balcony and snaked down the narrow staircase. When they emerged from the front door, Gonzalo stopped in his tracks. Still bloodied, a red and yellow butterfly, Doña Lambra approached the bull without hesitation.

The bull was splayed out on the ground in the same place where the lancer with the string had pegged him. The beast still struggled to breathe, but the butcher was coming through the barriers with his long knife to give the coup de grace. Doña Lambra leaned in close to the bull's ear, stepping in puddles of blood that still coursed out of his body. Gonzalo told himself to be revolted at the way she soiled her shoes and suspect she might spread such stains into his family, but at the same time, a deeper urge told him to take her in his arms and turn her bloodlust into pure lust.

"Stand back, Lambra," shouted Álvar Sánchez. At the butcher's shrug, Álvar lifted her up by the armpits. She kicked and struggled, but he turned her around several paces away from the bull, so that she faced away for the killing blow. Gonzalo and his brothers approached. By the time their aunt-to-be returned to the animal's side, he was dead.

She looked up at the butcher. "What are you going to do with it?"

"It's going to make several days of stew right here at this inn, even with the extra guests."

"No, it won't. This beast is too noble for stew. Tell the innkeeper to roast it whole. We'll have a great feast in honor of my upcoming wedding here in the plaza tonight."

The butcher scratched his head and eyed the front door.

"Don't worry, the count will see that it's paid for," Doña Lambra said. She looked up at the balconies and decreed, "You're all invited! Bring your relatives and friends!" Shouts and applause thundered around the plaza as the spectators came down and exited through the opening barricades to tell everyone they knew. Doña Lambra folded her arms and watched with obvious pleasure.

"This is quite a noble gesture, aunt," said Gonzalo, winking. The look she returned to him made Gonzalo feel as if he were a spider crawling among the filth. Gotina chose the moment to squeeze his hand where her lady couldn't see, then joined Justa and the Little Page.

Justa tugged on Doña Lambra's arm. "We need to get back to the tent so you can take off the yellow silk and I can sponge you off." But her cheeks were still smudged crimson when Gonzalo's mother and father joined the gathering from somewhere beyond the plaza.

"Boys, Lambra, my sister," said Doña Sancha. "I have wonderful news. My serving girl has seen my brother arriving through the city gate."

Lambra shook her head.

"My brother, Don Ruy Blásquez," Doña Sancha specified.

Doña Lambra looked as if an icy breeze had penetrated her.

"We'll have to go and meet him right away," Álvar Sánchez said, stooping to take her hand.

Gonzalo refused to give Álvar Sánchez the opportunity to parade Lambra around the city as if she were his bride, bloodied or clean. "I'll find our uncle and escort him here to meet Doña Lambra." His mother kissed him and sent Rodrigo and Fernando with him.

As they made their way through the crowded streets, Gonzalo wanted to ask Rodrigo, who knew the most about honor and matters of family, and Fernando, who was the most loyal of his brothers, whether they thought Doña Lambra was the best match for their uncle. He knew if he asked Gustio or Diego, they would only tease him about wanting Lambra for himself, and the idea was too true to bear speaking aloud. But before he could say their names, the crowd opened up to allow someone to pass. After the count's banner carriers and the count himself, the three brothers came face to face with Ruy Blásquez's straight-toothed grin. They each embraced him.

"Come, uncle, your bride awaits you," said Rodrigo.

"She's ready so quickly?"

"We've been preparing for six days, and she arrived this morning," said Fernando.

"Tell me," said Ruy Blásquez, grabbing Gonzalo's sleeve. "Is she as beautiful as they say?"

"Nothing anyone could say would capture her beauty, uncle," said Rodrigo.

"Oh no," said Ruy Blásquez. "I haven't had time to wash from the journey. She'll think. . . ."

"I hardly matters what she thinks," Gonzalo started. Before he could imagine how to describe Lambra beyond her physical beauty, they had arrived in the plaza behind the standard-bearers and Count García.

The group with his brothers, his parents, Álvar Sánchez, Gotina, Justa, the Little Page, and Doña Lambra seemed not to have changed. Looking closer, though, it appeared that Justa had succeeded in taking Doña Lambra somewhere to wash up. Her cheeks no longer displayed bull's blood, although the headdress still surrounded her face with discolorations. Justa looked nervously between the stains and Ruy Blásquez, and Gonzalo's eyes were drawn to where the silk skirt had picked up a neat line of blood when Doña Lambra had stood next to the bull. The hem brushed over the tops of her shoes as she moved, but it had dried.

Gonzalo went to stand with his brothers while his uncle embraced his mother and father and the count showed his flag bearers where to stand. Lambra ignored everyone but Gonzalo, or rather the blue tunic outlining his shoulders and gathering in folds over the front of his waist. He felt his cheeks getting hot and poised his face in the direction of Ruy Blásquez.

His uncle was only a little taller than Doña Lambra: Gonzalo was glad he wasn't shorter. She looked into Ruy Blásquez's eyes without tilting her head and he stared back with the intensity of someone awakened from a days-long dream. His hair and beard were a blend of brown and white. Gonzalo wondered whether she knew her husband had already completed thirty-five years. He wasn't smiling, which was to his disadvantage. Lambra might assume his teeth were broken and brown to match his rumpled, dust-covered travel cloak.

"At last you grace us with your presence, my lord." She curtseyed and held her hand out to be kissed, but he didn't move. "Has he never seen a beautiful noblewoman before?" she whispered to Justa, who laughed nervously. Ruy Blásquez blushed. Gonzalo gave his uncle an encouraging pat on the shoulder. His wife would have to learn either to keep her thoughts to herself or to whisper more quietly. She certainly couldn't go on shaming her husband with such words.

Finally, Ruy Blásquez took his bride's hand. A delicate sigh escaped him. "Doña Lambra." He seemed to savor the shape of the words in his mouth. "I'm sorry I couldn't meet you sooner. It takes at least three days to get to Burgos from Vilviestre, and I was absorbed into a group of pilgrims going all the way from Toulouse to Santiago de Compostela. They were slow and always complaining about blisters. I let the weaker ones take turns riding my horse, although I'm not sure it counts for the pilgrimage when they don't walk. I invited them to rest in Burgos for a few days and see the wedding. But what am I going on about? I'm honored to meet you." His lips touched the back of her hand and Gonzalo flinched, imagining the scraping of their dryness against her soft skin. No, he must not think about her soft skin or any other part of her. She was going to be his aunt.

Count García waited for Ruy Blásquez to let go of Lambra's hand. "Unless someone has an objection, we could have the betrothal right now."

For a moment, Lambra stood staring at nothing. Gonzalo thought he saw a tear forming at the tip of her eye, but just as swiftly, it was gone. "There is no impediment, cousin."

Doña Sancha passed in front of her husband and sons and held out a thick cord. "Begin, brother," she said smiling. "We're here to witness."

"I take your hand as a sign of my intent to marry you as soon as the count permits," Gonzalo's uncle said. He reached for Lambra's hand, but she didn't close the gap. Sancha looped the cord around their wrists, binding them together in a spiral although Lambra's fingers hung limp.

It was too quiet and solemn for Gonzalo. "Go ahead, kiss her, uncle!"

Álvar Sánchez moved his blond bulk between Gonzalo and Doña Lambra, so he couldn't see his mother take the cord back and free their arms. He heard only Lambra releasing her breath as if she had been holding it the whole time.

When Gonzalo nudged Álvar out of the way with snarls from both sides, he saw Ruy Blásquez pulling something small out of the satchel he carried under his traveling cloak. "I have this ring. . ." he began. He took Lambra's right hand and worked the object onto her finger. She pressed her hand into his as if it had great weight. "My scribe told me that St. Isidore says the fourth finger of the right hand has a vein that runs directly to the heart."

Through blanched lips, she rasped, "Thank you, my lord."

Count García conferred with Ruy Blásquez and the wedding ceremony was set for Thursday morning. Gonzalo smelled the bull beginning to roast in the inn. He watched Doña Lambra dart her gaze around the plaza, only to settle on him. He stared back at her, determined to see into her soul. She started and clasped Álvar Sánchez with more passion than she would ever show toward Ruy Blásquez. Gonzalo knew it in his heart.

He didn't know what to do. She wasn't suited to his uncle, but she was marrying him. If she was going to join Gonzalo's family, she would have to turn all her devotion to Ruy Blásquez, whether he deserved her or not, and forget about her passion for her cousin. Gonzalo needed to show his brothers the problem. Suero was holding the blinkered goshawk on his left arm and looking much more at home for it. Gonzalo caught his eye and gestured subtly toward Lambra's grip on Álvar, but Suero's only concern was that coddled bird. Gonzalo's mother linked arms with Ruy Blásquez. The whole family waved to Doña Lambra and Gonzalo's father promised they would return for the feast that evening. The count, preceded by his flag bearers, headed up the hill to his palace. The seven brothers accompanied their elders to show Ruy Blásquez to his lodgings on the riverbank. Gonzalo lingered, unwilling to leave Doña Lambra alone with only her closest servants and Álvar Sánchez. When the rest of his family had already left the plaza, Gonzalo looked back to see Gotina wink at him yet again. Doña Lambra buried her face in Álvar's broad chest, his thick arms encircling her the way a man's hand might cradle a sparrow.

Chapter III

For three days, Gonzalo had taken every opportunity to return to his family's tent and sleep. It was better than playing passive witness to Doña Lambra's antics, unable to convince anyone else of the problem of carrying on with Álvar Sánchez when she was to marry Gonzalo's uncle. Why couldn't they understand the risk Lambra posed to their family's honor?

By Thursday morning, he felt so well rested, he smiled at Gotina, waiting as she had every day outside his tent. He could still feel a little ache on his sides and shoulders where her fingers had prodded him to go dancing or run in the joust and not sleep his life away—what was he, an old man? But today, she blew him a kiss and waved and headed back to Doña Lambra's tent, where she must be needed to prepare the bride. Gotina's braided hair, shining like strings of black pearls in the morning sunlight as she walked away, made Gonzalo sigh with relief. He couldn't do his duty by his family and entertain her as well. Now he wouldn't have to.

He followed his mother, father, tutor, and brothers to the plaza, where Ruy Blásquez already paced outside the stone cathedral with its square tower and gabled roof, his hands clasping and unclasping as he watched his shoes and the hem of his tunic.

"Nervous?" said Gonzalo's father, taking Ruy Blásquez's arm. "It's not your first wedding. What could bother you today?"

"My first sister-in-law was nothing like Doña Lambra," admonished Gonzalo's mother. When Ruy Blásquez gave a strangled cry of panic, she embraced him. Gonzalo knew her arms provided great comfort, even though she only came to the middle of his chest. "But my husband is right, brother. You've been married before, happily, although she couldn't give you children. Never mind anything else. We'll be here with you to make sure all goes well."

With that, she shooed her sons away from the cathedral door and drew dried herbs and flowers from pockets Gonzalo hadn't known were inside her tunic and cloak. With a stick, she carved a large circle on the hard earth. More people arrived to take their places around the square, including guests from León, Navarra, and France, monks, nuns, and priests, and the plain folk of Burgos. Doña Sancha set the herbs and flowers inside the circle in a pattern with meanings she might have shared with a daughter, but were a mystery to Gonzalo.

"You'll stand here," she told her brother. "When your bride comes from that side, you'll step inside the circle together." She arranged her husband and sons on Ruy Blásquez's side of the circle with as much care as the flowers. Gonzalo, always last, ended up next to his uncle, so close he could hear each shallow breath he took.

Count García arrived with a full complement of knights and squires and four banners in white with red castles, as well as a fiddler and a flutist who made ready to play. So many people in the plaza must have been making the loudest ruckus since the city had been won from the Moors, but Gonzalo heard nothing.

From between the buildings at the far end of the plaza emerged Gotina, dancing to make her braids fly through the air and strewing flower petals before forty women who walked with their hair covered to emphasize their married status. Their laughter and singing couldn't distract Gonzalo from Doña Lambra, who tottered on their shoulders.

An heirloom beaded necklace competed with her yellow hair, shining in tight plaits on her shoulders with ornamental brass tips that looked as if they had come out of a treasure chest long ago. A mail girdle, inlaid with brass and pieces of jet at the edges, cinched her bright blue tunic from under her breastbone to down over her hips. Gonzalo shivered at the thought of the bitter touch of the matching mail sleeves, from the decorated wristlets up to her shoulders. A burgundy-colored cloak edged with three rows of golden braid was fastened over her shoulder with a gilded brooch in the shape of a lion rampant. The brooch must have entered her family to be worn in the court of León long before the County of Castile had been reconquered from the Moors. A square cap, decorated all around with braid and gold carbuncles, looked like a royal crown. Gonzalo imagined he wasn't at his uncle's wedding, but that this bride had come from the farthest reaches of Christendom to marry the King of Navarra or León.

The married women set Lambra down in the middle of their ranks, then filed out in two rows to make a path to guide her. She let the cloak fan out behind her unsteady stride. Her face was frozen into a grimace like the one the Virgin Mary wore as she cradled the Savior's dead body inside the cathedral.

The contrast made Gonzalo remember Lambra's grin at the banquet days before, when her mouth had dripped red with juices from the roasted bull's testicles and the sauce-engorged bread trencher. Each time she received the goblet, she had made sure to turn it so that her lips didn't touch the same spot as Ruy Blázquez's. She didn't take the same precaution against Álvar Sánchez, seated on her other side. Gonzalo could hardly taste his food through a choking desire to throw his eating knife across the table into the gloating knight's hand so it could never touch Lambra so familiarly again.

There he was now, that upstart Álvar Sánchez, wearing just as juicy a grin, so close to Doña Lambra that the obnoxious curl on the toe of his boot intruded on the magic circle.

"What is that blasphemous behemoth doing there? Shouldn't a member of the groom's family stand next to the bride?" Gonzalo whispered to Gustio.

Gustio knocked his elbow into Gonzalo's ribs. "Why? Were you hoping it would be you, little brother?" He chortled until their mother hissed at them to be silent.

Count García was addressing the crowd, "... with these deeds, Ruy Blásquez has earned as a bride my most lovely cousin, probably the most beautiful woman Castile has seen since my mother joined the Kingdom of Heaven. May they live many more years and have many loyal Castilian children." He raised his arms high, which the crowd took as a sign to cheer and shout.

Gonzalo noticed that his uncle had already moved into the circle and reached for Lambra's hands, still weighed down with that prodigious ring. She was looking at Ruy Blásquez, but not with love or even curiosity. It was a look of judgment. Gonzalo tried to imagine how his uncle's soft eyes, long nose, and weak chin fared on Lambra's scale. He crossed his arms with impatience.

"I receive you as mine, so that you become my wife and I your husband," Ruy Blásquez said. Gonzalo was relieved to glimpse him smiling widely, displaying his straight, white teeth — undoubtedly his best feature — to his judge in the form of a bride.

Ruy Blásquez smiled and waited, waited and smiled. Gonzalo witnessed a thousand expressions cross Lambra's face like clouds in a stormy sky. At last, Justa emerged from the crowd and leaned over the circle so as to reach Lambra without invading it like Álvar Sánchez on the other side. "I receive you as mine..." she prompted so quietly that Gonzalo had to read her lips.

"I receive you as mine so that you become my... husband... and I your... wife," said Doña Lambra, her eyes narrow. She pulled her hand away from Ruy Blásquez to wipe at her plump lips, as if the words had sullied them.

She craned her neck to look at Álvar Sánchez and Gonzalo knew she wished she had said the words to him. His heart beat faster. Then she shifted her gaze to Gonzalo. He felt as if he were smothered with the parsley, fennel, red carrot, and beet sauce from the banquet. Such was the hunger he saw in her eyes, a hunger he couldn't help but feel, too, and which raged all the more, the more he tried to contain it. He remembered the way the bull's testicles had flopped onto Doña Lambra's trencher under their own weight and the way they deflated when she plunged her knife into the center of the sacs.

He stopped a startled cry in his throat.

The crowd shouted and clapped until his ears rang.

Justa took Lambra's hand and slid something into it. Lambra held it over Ruy Blásquez's hands and let five *sueldo* coins fall into the cradle he made.

No one spoke for a moment. "Those stand in for the dowry," Justa explained.

"My parents died five years ago. We'll be Lord and Lady of Bureba, but that's the only dowry I have." Lambra squinted at Ruy Blásquez as if awaiting a response to a challenge.

"It's enough," he said. He folded her hands into a cup and poured the coins back in. "And this is my bride price."

She accepted the coins with a blank expression and Justa took them away. Two of the married women approached and tugged the regal cap from her head to let the sunlight fall onto the part down the center of her scalp. They untied her braids and smoothed her long hair into a sheet that covered most of her back, then placed a garland of wildflowers as a new crown. One of the women set another garland on her new husband's head. Doña Lambra's face loosened into a smirk at the sight.

Count García led the crowd in jubilant roar. "And now, Ruy Blásquez makes Doña Lambra Lady of Vilviestre, and they hold lands together, wedding gifts from me."

"Long live the newlyweds! Long live the newlyweds!" The crowd shouted until they were the only words Gonzalo remembered ever hearing.

Doña Lambra's mail girdle made a metallic sound as the married women swept her onto their shoulders. A crowd of men from Burgos raised Ruy Blásquez in the same fashion, and Gonzalo and his family followed as the newlyweds rode through the streets atop the strange, lumbering animals. The bride and groom were ferried past the city gate and set on the riverbank in front of Doña Lambra's red and gold tent.

A priest entered the tent as if it were his own, and other priests held the flap open. A choir boy tossed flower petals over the colorful pillows on the bed with a giggle. The priest swung a burning censer over the bed in the form of the holy cross three times. He exited the tent and placed his hand over the garlands on both of the newlyweds' heads in blessing. Ruy Blásquez took Lambra's hand in his and led her inside the tent. When the priests dropped the tent flap, the crowd gave a final cheer, then dispersed.

Gonzalo's family turned to each other to talk over what they would do next, so he slipped out of the confusion to stand right beside the tent and listened.

"Alone at last," came his uncle's voice, only slightly muffled.

"Yes," Lambra answered, more difficult to hear. "Now we have a chance to talk. Sit with me a moment."

Gonzalo leaned closer. The bedstead with its mound of pillows was on the other side of the barrier.

"Listen," she said with no deference to her new lord. "You and I are nothing separately. We each hold small territories, and now the count has granted us some little bit more. But together we can become the most powerful family in Castile."

"Do you think so?" He sounded surprised or puzzled even through the tent fabric.

"Who is the most powerful family now? The Gonzálezes of Lara. Your sister's family. But you are the male heir of your father, so who is she to prosper so and share none with us? You should be the one sharing wealth with her, don't you agree?"

"I never begrudged..." he began.

"Together we can find the way to make the count choose you as his *alcaide mayor* over Diego González. Your sister's family must yield their rank to you. Then all will be right in Castile. Will you let me help you... my lord and husband?"

As Gonzalo drew his hands to his dry throat, he thought he heard low murmurs and the sound of mail crushed against wool.

He put his hands over his ears, made the sign of the cross over his chest, and clasped his hands over his pounding heart. He must've heard wrong. Doña Lambra wouldn't hate his family so much, and certainly his own uncle wouldn't join her in that cause since he was a part of Gonzalo's family. He felt himself beginning to fall against the tent, so he turned around, only to see Gotina's laughing face. She must have been nearby throughout the wedding and the procession, but Gonzalo hadn't spared attention for anything but Lambra.

"Everyone is wondering where you are, my lord G —"

He muffled his name with his hand. Her lips met his palm, soft and wet. He moved his hand away and kissed her. When she opened her mouth, accepting his will without question, he imagined her lips were as round and red as Lambra's. He remembered Lambra's clean, summery smell as he pressed Gotina closer. He pulled her out of sight behind the tent and she tumbled to the grassy riverbank with a giggle. She pulled her skirts up over her thighs and he pushed into her, placing his hand back over her mouth to mute her grunts. When they heard Lambra's cry of virginal pain through the tent wall, they froze, but only for a moment. He matched his rhythm to Lambra's moaning, which came louder each time.

Gonzalo might have forgotten what he'd heard through the tent and gone on to enjoy the rest of the celebrations after Gotina's timely embrace.

But looking into his eyes, she must have understood that her body served as a substitute for her lady's. She opened her mouth to let his fingers in, then bit down, drawing blood.

Chapter IIII

Doña Sancha woke to the glow of morning light inside the tent and shouting outside. She sat up, pushed back her hair, and saw the floor of the tent empty, as it had been the night before. She didn't know whether her seven sons had awakened already or hadn't come to sleep yet. "How do they keep up this pace for so many weeks?" she wondered aloud.

Her husband, Don Gonzalo Gustioz, stirred beside her, groaning. "It can't be morning already, Sancha."

"I'm afraid it is, dear heart. Haven't you heard the noise outside?"

He shook his head vigorously, his eyes still closed. She ran her fingers through his whitening hair — not as white as hers was grey — and traced the creases along his cheek. She loved her sons, but they were mysterious to her. Her husband, on the other hand, seemed like a portrait of her eternal soul.

"Do me the honor of finding out what's happening. It could be the Moors come to sack Burgos, for all you know."

"They'll never make it up here again." His eyelids fluttered. Only when he looked on Sancha with his laughing eyes did he still reveal the vigor he'd passed on to his sons.

"Well, the Navarrese, or the French, then. Go on, lazybones." She playfully pushed her husband until he rolled out from under the blanket. She washed with the bowl and linen on the table, slipped on her tunic, and smoothed and bound her hair while he greeted whatever was making that racket on the riverbank. She checked the crucifix on its long gold chain around her neck, and had finished fastening a curl-shaped brooch to secure her mantle when her husband appeared between the tent flaps, grinning.

"Come and see for yourself what your brother's having done."

Sancha held his hand and they took to the riverbank. The wind carried a fragrance of grass and late summer flowers. It stiffened the multicolored flags atop the tents and that marked the boundary of the jousting area, where a square-turreted Moorish castle had sprung up overnight. Twenty men worked in their undergarments, putting the finishing touches on a wooden scaffolding nearly the size of a real castle that tottered in the breeze on the edge of the river. People, some in rags and others in gaudy finery, stood staring at the strange bulk.

"Ha! I told you it was the Moors come to take Burgos." She spotted Ruy Blásquez, who was giving final approval to the project. "Did you do this, brother?"

"Yes. I'll give a prize to the winner. This is the only thing this wedding has been missing. I wanted everyone not from Lara to see one of our most exciting customs."

"Including Doña Lambra. Has she ever seen lancing the scaffold?"

Ruy Blásquez blushed. "I don't know. Do you think she'll like it?"

"She certainly will." Sancha looked into her brother's eyes and barely recognized the quavering man behind them. "Where is she?"

"Asleep in the tent, as far as I know. I hope the noise didn't wake her."

"I'll get her. She must see this wondrous present you've given her."

Sancha was still seeking a way to get to know her sister-in-law. In the three weeks since the wedding, Doña Lambra had spent little time with Sancha and her seven sons. Whenever they ended up together to watch a joust or hear music, Lambra hid behind the three who were always at her side: Álvar Sánchez, her serving girl Justa, and that funny Little Page. Sancha remembered her young self, timid and overwhelmed at her own wedding festivities, so many years ago. But there wasn't anything timid about Lambra, the way she'd waded through the bull's blood and torn through its testicles. Something must be provoking her coldness. She would have to move beyond it now that she was a part of their family.

Sancha snatched back the tent flap, calling for her sister-in-law, but the bride's residence was empty. She turned around and saw one of her own serving girls in the throng that had come to see the wooden castle.

"Luz, do you know where Doña Lambra is?"

The maid curtseyed. "No. I'm sorry, my lady."

Where was that girl? A bride's place was with her groom. "Have you seen my sons?"

"Yes, my lady. Don Martín is playing chess in the inn, and his brothers are watching. And betting."

Sancha took the maid's arm and they made their way through the crowd, toward the city and the inn. "They won't want to miss this, no matter how much they're betting. I wonder who would bet against Martín? Everyone knows he'll win."

"He's playing against Don Fernando, and if I may be frank, I think he's going to let Don Fernando win so they can collect the wagers. It was Don Gonzalico's idea."

"God save me!" Sancha exclaimed. "The devil gets into that boy every way he can." Sancha hadn't seen the Gotina girl near Gonzalico since the wedding ceremony. They must've had a spat. It was just as well, because he shouldn't spend time with someone below his station. "Luz, do you know whether they slept last night?"

"My lady, I would guess they think it's still night."

Doña Sancha threw open the door of the inn, casting daylight into the murk surrounding a crowd of gamblers pressed around a chessboard with her seven sons. Their symmetrical faces shone with interior light, like saints in an altarpiece. Sancha shook her head. If people who stayed up all night to gamble needed a patron saint, they should make their choice here.

"Mother! Good morning," the seven said in melodic unison.

Doña Sancha sighed. "I shouldn't even tell you. I should take you all back to Salas this instant."

"What shouldn't you tell us?" asked Gonzalico, grinning as he stood up to embrace her. He had been knighted the year before, but his mother still had a hard time understanding that this earthy, musky, male smell came from her youngest son. His soft boy-stubble scraped her cheek.

"Your uncle has set up a scaffold castle on the banks of the Arlanzón and called on all the knights to try to knock it over with their lances. He's going to give a prize to the one who does the most damage."

The whole inn shouted with glee. Everyone stood up and made to go to the riverbank, but Martín stayed at the chessboard. "I'm nearly finished here. What about the bets?"

"Oh, come on," said Gonzalico. "The prize will be much greater than any winnings we can take here, and one of us is sure to win."

Martín nodded and gathered up the pieces as the bettors scrambled to take back their wagers.

They surrounded their mother as they made their way back to the riverbank, with everyone else from the inn trailing along. Sancha thought perhaps Doña Lambra might warm to them if her sons would stop showing off so much. "I want you to promise me that you won't compete today," she pled with the seven of them. "It would be unseemly for your uncle to give you a prize. You're already the most honored knights in Castile. What more could you want?"

"Yes, of course," came the reply, uneven and muffled in the hustle. She thought they all agreed, but couldn't be sure she heard seven voices. Suero's goshawk squawked sleepily. If Suero hadn't slept, the poor bird hadn't slept, either. The strange young man Sancha sometimes couldn't believe she was related to now took the hawk with him always, in the name of training.

"And where is Muño Salido?" asked Sancha. "He should be keeping you from gambling."

"Oh, he went to bed ages ago," said Gustio.

Sancha sighed again. How could she expect their old tutor to keep up with a single one of these young men, let alone seven?

At the riverbank, Doña Lambra was standing with her maid Justa and the Little Page as if she'd been there for hours. In a new tunic and mantle sewn from the yellow silk, with no trace of a stain, she contrasted with the other ladies' wool dresses like a translucent piece of amber on a dry, dead trunk.

"Good morning, Sancha," she said. "What is this scaffold business?"

"It's a custom we have in the region of Lara. The men run against it with their lances as a test of strength. And they don't have to cover up in armor like they do in jousting, so we ladies get to watch them in their best clothes." Sancha pointed to the women alternately rushing toward the river to make sure they had the best view and stepping back when one of the men, knights who owed fealty to Ruy Blásquez, explained how much room the contestants would need. The women stayed back only when armored soldiers bearing the insignia of Castile formed a line running from the wooden structure to the starting point several yards along the bank.

A gasp of surprise went up from the onlookers when they saw that the first knight to ride his horse up to the mark was Count García himself. He paused just long enough to let his subjects see what a fine figure he cut in a tunic festooned with red and gold embroidered castles and a new lance painted bright red that looked as solid as steel. He dug his heels in and began the charge. A brown-haired girl slipped past the guards and scampered into the horse's path. Startled, the count steered his horse into the water, flinging the lance haphazardly toward the castle over the girl's head. Her shouting mother burst through the human barrier and scooped the girl up, unscathed.

Count García's strong-looking lance had snapped in two without making a dent in the castle's surface.

Doña Lambra looked in Sancha's direction. "I can see why this is interesting. A less able horseman than the count would've gone straight to the ground."

Sancha was pleased that Doña Lambra shared her thoughts with her, but then saw Justa standing between them, so the confidence was probably meant for her. Out of the corner of her eye, she saw the hoary head of Muño Salido, who must have joined her sons in the crowd during the spectacle. Don Gonzalo stood beside the tutor, so Sancha drew her husband to her and they stood with their arms linked while they watched what would happen next.

Count García brought his mount splashing through the shallow water to the riverbank and laughed for all to hear. Ruy Blásquez hurried to meet him. He took the reins and patted some of the water off the horse. "Are you wounded, my lord?" he asked in a thin voice that nonetheless carried to the crowd.

The count made some exaggerated nods and more guffaws. "The only thing wounded is my pride."

Ruy Blásquez turned toward the crowd and announced, "I will take a run at the scaffold before the competition begins."

Doña Lambra gazed at him anxiously, hugging her arms to her body, as he strolled to the starting line.

"Don't worry," said Sancha, "my brother, your husband, is the most talented knight among these here gathered."

"We'll see," the lady muttered. Her eyes glistened in the sunlight even more than her jewels. Sancha had asked a scholar she'd met during the festivities, and he'd explained that "Lambra" meant "little flame," but at this instant she seemed to grow into a raging fire.

Ruy Blásquez plunged forward without a horse. He looked at his wife, expectant on the sidelines, and ran as though his life depended on it. His legs flailed and he released the lance as he tumbled to the ground.

A gasp went up from the crowd. Doña Lambra bowed her head in disappointment, but Sancha witnessed the supernatural moment when the spear glanced off the scaffold and loosened two of the machicolations with a loud crack. Ruy Blásquez rolled himself into a standing position almost as quickly as he'd fallen. He stared at the unexpected damage and declared, "I pronounce this scaffold ready. Let the lancing begin!"

The laughter and cheers prompted Doña Lambra to look around at the faces, as if to detect any mocking. Sancha put a hand on her shoulder to reassure her, but Lambra shrugged it off her bright silk. Hurt, Sancha looked to Don Gonzalo, who smiled at her and shared comments as each contestant came to the starting line.

Fifteen or twenty knights, some on horseback and some on foot, tried in rapid succession to knock the false castle down, but obtained no better result than their count. Ruy Blásquez waded through the crowd to stand beside Doña Lambra, covered in streaks of dust and carrying his intact lance like a staff. Sancha watched as her brother's other hand hovered behind his new wife's back, never daring to rest on the silk, so close to the lady's skin underneath.

Justa leaned toward Lambra and was whispering something Sancha couldn't quite hear about her having the most virile husband, when a ray of light glinted at the starting mark on horseback.

He wasn't wearing mail, so the radiance of his person was inexplicable until he looked toward Doña Lambra and smiled. His eyes hinted that the same kind of flame burned inside him as did in Doña Lambra.

"It's Álvar Sánchez!" she exclaimed.

Sancha rolled her eyes at Don Gonzalo — they both knew only too well how proud Lambra was of her cousin. Sancha had allowed her some favoritism because there weren't many people from Bureba at the wedding. But could she be so blind to the virtues of the knights of Burgos, especially Sancha's sons? Still the lady went on, eying her new nephews. "By himself, Álvar is worth more than all the other knights together."

Gonzalico grunted behind Sancha, and she recalled how often he had narrowed his eyes across a table at Álvar Sánchez. For weeks, he had been trying to tell his brothers something about Álvar, that he was some kind of threat to the family. Beyond simple rivalry, Sancha hadn't been able to imagine what her son was seeing. Now she watched closely to find out if the knight would give some sign of whether he meant them good or ill.

A servant handed a lance up to Álvar Sánchez. He needed not a moment to ready himself: his raising the lance and the horse's charge were one motion. As soon as he'd aimed the spear, it made a cracking sound so loud it must have been heard within the city walls, if not back in Zamora. The scaffold broke nearly in half, such that one side of the castle, along with the loosened machicolations from Ruy Blásquez's shot, hung crazily from the other side. The throng of viewers remained silent in disbelief for a moment and then roared their approval. The trumpeters made it known that Álvar Sánchez had won the day.

Doña Lambra turned to Sancha and said over the continuing din of the crowd, "See what a great knight Álvar Sánchez is! He's the only one who could hit the scaffold." She turned away, and could not have meant what she said next to fall on anyone's ear: "If only he weren't my cousin, I wouldn't refuse him any token of my love."

Ruy Blásquez's face turned a deep shade of red, and Sancha's heart sank because she knew he'd heard. How could any lady say such a thing about another knight in the presence of her husband? Sancha chuckled to make it seem as if Doña Lambra had been joking, and most of her sons behind her joined in with hearty laughter.

But young Gonzalo emitted no sound. He took the arm of a page and marched to the starting line.

"Gonzalico, what are you doing?" shouted Sancha, but her voice was lost in the tumult.

She watched with her hands clasped around her crucifix as the page procured her youngest son a lance. Without ceremony, and with the multitude still celebrating Álvar Sánchez's blow, he ran at the castle, as precise and speedy as an arrow. He launched the lance into the middle of the undamaged section. The sound made the rest of the crowd look in time to see the top half of the remaining side follow the already broken section teetering to the ground.

Sancha's heart leapt with joy at her son's strength. She caught the breath she had been holding and she, her husband, and her other sons led the crowd in the loudest cheer of the day. All that remained of the scaffold was a single upright which, had it been a real castle, wouldn't have protected a single Moor. Soon enough, the trumpeters would sound their endorsement, most likely with Ruy Blásquez's permission.

But the tight enclave around Doña Lambra did not yell or even enjoy Gonzalico's capering as he accepted praise in the form of shouts and tossed flowers. Sancha observed that the silent group created its own energy, like the eye of a storm. Gonzalo made his way through the crush of spectators toward his family with his prizes.

"Ha ha! With those flowers, you look like the bride of this wedding celebration," said Suero, shifting the weight of his goshawk on his glove.

"Well done, little brother," said Diego.

"I wonder what our uncle's prize is going to be, now that you've won it," Gustio said.

Sancha took young Gonzalo into her arms. He wasn't as tall as some of the knights in Burgos, but he towered over her. "We knew you could do it, my dear one. But why didn't you keep your pledge to your mother not to compete?"

He bent down to kiss her cheek. "I never promised."

As her son escaped her embrace, Sancha felt a chill. She wondered when she had lost control of her son, or whether she had ever had any influence over him.

Álvar Sánchez led his steed through the crowd to come to Doña Lambra's side. She didn't smile, but he took her hand. "Don't fret, cousin. I have no need of your husband's prize, whatever it may be. I can earn all the wealth I need in the count's service with my bravery, my skills, and my horse."

Gonzalico turned to Álvar Sánchez. Sancha thought it must have been the first time they'd looked each other in the eye since before the wedding ceremony.

"You're a very good lancer, Don Álvar, and the ladies like you, too. They don't speak of any other knight but you."

Sancha imagined her son was attempting to be a gracious winner. Everyone there knew what he said wasn't true: the ladies had been cooing over Gonzalico ever since the family had arrived. Álvar was a good jouster and handsome enough, but the only one who preferred him to Gonzalo was Doña Lambra.

Álvar Sánchez let go of Lambra's hand, puffed out his already enormous chest, and bared his teeth. "They have every right to speak of me, since they understand that I'm better than all the knights here. Even you."

Gonzalo drove his fist into Álvar Sánchez's smirking face. Álvar collapsed at the feet of his horse, and it reared with a shriek that sounded the way Sancha felt. With nowhere else to land in the crush of people, its sharp hooves came down on Álvar's flesh. He grunted and threw his arms out to defend himself, but it reared again and again in terror and confusion, coming down harder each time. Don Gonzalo shielded Sancha's face from the flying dirt clods and tufts of grass. A few more sharp cries and Álvar was silenced even as men shouted at the horse and pages darted under it, dodging the deadly legs as they tried to pull Álvar to safety. His teeth bounced and rolled on the earth or landed on people's shoes like cast dice. Young Gonzalo reached for the horse and seemed to hold the mane in his fist, but the animal escaped his grasp each time. Finally Muño Salido seized the reins and led the horse, still kicking, away.

Blood sprouted from Álvar Sánchez's body and raced outward, covering the ground with a steaming red plague. Doña Lambra let out a scream louder than any of the lance blows had been on the scaffold.

Justa dropped to her knees and took Álvar Sánchez's bloodied head in her hands. The Little Page stooped and touched Álvar's limp hands and still chest. They looked up at Doña Lambra and shook their heads.

"Dead?" the lady asked, choking.

"Yes," Justa whispered.

"Fetch a priest," said Sancha. The Little Page nodded and squeezed through the stunned crowd. Sancha held on tight to her son's arm. "Gonzalico, what have you done?" she whispered into his ear. He opened his mouth and shook his head in disbelief.

He had wanted to stop Álvar Sánchez from outshining him during these entire festivities. Had it been more than boyish competitiveness? "Son, I have to know whether you did this intentionally. Tell me now."

"How could I intend his own horse to kill him? Of course I wasn't trying to kill him." She let him go and was sorry she'd doubted him. Her son would never murder even the most blasphemous traitor in the middle of a wedding celebration.

Doña Lambra tore at her silk, sending crisp sounds through the air along with her grating sobs. She strode among the crush of people, wading through the blood and the teeth, to face young Gonzalo. "He was my cousin. He won the prize. Never before has a bride been so dishonored at her own wedding. Ruy Blásquez will repay this betrayal!"

Sancha wiped at the tears coming down her own cheeks. "Oh, dear sister-in-law, he didn't mean to do it. Let us pay the homicide fee and have masses sung for Álvar's soul."

Ruy Blásquez, still holding the lance he had used against the scaffold, took Lambra's shaking hand in his and looked into her wild eyes. She wrenched away to point at Gonzalico. "Do something! Are you my husband by these nuptials or not?"

"Brother, he's your nephew!" Sancha shouted.

Ruy Blásquez struck Gonzalico across the face with the sharp end of the lance. Gonzalo fell onto his seat and blood streamed from a single streak that started on his cheek and gashed diagonally up the bridge of his nose to the opposite eyebrow.

At the sight of her son's blood, Sancha broke away from her husband and lunged toward the wound with a handkerchief grabbed from Luz's ready hands. But Gonzalo pushed her away, staining her sleeves with garish smears. The blood panicked her. She'd often wondered whether seven healthy warrior sons was too much blessing for one family. Sancha's other brothers had weakened and died before their training could even begin, and the last stillborn had killed her mother when Sancha had thirteen years. The first strong son had filled Sancha with joy. She tried not to gloat over the second. When Suero was born, she'd begun to cut herbs and place bundles on bedrolls at the instruction of the midwife, without telling her priest. The fourth son, she knew, was seriously tempting the devil, and she still had trouble believing Gonzalico had survived fifteen years with no mishap.

He got back to his feet, wobbling, refusing his brothers' help.

"For God's sake, uncle," he said blithely, "as your nephew, I never deserved such a blow from you." He turned to his brothers. "I beg you not to sue my uncle over my death if I die here."

"Sweet boy, you won't die here," said Sancha. She didn't feel as sure as she sounded. Perhaps her seventh son had been born in an evil hour, after all. She tried again to hold Gonzalo, to press the crucifix to his lips for protection, but he swiveled once again, tottering.

"But, uncle, for the sake of your love for me, I beg you not to hit me again, because you couldn't suffer the consequences."

"He doesn't mean it," cried Sancha.

Ruy Blásquez raised his lance once again, over the crowd's noisy objections. Diego and Fernando rushed their uncle and jostled him so that Gonzalo dodged the blow. The weapon glanced off his shoulder and did not cut him, but broke in the confusion. Gonzalo seized the goshawk from his brother Suero and, matching the bird's shrieks as it sank its talons into his arm, forced it into his uncle's face. The hawk struck out with its beak in indignation.

"Stop!" Sancha wailed.

Suero whistled the first three notes of its particular tune over and over, but before he coaxed the agitated hawk back onto his protected hand, Ruy Blásquez's nose was bleeding more than Gonzalo's brow.

Doña Lambra looked around her. "Justa, what can I use for a weapon?" she said, but Ruy Blásquez, holding his nose with both hands, mustered the strength to call into the crowd.

"My warriors! Will you abide this affront to your lord? To arms, to arms!"

Sancha wanted to hide her eyes, to disappear, to return to Salas with her babies swaddled, safe in her arms.

The onlookers made way as the knights under Ruy Blásquez's fealty came from their posts on the riverbank, pulling out their shields and unsheathing their swords. Gonzalo tipped over and his brothers held him, but his arms reached around in search of a weapon.

"Gonzalico, you're half dead, and there must be a hundred of them," Diego tried to reason with him.

Crouching close to his ear, Fernando told his youngest brother, "Don't you think it's unpardonable to have caused such a scene at our uncle's wedding?"

But even as he was unable to keep his own feet under him, Gonzalo shook his head and tried to wield a sword.

Sancha threw her hands up in despair. "Santiago Apostle, turn them away from each other!" She looked to her husband as the clattering soldiers crushed in upon them. With a nod toward her, Don Gonzalo took his youngest son into his arms and kept him from falling, from grasping at weapons, or even from speaking.

Count García arrived at the site of the commotion, parting the soldiers like the Red Sea. He made a sweeping gesture at Ruy Blásquez's soldiers. "Stand down."

Ruy Blásquez looked at Doña Lambra, who still flickered with rage. "Look at all this blood, my lord, at my own wedding. You should allow such a justified feud to take place," he said, holding his nose.

The count raised his voice in announcement. "Let it be known to all present that I, García Fernández, Count of Castile, hereby pardon

Gonzalo González for the unintentional slaughter of Álvar Sánchez. He will pay no homicide fee."

Doña Lambra let out a strangled cry and, in what looked to Sancha like an exaggerated gesture, toppled into the arms of her poor maid.

The count ignored her. "I further pardon Ruy Blásquez for his offense against Gonzalo González's person and consider that any debt incurred for such wounding has been paid with the breaking of Ruy Blásquez's nose."

Ruy Blásquez emitted a loud snort, then winced in pain, but Sancha's husband nodded in agreement. He handed his son to her and she held on even though his weight with the dizziness threatened to crush her.

Don Gonzalo knelt at the count's feet, saying, "As your humble servant, my lord, I am honored by your wise judgment."

Sancha smiled and nodded encouragement.

He stood and announced, "And to show my family's goodwill toward Ruy Blásquez and his wife, I give my seven sons, all peerless warriors with experience in the South against the Moors, to serve in Ruy Blásquez's army. There is no better place I could commend them to, since Ruy Blásquez's honor and power are feared by Moor and Christian throughout Hispania."

As usual, peace could only come about if Sancha sacrificed her mother's rights over her sons, and they would leave her yet again. But they would watch over each other and her brother would forgive Gonzalico. Harmony among the male family members must take precedence over her desire to kiss and hold the precious men she'd given birth to. She smiled her agreement, though it wasn't called for.

Taking Ruy Blásquez's hand in his as a sign of friendship, Don Gonzalo continued more privately, "You can send them on campaigns and they will do you proud, or you can use them as personal bodyguards and you will always be safe. As your nephews, they can do nothing other than obey your every command."

With dutiful nods, six brothers knelt at Ruy Blásquez's feet and kissed his hand. "Gonzalico will do it some other time. If he kneels now, he may not be able to get back up," said Sancha. She dabbed at his head wounds with Luz's handkerchief, although they were beginning to stop bleeding at last. As the last drop dried, Sancha spoke a prayer of gratitude.

And with this, the men seemed well pleased. Sancha looked at Lambra, who had abandoned her faint. Lambra refused to meet her gaze, but crouched and began collecting Álvar Sánchez's gore-covered teeth in an improvised pouch of her skirt. The blood and soil seeped through the yellow silk and spattered sinister flowerlets on Álvar's tunic, then sank deep into the earth.

Chapter V

Justa reached for the gold-covered tent flap, but a high-pitched moan inside made her drop it again.

Of course her lady was awake. She had sent her husband for Justa. Ruy Blásquez had then awakened Little Page in the male servants' tent and sent him to the maids', perhaps thinking his small stature excused him from the risks of manhood. Little Page had waited outside for Justa to dress and then brought her to Doña Lambra's tent, all the while rubbing his eyes with exhaustion.

After the previous day, it had been a relief for Justa to retire with her own private grief for Álvar Sánchez. She curled up on her bedroll, thinking of Álvar's fiery eyes and rumbling laughter. He had never failed to make Lambra smile. If they had been able to get the dispensation and marry, Bureba would have been the most benevolently administered territory in Castile. But that was never to happen, even if he had lived. Justa shuddered with the ache of seeing a man so brave, strong, and kind laid to rest, and fell into the cradling arms of sleep.

Doña Lambra, it seemed, had shared the burden of her grief with everyone in Burgos. With Justa's help after the lancing contest, she had collected Álvar Sánchez's teeth in a leather pouch. The next day, they laid Álvar's body in the ground wrapped in linen, close to other knights who died defending Castile. After the blessings, Doña Lambra set the pouch on his chest so it looked as if he held them in his folded hands through the cloth. She had wailed and beat her chest for hours and refused to take to her bed, but strode about the streets of Burgos flailing her arms in a continuation of the funeral procession. The count secluded himself in the palace in dismay, and Justa was left with a lady she couldn't calm down. She followed Doña Lambra everywhere, suffering along with her, until Doña Sancha insisted Lambra lie down. Ruy Blásquez and Don Gonzalo carried her to the tent and set her in the bed, where she moaned and lashed out at Justa long after nightfall, until the maid left without permission.

Justa wondered whether today would be more of the same. Had her lady already found the depth of her despair, or did she have farther down to go?

"Better go in," said Little Page beside her, holding a bucket with water for the basin.

Justa jumped. She'd forgotten he was there. "Will you come in with me?" she asked her little friend.

"I wasn't asked for," he said.

Justa knew how much he feared Doña Lambra. He always kept as far from her as Lambra allowed, even while gazing at her reverentially. He might not be much help if he came inside now.

"The only person who could bring our lady out of this is Álvar Sánchez." Justa wiped a new tear from her cheek.

Little Page set his jaw and opened the tent flap. Justa ducked inside and Little Page set about filling the basin with water. If Ruy Blásquez had slept the night in the tent, Justa found no mark he might have left. It still belonged only to Lambra, with the furniture and gifts in the same arrangement as before the wedding. The only items missing were Justa's pallet and bedroll.

Doña Lambra still lay atop the pillows. "It isn't right that someone so handsome should have to meet eternity without his teeth," she whispered. She licked her lips and coughed.

"We did our best for him, my lady," said Justa.

Doña Lambra rubbed her eyes. Little Page rummaged through the silks in the trunk and Justa stood over her lady. Doña Lambra's lips were cracked, her cheeks red. Her eyelashes and the hair near her face were crusted with the remnants of so many tears. How could Justa ever bring balance back to her bodily humors after such a day?

Justa offered her hand. Doña Lambra took it and pulled herself into a sitting position with a whimper. She cast her gaze about the tent, bright with morning sunlight. "It's probably getting too cold for the silks," she rasped. "Let's put on my grey wool tunic today and keep my maids close by me. It will take all of them to equal the good company of my late cousin."

Justa had witnessed the way Doña Lambra had miraculously stopped weeping only when Gonzalo González had stepped forward to express his remorse. Her look of condemnation was so dark, Justa made the sign of the cross in self defense. Unlike her lady, Justa doubted there had been malice in the terrible accident that had killed Álvar Sánchez. It comforted her to think of the ten masses lifting his soul up to dwell with the Holy Family and the saints.

"Don Gonzalo paid for ten masses in his honor," Justa reminded her lady, leading her to the table.

"Ten times ten masses couldn't comfort me. They won't bring back his smile, or the way he looked at me."

Justa was too exhausted to think of any other words of comfort. She dipped one of the linens in the basin to dab her lady's swollen face. Little Page held the other linen ready for drying. He made a show of looking away from their lady's curves outlined by the wispy underdress she'd slept in.

"Or his bravery, or his skill with weapons, or his loyalty to Castile," Lambra continued while Justa brushed her hair, dressed her and slipped her shoes on. "Paying for so many masses only shows how rich they are without sharing any of it with Ruy Blásquez."

To fetch the other maids her lady had requested, Justa left the tent, shook her arms to release some of the tension, and looked down the riverbank. For five weeks, it had been festooned with tents and banners and people in all manner of occupations. Now, the multitudes that had arrived in Burgos with such pomp for the wedding festivities had dispersed, returning to their own lands. Each of three mornings, a few more of the manmade features had disappeared, until finally the entire bank was plucked bald. All that remained as evidence of the merriment was a lamentable groove in the dust where men and horses had proven their worth against a wooden castle.

The maids had washed and dressed by the time Justa came for them. When she led them back out, Adalberto, who tended Doña Lambra's horses, caught her eye. He was standing idle with the male servants, those from Bureba and the ones who had been given as wedding gifts.

"Where are you headed?" he asked with a warm smile.

"We have to stay by Doña Lambra today," Justa answered.

"Would it help if we joined you?"

"It might," she said, fighting a grin of her own.

Doña Sancha and her sons with their tutor Muño Salido were approaching Doña Lambra in a somber procession that recalled the funeral of the day before. Doña Lambra's hands were busy wiping away teardrops and twisting her braid as she waited for them. Justa, Adalberto, Little Page, and the other servants came to stand beside their lady. Justa was glad to surround Doña Lambra with so many people before she faced her crowd of in-laws. She took special consolation in Adalberto's steady and, yes, handsome, strength as he fulfilled this task beyond his duty.

Doña Sancha stayed several paces away and her men stayed behind her. Doña Lambra furrowed her brow and Justa crossed herself again, mouthing a prayer to the armored angel Michael for protection.

"We're here to express our condolences once again," Doña Sancha said across the space between them.

The young knights and their tutor bowed from the waist. "We're so sorry for your loss, aunt," said Diego.

Young Gonzalo surged forward from the crowd and knelt before Doña Lambra. His face had healed much more quickly than Ruy Blásquez's nose. Five faint reddish spots were the only reminder of the gash that had made him lose so much blood. Witnessing his vitality, it was hard to understand that Álvar would never recover from a single punch to the face. Gonzalo kissed Doña Lambra's hand and said, "I'm especially sorry. Can you ever forgive me?" Justa granted her wordless forgiveness to his sincere brown eyes.

But Doña Lambra pulled away as if his touch burned. "I've accepted your apology, and the Count of Castile has arranged for civility on both sides."

No one spoke for a moment, waiting for Doña Lambra to continue. The goshawk squawked from his perch on Suero's specially padded shoulder. He still carried it everywhere, and Justa knew the sight of it brought Doña Lambra nothing but shame. She'd had plenty of time to tell Justa that the count should've had the bird killed after what it had done to her husband's face. Gonzalo went to stand beside his mother, who took her turn to speak.

"My husband told me he's spoken with Don García this morning. The count wants to leave Burgos in order to observe his holdings in the rest of Castile, and among the many knights he's decided to take with him are my husband and my brother."

"Oh, is that where my husband is now?" said Doña Lambra. Since Álvar Sánchez's death, she had seemed hardly to notice the man she was married to. They'd exchanged only necessary words in Justa's presence, and where Ruy Blásquez slept, if it hadn't been inside the bridal tent, was a mystery.

"Yes, the count must be talking to him now," said Doña Sancha. "I understand they're to leave soon, perhaps as early as tomorrow. I think I'll take my sons back to Lara, since they haven't been singled out for this mission."

"I wonder what I'll do, losing my husband so quickly," said Doña Lambra, fluttering her eyelashes. She reached for Doña Sancha's hand and smiled with her mouth only. "Ruy Blásquez must abandon me to my fate. Don't you leave me, too, dear sister."

The sudden brightening of her humor alerted Justa that something was wrong, worse than when Doña Lambra had been weeping inconsolably. In Bureba, such quicksilver changes had only ever led to some unlucky servant going hungry or getting a beating.

But Doña Sancha wasn't aware of that. She clasped Doña Lambra's hand and smiled back, a joyful smile that softened her eyes. "There's nothing to do in Burgos now. Would you like to come to Salas with us?"

"Well, that's generous of you to offer. But I was thinking I should visit some of Ruy Blásquez's holdings. Perhaps there's somewhere with good hunting now?"

Suero's face lit up behind the goshawk. "Barbadillo could be good now."

"And Barbadillo is on the way back to Salas. What a wonderful idea," said Doña Sancha. "My sons are excellent hunters, especially with Suero's hawk. It would be such a treat for them, since they couldn't go with their father and the count. And I know you'll be pleased to see a part of Lara you now govern with my brother."

"Yes, a wonderful idea," Doña Lambra exclaimed. "Is it terribly cold in Barbadillo at this time of year? Will our tents be adequate?"

"Not to worry, sister-in-law," replied Doña Sancha. "You now have a vassal in Barbadillo with a farmhouse on a large estate."

Doña Lambra turned to Justa with a hop. "We must start packing at once."

"We can leave today if it pleases you so much." Doña Sancha chuckled. She promised to return to the tent when they were ready to set out, which prompted Justa to usher the maids into the bride's tent after Doña Lambra.

Seeing Adalberto depart with the male servants, Justa grasped his sleeve. Even before he turned around, she was blushing. "I'm sorry. I was going to ask you to oversee the packing of the male servants' tent. I don't think I can watch over both."

He took her hands in his and she felt a rush of unexpected pleasure. "Of course, Justa. Have no worries. I'll even ready the horses and drive the carts right up here."

"Thank you," she breathed, turning to the tent.

Gotina and the other maids were working mirthlessly to get Doña Lambra's belongings and wedding gifts ready for the carts. Justa held up one of the multicolored pillows. "Are these soft things for you to keep, or only for using here?"

"We can pile them into the carts and sit on them during the journey," Doña Lambra replied dismissively. "But where are the needles and sharp instruments?"

Justa stopped tossing the pillows into the doorway. "They must be in the servants' tent, my lady. Adalberto will make sure they're packed and ready to go."

"I only want to make sure you can work with the rest of the silk while we're in Barbadillo," Doña Lambra said. Justa might not have remarked upon the request, but the unsolicited justification added needles to her list of items to worry about.

Ruy Blásquez's foot jutted inside the tent flap and carried him over the pile of pillows. He held his arms out, but Doña Lambra waited for him to come to her through the maze of folding, packing maids.

"I've been talking with the count, my dear wife. He's making rounds all over Castile to confirm town charters and grant privileges."

Doña Lambra backed away. Justa couldn't blame her. He looked bizarre with bandages wrapped around his head in a cross, avoiding his eyes. He kept his mouth agape to breathe, and his voice seemed to come from deep inside a hole. "There's not a lot to do in Burgos now," said Lambra.

"The bad news is that Don García has specifically asked me and Gonzalo Gustioz to go with him."

"It's right that he should choose two of his best and noblest knights, my lord. And maybe he'd like to see you become good friends, to make sure there are no hard feelings about what happened." She kept her voice steady, above an undercurrent Justa was afraid would burst out at any moment. "It's not worth the risk of fighting amongst nobles when Castile has serious enemies to consider."

"I didn't know you were so politically astute. It grieves me to leave you so soon, my love. Gonzalo Gustioz convinced me his sons would protect you in my absence, but tell me you'll miss me. Give me that small comfort among so many sorrows."

The ladies stood in their places, soundless, and their lady remained as motionless as they did. Ruy Blásquez seemed incapable of looking away from her. He wrapped his arms around her. Justa gestured to the other ladies to keep working and Doña Lambra took her lord's hands in hers as if to escape the embrace. "Do your duty, husband. I'll be safe with my nephews looking out for me."

He kissed her forehead and squeezed her hands. Finding no more words, he turned and went out, tripping a little on the pillows.

"Do you think I made him suffer enough for abandoning me unavenged?" Doña Lambra asked Justa.

Justa swallowed, but her mouth had gone dry. "Certainly, my lady."

"I don't need him. I only need an opportunity."

Doña Lambra whipped the tent flap open to find Doña Sancha, the seven brothers, Muño Salido, their horses, and two squires. "Where are your carts? Your pages and cooks?" she asked. Justa, twenty other serving girls, Little Page, Adalberto, twenty other male servants, two cooks, and fifteen horses surrounded Doña Lambra's two carts.

"We'll have anything we can ask for in Barbadillo, and my husband is taking most of our squires with him," said Doña Sancha.

"We have to support our father," said Diego.

"But you'll be so much faster than I will, with my wedding presents and possessions." Doña Lambra seemed to be bragging more than protesting.

"Of course we'll stay with you, aunt," said Gonzalo. "We'll protect you from any danger you can imagine."

"I'm sure you will," she said, turning toward her traveling crew. Justa felt uneasy that their party vastly outnumbered the González family, but didn't think any of them but her lady felt enmity toward them. She held out her hands to cup Doña Lambra's foot so she could mount her palfrey, taking up the reins.

"Are you ready to leave?" asked Doña Sancha. "Did you bid farewell to my brother?"

"Yes," Doña Lambra said. "Do we cross the Arlanzón here, or later?"

The first day, they paraded over the plains, through farmlands and vistas that stretched southward to the end of the world. Over the horizon lurked the unimaginable Caliphate of Córdoba. The sun warmed Justa's skin and illuminated their path, making lace patterns through the treetops. Did the same sun warm the black faces in Córdoba? The way Doña Lambra looked south, Justa knew she was thinking about it, as well. Her nephews had saved Zamora from the Moors and gone on raids to the south, but she didn't deign to ask them. They progressed unharrassed even by the mountain-dwelling Basques, so the brothers had no chance to show off. They noisily play-fought with each other when they camped where the ground undulated into foothills full of burbling streams and oak trees.

The second day, as they entered narrow passageways between rocky outcrops shaded by pines, the seven brothers surrounded Doña Lambra and Justa on their horses like her personal guard. She cleared her throat and said loudly for Gonzalo to hear, "Oh, Justa, do you think there are robbers hiding in these hills?" Justa felt herself blushing at the mention of her name. She didn't want to be included in whatever game her lady was playing, but couldn't release the reins to hide her face. "It doesn't matter, anyway," Doña Lambra continued, "with my nephews here to protect me."

Every one of the brothers grinned, baring white teeth, and sat up a little taller in his saddle. When they came to a creek, the brothers pushed her male servants aside and worked to get the carts across. Justa turned away from their bare chests to see Doña Lambra narrowing her eyes. She moved her lips with what Justa didn't doubt were curses on their strong muscles. Justa said her own quiet prayers to all the saints she could think of that the devil wouldn't come to help Lambra unleash her fury.

Little Page was standing to the side, impassive, and when he glanced at Justa, she recognized the God-sent distraction and mouthed, "Help." He nodded and disappeared behind a boulder to emerge moments later in his undergarment, his flat white chest a parody of the brothers' tanned sinews. Justa would've thought he had done it every day of his life. He put his hands behind his head to show his absurdly hairy underarms, stuck his tongue out, and did a strange dance, setting one foot out at a time. Soon the laughter from servants and ladies kept the rhythm for him. Justa was beside herself to see that Doña Lambra's smile was no longer superficial, but filled her entire body with mirth. She looked radiant, as beautiful as she had been when she was a child with a mother and father.

Little Page capered back and forth to everyone's amusement until the carts were across and the brothers put their tunics and mantles back on, laughing and smiling with everyone else. Doña Lambra dismounted to plant a kiss in Little Page's hair. He looked up at her, questioning, but she told him, "You are the best gift I've ever received. You must never stray from me."

Justa smiled at him, too, relieved she could still predict her lady's behavior.

"What a delightful servant you have," Doña Sancha told Doña Lambra when she returned to the horses.

"Yes," said Doña Lambra. "But I only hope to have one child as perfect as your seven perfect sons."

The way she watched Gonzalo and his brothers, Justa knew Doña Lambra didn't think there was anything perfect about them. She helped Little Page dress and climb into the cart again. "Thank you," she said.

"It's below my dignity," he whispered back to Justa. "But truthfully, I'd do anything to keep her happy. Her unhappiness is terrible to behold. Is there something wrong with her?"

"Too much choler," Justa replied quickly, then returned to her place beside her lady.

Something wrong with Doña Lambra. Perhaps there was. Justa had lost her parents before she had time to make memories of them. Lambra's parents had fostered her, and the girls received the news of their deaths standing together at the main house in Bureba as if they were twin sisters. From that moment, Lambra had become a haughty lady and Justa little more than a pledged serf. A different woman might have afforded Justa the dignity of her station in honor of their relationship as foster sisters. But Lambra was no other woman, she was Doña Lambra, Lady of Bureba, and Justa had learned to respond before she was called.

They came upon Barbadillo, nestled between two humps of hills and with a view to sierras in every direction beyond the forests, as the sun declined behind them. The main farmhouse reminded Justa of their home in Bureba, with thick thatch on the roof, but with golden brown stone walls instead of grey. Spread out before them were several other huts — probably stables — hogs, chickens, a fountain spouting water for anyone's taking, and a slaughterhouse. A man with an open face came out of it and shut the door behind him. Seeing the visitors, he approached, wiping dirt onto his apron.

The travelers dismounted and Doña Sancha was first to speak. "Ermenegildo Antolínez! I hope our visit isn't inconvenient. As you can see, I've brought my sons for hunting, and my brother's new wife to see her lands."

He took Doña Lambra's hand, kissed it, and smiled. "You have my loyalty, my lady."

"Thank you, Don Ermenegildo. Would you be so kind as to show us where we may rest from our journey?"

Before she finished her sentence, the seven brothers had abandoned solemnity and darted to the fountain, where they washed the dust from their faces and drank out of their cupped hands, then splashed each other and made such a noise that the hunting hounds emerged from the hills, barking and howling.

"You would never know the eldest of them is a score and five years old," Ermenegildo Antolínez said, waving the rest of the travelers toward the farmhouse.

It was only as large as the main building in Bureba, with a long table running down the center where they might break bread before going to sleep.

"I've never hosted this many people before," explained Ermenegildo Antolínez. "But there should be room for everyone."

After a supper of freshwater fish stew with leeks and carrots, the landholder and the seven brothers moved the tables and benches to make room for two long rows of bodies to sleep side by side. Doña Lambra claimed the spot nearest the fireplace and insisted that Justa set her bedding next to her. That way, Doña Lambra wouldn't be near anyone else. Justa knew to direct the sexes to be segregated like they were in Bureba, with women in Lambra's row and the men on the other across a cleared aisle, although Ermenegildo Antolínez's wife took her place next to her husband, at the fireplace. Toward the end of the hall, where they'd placed the chamber pots, it was found that there weren't enough bedrolls, so Little Page, Adalberto, and other male servants followed Ermenegildo Antolínez to the barns to get more straw. Once every last person had a straw tick of some sort to lie atop, and all the spiders that ran out of the straw had been stepped on, swatted, burned, or drowned, travelers and hosts could finally rest.

Justa listened to Doña Lambra's breathing all night, and it was not the breath of a carefree sleeper. Her lady woke several times to sigh, to shift on her crackling straw tick, to throw off her blankets or to gather them up again. "Do you need something, my lady?" Justa whispered.

"Blood," she whispered back, choking on a sob.

"Do you mean your courses have come upon you?" It wasn't that time yet.

"There will never be enough blood to pay for the loss of Álvar Sánchez."

Justa made the sign of the cross over her pounding heart and hoped she'd misheard. To her dismay, the pattern repeated: nights in dreary vigil, days of drowsiness.

Doña Sancha accompanied her sons and their squires on their hunting expeditions most days, though they brought back no game. Doña Lambra stayed at the farmhouse, relieving Ermenegildo Antolínez's wife of her day-to-day duties and taking care of the household as if it were her own. Where did she get so much energy? She never seemed to sleep.

Justa snapped awake one afternoon as Doña Lambra cornered her vassal at the hearth several days later, after he had conferred with her cooks about what was to be served that evening.

"Ermenegildo Antolínez," she said, "you swore your homage to Ruy Blásquez as soon as you came of age. Do you maintain loyalty to me now?"

"Of course, my lady," he replied, nodding in deference.

"And do you love me well?"

Ermenegildo averted his gaze. "More each day, because even over this short time, your nobility has only grown and my love and honor for you have grown with it."

She took his arm and made to stroll about the grounds, leaving the maids and pages busy sewing or preparing food, except Justa, who followed them silently.

"I assume the news of the way my wedding festivities ended has arrived here," said Doña Lambra.

"Yes, my lady. It is most unfortunate." Ermenegildo kept his gaze focused straight ahead, such that Justa couldn't judge his face.

"In that case, faithful Ermenegildo, know that the seven knights I have brought with me to your lands are the seven brothers from Lara who caused me and my husband such grave affronts at the celebration where we should have been most honored."

The vassal gave an appropriate gasp of surprise.

"So you'll understand when I tell you," the lady continued, "that I've brought them here not so they may amuse themselves hunting, but to gain your support in my revenge."

Ermenegildo Antolínez stopped short. "What would you have me do?" he murmured.

"As a woman, I cannot carry out this revenge myself. I need you or your servants to take on this burden and maintain the honor of my house, since my husband is under the thumb of the Count of Castile and refuses to defend me properly. In order to pay for the death of my cousin Álvar Sánchez, all the brothers must be killed or maimed."

She grasped his shoulders and turned him toward her, but he looked at the ground. "My lady, I bear no blood relation to you, so this would be a tremendous sin."

"Justice is no sin."

"They're strong knights. I have no one who could confront them. I myself am too old to consider it."

"I must avenge Álvar Sánchez. Suppose your servants were to gang up on just Gonzalo González. He's the youngest, and also the one who's most to blame."

He looked up at her, his eyes glassy. "My lady, I beg you not to ask this of me. My family has no quarrel with the Lara family, of which our lord Ruy Blásquez is a part. We're simple farmers. Not a single one of us has his own weapon."

"No, but on a farm there are many dangerous implements." She looked around her. "My maids have pins and needles. You could run over him with a cart. Or, you must have knives to kill the livestock. Help me! Slaughter him like a pig!"

The man started as if a bull had butted him, and Justa gasped, giving herself away. She turned and ran back to the house, where her heart didn't stop resounding in her ears until hours later, when Ermenegildo Antolínez confirmed with the cooks that that evening they would have a pork stew, made from fresh cuts from the latest slaughter. It was the only swine whose flesh was sacrificed that day.

All night, Justa used her wakefulness next to Doña Lambra to pray for the brothers and their innocent mother. How might she get away from her lady to warn them? Surely, such popular and strong knights needed no warning about their own aunt. The bride of their flesh and blood. No, her lady would never find the support she needed to carry out her revenge. It would be all right.

At breakfast, Doña Lambra sat necessarily in the midst of her relatives. She projected a vacant stare that unnerved Justa as the bread and wine were served. The lady's breath was labored, her fists clenched.

"Don Gonzalo, how have you been faring on the hunt?" Justa said at her end of the table. Anything else would have been better to distract her lady, she realized too late.

"We've been getting excellent exercise," Gonzalo said in his aunt's direction.

"But that's all," added his brother Fernando.

"I was expecting to be able to bring more fowl back for the dinner table, to impress Doña Lambra with the abundance of our region of Lara," said Gonzalo.

Thinking only of sending her lady away so she might be able to sleep a little, Justa said loud enough for the table to hear, "My lady, the weather seems to distress you, and you haven't seen much of Barbadillo. Why don't you saddle a horse and ride out with your nephews, Doña Sancha, and Muño Salido, in search of game? The exercise could warm your heart."

Justa had never seen Doña Lambra's cheeks so red, and she knew her lady didn't need warming.

"It's an excellent idea," said Doña Sancha. "Join us, sister."

"Who knows?" said Gustio González. "Maybe adding another hunter will change our luck."

"Yes, yes," the other brothers chimed in.

"You can't change luck that way," said Muño Salido, clearing his throat around his bread.

Doña Lambra set her jaw. "I'm happy staying here and helping to take care of Ermenegildo Antolínez's household."

"Well, maybe the maid can join us, then," said Gonzalo González to the thunderous approval of his siblings.

His mother smiled at Justa. "Of course you may come with us, dear girl."

When she looked back into Doña Sancha's brown eyes, Justa sensed something she hadn't experienced in years: kindness. She checked with

Doña Lambra, who made a gesture with her hand that Justa took to be permission. Should she stay and watch over Doña Lambra? The brothers couldn't be safer than out hunting, Justa decided.

She had never been hunting before, so she stayed close to Doña Sancha and tried to keep out of everyone else's way. She felt like a part of the group as they rode out, each on their own horse, even though she was the only female besides the knights' mother. She clutched her cloak at her chest and breathed in the moist air and almost believed she was in the woods at Bureba in the autumn. Not knowing the signs, to Justa it looked as if their luck was unchanged that morning. But as they delved deeper into the trees, the goshawk perched on Suero's hand flapped its wings impatiently.

He let it go, and it flew high above the trees to plummet downward they knew not how far away. Invigorated, they urged the horses forward and met the goshawk halfway. Diego released the hounds and they searched out the prey among the trees, barking. Gonzalo rode in after them and returned in a few minutes with the goshawk on one hand, this time with the proper protective glove. A bleeding pheasant in his other fist flapped its wings frantically. The dogs barked and the humans couldn't repress a few shouts.

"At last. At last!" exclaimed Fernando González.

"Ha! I knew we couldn't fail," Gonzalo told him. He handed the bird of prey back to Suero and set about tying the pheasant to his saddle.

Justa looked at the goshawk and then at Gonzalo, back and forth, so many times that he volunteered, "I helped Suero train this hawk, and it answers to me almost as quickly as it does to him."

"I wouldn't lend my bird to anyone else. We've broken it so well, it could keep any hunter in fowl and small pelts. It's worth a fortune," added Suero.

Fernando's doubt, Suero's fixation, and Gonzalo's confidence charmed Justa and convinced her again that the brothers had meant no harm at the wedding. Remembering the signs from Doña Lambra, she wanted to tell them to leave for Salas and not to stop until they were home. But in spite of her lady's obvious intent, she couldn't come up with a single thing Doña Lambra could do to harm the brothers. Even so, riding next to Doña Sancha the rest of the day, she was thinking of what her lady might be doing or considering back at the house to the detriment of her soul.

They covered more ground that day, going farther out than they said they'd been before and, by the grace of Suero's goshawk, they took a clutch of two partridges and two pheasants. The crowning achievement came when the group had already turned back. Suero spotted a gigantic wild goose.

"Is it too big for the goshawk?" he wondered. Fernando put an end to the question by shooting a true arrow. The heavy bulk of the dying bird plummeted below the horizon created by the pines and, on an unseen pond, made a splash that echoed off the trunks.

"You should have let it fly," said Muño Salido. "I could have read the augury from its pattern."

Justa thought the goose had probably been flying south to a meeting place with others of its kind before heading at the right time to Andalusia and farther south, and none other than Gonzalo echoed her thought.

"A straight-flying bird isn't likely to give omens."

"I'm very sorry, tutor," Fernando was saying to Muño Salido. "Why didn't you say something?"

"It's been many years that you're too fast for me, boy," replied the white-haired man as the hounds came back out of the trees, soaking wet and laden with the surrendering goose.

Their cheeks rosy with exertion, the hunters returned jubilant to the house. With help from one of the squires who had also been on the hunt, smiling and panting, Justa took the birds to the kitchen and passed on the brothers' instructions for the cooks to prepare a feast right away. She came out of the farmhouse to see the seven knights laughing and splashing around the fountain, attempting to slake the thirst they had worked up.

Gonzalo held Suero's goshawk. He'd stripped down to his breeches in order to bathe the bird. Justa watched them from a hundred feet away, unable to extract her gaze. She hadn't had the luxury of staring when the brothers had stripped at the ford on the journey, so she had never seen such a beautiful man in such detail. Steam rose off his skin. His nipples compressed to hard red points under the water. He left her breathless, too distracted to consider whether she would need to confess her voracious eyes the next time they met a priest.

Doña Lambra emerged from the slaughterhouse with Gotina by her side and came to stand next to Justa.

"He's doing that so we'll fall in love with him," Doña Lambra said.

The serving girls didn't answer, too enthralled with the vision before them.

"Well, he has no right to take advantage of us out here with almost no other men around. I won't let him get away with it. Gotina, find Little Page for me."

When he arrived an instant later, she held his shoulders and murmured. "Go to the kitchen and find a vegetable of some kind. I think they're using some old cucumbers today—the bigger, the better. Soak it in as much blood as you can, then go to the brothers over there by the well and hit Gonzalo—the one holding the falcon—hit him with it as hard as you can."

Little Page stared at her dumbly. Justa wasn't sure what to think of such bizarre orders. Doña Lambra erased all doubt about what she intended: "Don't worry. I'll protect you if they come after you. I'll have my vengeance for my cousin Álvar Sánchez and no one will be harmed."

Still Little Page hesitated. "But, my lady, where can I find blood?"

She snapped her fingers in the direction of the slaughterhouse. "They drained an enormous hog yesterday. Some of the blood has been left in the collection bucket. Hurry!"

Propelled by his lady's intensity, Little Page's stumpy legs carried him into the kitchen and then to the slaughterhouse. More quickly than Justa expected, he darted out again holding a cucumber in front of himself so as not to stain his fine tunic with the sludgy, reeking red-brown blood. The cucumber had been peeled in the kitchen and become engorged when Little Page scraped it along the inside of the bucket. The brothers saw him approaching and stopped their playing. Their voices carried to where Justa was standing with Doña Lambra.

"Do you suppose Doña Lambra's sent us something to eat?" asked Suero.

"I hope so," said Gonzalo. "Food can't come too soon for me."

Before their expectant eyes, Little Page ran. When his aim was true, he hurled the cucumber with all his might and hit Gonzalo squarely in the chest with it. Little Page didn't wait for the reaction, but turned and ran back toward Doña Lambra. The six brothers howled with laughter and the goshawk flapped its wings and squawked until Suero took it back. Blood had splattered over the bird and Gonzalo's chest and breeches, ruining them.

"You shouldn't be laughing. If this had happened to any of you, I wouldn't rest until you were avenged. He was proving he could wound and kill me if he wanted to. Stop laughing!" Gonzalo splashed water in a vain attempt to clean himself.

Diego González brought his younger brothers into a circle and murmured to them for some minutes. Then Gonzalo pulled his tunic over his bloody undergarment and, with the rest of his brothers, headed toward the house with his sword unsheathed, but under his belt.

Little Page trembled violently. Doña Lambra motioned him toward her, and when he knelt at her feet, she threw her skirts over his head, covering him completely. At that, the brothers sprinted.

Diego was first to arrive. "Aunt," he demanded, "don't protect this man."

"Why not?" she retorted. "He's my servant and my responsibility."

Diego González pointed his sword at her skirts. "I respectfully advise you not to get in the way. The fact that he shows fear means he threw that cucumber with malice, and we can't let it go unpunished. Just a slap or a tear in his tunic will do."

Doña Lambra was unshaken. "His tunic was a gift to me from Count García at the same time he was. If this page has done something to offend you, then he will make amends in due course."

Justa stared at Little Page's hidden bulk while her lady smoothed the fabric over his quivering head.

"While he's under my care, I advise you not to touch him," said Doña Lambra.

Gonzalo erupted. He dragged Little Page kicking and screaming out from under her skirts, ripping and tearing as he went. She pulled against Gonzalo by Little Page's ankles, but in his confusion the little man kicked at his savior. Surprised, Doña Lambra released him and clapped her hands to her face.

By the time Justa screamed, "No," it was over. There at his lady's feet, Gonzalo inserted his sword into Little Page's gut. A whimpering cry punctuated the blade's withdrawal. Justa and Gotina went to the victim and held his head up. Gonzalo backed away while the other brothers sheathed their swords and bowed their heads.

Little Page choked and gurgled. Justa patted his smooth face, saying, "Hush, hush. We'll take care of you." She said the Latin prayers she knew and tried to keep him awake, but he blinked and then opened his eyes wide to give his last rattling breath up to God. Justa closed the eyelids. His blood had splattered Doña Lambra's skirts and even her hands and bodice. It looked as if she had barely survived a brutal attack. But Justa was most disturbed because she stood still, not shaking with rage or shock.

Diego ushered his little brother away from the scene and the other five followed. The ladies were still standing around the page's body when they saw the brothers, their mother, tutor, and servants leaving in a silent procession along the road they had lately used to find wild game. Doña Sancha kept her eyes forward and avoided looking at Doña Lambra, and most of her sons imitated her. The youngest, on the other hand, stared at Justa's lady even when it meant twisting around in his saddle. Bringing up the rear, Muño Salido gazed upward, probably scanning the skies for an augury, or any kind of guidance.

Justa castigated herself for wanting to warn the brothers. Then again, if she had betrayed her lady to them, Little Page might never have been in danger. But what had caused Gonzalo to lash out? Something, a glance or gesture, must have happened between him and her lady. Something had caused her protection of Little Page to enrage him. Whatever had happened, they should stay to make amends. Gonzalo knew law; there must be some recompense due.

Once they were so far away Justa couldn't see them through the trees, Doña Lambra swept into action. She tore at her clothes, making rips in her sleeves to match the ones in her skirt, and disheveling her hair: no one could mistake her state of grief. How could the brothers even talk to such a person? Perhaps it was just as well they'd left.

"What are you waiting for?" Doña Lambra snapped at the maids and the other servants who had come to see what had happened. "Show your loyalty to me. Grieve the loss of this excellent servant!" They imitated her, tearing at their clothes and moaning.

Justa shook her head, feeling she might faint, if only to escape. "Someone needs to go for a priest. Does anyone know where the church is?" she said over the keening.

Adalberto touched her shoulder to comfort her. "I'll go." She watched as he took another male servant and asked Ermenegildo Antolínez where he could find a priest for the poor soul.

After Little Page had been blessed with the bare ceremony his status merited, Doña Lambra put a bundle of cloth about the size of the man on the straw tick where Little Page had slept and had Ermenegildo Antolínez place it in the farmhouse where it wouldn't be disturbed over the course of the day. She lay beside it, weeping until it seemed she would cough up her insides, and refused to eat or drink. Justa couldn't convince her lady to change her clothing until more than three days had passed, and when she finally held the destroyed garments with the last evidence of Little Page's life in her hands, Justa found herself unable to move.

Through the new tears, Justa was able to make out Adalberto's olive-toned face and kind eyes. Without a word, he took the clothes and disposed of them somewhere out of sight. Relief filled out the corners of her grief. She blushed and thanked him over and over when Adalberto returned to Justa's side to help patrol the estate and ensure no one was acting sanguine in Doña Lambra's presence.

Justa wondered how long it would be before Ruy Blásquez came for them: they couldn't travel without getting lost or running into bandits now that their escort had abandoned them. Everyone assembled in prayer for Little Page's soul every day, even after he was wrapped in linen and buried in the earth on Ermenegildo's estate.

Justa began to believe it was not the page Doña Lambra mourned.

"I am a young widow," she whispered one night as she reached over the blanket for Justa's hand in the dark. "Betrayed and abandoned with no husband to protect me in this strange land."

The words sounded like the deepest secrets of Justa's heart.

Chapter VI

Don Gonzalo Gustioz opened one eye into the brightness of the tent. The count had let him sleep later than the other troops, again. He stirred, thinking to turn onto his side, and felt a familiar pain shoot up his left leg. It still made him grit his teeth in an effort not to yell. Why had the count brought him on this ridiculous tour, dragging his forty-five-year-old bones from place to place, day after day, for four weeks, when a couple of his sons could have done the job without complaint and with no damage to their young bodies?

He opened both eyes and saw his brother-in-law, Ruy Blásquez, sitting up on his bedroll, lacing his boots, his nose wheezing under the bandages. Those must surely come off soon, but if the racket Don Gonzalo had had to endure every night was any indication, that nose would never be the same again. He thought of his namesake son's rashness at the wedding celebrations and marveled that he must be the one to pay for it — in tormented nights and lost sleep.

Ruy Blásquez grunted as he stood and looked back at Gonzalo. "Need some help getting up, big brother?" He flashed his white teeth.

Don Gonzalo couldn't help but smile. This was why he was here: to spend time with his brother-in-law and strengthen their reconciliation. It was difficult to remain angry with Ruy Blásquez about striking his son and calling his soldiers to attack. He was so good-natured with the rest of the soldiers and with the count, and always quick to follow orders. Gonzalo was sorry about Álvar Sánchez and about Ruy's nose. He got up under his own power and stood before Ruy Blásquez, considering this man who was, after all, a little bit like his beloved wife, Sancha. He threw his arms around him in a rough embrace. "My dear brother-in-law," he grunted.

Ruy Blásquez pulled away, but whispered, "You are dear to me, too. We can't let these legal matters come between us." They stood for a moment in a silence that respected the renewed peace between them.

"When do you think the count's going to let me go back to Salas and you to Doña Lambra?" asked Gonzalo, expressing his dearest wish.

"We're not a day's journey from Burgos now, so perhaps Don García intends to return today. I think we've covered most of Castile now, and I don't want Lambra to forget me."

"If my cousin forgets you," said Count García, entering the tent with a sudden burst of authority, "then she doesn't deserve you, my most valued vassal."

"My lord, you've let us sleep later than the troops, again, and now you flatter us?" said Gonzalo with a wink, then a respectful bow.

"I've come to your tent because there's a messenger for both of you. He says he's been trying to find us for weeks." The count gestured to follow him and stepped back outside the tent with Ruy Blásquez behind. Gonzalo ran his hands over his clothes, seized his boots, and opened the tent flap onto a clear morning. The smell of burning wood and the slant of the sun told him the summer was finally waning.

The messenger looked out of place, disheveled and urgent in the well ordered campsite where soldiers were dismantling tents, feeding horses, and sharpening blades, unhurriedly getting ready for another long day of riding. "Are you truly Don Ruy Blásquez and Don Gonzalo Gustioz?" the messenger said as if he'd never dreamed he'd meet them.

"I'm Ruy Blásquez."

"And I am Gonzalo Gustioz."

"Praise God, I've found you at last."

The count held the messenger's shoulder to calm him. "You've found them. Now tell us what's happened. Take a deep breath first."

The messenger looked at the count, then heaved a sigh. "There's news from Barbadillo, where both of your wives and your sons were staying."

Gonzalo saw Ruy Blásquez stiffen, as if taut muscles would help him hear the news better. "Something has happened, hasn't it?" It wasn't a question.

"Gonzalo González killed one of Doña Lambra's pages."

Ruy Blásquez turned to Don Gonzalo. "What is wrong with your youngest son?" Gonzalo shook his head and held his hands up with the boots still in them, unable to answer. Ruy Blásquez softened and said to the messenger, "I'm sure it's a mistake."

"Doña Lambra has her attendants in mourning and awaits her lord Ruy Blásquez in Barbadillo, but Doña Sancha and her sons have returned to Salas." The messenger lowered his head as if expecting a blow.

Ignoring the aches in his back, Don Gonzalo laced his boots while he spoke to the count. "My lord, Burgos is near. Were you planning to end the tour today or perhaps tomorrow?"

"Yes, of course," replied Don García. He held out his hand to help Gonzalo straighten up. "You two must return to your wives and understand what happened." He took Ruy Blásquez's hand in his. "You're both dismissed with your knights as soon as you can be ready. I hope it's nothing serious. Go with God."

Gonzalo's mind continued to race even as he rode eastward next to his brother-in-law through manicured farmlands, their knights in formation around them. Indeed, what was wrong with his youngest son? What murderous impulse had he failed to quash during the boy's instruction? What else could he have done to make him as reasonable as his brothers?

But then again, perhaps there was no dead page at all. Perhaps the messenger was mistaken. Muño Salido would never have allowed any of the boys to act so rashly. "It's got to be a mistake," he said.

"I agree." Ruy Blásquez nodded. "I wonder what happened to result in such a strange message."

"Only one way to find out," said Don Gonzalo, and they quickened their pace.

When they came to the turn that allowed them to spy the golden stone buildings of Barbadillo between the rocky hills in the afternoon, a male servant, apparently the sentinel, turned and ran back to the main house. As they rode nearer, Doña Lambra emerged from the door, her hair loose and flying as she worked her arms up and down in a hundred different gestures. Don Gonzalo was reminded of crazed Moorish raiders who gesticulated to strike fear into their enemies' hearts, and his own heart stilled in his chest. They stopped their horses and the soldiers stayed where they were.

Ruy Blásquez found Gonzalo's eyes and said, "Perhaps it's best if you take your troops back to Salas immediately. I'd love to host you in Barbadillo for the night at least, but circumstances...."

Doña Lambra was howling now, a sound unlike anything Gonzalo had heard between the earth and sky.

"Agreed," replied Gonzalo. "Find out how to remake the peace between our families."

"I pledge it," said Ruy Blásquez with his hand over his heart. Gonzalo raised his arm high as a signal for his soldiers to follow, and they progressed on the road to Salas without looking back.

They traversed the mountain pass without any creature, wild or human, coming out of the trees to meet them. As the land flattened, revealing darkening clusters of cypress and pine, the sickness in Gonzalo's stomach lifted. The moon lit the new stone church of San Pelayo, signaling the entrance to Salas, nestled in the shadow of the primeval rocky outcrop. He couldn't help breaking into a run across the bridge, leaving his warrior escort to find their own way, as they surely could. It peeked between the trees like a shy bride: home.

Someone must have seen him and told Doña Sancha, for she emerged on the road in front of the house, her arms open. A pearlescent halo from the candle she held made her even more beautiful than the first time he'd seen her.

"Sancha, Sancha!" he cried, tripping over the saddle. His feet found the road and he took her in his arms and smelled the garlic of some home cooked meal. "How long has it been, my dear Sancha?"

"Six weeks at most, my sweet lord," she whispered into his bristly neck. Looking into his face, her brown eyes glazed. "But what six weeks they've been. I'm afraid there's no remedy anymore."

"I've heard something of what happened in Barbadillo," Gonzalo started.

"Perhaps it's best if your son explains it to you," said Sancha, looping her arm through his and leading the way with her candle. A page emerged from the shadows and led Gonzalo's horse by the reins to be curried and fed.

"It's late. Are my sons awake?"

"Have you forgotten them already? I don't think I ever have seen them sleep! Muño Salido, however, he's curled up by the fire like a cat."

"He's getting very phlegmatic. I suppose it's normal for his age," Gonzalo had time to say before the door squeaked on its hinges to reveal his seven sons variously pacing up and down the hall or sitting at the table in occupations that were abandoned as soon as the door opened.

"Father!" they shouted. Don Gonzalo saw Muño Salido by the hearth start awake and settle into deep sleep in the same instant. Six of his sons embraced him in welcome. Only young Gonzalo hung back as if assessing his father's mood. When the others had finished, he stood before the master of the house, his eyes lowered in deference.

"And you, son? Have you no welcome for me?" asked Gonzalo Gustioz.

Young Gonzalo lifted his head. "My lord, have you heard about Barbadillo?"

"I've heard something about it. Come and tell me what really happened." Don Gonzalo sat down on the bench, facing away from the table, and his sons arrayed themselves in front of him as if he were the judge in a court case. Sancha sat next to him and held his hand in her lap while Luz busied herself looking for wine and refreshments.

"It's not easy to explain," began young Gonzalo.

"It's good and simple," cut in Gustio. "Doña Lambra made a veiled threat on Gonzalico's life and he defended himself."

"How did she threaten you?" Don Gonzalo asked.

"It was passing strange," said Diego. "She had her page . . . well, you may not believe it, but she had him throw a bloody cucumber at Gonzalico."

Their father licked his lips in preparation to speak, but could think of nothing after such bizarre news. He looked into the eyes of each of his sons. He was about to ask whether he'd heard correctly when Diego mercifully continued.

"We all laughed, didn't we? It was so strange. But then Gonzalico explained to us that in so doing, the page was proving Doña Lambra could hurt or maim us."

Young Gonzalo nodded solemnly.

"His honor was at stake," exclaimed Fernando.

"Is your honor so fragile that you have to kill innocent messengers? Why didn't you think it over? Ask Muño Salido?" said their father.

"We discussed it amongst ourselves," replied Diego. "We decided if the page had laughed and acted as if it were a joke, there would've been no fault, but because he ran away, Doña Lambra must have meant us harm. Otherwise, everything would have been fine. We only intended to tear his clothes to match the damage to Gonzalico's, but. . . ."

"So, when he ran from you, he acted afraid?"

"He was so afraid, father," said young Gonzalo, "he hid himself under Doña Lambra's skirts. I had to pull him out screaming. If he hadn't been wriggling about so much, he wouldn't have died."

Don Gonzalo pursed his lips. "Did you pay a homicide fee?"

"It wasn't necessary because of his rank, and besides, I'd been offended." Young Gonzalo's face was placid, as if resting his case. "Although I'm very sorry our aunt let it go as far as the death of someone so innocent." His brothers sighed or grunted and their father nodded in agreement.

Don Gonzalo wasn't sure how gravely his son had been offended. There was a hint of something his sons weren't saying, something that had escalated the situation by itself. He also felt for the beautiful young girl, who must prefer to be with young men, men like his sons, over marrying Ruy Blásquez, who must have a score of years over her, no matter his reputation and prestige. It was nature at work.... Perhaps young Gonzalo's exaggerated reaction was also natural under the circumstances. His youngest son had studied the law much more than his father had, and he wanted to believe his son, but the whole story was so strange, the unofficial judge couldn't help feeling indecisive.

"Did you attempt to make any recompense?"

Young Gonzalo shook his head gravely. "Mother instructed us to pack up and leave," said Gustio.

"And what do you say, Sancha? Is that how it was?" asked Don Gonzalo.

She furrowed her eyebrows and wrung her hands. "Though I didn't witness the event, I believe my sons are in the right. All the same, I knew we wouldn't be welcome while Doña Lambra was in Barbadillo, if you understand my meaning." Remembering her wild gestures at the entrance to Barbadillo and the fear they struck into his heart, Don Gonzalo nodded. "So we came back to Salas."

"And in Salas we'll stay," pronounced Don Gonzalo.

"I've been giving alms in the Little Page's memory, and I've sent the boys to church every day since. The priest heard their confession, so I'm not sure what else we can do to show our regret," his wife continued. "But we're all deeply grieved, none more than Gonzalico."

His seven sons — such large and unpredictable men — nodded and waited silently with their hands at their sides.

"You must watch yourselves and avoid attacking defenseless men. But I don't forgive you, my son, because I do not judge that you've done wrong."

The brothers' shoulders relaxed in unison. Rodrigo ran his hand across his brow and Suero heaved a sigh.

"But it has been a very unfortunate incident, especially after the way your uncle's wedding ended. We'll wait it out here to see what happens next."

Their relief turned to groans. "It's just like you to get us grounded!" Gustio said to young Gonzalo.

Over the mornings that followed, Don Gonzalo found that his wife wasn't exaggerating. By the time he woke up, his sons would already have gone off somewhere. Sancha instructed Muño Salido to take them to church in the mornings, in the hope that the instruction would stay with them all day. Even though the old tutor awoke before the cock's crow, more often than not, he couldn't find them until midmorning, when they returned to the main house for some kind of breakfast and a scolding from their mother.

Don Gonzalo learned to enjoy the quieter moments when his sons were otherwise occupied. He witnessed his wife's confident directions at the hearth for the day's meals, not only for their family, but also for the families of the vassals and servants. He made the rounds with her as she inspected a different aspect of their lands each morning. He'd assumed he would most enjoy seeing after the curriers and how they cared for the horses in the stables, but when Sancha headed through the wooden stakes to the henhouse, he was captivated. He petted the soft feathers of the ones that didn't run away from him and cooed encouragingly as Sancha reached into the nests for their eggs.

"I think this one is on her last legs. It's been a week since her last lay." She clucked her tongue disapprovingly, then turned to her husband. "Well, I guess we're having chicken for supper." She pointed to the intended dinner, pecking away at the feed grains in the yard with the others.

Gonzalo regarded the disappointing chicken. "It's been fifteen years since you last laid, my darling, and yet I wouldn't even consider dicing you up in a pot." He reached for her, nearly tipping the eggs into the straw.

"Don't be ridiculous," Sancha said, blushing. She handed him the product of another successful chicken and moved on to something she must have been considering for some time. "My lord, I've been thinking it might be time for Diego to settle down and find a wife."

"Hmm. He is the eldest. He must have more than a score of winters behind him."

"Twenty-five. He's one of the highest honored knights in all Castile, but I wonder whether his brothers might be holding him back. I'd like to grant him some land in the region of Lara so Count García doesn't take it into his head to settle my son in the farthest reaches of the realm."

She came to the end of the row, so she modestly held up her skirt and he set the eggs into it. "We could give him Canicosa so he'll be near your brother," Don Gonzalo said. "If the present confusion is settled favorably, of course." They started back to the main hall. She stepped gingerly over grasses and egg-sized stones, and he watched to make sure she wouldn't trip.

They heard the commotion before they saw the seven brothers coming. Serfs and animal caretakers paraded behind them, shouting and whooping.

Don Gonzalo ran to meet them, followed by Muño Salido and Sancha, after she set down the eggs.

"Look what we've done, father," said Fernando over the clamor.

They carried between them a monstrously large cat with black tufts of hair at the points of its ears, a black-and-white-striped beard, black spots down its tawny back, and a fresh, gaping wound near its shoulder. Each brother held a leg, the head, or the tail, except Suero, who clutched his bow and arrows.

"What is it?" asked Sancha, not moving any closer. The animal twitched, throwing half the group off balance and silencing the other revelers. "It's not even dead!"

"That's a lynx, isn't it? Where did you find it?" said Don Gonzalo. "And for the love of St. Peter, be careful."

They lowered the cat to the ground and some set a foot on the paws to hold it down. "We were going out to see if we could catch some rabbits or birds," reported Fernando. "But we found Leo here in a panic over this animal invading the pig sty."

Leo approached Don Gonzalo and kissed his hand. "Without your sons' help, who knows how many hogs we might have lost."

"What was the manner of it?" asked Don Gonzalo.

"Your sons heard me shouting at the beast," started Leo, but Gustio cut in.

"We took out our daggers and tried to corner it, but it was so fast we could hardly keep our eyes on it. We chased it around the sty and it leapt over the fence and was running away when Suero felled it with his arrow."

The brothers led the serfs and animal husbands in a round of applause. Suero made a half serious bow.

"Why in the name of all the saints are you bringing it closer to the house?" said their mother.

"We thought we might be able to trade for the fur," said young Gonzalo.

Sancha crept forward and her husband witnessed her face light up at the elegant dotted pattern of the pelt. Don Gonzalo imagined it would make a fine rug or blanket, or perhaps trim a winter cloak. She straightened up and ordered, "Take it to the slaughterhouse. There's no need to skin it right here." She shook her head and looked pointedly at Don Gonzalo.

They cautiously picked the cat back up, although it was unresponsive, and started away with it. The serfs and animal husbands cheered again. Before Suero followed them, Don Gonzalo kissed him on both cheeks. "Good job, son, saving the sausage."

"Thank you, father." Suero chuckled and rejoined his brothers for more admiration.

"It was thoughtless to bring the animal here," said Muño Salido.

"But brave and worthy to take a lynx down," added the father.

"I don't think there can be any doubt now," said Sancha.

Don Gonzalo nodded. "We have to find something for them to do."

The hall was deserted yet again one early morning. Gonzalo reached out to find Sancha, warm and fragrant like honey. He kissed her responsive lips and stared into her eyes, only to be interrupted by the shaft of light coming through the front door.

"Good morning, my lord and lady," said Muño Salido.

"Not now, Muño," Gonzalo grumbled.

"I'm afraid there's a surprising visitor, Don Gonzalo." He moved from the doorway to remove his lord's tunic from its hook and hold it toward him.

"Who could be so surprising?" asked Sancha.

Muño Salido hesitated. "It's your brother, my lady."

"God save me," cried Gonzalo, standing up and thrusting his arms into the tunic sleeves. "What did he look like? And where are my sons? Find them and bring them here."

Sancha had climbed into a long-sleeved tunic and run her fingers through her hair. Gonzalo stopped her. "Stay here until I know his intentions, dear wife."

"But he's my brother," she replied. "If his heart needs softening, I'm the one to do it."

"Grant me this, darling, and I'll make sure all is well."

She nodded and moved about the hall, opening the shutters and clearing away her sons' bedding. Gonzalo opened the door a crack and peered out. Sure enough, Ruy Blásquez stood next to his horse, casting long shadows in the morning glare, unaccompanied, which was a good sign. He appeared to wait patiently, looking about. He no longer wore a bandage over his nose. A twisted red scar provided a vivid reminder of the wrong done to him and was also the likely culprit of the disturbing whistle going in and out of his face with each breath.

More quickly than Gonzalo would have guessed, he saw the noble retinue of his seven warrior sons and Muño Salido approach Ruy Blásquez. He noted that their hands rested on their hilts, as if they had been invited to a fray. He nodded to himself in approval, then opened the door and stepped into the sunshine.

Ruy Blásquez opened his arms and smiled. "Is this any way to approach your uncle, my boys? Come into my arms, without weapons."

The knights looked to their father, who opened his arms to indicate that they should welcome the visitor. Muño Salido stood back, his arms folded, and let his students approach their uncle. As each son embraced Ruy Blásquez, Gonzalo watched his face glide from joy to inscrutable stoniness. But as his own arms encircled the man's chest, the camaraderie from when they had roved Castile together wafted up around them with the dust of the road.

"Your aunt forgives you and graciously acknowledges that the incident in Barbadillo was her own fault," Ruy Blásquez announced to his nephews.

Don Gonzalo nodded with satisfaction. His brother-in-law had kept his promise to create peace between them.

But Gustio said, "That doesn't sound like our aunt."

"I agree," said young Gonzalo. "Uncle, are you sure?"

"Have you no confidence in me, who helped to raise and teach you? I'm her husband, and I convinced her."

"Imposed your will on her, rather?" said Don Gonzalo.

"Of course. I've been married before. I can handle Doña Lambra. She forgives you completely. There's one thing I'm not sure I can forgive." The brothers reached for their hilts again, but released them as Ruy Blásquez continued, "And it's that you all went back home when your father had promised you to me for soldiers. But if you'll honor the agreement now, even that omission will be forgiven."

"Of course we will, uncle. It's our duty." Young Gonzalo gave a sigh of relief.

Diego looked instead to his father, who recalled what he and his wife had agreed after the lynx incident. "Your mother will miss you, since she needs to stay in Salas to oversee the harvest tributes. But it's true, we had an agreement, and I insist you go back with your uncle right now," Don Gonzalo Gustioz said.

Muño Salido gripped Don Gonzalo's arm with a surprising suddenness of strength that drove his tunic sleeve grinding into his flesh. The tutor brought his lips to Don Gonzalo's ear, but Ruy Blásquez was already speaking in a voice that seemed louder in Salas than it had been anywhere else.

"Doña Lambra told me she knew you would be so gracious and generous. My wife is proving to be wise beyond her years. But I'm afraid I have to send my nephews to Barbadillo without me at first."

"Boys, start getting your things and squires ready for the trip. You'll go this very day, so start saying farewell to your mother," said Don Gonzalo, ushering each son into the front door. Muño Salido followed them, but not before he threw a stern look at his lord and at Ruy Blásquez in turn.

Any doubts forgotten, Don Gonzalo turned to his friend. "What keeps you from Barbadillo and Doña Lambra?"

"Well, I'll be kept from Barbadillo unless you help me and benefit yourself by taking advantage of the opportunity I'm about to offer you," he explained. "You remember my wedding to Doña Lambra and how grand it was. Well, it cost a lot more than I expected, and I only put on so much of a show because Count García had promised to help.

I understand he has a lot of expenses as Count of Castile, but he hasn't yet paid me the debts from the wedding like he ought. On the other hand, Almanzor, the Caliph of Córdoba, promised me a lot of gold, too, and the goods they have in Andalusia are worth much more in Castile, so even if he gives me one fifth of what he pledged, it would be more than enough to settle the accounts. As you said, I would really like to return to Barbadillo with Doña Lambra now, since I had to leave her so soon after the wedding. So I wonder if, as my beloved friend and brother-in-law, you would take letters to Almanzor in Córdoba, and bring what he gives you back to me. If he's as generous as I think he will be, I can let you keep half of it for your trouble. What do you say?"

Don Gonzalo stared into the morning sunlight, considering. "It does sound like an opportunity I shouldn't miss. Might I take my eldest son with me? He knows the south well and can command my troops."

"Oh, no," said Ruy Blásquez, patting his hand reassuringly. "There's no need for you to take anyone with you. I can see you to Silos, but if you'll permit me, from there I'll go back to be with Lambra and your sons. The no-man's-land is just that, and when you cross into Andalusia, just show your letters for safe passage."

"Truly?"

"Oh, yes, everyone can read there, and Almanzor's name is so respected, no one would think of interfering with someone who had business with him."

Gonzalo was still doubting whether every single citizen of Andalusia could read when the door swung open and Sancha, now with her hair properly smoothed into a twist at the base of her neck, marched toward them. "Brother!" she shouted at Ruy Blásquez. "You would leave me alone and destitute without my sons?"

"Sister, there's no cause for worry. Salas is the safest city in Castile. It is eternally protected by the mere reputation of your seven warrior sons."

"Not to mention that things are so calm right now that Ruy Blásquez insists I go to Córdoba alone," added Don Gonzalo.

"You're leaving, too? Without even a squire?" shrieked Doña Sancha.

"Not to worry, Sancha. All he has to do is show his letters for Almanzor, and no one will bother him," said Ruy Blásquez.

Don Gonzalo was warming to the idea. He wanted to see for himself the fabled riches of Andalusia. "Remember Doña Lambra's silks from Andalusia at the wedding? I can bring you back cloth that's even better, and more stones than you know how to string together. It will be enough to make us rich forever. Please, my love, you can administer Salas in my absence. Let me bring you back these gifts so I can honor your station." Sancha stared at each man in turn. She wordlessly threw her arms around Gonzalo Gustioz as if she would never see him again.

"Sancha, dear, I'll no sooner arrive in Córdoba than I'll leave again for Salas. You won't even notice I'm gone," he whispered into her ear.

"If you can say that, you can't understand how much I love you." She pulled away and turned back into the hall.

When the two men followed her inside to pack Don Gonzalo's knapsack, the light seemed to have gone from the building. The brothers took mounted swords from the wall or searched out daggers in trunks, then opened the shutters and proved the shimmer of the blades at different angles in the still slanting sunlight. They had already stacked their boiled leather breastplates and yards of chain mail in the far corner. Sancha moved about the hall, placing items into her sons' packs and taking care to keep her back to her husband and her brother.

Muño Salido followed her wherever she went. "Do not mourn for what hasn't happened. This is a safe and easy mission your sons will utilize to bring honor to the region of Lara."

"They should stay here and protect me in my old age," she insisted, still intent on her tasks.

"Not a single person in Castile would say you're old, mother," said Diego as he fastened a belt that could carry three swords. "You had me when you were only fifteen..."

Sancha set aside the knapsacks and interrupted each of her sons in their tasks in order to kiss their faces. Hers furrowed deeper into grief with each one. "Don't go," she whispered when she had planted the seventh kiss on young Gonzalo's forehead.

"Permit me to say, Doña Sancha, that they're obliged to go for the sake of honor and fealty," said Muño Salido, patting her shoulders for comfort. "And things are so quiet here that there aren't even any birds flying overhead. In fact, I may want to go with your sons. How would that be? I may be getting along in years, but I have a lot of experience. I can guide your sons out of any danger — not that there will be any danger. No, I'm sure the complete absence of auguries is a good sign."

Having made his point, Muño Salido turned to the brothers and told them to prepare the horses for the journey. They filed out of the hall and headed for the stables, nodding to their father as they went.

At the fireplace, Sancha sank her face into her hands.

"Perhaps you'd like to leave today, as well?" Ruy Blásquez whispered to Don Gonzalo.

"Yes, why don't I?" he replied. Disturbed by Sancha's snubbing, he took out a knapsack and Ruy Blásquez laid a folded and sealed parchment in the bottom.

"These letters are for Almanzor only, not his page, not his generals. Almanzor."

Don Gonzalo picked up the parchment and held it in the light from the window as if it would gleam like his sons' swords. "Ah, it's in Arabic writing, anyway."

"Yes, I found a scribe to translate my dictation. I thought it would make it easier on Almanzor not to have to bother with our Latin."

"Will I have trouble making myself understood in the south?" asked Gonzalo.

"No, no," said Ruy Blásquez. "Everyone can speak Christian. I thought it was a diplomatic courtesy to write the Arabic letters."

"Of course," said Gonzalo, unaccustomed to courtly subtlety. He thought about what else should go into his pack, but before he'd made any determination, Sancha laid hard cheese, sausage, crusty bread, and a variety of knives both for eating and defense on the table before him. He looked at her gratefully, and she threw her arms around him again, upsetting his balance.

"Come home to me soon, dear husband," she murmured into his neck.

Don Gonzalo tried to speak over the knot in his throat, but Ruy Blásquez reassured her instead. "He'll be home probably before the harvest tributes. I'm going to accompany him as far as the new monastery of San Sebastián at Silos, so we can be sure he's starting off well rested and as safe as can be."

Sancha let Gonzalo go, so he busied himself packing the knapsack, willing his eyes to stay dry. Behind him, Sancha replied to her brother, "You take good care of my sons."

"Of course. Better than you can imagine."

When Gonzalo was finished packing, he turned around and kissed Sancha goodbye. He looked into her eyes, which reflected his gaze with love and devotion intense enough for an epic poem.

With Ruy Blásquez, Gonzalo walked out into the sunlight, where his seven sons waited with their pages, horses, and accoutrements.

"Farewell, father," said Diego, before all seven crushed the air out of him in an embrace.

Half laughing, half gasping, Don Gonzalo couldn't keep the tears from welling up. "Fare ye well, too, my sons."

"I'll take good care of them," said Muño Salido, standing tall.

"There's no cause for sadness. We'll see you again soon, father," said Fernando.

Ruy Blásquez, outside the family circle, announced, "And you'll see me even sooner," which the brothers took as a signal to release Don Gonzalo and variously kiss Ruy Blásquez's hand, embrace him, or kiss his cheek goodbye. Then they mounted their horses and swept their retinue past the church along the Barbadillo road while their uncle and father left Salas and headed south.

"You know, little brother-in-law, this couldn't have come at a better time," Don Gonzalo commented as they crossed the bridge.

"My sister doesn't seem to agree."

"I must apologize for Sancha's reluctance. Perhaps it's my own fault for not making our finances available for her inspection, but she doesn't realize that without this windfall, Salas might be deserted within a few weeks' time."

"Really," exclaimed Ruy Blásquez. "See how well I love you. I bring you what you need without even knowing about it."

Gonzalo laughed, a deep-throated relief that echoed off the trees as they rode. He wiped the tears from his cheeks and enjoyed the easy day's ride to Silos, where the tonsured monks welcomed them with vegetable soup in a bowl of coarse rye bread. They took their meal on the steps outside the front portico to allow the friars to eat in the refectory in their customary silence. A gentle breeze carried the scent of pine to Gonzalo's nostrils every time he brought the bowl to his lips. Watching the sun glint behind the trees, Gonzalo found himself buoyant with friendship and the prospect of great riches.

"Do they have pine trees in Andalusia?"

Ruy Blásquez lowered his bowl and sucked the air in through his mouth. "Of course they do."

"Are they like the pine trees in Castile? Do the cities have plazas and cathedrals? What are the houses like?"

Ruy Blásquez chuckled. "You'll see all that soon enough, big brother."

The abbot came through the archway. "We're still new, gentlemen, but we have a special space reserved for lay travelers. Permit me to show you." Gonzalo and Ruy Blásquez stood and followed the swirling skirt of his habit down a hall. The abbot pointed out the rough wooden archways in the cloister as if in the hope that these noble knights would give alms for stonemasons. Achieving little reaction, he showed them a small bower, the first room off the cloister with one tiny shuttered window. "It's three times as big as any of our monks' cells," said the abbot, committing the sin of pride. "I hope you pass a restful night." He left a candle burning and drew the door closed after the visitors offered their thanks. They rolled out their mats and settled in.

Ruy Blásquez smacked his lips, settling under his blanket the same way he had on their tour of Castile. Gonzalo eased into a heavy slumber. For those short hours, he was overwhelmed by the same delicious wellbeing he had felt as a young man starting out on a new campaign in Navarra or France in the service of the King of León.

Don Gonzalo thought he could have slept all day in that darkness, but a novice knocked on the door in what turned out to be the late morning, after the monks had finished Lauds. "Good morning, young man," said Gonzalo, sitting up. The boy smiled and nodded. He placed two wooden bowls on a raw timber perch on the otherwise blank wall and made half a bow as farewell, leaving the door open. Gonzalo opened the shutter to let in yet more light, helped himself to the flavorless porridge, and then noticed Ruy Blásquez standing in the corner, his bed already rolled up, his belt cinched, his face a blank mask.

"Um, early riser?" said Gonzalo.

Ruy Blásquez's face morphed into a wide smile faintly twisted by his new scars. "I'm sorry to be leaving you, big brother, but I have to get back to Lambra."

"Of course," replied Gonzalo. "I have to get on the road, too. I'll be quick." He downed the porridge in one gulp before Ruy could say anything else. He rolled up his bed, and Ruy Blásquez helped him tie it off and then gird his belt. "Thank you," said Gonzalo. Running his fingers through his hair, he followed as his brother-in-law led the way to the main door of the monastery, muttering to a stray monk about collecting their horses.

"There are a few more monasteries a day's journey apart where you could stay the night, if you take the western route," Ruy Blásquez commented as they found their horses groomed and waiting for them. "Of course, going directly south, you'll get there faster."

"I think I'll go south, then. I want to get your money back to you quickly, and you said there's no one around, so I could camp safely, right?"

"That's right," replied Ruy while he mounted. "It should take you no more than fourteen mornings to get to Córdoba, and only two or three to arrive where you can trade for more provisions." He turned his horse for the northern road, then looked back and waved farewell.

Gonzalo stood for a few minutes, breathing in the pine-filled air and looking at the trees, again wondering what sorts of buildings and forests they would have in Córdoba once he had completed the long journey. He smiled and waved each one of the seven times he saw Ruy Blásquez look back at him.

The silence was so profound that at times it hummed in his ears. He couldn't stop himself from swatting at it, when a single man appeared on the road ahead as he rounded a curve. He reined in his horse. The upturned shoes, bright green tunic, and wooden flute peeking out of his knapsack told Don Gonzalo this must be a jongleur.

"What are you doing out here?" he asked. "Are there towns to the south?"

"Very few, Sir Knight," replied the minstrel after he doffed his pointed cap and made a theatrical bow. "I've been wandering for days, after the rest of my troupe said they wanted to find a Moorish court to play at. I didn't think we would be welcomed, but it was probably better to have risked it than to have wandered off by myself. Can you tell me if there are Christian towns nearby, sir?"

"I've just come from the monastery at Silos, where I'm certain they'll take you in for the night if you're weary. From there it's only another day's journey to Lara, where we have many towns full of lords and ladies who would delight at your talents."

"I've heard of Lara, home of the famous seven noble knights. Do you know that land well?"

"I am the Lord of Salas. Most of the towns belong to me or my wife."

"And the seven noble knights are your sons! What an honor to meet you, my lord."

Gonzalo held out his hand and the jongleur kissed it.

"But why are you leaving Lara in the direction of such desolation?"

"I have business in Córdoba," he replied, straightening up in the saddle and running his hand through his hair as if he were too important to have concerns about the crossing.

"I'm sorry to say that you have a long, unfriendly journey ahead of you. It's desert for miles, and a warrior like you might run into enemies at any moment."

"No need to worry," said Gonzalo for the benefit of both of them. "My business is so important, no one will bother me."

The jongleur held his breath for moment. Gonzalo wondered what he wasn't saying, but didn't deign to ask. "Well, Godspeed, my lord. And God reward you for the good news you've given me about my road ahead."

Gonzalo nodded, giving the man permission to continue on his way. His voice didn't want to leave his throat, so he nudged the horse's sides with his legs, and that was enough to provoke a smooth, even pace. The sky above him changed from a bright blue to a greenish color he couldn't imagine trying to explain to Sancha. He advanced without seeing any other travelers, but a cold sensation crept along his hands and up to his elbows when off the road he spied an abandoned farmhouse. There was no roof and the stone walls bore scorch marks. A lone rabbit bounded up and down what looked to have been a chicken coop. His stomach clenched. He considered the rations Sancha had placed on the table in spite of her objections to the trip, but then thought if he stopped, he might turn back. Disturbing the horse as little as possible, he rummaged in the knapsack and pulled out only the wineskin and took a swallow every so often. Before he came across any person or landmark, it became too dark to continue. He found a space off the road with enough room between trees to lay out his bedroll. He dismounted against the protests of his legs and tied his horse to one of the trees, hoping they would be hidden if anyone happened by.

"I'm sorry I let it get so dark," he told the horse as he patted its neck and scratched its ears. "There's no way I can find you any water. First thing tomorrow, I promise." He lay down and had to brush some crawling thing off his arm. He wiped at his eyes, so useless in the dark, and most of the night he listened to his horse's breathing as proof that he wasn't alone.

The sun came through the branches to Don Gonzalo's eyes like the tip of a firebrand. His stomach felt like a giant hole. He sat up and rummaged in his pack, pulling out the crusty bread. He was able to swallow with the aid of the last dregs of the wineskin. The sausage, with its layer of grease, was a little easier. He thought he could taste Sancha's love in the food and a tear escaped his eye before he knew it was coming.

"Stinking, crying Christian. What are you doing here?"

Gonzalo hadn't known he could feel any worse, but his heart hit his throat at the sight of three knights wearing turbans on horses with plumed headdresses and studded saddles. The sheen of their chain mail and their metal shield bosses strained his eyes further. They grasped their daggers as if ready to swing low and gut him before he could cry out.

The one who appeared to be the leader continued, "We're under special orders from General Ghalib in Medinaceli to keep the no-man's-land clear of hostile elements."

"I only need water for my horse. I'm on my way to Córdoba," Gonzalo croaked through dry, heaving sobs.

"Alone?" said the head knight. "Are you stupid or insane?" His companions chuckled.

Gonzalo collected himself in response to the challenge. He wiped his mouth, took the parchment out of his knapsack, and stood up, trying not to groan. "This is my safe conduct. It shows I'm on a peaceful mission to see Almanzor."

The knight took the parchment and broke the seal without hesitation.

"That's for Caliph Almanzor alone!" shouted Gonzalo, reaching up, realizing he should never have let go of his only possible protection.

The head knight ignored him, intent on the contents of the parchment. One of his friends said, "Almanzor isn't the caliph, he's the chamberlain, you worthless piece of pagan dung."

The other knight finished reading, and without glancing at Gonzalo, he spoke to his companions in a language that sounded to the Christian lord like a burbling waterfall. They guffawed, sending chills through Gonzalo's body.

The knight handed the letters back to Gonzalo with a smile. "A *wadi*, where you can refresh your steed and fill your wineskin, crosses this road within another hour's time. You're going the right direction, but travel swiftly today and try to make it past the no-man's-land. Once you're in al-Andalus, stay with Christian farmers and avoid the roads. Keep that letter very, very safe." He waved to his compatriots and they proceeded north, chuckling.

Gonzalo stood in stunned silence for a few minutes. He wondered what magic had produced such a dramatic turn in their treatment of him. He had never seen so much hospitality from Moorish warriors, but maybe that was because they had been fighting in Christian lands, so they had no hospitality to give. Or perhaps the scribe Ruy Blásquez had used was a sorcerer and had put some kind of charm on the paper. He crossed himself, hoping God would forgive his transporting such a document into pagan lands. He walked his horse at a brisk pace to the watercourse, just where the Moorish knight had said it would be. He cleared away some stones and filled his wineskin while the horse slurped greedily.

"Better now?" Gonzalo said, patting the horse's neck. He mounted, and at a gallop, they emerged onto a plain. The sky opened up above him and beneath, short grass and wilting wildflowers. He felt himself at an advantage because now he could see anyone coming from miles away. But then of course, they could see him, too. He stopped by the side of the road to eat the cheese Sancha had packed and more of the bread, but when he spied movement on the eastern horizon, his heart told him to be on his way. He didn't wait for whoever it was to come any closer, but set off at a gallop again.

Gonzalo learned that it was one thing to campaign through Christian territory he'd known all his life accompanied by lords, friends, and an entire army, and something else to venture into unfamiliar lands with surprises at every turn and no ally but his horse. He found no one who was obviously Christian, but when he showed Muslim or Jewish farmers a coin, they would bring him bread, meat, or fruits that remained unidentified because of their lack of a common language.

A few times he received a bowl of rice with spices, and once, a leather bag full of fermented milk he was reluctant to try. He hung it from his saddle to ride for the day, and by the evening it had turned into a loose curd cheese he was happy to recognize. He tried to grab at fish in a river, but his lack of success indicated the activity was too close to animal behavior to be appropriate for a Christian, and a noble one at that.

Sometimes he slept in a stable next to his horse, but too many times he lost consciousness under the stars to regain it beneath a stark sun that seemed to burn his eyelids right through. Sometimes he stared into the brightness and let his horse plod forward while he muttered to himself how this was not the way his brother-in-law had described Andalusia.

Halfway through his journey, having crossed sierras, plains, rivers, and forests, he squinted to see a city that appeared to be at least as large as Burgos on the horizon. It looked blurry although there was no fog: on the contrary, the sun's glare had increased steadily, making his eyes water more each day. In spite of its indefinite look, or perhaps because of it, the city rose majestically above the river he was about to cross. A notion leapt into his mind, and when he met a caravan of traders, their carts filled with anonymous packages from the east, he pointed in the direction of the city and said, "Toledo?" to all of them in general.

One of the mule drivers conferred with his partner, then said, "Yes, Toletum."

Gonzalo was too astounded to try to ask what they were trading, so they continued onward. This was the ancient seat of the Visigoths, who ruled with Christian faith and written laws until the besotted King Rodrigo set loose the Moorish scourge over the whole peninsula almost three hundred years before. He thought about following the traders into the city, to sample whatever civilization the old capital could provide, but he worried the people would look on him with suspicion or even delay him somehow. He put Córdoba at the front of his mind and the name of Almanzor at the tip of his tongue, although he wasn't the caliph but some other title.

The confirmed existence of Toledo, a fabled city from songs and lore, showed Gonzalo that in Andalusia anything could be mythic. A pebble or a wildflower could have ties to the history of Hispania, that once unified peninsula, one small corner of which was his home. They had to bring that bountiful land back under the Christian control it was destined for. He could hardly wait to return to his sons, now that he fully understood the meaning of the Reconquest in which they had played some small part. The first task would be to eliminate that General Ghalib who'd sent those Moorish knights into the no-man's-land out of some sense that it was his to clear out. Don Gonzalo would show him whom Hispania belonged to.

Chapter VII

Young Gonzalo paced the entry road to Barbadillo with steps that scared away small animals and birds. Nothing had happened since he'd welcomed his uncle and reunited him with a standoffish Doña Lambra some fourteen mornings previously, but in the absence of other duties, he contented himself with standing sentry.

The monotony broke when a man in a green tunic and pointed cap appeared on the road. Gonzalo thought he could hear bells jingling as he approached. The knight changed the spontaneous grin on his face into a frown and maintained what he hoped was frightening eye contact. When the jongleur stopped and raised his hand in greeting, Gonzalo dropped his lance into his other hand, creating a horizontal block. The jongleur jumped backward.

"Halt," said Gonzalo. "Who goes there?"

"I'm a simple entertainer, come to alleviate the sorrows of this place for as long as the lord and lady will allow me." He cocked his head, sizing Gonzalo up. "Who goes there?"

"I am Gonzalo González, Lord of Salas, son of Gonzalo Gustioz, Lord of Salas, and brother of Count García's highest ranking *alcaide*."

"You're one of the seven noble knights of Lara? How can such fame have come to one so skinny?"

Gonzalo judged the other man no bulkier. He took the lance back into his right hand and put the other on his hip. "I've completed fifteen years. I was knighted last year."

"Impressive," replied the jongleur. "Did you prove your skills against five-year-olds or some babes in their swaddling clothes?"

Gonzalo gripped the lance so tightly that the wood cracked under his palm. But then the entertainer laid his pack on the ground and did a hopping, kicking dance that made his small audience laugh out loud.

Gustio appeared between a multitude of tents and ran to his little brother's side. "You've found us an entertainer. What a godsend!"

"I don't know about a godsend, but the guy is all right," said Gonzalo, winking at the jongleur. "Come and play for us."

At the knight's beckoning, the jongleur picked up his sack and moved beyond the point that had been so well protected moments before. They twisted along a path between the tents and countless knights, many of whom dropped what they were doing in delight and surprise.

"Good going, Gonzalo!"

"Excellent idea, my lord!"

"There's nothing to do here at all, unless you really like goats," explained Gustio.

The traveler considered his surroundings. "I took a risk saying 'lord and lady.' Is this some kind of military encampment?"

"No, this is Barbadillo," said Gonzalo, "an estate protected by the seven noble knights of Lara you're so willing to make fun of and about two hundred of their most loyal fighters."

"Is this place strategic?" asked the jongleur. "I wouldn't have imagined so, but with so many soldiers...."

"Of course it's not." Gustio chuckled. "We're under obligation to the lord and lady, and we thought it would be more interesting if we brought a lot of friends with us." His voice became quieter as the sentence went on, and Gonzalo provided some loud laughter as they opened the door to the main house to make sure no one inside would hear his brother's frankness.

Doña Lambra stood up from her seat at the window and gave a gasp of surprise. Gonzalo couldn't help noticing the way her eyes glittered in the low light. She made a smooth gesture with her thin white hand and Justa put down her sewing and stood up, too. The cooks at the hearth turned to see who it was and cried out with delight. "My dear aunt, I've brought you some entertainment," Gonzalo said.

She strode up to the minstrel, who backed away before regaining his jovial attitude. He took off his pointed cap and made a deep bow. "It is a profound honor, lady."

"Where do you come from?" she asked, looking him up and down.

"I've been wandering Castile for five years, and am just come back from the no-man's-land to the south."

"Your accent isn't Castilian."

"I was born in Asturias."

Gonzalo watched, fascinated, as the jongleur stood up straighter and straighter in response to Doña Lambra's challenges.

"Asturias, near Covadonga, where King Pelayo first rose up against the Muslim invaders," the jongleur added.

"We have no need of a full life story when he's here to tell us so many more interesting ones," Gonzalo said.

"What instruments can you play?" Doña Lambra continued.

"I have a flute with me, noble lady, and a three-string rebec, but it may take me some time to tune it back up."

"Can you sing at the same time as you play?"

"The rebec. Not the flute." He smirked.

"It's not your job to laugh. It's your job to make us laugh. What songs do you know?"

"I know the epics, most hymns, and many popular songs, kind lady."

Doña Lambra met Gonzalo's eyes with flashes of light. "Lead him to a clearing where all of us, and all your knights, can sit around and hear him." Already taking Justa by the arm to return to their previous task, she told the jongleur, "You may begin tuning your rebec. When everyone has gathered, you may play for us. If you entertain us, we will give you supper and a place to rest."

Gonzalo watched the barest suggestion of hips and calves show themselves under his aunt's tunic as she walked away. When he turned to the jongleur, a grin had overtaken his animated face.

"You can't know what this means to me to practice my art again among Christians. The Moors were none too interested, and the monks demanded silent meditation almost all day long."

"The monks?" asked Gonzalo as he struck out on another zigzag between the tents.

"What a dreary bunch. Restful, though. I was at Silos fourteen mornings ago."

Gonzalo brought the minstrel to a clearing in the tents with a backdrop of trees. "My father left for Córdoba from Silos about two weeks ago," he said. "You didn't happen to meet him, did you?"

"I did, now that I think of it," he replied. He set his pack down in the center of the clearing and pulled out his flute and a rebec with strings that were near to falling out of their tuning pegs. He didn't even fish out the bow, but began tightening the catgut.

"Did he seem well?" asked Gonzalo.

"Very well, young knight," said the jongleur. "He was pointed in the right direction, although he had a long journey ahead of him. I wouldn't expect him back for another month."

"No," said Gonzalo. "I expect he'll go back to Salas, and we won't see him for some time after that, anyway. Well, you can tune up while I get everyone assembled, all right?"

Gonzalo looked inside the tents, rousing the company for the most interesting thing to have happened since they'd arrived in Barbadillo. All two hundred dropped what they were doing in the farthest reaches of the farm and happily clustered in the middle of the empty space. Gonzalo's brothers roused the pages, and between them, they brought the two benches from the dining table in the main hall and set them off to either side of the warriors, creating a front row for the estate's nobility.

"I wonder where our uncle is," said Gonzalo over the roar of the two hundred waiting knights.

Muño Salido appeared from somewhere near the stables, Ruy Blásquez on his arm. During long hours of sentry duty, Gonzalo had reflected on their uncle and wondered what he was doing all the time. They hardly ever saw him until late at night, but when he or one of his brothers asked, they never received more than a chuckle in response, as if they were too young to understand the duties of a lord and landowner. The true owner of the estate, Ermenegildo Antolínez, had absented himself with his wife and some servants with no goodbye the day following the seven brothers' surprise arrival. With such strange portents playing out in the people around him, Gonzalo felt something momentous and exciting was about to happen.

"Come and sit with us, uncle!" Gonzalo shouted.

"Gladly, my nephews," Ruy Blásquez bellowed in return. He crossed the expanse of laughing, joking, shouting soldiers and seated himself next to his youngest nephew. He said, "Thank you for this welcome festivity," but Gonzalo could not catch his eye, which seemed focused on some point beyond Gonzalo.

About twenty pages and serving women came from between the now deserted tents and stood in a clump, waiting to see what their lady would have them do. Doña Lambra emerged last, her favorite maid Justa before her, finding the route for them. Gonzalo had often contemplated the maid and thought that with such similar figures and coloring, she could have been Doña Lambra's sister. But while she lacked Lambra's noble station, Justa was vastly sweeter. She was prettier than Gotina, who had pointedly disdained him since the wedding, anyway. If only he could have found Justa by herself, perhaps he could calm those nerves. But the two women were never apart, and the haughtiness of the lady was enough to keep suitors away from the maid.

With a series of impatient gestures, Doña Lambra ensured the house servants spaces in front of the knights, but still sitting on the ground. She placed Justa on the bench across the way from the brothers and made to join her.

"Come and sit with us!" Gonzalo repeated.

Although he felt her energy upon him as distinctly as sparks from a roaring fire, she pretended she had neither seen nor heard anything beyond the midpoint of the crowd on the ground, and continued conferring with Justa as always.

Beside Gonzalo, Ruy Blásquez stirred. "I guess I'll go to her, then."

"No sense wasting all that bench space," said Gonzalo after him.

The crowd hushed to a low rumble as attention focused on the minstrel. He held the body of the rebec up to his ear, plucked a few strings, and nodded to himself. "If I may begin, noble lady?"

Doña Lambra closed her eyes and nodded, granting permission to draw the bow across the strings in a frenetic melody that matched the previous rowdiness of the knights. "It's the summer! Men are lusty! Maidens — "

"It's hardly the summertime." Doña Lambra's voice issued forth as from inside a well and echoed off the tents as she stood up, shaking off Ruy Blásquez's hand. Gustio shook his head at Gonzalo, and Gonzalo nodded agreement at his condemnation of their aunt's objection.

The jongleur, however, nearly dropped his rebec. His voice wavered. "My apologies, dear lady. Mayhap you'd prefer an epic story. Battles between good and evil?"

"Yes, certainly. Which ones do you know?"

"King Arthur, King Pelayo, Count Fernán González. . . ." His voice recovered its steadiness. He ran the bow across the strings, testing his ideas, then raised it as if he'd solved the problem forever. "Perhaps you'd prefer something new. I've just learned an exciting song about the wedding of Ruy Blásquez, uncle of the seven noble knights of Lara."

His wry smile faded as the crowd fell unnaturally silent. Gonzalo heard one of the knights whisper, "What did he say?" to the man next to him. As soon as Gonzalo had the minstrel's gaze, he shook his head emphatically. The musician's face became as red as an autumn berry. He looked down at his pack as if preparing to leave Barbadillo all together.

Doña Lambra, still standing, spoke again. "I don't think that topic would interest anyone here."

"My lady, what about Roland? That was your favorite in Bureba," Justa whispered.

Doña Lambra nodded. "Yes, tell us about King Charles and Roland at the pass of Roncesvalles."

The jongleur cleared his throat again, sounding much drier this time. Someone passed a wineskin through the knights to lay at the minstrel's feet amid laughter. He appeared to gain courage making flourishes with his rebec, and then he began to sing.

"Charles the King, of the Franks lord and sovereign,
Full seven years has sojourned in Spain,
Conquered the land, and won the western main.
Now no fortress against him remains,
No city walls are left to him to gain,
Excepting Zaragoza that sits on high mountain."

Doña Lambra seated herself, and the jongleur sang with gusto. Satisfied silence settled over the audience, the entire estate of Barbadillo, from Ruy Blásquez to the seven brothers to the knights and through the ranks of pages and farmhands.

"Passes the night and opens the clear day
That emperor canters in brave array—"

"No," said a voice that was unmistakably Doña Lambra's. Gustio elbowed Gonzalo in the ribs. Gonzalo emerged from his trancelike listening to see his aunt drawing herself up to her full height again. "That's not the way they sang it in Bureba."

Ruy Blásquez stood beside her and attempted to catch her waving hands. "Now, Lambra, I'm sure each region has a different manner of telling. This man is a foreigner, isn't he? Let's hear his version."

"He's skipped the Emperor Charlemagne's dreams. There's no point to the story without them." She folded her arms.

"I've never heard another way to tell this most veracious tale," said the jongleur.

Doña Lambra heaved a sigh and launched into a spoken recitation.

"Passes the day, the darkness is grown deep,
That emperor rich Charles lies asleep
Dreams that he stands in the great pass of Size,
In his two hands his ashen spear he sees
Guenes the Count that spear from him doth seize
Brandishes and twists it with such ease..."

"I've never heard those words, I swear it, my lady," the minstrel broke in. "They are excellently conceived and you recite them well, but...."

"That's because they belong there. I think I know this poem better than you, whose office it is to remember these lines for our edification." She took a few threatening steps toward him.

"My memory is perfectly suited to my occupation," the jongleur said. He set his instrument down and slipped his hand into a pocket of his tunic, pulling out what looked like a small piece of folded parchment. "The proof is right here." Gonzalo followed his brothers and uncle, who stepped up to see what the object proved. It turned out to be a tiny book, about half the height of Gonzalo's palm, without a cover and stitched down the center with black thread.

"Who gave you that book?" Doña Lambra huffed.

"I made it myself, lady, from spare scraps I've found over the years. This way, I can be sure never to forget." As the jongleur turned a surprising number of pages with a practiced thumb, Gonzalo saw the words making up the first few lines of all the epic songs he had ever heard, followed by a list of words outlining the basic plots. When he'd located the *Song of Roland*, the jongleur put the page under Doña Lambra's face. "See there? No dreams at all."

Doña Lambra glanced at her husband in bewilderment and Gonzalo guessed that she had never been taught to read. Her cheeks reddening, she said, "It only shows that my memory is better than your letters. Be gone from here. Now."

The minstrel stood still, as if seized with fear.

"I'll escort him out, aunt," said Gonzalo. "I'm the sentry." As he knew she would, she ignored him, and turned back through the tents toward the house, Justa joining her without need of words. The two hundred knights shouted and pounded their fists on the ground. Gonzalo leaned close to the minstrel's ear to make sure he could hear. "I'll take you to a hiding place, and once we get the benches back inside and my aunt settled, perhaps you can still play for these cavaliers and stay with them."

The jongleur relaxed and gathered up his pack. "That is most kind, noble knight. I don't know what happened. I'm accustomed to speaking my mind."

"So is my aunt," replied Gonzalo. "I'm afraid it's her mind that holds sway here."

After he had settled the jongleur in to hide for a while in the stables, Gonzalo returned to the scene to find that one of the benches had already been returned to the main house and the two hundred knights had scattered like autumn leaves. His brothers, however, were standing in a circle speaking with Ruy Blásquez.

"Ah, Gonzalo," he said, "join us, join us."

"What's going on?" Gonzalo asked Diego.

"Our uncle has a proposition for us, and we're debating it," he answered brightly.

Gonzalo knew this was the exciting event he'd sensed in his uncle's absences. "What sort of proposition?"

Ruy Blásquez took him by the shoulder. "Are you enjoying your idle time here with Doña Lambra while your father seeks glory in Córdoba, or would you prefer to shake off the cobwebs on the field of battle?"

Gonzalo took a moment to add a bit of deference to his eagerness for something to do. "Uncle, although our aunt is most gracious and beautiful, I think I speak for us all when I say we hold no cause more dearly than putting the Moors in their place, which is to say, outside of Hispania. Do you have a specific plan?"

"I have it on good authority that Almenar is unprotected and practically deserted at this time. Imagine if we could take it for Count García. Imagine the honors at so increasing the southern border."

Six of the brothers inhaled as if snatching the idea out of the air and grinned.

"Uncle, doesn't it seem to you that taking advantage of the vulnerabilities of such a strategic location, when we ourselves are so strong and could take a much better protected city, is a little dishonorable?" Fernando said.

"The only ones without honor are those who've left Almenar unprotected. I intend to go and take it. You certainly don't have to come with me. You're perfectly welcome to stay here with Doña Lambra for the rest of your earthly lives."

"Come on, then. You don't want to look like a coward!" Gustio exhorted his brother.

"No, we don't," agreed Fernando.

"When are we leaving?" asked Gonzalo.

"There are many knights who want to come with me, since they know how successful I tend to be at these enterprises. They're supposed to meet me at the entrance to Barbadillo tomorrow morning."

"Perfect," said Gonzalo. He waited for his uncle to weave back through the tents, doubtless to report to Doña Lambra. "He doesn't give much time to prepare, does he?"

"No, but it doesn't matter," said Diego. "We can have these knights packed, ready, and willing in a few hours."

"True enough," said Gonzalo. He headed back to the stables to check on the horses and make sure there weren't any problems before they needed them the next day. He found the jongleur petting the nose of one of the stallions. "Oh," he said. "I'm afraid our arrangement won't work. We're leaving tomorrow in the morning, our knights are coming with us, and we'll be too occupied the rest of the day to hear your music."

"It's a good thing I'm well rested," he replied, stepping away from the horse and taking up his pack to make his way.

"Don't leave yet." Gonzalo took his hand and cupped it around a gold coin. "I need to ask you a favor for tomorrow. Some of the knights will let you stay in their tent overnight. Continue to Salas. You'll be welcomed there by my mother, Doña Sancha. Please, for the sake of a knight who tried to do right by you, tell her that her sons are well and are headed to Almenar."

"You're certain I'll be well received?"

"Trust me, my mother is a much better hostess than Doña Lambra."

In spite of her unpredictable moods, Gonzalo knew he would miss Lambra's golden hair and flashing eyes when they left.

The seven brothers met Ruy Blásquez's volunteers before he did. The previous night had been the last for some foreseeable time in which Gonzalo would have to endure the sweet torture of sleeping across the chamber from his untouchably beautiful aunt and her maid. Gonzalo had seen the minstrel off within an hour of sunrise, and knowing good news of them would reach his mother made his heart light. The brothers and Muño Salido waved goodbye to Doña Lambra and left Ruy Blásquez to say a perhaps more intimate farewell. Astride steeds with shining coats and polished saddles, under leather breastplates and chain mail that glittered in the early light, Gonzalo thought they cut fine figures as they led their two hundred equally spruced knights out to the post where he'd stood sentry so many days. Even hoary-headed Muño Salido sat up as straight and strong as the sword he kept at the ready in its sheath.

The sentry post was not the same deserted area Gonzalo knew so well. Crowded together on the road so tightly he couldn't begin to count them, a swarming mass of cavaliers and foot soldiers waited.

"Who goes there?" he questioned out of habit.

"We're vassals of Ruy Blásquez, gathered to sally to Almenar," one of the knights in front replied.

"Welcome, friends," said Martín.

"We're the seven noble knights of Lara and our vassals, and we're going forth to Almenar as well," said Diego.

Gustio cut in. "I hope there will be enough riches for all of us."

The enormous mass of armored warriors was laughing when Ruy Blásquez appeared behind the brothers' knights. He had to shout to be heard before Gonzalo noticed his arrival on foot, weaving his horse through the chaos. He confronted Diego.

"I didn't know you were bringing all two hundred of your knights with you."

"Of course we are, uncle. They're as bored as anyone else," said Gustio.

"Who is going to stay and protect my wife?"

Perhaps because it was so unexpected, Gonzalo hadn't even seen Doña Lambra standing on the other side of her husband's horse. He started, unsettling his steed.

"No, no, no." Doña Lambra shook her head and set her jaw.

Gonzalo realized she thought he was volunteering for the task. He wasn't sure how to explain that he would much rather go and battle Moors without insulting both the host and his lady, but luckily, she was adamant.

"I won't need any knights with me. It's perfectly peaceful here and Ermenegildo Antolínez will return soon."

Ruy Blásquez came around the front of his horse and took her in his arms. She visibly stiffened. "In that case, my brave wife, we must be headed out. The day is getting late."

She kissed him on the cheek and whispered to him, ending with an encouraging clap on the arm. The exchange was so unlike anything Gonzalo had seen his mother and father do that he shook his head in wonderment.

Ruy Blásquez mounted his horse. Doña Lambra patted his leg and turned back toward the estate, but not before she shot a look at Gonzalo that he thought he could hear snapping in the air around his ears. He couldn't tell what she meant by it, so he turned his mind to the simpler matters — battles, raids, maybe a siege — facing them.

Ruy Blásquez rode ahead in order to be at the vanguard of his vassals and the brothers followed with their tutor and knights under bright blue skies made crisp with the coming autumn.

For two days, they had been traveling at a steady pace that was faster than such a large number could usually manage. The brothers' warriors followed close behind the brothers, and the brothers followed Ruy Blásquez's soldiers narrowly. Ruy Blásquez in turn seemed motivated by a superhuman force.

"Maybe he really needs some money," mused Gustio that afternoon on the road.

"He did send our father after a large treasure. Can his wedding have been so expensive?" wondered Gonzalo.

"I'll never get married if weddings cost that much," said Gustio.

"What father would marry his daughter to you, anyway?" Gonzalo's remark elicited chuckles from his brothers.

"Boys," Muño Salido reprimanded.

"What?" Gonzalo was saying when a rook, flying much lower than usual and by itself, zipped through their disorganized ranks from the back, sending the soldiers to the sides of the road. Its slender wings pulled it higher up before it would have reached Ruy Blásquez, who advanced down the road unaware his nephews and their knights had stopped.

"That was unusual," puffed Diego, shaking off his surprise.

"God save us!" Muño Salido's voice resonated in Gonzalo's ears. When the brothers looked at their tutor, he was pointing into the sky, where the glossy black bulk of a carrion crow traced a path over the road.

"What's the problem?" asked Gonzalo.

"The rook and the crow. This doesn't bode well for our campaign." He clutched at his heart.

An eagle came screeching through the sky, passing back and forth over the brothers and their tutor, increasing the volume and frenzy of its call with each pass. As Gonzalo watched, it tried to land in a pine tree, but each claw grasped at a separate branch, upsetting the raptor's balance. It fell headfirst, wings flapping, and brought the branches around itself in a tangle, constricting its own neck. Suero rode toward the tree, probably sympathetic with a bird of prey, but he could never have reached the tragedy in time. The more the eagle flapped and struggled, the faster it happened. Its dead weight bent the branches so that the tree released it to the ground it had never visited in life.

The brothers looked to Muño Salido again. He hung his head briefly, but when he looked back at them, there was no doubt in his voice. "We must turn back."

"Back to where?" said Fernando. "There's nothing for us in Barbadillo, and if we go back to Salas, we won't be fulfilling our obligation."

"We can come back when the omens are better," said Muño Salido. "A carrion crow higher in the sky than a rook is enough of a warning, but that eagle killing herself..." He turned his horse and came back through the clear space in the center of the road.

"Shouldn't the omen apply to the leader of the expedition rather than to us?" asked Martín.

The question seemed to give Muño Salido pause. "If you insist on continuing on, I ask that at least we send a page to your mother, to tell her to cover seven cots with dark cloth and mourn over them. That may help to undo the augury."

"Muño Salido, that's un-Christian," shouted Gonzalo, his hand gravitating toward the hilt of his sword. "I would strike you down right here for such beliefs if you weren't the man who taught me everything, including Christian doctrine."

Muño Salido shook his head. "You all refuse to turn back?"

Gonzalo looked to his brothers and, reading their consensus, nodded once.

"I curse the hours in which I raised you not to take my advice. I will return to Doña Sancha and await your news." He urged his horse onward, but then stopped short and returned. "Come to me, each of you, and let me kiss you, since it could well be the last time I see you."

Maneuvering the horse to each brother in turn, he kissed both of Diego's cheeks and Martín's forehead. He clasped Suero's gloved hands and held Fernando in the closest hug he could manage. Gonzalo saw he would be last, as always, so he tried to cut the tension.

"So much tragedy for such an old man!"

And so the brothers were laughing when Muño Salido kissed Rodrigo and Gustio.

"Farewell," Gonzalo whispered in Muño Salido's ear. The old man wiped a tear from his own eye.

Muño Salido turned and headed back up the road without saying anything more.

The brothers gathered together and led their knights in pursuit of Ruy Blásquez. Two miles up, they found the troops and their lord stopped and waiting.

"What happened?" asked Ruy Blásquez. "Where is Muño Salido?"

Gonzalo wasn't sure how to explain it, so he was glad when Gustio spoke for them. "He turned back after reading an augury he thought pointed to our deaths."

"Ah, is that so? I always knew he had something of a sorcerer about him." Ruy Blásquez's mouth twisted as if he were in deep thought when he brought his horse closer to Gustio. "What sort of augury was it?"

"The flights of birds, his specialty," Gustio explained. "A carrion crow flying above a rook, and then an eagle that screeched its heart out and strangled itself in a pine tree."

Ruy Blásquez smiled. "So, it's all been a simple misunderstanding. That kind of sign means our venture in Almenar will be an unmitigated success."

"I never knew you could read the flights of birds, uncle," said Gonzalo.

"Oh, yes, elementary. Nothing bad at all. Actually, I'm very upset with Muño Salido for abandoning you like this. Guard yourselves well, knights, since your tutor refuses."

"I do not refuse," came a vigorous voice from the back ranks of the brothers' knights. It belonged to an old man on a horse that had been running too hard.

"Muño Salido, you've come back," said Gonzalo with a grin.

"I couldn't leave you," he said as he made his way back to his students. "It's my duty to stay. Besides, what do I have to fear as a man who has already lived his life when you young saplings never hesitate?" The brothers clapped him on the back with smiles and chuckles.

But Ruy Blásquez had become stern since the tutor's reappearance. "Muño Salido, you were always against me, and you're working against me now, making up lies and witchcraft about omens to make my soldiers abandon me. I deserve satisfaction from you."

"Listen, Ruy Blásquez," Muño Salido responded. "I came here in good faith to help and support my charges in any way I could, and never with any interest against you. But I would have to accuse anyone who interprets that augury as favorable of lies and treachery."

"You words are violent, old man." Ruy Blásquez folded his arms in self-defense.

"Only as violent as your denial that the omens are bad," Muño Salido said.

"What use are campaigns if you won't even protect me when you see me so dishonored?" Ruy Blásquez cried to his soldiers.

One of the soldiers advanced, sword drawn, on an unprepared Muño Salido. Before he reached his prey, Gonzalo drew his weapon and sliced at the offender's shoulder. The knight fell bleeding to the road among the horse's hooves, startling them. In the commotion, the only distinct sound Gonzalo heard was Ruy Blásquez's voice calling, "To arms! To arms!"

"He wants to kill us!" shouted Diego to his brothers, and they started riding away, each as he could, with Ruy Blásquez's faithful minions in close pursuit.

Gonzalo couldn't continue running away after such a strange event. With rage building in his chest, he halted and shouted back to Ruy Blásquez. "Why are we about to kill each other when we came here together to fight against Moors?"

The galloping and clanking died away as his brothers and their knights and then Ruy Blásquez's troops stopped, ready to hear what the leader of the campaign would say.

Ruy Blásquez studied the faces of the soldiers around him. He gestured behind him at the bloody knight on the ground. "You killed my vassal," he said weakly.

Gonzalo dismounted and signaled to his brothers and Muño Salido to follow. When they came upon the wounded knight, he didn't move, and his face stared at the sky with no recognition. Rodrigo knelt and slid his hands under the knight's breastplate. "He's dead," he confirmed. When he pulled his hands out, they were covered in so much blood that Gonzalo felt shoved back by its warmth and metallic smell.

"I think you pierced his heart," Rodrigo said to him. "How did you manage that?"

Muño Salido brought Rodrigo to a patch of grass to wipe off the blood and kept tidying him with an ancient handkerchief. Gonzalo looked up at his uncle, still mounted and with his hand on his hilt. "I'm very sorry about this, uncle. Your knight attacked Muño Salido, and I was defending him as well as I could. But if your knight is your only grievance, then we're willing to pay his homicide fee, which is fifty *sueldos*, and by rights you should accept it." His brothers searched the pouches in their belts to contribute to the fee.

Ruy Blásquez mutely observed the way his own troops seemed to fall in with the wisdom of this resolution. When they had assembled the sum of fifty *sueldos*, Ruy Blásquez held out his hand in tacit agreement. Both groups of armored men nodded their approval.

Ruy Blásquez stowed the coins in a fold of his tunic. "That knight must be given a Christian burial. Ten of your soldiers must take him back to Vilviestre and see to it."

"Who will take this knight back to his home in an honorable fashion?" Gonzalo saw no hands raised. To his uncle, he said, "No one wants to miss the riches at Almenar. My brothers and I will go."

"Nonsense," said Ruy Blásquez. "If there are not ten volunteers, I will choose twenty and oblige them."

Two soldiers stepped forward.

"Thank you, gentlemen. Two will be plenty for this task," said Gonzalo.

During the hours it took for the brothers and Muño Salido to say what prayers they could for the knight's soul, clean the body, wrap it in linen, and lay it in the supply cart, Ruy Blásquez paced the road, hesitating and tapping his foot when he faced the direction of Almenar. Gonzalo marveled at the change in his uncle since the wedding. He whispered to Gustio, "I think our uncle is becoming more like Doña Lambra every day."

And so the accidental casualty of the Almenar campaign started back home between resisted smiles and repressed snickers.

Chapter VIII

Don Gonzalo moved doggedly onward over more plains and a sierra that lowered him bit by bit. Every time he said "Córdoba?" he received nods and directions. The people he met offered him water and soap to wash with because his body was so caked with stinking, itchy grime. At first, he thought the dirt layer must protect him from the burning of the ever-increasing glare of the sun. When the flakes of his scalded skin sloughed off to prove that the dirt had no benefit, he accepted the charity, wishing it were Sancha scrubbing the thirst, hunger, and heat away and offering him clean clothes.

Every day, he found a new piece of evidence of the sensual way the Moors lived in Andalusia, and it inspired a new battle plan he would take home to Count García as soon as he collected Almanzor's debt. So many thoughts and the constant, sore-inducing, movement of his horse under the stretching sky made his head so heavy he usually lay down near a water source and fell asleep without eating or brushing off his companion.

Palm trees lined the widest river he had ever laid eyes on the morning after he'd passed between extensive farms with olive groves and tangled grape vines. From the sound of it, he judged several waterwheels to be at work out of sight. Beginning outside the riverbank, a solid crenellated wall of golden stone blocks rose in a semicircle.

A stench he recognized from his victories on the battlefield wafted into his nose. Hung on ropes from the top of the wall, heads with decomposing eyes gaped down at him. These must be the criminals and enemies of Córdoba. Well, Don Gonzalo wasn't an enemy. An opening in the wall stood before him, wide enough for two men on horseback.

He hesitated. When he looked down, he saw the dust of the road all over his tattered tunic. He could feel the sweat welling up on his forehead and in his armpits and imagined his face as a pool of mud where it wasn't bright red, scorched by the sun. He dismounted and shook himself off, raising more dust. Taking his horse's reins, he tied it where it could drink from the river if it wanted. Then he stepped though the archway, where narrow cobblestone streets twisted between whitewashed walls of one and two stories. He wandered for a few minutes, stepping as if he were trying not to disturb a sleeping dragon. A man in long robes and a turban darted in front of him and another hurried past. Gonzalo wanted to stop someone and ask where the main square was, thinking that from there he could get his bearings, but his intentions were interrupted by a sudden voice from above that filtered into the streets below, reverberating against the walls in a mournful tone Gonzalo wouldn't have called a melody. The doors in the buildings opened to pour men, women, and children into the streets. It should have been a confusing jumble, but every last person was headed in the same direction in a purposeful manner. Gonzalo let some of them pass, then held out his hand to catch a turbanless man by the shoulder.

"Main square? Principal plaza?" he asked as simply as he could.

The man nodded and pointed in the direction everyone was already going, confirming Gonzalo's suspicions. They must be holding a meeting in the main square.

Smiling at his luck, he allowed himself to be swept along by the tide of humanity. After only a few more twists and turns, the close-huddled buildings opened into a space from which he could see that enormous river again. The space was not empty, however; in the center was a gold stone building with arcades through which everyone was walking, women through one side and men through another. He craned his neck to see a tower, taller than any tree or building, reigning over the movement below. The notion of a cathedral entered Gonzalo's mind. When he passed through the archways, he found himself standing in a patio as big as the main square in Burgos, with pruned fruit trees at regular intervals, straight rivulets of water that appeared from nowhere in channels dug into the soil, and pools in which the men washed their faces, hands, and forearms before going through a set of archways at the far end. The women, colorful and at the same time discreet, disappeared behind a wooden screen with floral perforations that let light inside, but not gazes.

Reaffirming his notion that this was their cathedral, Gonzalo stepped toward the men's entrance, but paused when instead of a central altar and side chapels, he saw a forest of marble columns supporting arches made from alternating stripes of white and red brick. They seemed like fanciful creatures that might start moving at any moment. Gonzalo couldn't see the far wall past all the men, who placed their rugs on the floor in rows facing away from him. He stood dumbfounded until someone with a long nose and teeth that stuck out even when his mouth was closed grabbed his tunic sleeve and grunted, "Christian? Not here."

"Is this Córdoba?" Gonzalo asked in bewilderment. "I need to find the caliph, Almanzor."

"El Mansur," repeated the Muslim. His eyes darted around the patio and found a likely candidate, a clean-shaven man with blue eyes and light eyebrows under his rose-tinted turban. The first man spoke in Arabic to the second, who looked at Gonzalo with impatience.

The blue-eyed man led Gonzalo outside the patio and took him by the shoulders to situate him. "This is Qurtuba, but El Mansur isn't here. He lives and works in Madinat al-Zahra, which is four miles up that road you see there."

Gonzalo looked where he was pointing in the distance, away from the river, where a clear road jutted through the hills of wild grasses. He grimaced. "Well, I've come this far. What's four more miles?"

"I have to get back to the mosque for prayers. You can find Madinat al-Zahra?"

"Of course," replied Gonzalo, relishing the long-awaited civility. "I am most grateful to you." The man hurried off. Gonzalo slipped beyond the wall and found his horse by the river. "Just a little farther now, my faithful friend," he said.

The road stretched as wide as a Roman one Gonzalo had seen near León and was flanked every few feet by tall poles, the purpose of which he couldn't fathom. Dead ahead of him lay a fortress or city he thought he'd heard the man call Medina Azahara. No one was out at this time, Gonzalo thought, because they were in the mosque. He was pleased with himself for having figured out that the singular building was their cathedral. He was musing about how such a strict habit made them vulnerable to an attack, if a Christian army ever made it this far south, when, more quickly than he'd predicted, he arrived. He covered his nose, said a short prayer, and looked away as he passed a line of four crucified bodies — yet more enemies on display.

A series of white stone archways marked this new city off from the road. They were large enough for Gonzalo to pass through without dismounting, so he rushed forward, noting as he did that the middle arch was presided over by a life-sized statue of a robed woman. A man in a turban standing outside the building on the other side of the gate raised his hands and shouted. Gonzalo stopped and fished about for the letters that would grant him admittance.

"I'm a special emissary to Almanzor," he said, looking past the guard. He hadn't imagined such an elaborate palace, and had to stick to his original plan to bluff his way in to see the man who would pay him so much wealth.

The guard reached up for the letters, but Gonzalo didn't let go of them.

"I will accompany you to the monumental gate, *sidi*," said the guard, taking hold of the horse's reins. Gonzalo felt perplexed by the idea that there was another gate. They eased up a slope and passed through a gate that seemed monumental to him, taller than the first. A vaulted dome soared over them as they continued forward. Men hurried about between the buildings on either side of them, which had archways rather than doors, so that the outside and inside flowed together. These men observed the guard with Gonzalo and let them pass. He only understood what the guard had meant by monumental when the man led him to the end of a queue and waved farewell before turning back toward his decidedly preliminary gate.

Before Gonzalo towered fourteen archways in the red and white pattern he recognized from the mosque, three times the height of a man, mesmerizing in their regularity and awe-inspiring in their reach for the clear blue sky. The central archway was higher than the others, and as Gonzalo watched, men in turbans flowed out of it while a line was forming behind the first man trying to get inside. He had been stopped by another guard who glanced at a parchment, took his weapons, and spoke at length before waving the traveler through. Gonzalo jumped down from his horse and held it by the reins, making the arches seem even taller, and remained spellbound, unaware of the passage of time before he became the first in line. He nodded to the guard, who maintained a creased frown. Gonzalo unfolded his letters for the muscular guard to see his importance as envoy of his brother-in-law.

A rush of disconnected sounds came out of the guard's mouth. Gonzalo shook his head. "I don't know what you're saying."

"I'll take your horse and weaponry. You go through this gate, *sidi*."

Gate, thought Gonzalo. If this was a simple gate, what were the wooden entrances to the chicken coops in Salas? He took the dagger and sword out of the sheaths on his belt, folded his parchment back up, and walked through, ducking his head as if he were entering a cathedral. Now he was confronted with more passageways that seemed to be half indoors and half outdoors. A sliver of sunlight gleamed on the smooth stones that showed the way in and out of secret corners and routes that led who knew where. He turned, and another man, similar to the guard in stature and attitude, was waiting for him.

In his growing confusion, Gonzalo handed over the parchment. It was the first time it had left his hands since the ugly incident in the no-man's-land. The man glanced at it and began speaking in that bubbling Arabic, but then appeared to think better of it. "You don't know what these letters say?"

"Not for certain. But I'm here to collect a debt the caliph owes my brother-in-law."

"The letters are addressed to the chamberlain, *sidi*."

He remembered the word from his encounter with the soldiers, nearly two weeks before. "Yes, that's what I meant. Almanzor, to be specific."

"The chamberlain holds the most honored rank among us, but El Mansur would never usurp the caliph's noble title." The guide considered for a moment, then clapped his hands. A beautiful woman appeared at his side, and he spoke short words to her before she scurried away again.

"You've come from the north? You must be exhausted and filthy from your long journey. Let us prepare you a bath and some food before you see the chamberlain."

There could have been no greater temptation to him after the grubbiness of the journey, but Gonzalo felt vulnerable and waivered for a moment until the idea of soap and some undreamed-of dish of food made him follow the guide without question. They passed anonymous walls, archways carved in alternating patterns he didn't have time to appreciate, a sculpted marble pool, an artificial pond full of orange fish, doors that were black as pitch and others that were white as bone, and a few wooden doors with that loopy writing engraved on them. His guide stopped at a door with leaves and flowers carved into it and Gonzalo walked inside. Smaller versions of the omnipresent archways along the top of the walls vented the room and provided light while maintaining privacy within. The woman Gonzalo had seen before was filling an enormous green, blue, and white tiled basin from a clay jar. She nodded to the men.

"It's nearly full. Take off your clothes and step in," said the guide.

"Take my clothes off?" repeated Gonzalo. "No thanks, I'll wait."

The man spoke to the woman briefly, then excused himself from the room. Gonzalo watched as the woman refilled the jar under a stream of water that came running out of the wall. The water she didn't use dropped into a small tiled pool that directed the flow into the floor. Next to this miraculous artifice, Gonzalo recognized a brazier for warming the jug, but it hadn't been used for months. Wiping at his sweaty forehead, he knew why not.

The woman wore a kind of dress made of flowing golden silk not unlike the material he had seen Doña Lambra wear at her wedding. Gonzalo dreaded to calculate the wealth of a city that could afford to dress the servants in such finery. Her chestnut hair was combed forward and trimmed at the eyebrows so that she never had to tie it back or brush it out of her eyes. Her glance from under the fringe looked wryly askew to Gonzalo as she gestured him into the filled tub.

He didn't make a move until she was gone. Then he peeled off his tunic, shoes, and undershirt, unleashing a world of odors. He decided to leave his breeches on. He lifted his leg high and pushed his foot past the layer of dried rose petals into the cool water. The pleasure against his sun-heated skin forced him to put his other foot in. He stood in the tub for a moment, rubbing the slick tiles with his toes, before sitting down and letting the water soak into his breeches. After he ran the fragrant liquid through his crusted hair, he relaxed and watched a complicated pattern of red and gold paint as it danced on the ceiling.

Ruy Blásquez hadn't said Andalusia would be so gratifying. Gonzalo wondered about this Almanzor. He thought the caliph was like a king, but then the chamberlain seemed to be in charge. Something else inscrutable about this decadent land.

Gonzalo awoke with a start when he felt his beard slide under the water. He climbed tottering out of the tub, squeezed the drips out of his breeches and shook his head to send the drops flying. He peeled off the rose petals he could find by sight and by feel. He dried off the rest of his exposed skin with a soft blanket that appeared to have been placed on a ledge for the purpose. The white fabric was brown when he carefully folded it back up. Hurriedly placing the stiff clothes over his body, he shivered at the contrast of their retained heat. Something that looked like a lamp was suspended by a chain at head level, and he looked inside to find that its fabric wick was soaking in fragrant oil.

The door opened and the page who had guided him to this bath room entered. He raised his eyebrows at the water splattered all over the room. "Finished, *sidi*? Are you refreshed? You didn't want to change into the robes we laid out for you?"

Suddenly, Gonzalo understood what the other folded fabric was for. Disoriented in his cleanliness, he couldn't think of anything to say. He patted at his tunic to make sure his parchment was still where he could get it.

"I understand. You're hungry. We've prepared some food I think you will enjoy if you come with me."

Don Gonzalo blindly followed his guide through more corridors and stumbled into another chamber, this one airy with windows on two ends that looked out on green plants and a shiny marble ledge to sit on near a basin that burbled with its own running water. On the ledge was an earthenware platter painted white and green and heaped with rice the same color as the serving woman's silks. Gonzalo's stomach rumbled at the smell of it.

"It has shellfish, white fish, and chicken as well as vegetables. I hope it doesn't contravene any fasting you might be observing in the Christian calendar," said the guide.

Gonzalo thought it was probably about the first of September. He had always relied on Sancha to keep track of the menu rules, anyway. "No," he replied.

"Then please enjoy. I will return to take you to Almanzor after prayers." The page disappeared in one of the many turning passages.

As Gonzalo set his travel-weary bones on the ledge atop yielding silk squares, he could imagine how his sister-in-law Lambra had felt sleeping each night on such things at her wedding. The caliph himself, probably raised on them, had never experienced the luxury of feeling so comfortable for the first time in forty-five years. Gonzalo pried open mussels and sucked out the sweet, spongy flesh.

He pushed the shells aside and ran his fingers over the plate to savor the spices and stray rice grains. Then he went to the basin and drank copiously from hands that still smelled like roses. At the window, he searched for the birds that were making a steady, soft cooing. A floral breeze came through the window with another one of those warbling chants he'd heard before everyone had flooded into the mosque hours earlier. When the guide returned for him, he was in such a stupor that he couldn't tell how much time had passed or whether he had been asleep again.

"The ministers have returned from prayers in the mosque. I'll take you to see Almanzor now."

Eager to show what he knew, Gonzalo asked, "The mosque in Córdoba?"

"Of course not. The caliph's mosque here in Madinat al-Zahra."

Gonzalo had no time to feel embarrassed. His guide rushed him through a garden he hardly had time to glimpse, straight to an airy hall. Two rows of red and white striped arches supported on alternating black and salmon-colored marble columns divided the space into three equal oblong chambers. They stopped in the first chamber, where countless men, fragranced with what were most likely expensive resins, sat in rows along the walls, conversing or waiting quietly.

The guide gestured to an open space, which Gonzalo took to be an invitation to sit down. As the guide disappeared, he folded his legs in imitation of the other men. Their robes were a rioting contrast of colors and stripes of which he couldn't guess the meaning. Such differences in the fabrics were probably geographical or social. Nearly all of them wore turbans, and his hands went to his scalp, feeling oddly exposed. But then, he guessed that they were all equal while they sat here shoulder to shoulder, awaiting an audience with Almanzor. He had taken the last available space along the wall, so he wondered how many days he would have to wait. Not that it would be disagreeable, even though he understood nothing of the low, serious-toned conversation around him. He imagined spending days staring at the lobed column capitals, at the marble walls sculpted in the most minute detail to create leaves, vines, and trees in every available space. Aside from the entrancing color contrast, with the deepest red yet, Gonzalo reckoned the archways must be made of sandstone to create such fine arcs and whorls. From his position, he couldn't quite see past the columns into the next chamber, but he guessed that craning his neck or getting up to look wouldn't be a favored activity. His only remaining desire was that Sancha could see it, too. He shook his head, trying to describe it all for her.

The man seated next to Gonzalo was staring at him. He was sitting up straight as a rod, balancing a sand-colored turban on his head and a ring on each finger, but his black eyes slanted downward into the newcomer's space.

"This is my first time in Córdoba," Gonzalo said, by way of friendliness.

"Clearly," replied his companion.

"What are these soft things called?" Gonzalo tried again.

"Do you mean the pillows?"

"Puh-laos?"

"Not quite."

Suddenly—or had it been announced by one of those men who rushed in and out constantly?—a tall, slim man wearing a brilliant white turban with a polished green stone centered in the twist came in to the middle of the chamber and lowered himself onto a pillow that had been placed there moments before by one of those running pages. He held a long hollow object that looked a little like a rebec, with five strings running down in front of a hole decorated with perforations and scrolls, but this instrument was so large, the player had to set it across his body and support it in his lap. The neck turned dramatically toward the player at the tuning pegs. His fingers strummed across the strings, and the murmuring died down. The chamber amplified the performance and Gonzalo, as much as the rest of the patient dignitaries, felt the sounds cascade over him like a late summer shower.

The musician cleared his throat and began to sing in Arabic. Gonzalo looked at his companion, but his rigid attention told Gonzalo this was the wrong time to ask questions.

All of a sudden, the nonsense congealed into words Gonzalo thought he could understand. Although sung with a strong southern accent and peppered with Arabic vocabulary, he was sure it was some version of the Latin he spoke every day and that some of the people he'd met in Andalusia had tried to speak to him. He closed his eyes to concentrate, and the voice swept back into incomprehensible trills and moans. Ah, there it was again. Gonzalo committed what he heard to memory.

So much love! So much love!

Habib, so much love.
My eyes that were so happy
Are now in so much pain!

After several more cycles of Arabic and that strange Andalusian Latin, the singer silenced his throat and played the instrument more and more feverishly until the piece came to a climax that provoked applause all over the chamber. He stood, bowed to each corner of the room, and exited.

Gonzalo gave himself a moment to absorb the surprise of the skill and beauty, then leaned toward the man next to him. "That was amazing. That instrument would be popular back home. Say, how come I could understand some of the words?"

He sighed, and Gonzalo was sorry to have made him impatient. "Well, he was singing a muwashshah, and it's the new fashion to put a quaint strophe in the language of the Christian or Jewish folk as the *jarcha*."

Gonzalo frowned. He resisted asking, but his companion seemed to have taken it upon himself to relieve his ignorance. "The *jarcha* is the exit, the ending, so it comes at the end of each movement of the muwashshah."

Gonzalo nodded as if he understood. Thinking what he could do to look less stupid, he fumbled in the folds of his tunic and drew out the parchment for Almanzor. He held it open to where he thought the addressee's name must be apparent.

Out of nowhere, one of the attendants was standing before him. Staring for a moment at the letters, he bent and snatched it out of Gonzalo's hands. His eyes went from right to left again and again with the barest movement of his lips. It looked as if a cloud covered his face, then he crossed the hall and darted between the arches, taking the parchment with him.

Gonzalo started upward, saying, "Hey!" but his seat companion lay a gentle hand on his arm.

"Let him do his job. I think your audience will take place very soon now."

The same page darted back out and, proving Gonzalo's seat mate correct, looked at him and beckoned. Gonzalo glanced at his only ally, who nodded vigorously, so he used his hands to raise himself up and, ignoring the way his legs had gone to sleep, walked deliberately to the attendant, who ushered him through the arches.

Each column along the central hall had a man in a white tunic stationed at it, turbaned and grasping the hilt of a scimitar in a sheath that glittered with gold and gems. Glancing upward, Gonzalo was astonished by a pearl, as large as a man's head, dangling over him. The attendant pointed, and Gonzalo looked to the far end, where Almanzor sat framed by a blind archway, red and white and carved like the others. He wore white robes and a turban, and might have been unremarkable if not for the couch, elaborately constructed of dozens of pillows, on which he sat. Flanking this soft throne, two scribes sat with inkpots and scrolls ready. Against the mathematically celestial wall, and with the warriors prepared for anything, he looked like a Melchior painted on the walls of the churches in Castile.

Gonzalo approached smiling, thinking of the riches he would hardly be able to carry.

Almanzor snapped so quickly that Don Gonzalo didn't see the long fingers move, and almost as swiftly, four turbaned guards stood and surrounded him, close enough to touch, but with their scimitars still sheathed.

"My bodyguards will not harm you unless I tell them to," said Almanzor with a lilting but powerful accent. He lifted himself from the pillows and towered over Gonzalo like Goliath on embroidered silk slippers. He held the parchment between his thumb and forefinger as if it were a piece of garbage. "Do you know what these letters say, Christian?"

Gonzalo bowed his head, then thought better of it since he was already short enough in comparison to the warlord. "My lord, I do not."

"Permit me to tell you. Ruy Blásquez instructs me to behead you."

Don Gonzalo felt his face flush and the hairs on his neck stand up. He seized the parchment and stared at lines of meaningless curls and flourishes. "How can that be? Ruy Blásquez is my brother-in-law and greatest ally."

"I would do many things to a Christian, but I would not lie to a man in your position. The truth is the least you deserve," Almanzor said.

"I mean no disrespect, my lord, but this is not believable. Might you bring someone who could interpret this for me in my Latin?"

One of the seated scribes answered Almanzor's gesture, took the letter and raised his eyebrows. Then he read for the entire gathering to hear:

"To you, Almanzor, from me, Ruy Blásquez, greetings as to a beloved friend. Be it known that the sons of Gonzalo Gustioz of Salas, the bearer of this letter, have grievously dishonored me and my wife, Doña Lambra of Bureba. Because I cannot take revenge in Christian lands the way my honor demands, I send you their father so that you may behead him, if you respect and love me well. After you have done that, I will bring out my troops, his seven sons among them, and I will wait in Almenar. You should bring all of your host and come there as quickly as you can, because I'll be waiting for you. Let your generals Ghalib and Viara come with you, since they're good friends of mine, and tell them to behead my seven nephews, since among the Christians these are the men in all this world who are most against you and seek you the most ill. And once you've killed them, you'll have the Christian lands of Castile at your will, because these sons of Gonzalo Gustioz are Count García Fernández's best knights."

"God save me," Gonzalo shouted. "Nothing is as I believed!" His voice cracked into a sob. He wiped at his burning eyes and covered his hands with tears.

He looked up when Almanzor began speaking again, this time with a gentler voice. "Despite what this letter claims, I do not consider you a threat to Córdoba, and so I will not kill you. But it seems that your family has committed crimes in Christian lands. I have no choice but to put you in prison until I can discover the true meaning of this." Almanzor gestured to his bodyguards and they took Gonzalo by the arms.

He didn't know what to do. He couldn't reconcile his hopes for riches and his friendship with Ruy Blásquez, doting uncle to his sons and the hero of Zamora, with the contents of that letter. He offered no resistance to the guards. He walked through the waiting hall with his head high, as if he were being shown to a richly arrayed chamber with some of those fancy pillows on which to rest after the long journey.

Chapter VIIII

Young Gonzalo sat astride his mount on the valley crest with his brothers, his tutor, his uncle, and both companies of troops behind them. The valley of Almenar opened out green beneath them, fragrant as the morning sunlight warmed the dewy grasses. A hundred head of cattle grazed lazily, surrounded by droves of bleating sheep, their shepherd perhaps resting, hidden among the brush. Young Gonzalo heard the animals' calls beckoning him.

"It's everything our uncle promised." A jackrabbit bounded between his horse's legs.

"It looks even better than I expected," Ruy Blásquez exclaimed. "How would you seven like the honor of first run at the place? You could go down there and sack it, and get the best prizes, then come back here once any defenses have been weakened."

The brothers nodded at each other, and Diego waved their soldiers on, but their tutor barked, "Wait!"

"What is it now?" asked Gonzalo.

"You didn't listen to me before, but I hope you will now," said Muño Salido. "It's quite plain that this place cannot be as poorly protected as it looks. Listen to my advice and stay right here while your uncle investigates."

"Always doubting," Gonzalo shouted back at him in frustration. He started down the slope, anyway, but Diego called him back.

"Wait, little brother! Don't you see those banners coming over the hill?"

The opposite crest was swimming in the red, blue, white, black, yellow, and green banners of Moorish soldiers as they appeared to rise out of the ground, sending the cattle lowing in every direction. The fluttering obscured the men beneath the flags and made it difficult to estimate their number, but if their hill was as wide as the one from which he now looked, there could be as many as three hundred.

Gonzalo tore his gaze away to stare instead at his uncle. "Whose colors are those?" he demanded.

Ruy Blásquez chuckled. "Not to worry. The Moors come out like that to scare us, but I've sacked this area three times before with no problem. If you're bold, and act as though you have every right to be here, which you do as Christians, then you'll be fine. Even Moors have some honor in that regard. Of course, I'll be here with my troops to protect you."

Diego González waved his brothers into a mounted huddle. "What do you think?" Gonzalo noticed Ruy Blásquez turning his horse and retreating around the valley ridge.

"Muño," Gonzalo whispered to his tutor, "see how my uncle sneaks off. Please follow him and tell us where he goes." The old man cantered some distance behind Ruy Blásquez, careful not to be detected.

"Imagine, we could take this valley for Castile. The honors would be endless," said Fernando in reply to Diego.

"There are only about three hundred of them," said Gonzalo. He was tired of relentless riding and longed to exercise his training against audacious enemies.

"I agree with Fernando and Gonzalo. With our two hundred and our skills, they barely outnumber us," said Rodrigo.

"But where has our uncle gone? Why doesn't he want a part of the first prizes?" reasoned Martín.

"Yes, we've already observed that this valley isn't what it seems," said Suero. "We thought it was unprotected, and now see how three hundred knights are marching to a strategic advantage before we even start down the slope."

"Look how fast they are," said Gustio. "Let's not allow them to advance any farther."

Muño Salido burst into the huddle, his horse foaming, his voice scratching out the words, "Betrayal! We have no choice but to fight!" He urged his horse down the slope, and before any of the brothers could react, he collided with the line of Moorish soldiers, thrusting his sword wildly. A mass of sparkling scimitars cut his horse from under him, and he disappeared.

From his place on high, Gonzalo could see only the backs of the warriors working and the occasional flash of a sword like the tooth of a war machine that was chewing up his teacher and lifelong friend. The movement stopped abruptly and in the pause, Gonzalo heard Muño Salido shout, "God protect... seven sons... house of Lara!"

"What is going on here?" Gonzalo demanded, but none of his brothers could answer. One of the Moorish soldiers held his hand high so the brothers could see a lopsided orb covered in hair and blood that splattered down his white tunic. As the warrior turned his horse and galloped behind a ridge, Gonzalo guessed that the orb was his tutor's head.

Gonzalo glanced back at his brothers. "For Santiago and Muño Salido!"

He heard the thundering of his brothers' horses on the ridge behind him, then next to him, and finally their one hundred ninety-eight knights surrounded them in a protective cocoon. As he descended into the Moorish army, Gonzalo observed great numbers of soldiers forming fifteen different ranks in different parts of the valley he hadn't seen from above.

"There must be ten thousand of them!" he shouted to Rodrigo, who was closest to him.

"Maybe more!" Rodrigo yelled back over the clashing and neighing.

For a few minutes, the brothers could only watch side by side in the center as their knights faced the onslaught in their stead. In spite of the groans, shouts, and screams, nothing seemed to happen. No movement took place to either decrease the circle of Christian knights or cause a Moorish retreat.

"Never give up, warriors!" shouted Rodrigo. Gonzalo felt the air move as a long, colorful object fell from a great height to his left. The first was followed by countless more arrows the archers must have been shooting into the air in hopes of getting at the brothers inside their core of fighters. Gonzalo fumbled for his shield and held it over his head so that the arrows thwacked against the hardened leather while others glanced off the helmets of the warriors around him or penetrated their shoulders. A knight next to Gonzalo fell and was trampled as his comrades clambered to avoid the arrows and reach the attackers.

Under his shield, Gonzalo felt the bile rise in his throat while his horse turned in tight circles, bumping other horses and knights and throwing foot soldiers off balance. "What can we do?" Gonzalo asked Rodrigo, who, like all the brothers, held a shield over his head. The arrows created an unceasing downpour. He couldn't see any of their faces.

Rodrigo peered back at him from under his shield, his mouth open but making no sound. Gonzalo was familiar with the deafening roar in his ears, the stench of blood, sweat, and fear, and the press of other men's gasping breaths that could be their last. Another knight fell in front of him with a scream and an arrow in his neck. Gonzalo had never been so outnumbered. He had never had to watch as his vassals peeled away from him like layers of an onion. He knew that the thousands of Moors wouldn't stop when they reached his family. His heart seemed to fall and split in two. His feet grew cold and he could no longer feel his toes. An image came into his mind of the painted wooden tableau in the church at Salas: twelve apostles and Christ arranged in order, strictly symmetrical, only Judas looking off to the side. Gonzalo made himself rigid, like those sculptures, imagining that the peace, silence, and lack of movement belonged to the Kingdom of Heaven. His judgment day was here, so he prepared to give up the pleasures of the flesh.

The apostle Santiago was the saint most likely to understand Gonzalo's soul because he had helped so many warriors take León and Castile back from the Moors already. Yes, Gonzalo thought, he would like to sit next to Santiago at that supper. He decided to enumerate the reasons he might not be allowed into Heaven and prepare counterarguments, the way he had practiced so many times with his tutor.

Muño Salido seemed to reach into Gonzalo's chest and draw out Ruy Blásquez's knight, his heart pierced and bleeding out like Gonzalo's knights now.

"Please tell our Lord to forgive me, great Santiago," he whispered into the back of his shield. "I didn't mean to kill him, but I had to save Muño Salido from him." It now seemed God had wanted to take Muño Salido no matter what Gonzalo wanted. "Does He want to take me now, blessed Moorslayer?"

He remembered Little Page, a lifeless heap at Doña Lambra's feet. The sense of sticking his sword into the warm, alive gut and pulling it out of a dead body made him lurch atop his steed. "I believed I was doing the right thing. If the Devil was leading me astray, please have mercy on me and plead for my soul in Christ's celestial court." He blinked back tears thinking of Little Page's tiny feet. What a nimble dance he would have done if he'd lived until the jongleur arrived in Barbadillo.

Then Gonzalo recalled why they had spent so much time in Barbadillo. He saw his beautiful aunt through a veil of dizziness, picking up scattered teeth.

"I'm sorry about Álvar Sánchez. But the count passed down a judgment already, and we've made amends as best we can on Earth. The only other people I've killed have been Moors, and I know that's what you would have me do. Don't let Satan send me to Hell, please, Santiago."

Finally, the arrows relented. The last one Gonzalo saw planted itself into his horse's forelock. He felt the doomed animal buckle beneath him and, somehow, Rodrigo's hands under his arms, pulling upward.

"Use your arms, Gonzalico. Get up here," Rodrigo shouted. Gonzalo kicked his legs to find them working. He released his shield and struggled onto his brother's horse's back, weaving his body around the arrows stuck into the flesh of the hindquarters. The horse lurched and reared with the pressure of the Muslim troops, who pressed ever closer.

Gonzalo held tightly to Rodrigo's waist and tried to get a visual understanding of the battle now that the arrows weren't in the way. He knew the time was near because only ten Christian knights insulated them now. The Moorish warriors propelled their scimitars over and over again. A few of them from the rearguard had dragged the dead and wounded into a clear area, away from the fighting, only to return to create more corpses for the pile. When Gonzalo looked to his inner circle, he saw Martín behind Gustio, another fallen steed on the ground, and Diego, Suero, and Fernando still atop their own mounts, which also writhed and panicked to keep their footing.

"Let's see if we can make it to that hill," Fernando said, pointing straight ahead and likely giving away the strategy. Each brother nodded slowly, agreeing for lack of a better plan.

Gonzalo looked at each of their faces, knowing that each eyebrow, nose, and curve of a lip, different as they were, reflected his own in some way. He suddenly felt his mother's last embrace around his torso, followed by an urgent need to survive.

"Don't let our mother suffer. Spare us for her sake," he whispered to Santiago. Then he straightened as best he could. "For God and Santiago!"

"God and Santiago!" replied his brothers, and raising their swords, the seven of them charged atop five horses. They pushed the Moorish soldiers aside, cutting a narrow swath toward the hill by striking downward with their swords and deflecting swipes and punches at their legs.

Then, abruptly, they could go no farther. They had made it halfway to the hill only to be stopped by soldiers who carried themselves with so much grace, Gonzalo felt time slow down as he watched them. They wore turbans with flashing jewels. Gems glinted on their fingers as they wielded scimitars inlaid with gold. Gonzalo thought it was a shame to dirty such beautiful craftsmanship in the field, but then Rodrigo's steed faltered beneath him.

Gonzalo jumped off. His feet hit the grass before the horse fell in front of him. One of the turbaned warriors approached the kicking legs to get at Gonzalo over the beast's dying breaths. He swung his sword toward Gonzalo's neck. It would have been enough to kill any other soldier, but Gonzalo repelled the arm carrying the blade with a crack, then brought the tip of his sword noisily up through the bottom of his attacker's ribcage. Only then did another Moorish soldier approach him. Gonzalo punched him in the face even harder than he'd punched Álvar Sánchez. A sickening crushing sound in the soldier's face accompanied his collapse to the ground. As the next enemy prepared to engage him, Gonzalo glanced around at his brothers, who had all been unhorsed, and comprehended that the enemy soldiers were waiting patiently for each of them to dispose of their first opponent before stepping in to fill his place.

"They play fair!" he shouted.

"Most Christian of them," he heard Gustio grunt back.

"What game is it?" yelled Suero.

The next Moorish knight ran at Gonzalo to tackle him.

"Ten thousand to one," Gonzalo heard from Diego. "A game we can't win."

He pushed a knight's body off his sword, and the Moor grasped at the blade as if to climb back up and keep fighting, apparently cursing him in Arabic. Gonzalo knew he could not do this ten thousand more times. The specter of weariness hovered over him, closer with each blow.

Fernando raised his voice over the clash of armor and swords. "Brothers, try with all your hearts. Our uncle abandoned us. Only God is helping us. Honor Muño Salido and our lost knights." Gonzalo saw Fernando through the flying dirt clods, blood, and weapons. He had his right foot atop the chest of a Moorish soldier in a sign of victory, daring his next attackers.

The other six brothers roared and attacked their enemies with all the more strength. Gonzalo pulled on his enemy's beard until he was on the ground. He held the Moor's arm behind his back with his right hand and kept pulling on the beard, twisting the neck until he heard the cracking sound he was waiting for. Whether it had been the man's neck or his jaw, he was out of the game. Hairs flew out of Gonzalo's opened fist. He left the enemy where he was and kicked his scimitar into a pile of claimed weapons where he could keep an eye on them. He tried to keep watch on his brothers, too, and whenever they gained a tiny bit of ground, he kicked the weapons pile forward and closed the gap.

In such a painstaking way, they edged toward the hill. By the time they were at the foot of the slope, he had used each one of the taken scimitars at least once and switched sword hands so often he no longer remembered which he normally preferred. They had started into the valley in the morning, and now the hill cast a shadow across the waiting enemy army. Even the bodies of cattle, unintended casualties, provided shade in the slant of the sun.

When Gonzalo extracted his sword from what seemed like his ten thousandth opponent of the day, Fernando shouted, "All clear! Up the hill!"

Without another thought, Gonzalo shoved an attacker aside and climbed to the summit. It was perched at only the height of a man and a half, but the enemies seemed to interpret the movement as a retreat and stayed below. The deafening sounds of battle ceased. Gonzalo went to a little pond and scooped the cooling water into his parched mouth. Feeling the relief on his cracked lips, he turned around to see his brothers clearly for the first time in hours. Diego stood as though something were wrong with his foot. Martín sat and rubbed at his face, which was so obscured with caked blood that Gonzalo couldn't tell whether he was injured or not. Suero cradled his right hand in his left, and Gonzalo beckoned him toward the water. Gustio had a gash on the side of his tunic and blood seeped through his chain mail. Gonzalo inspected himself and found the barest scrape on his calf. They were all so splattered with blood and dust that no one but family could have recognized them, but Gonzalo was amazed they had come through that Calvary as well as they had.

"Where's Fernando?" Rodrigo said then.

Gonzalo cast his eyes below at the silent throng of swords, shields, turbans, and helmets. Fernando's body must have been claimed on his way up the hill with them. Gonzalo looked at his brothers, now only five, and they understood. They hung their heads and placed their hands over their hearts for Fernando, too exhausted to speak.

The six remaining brothers lay beside the pond far out of the reach of their organized and respectful enemies, sometimes taking water into their hands and bringing it to their parched lips. Young Gonzalo imagined those thousands of knights below having laid down their weapons, resting like him and his brothers. He couldn't understand how this had come about. In the growing shadows, on the hillcrest opposite the one they had come down in the morning, he glimpsed the outline of yet more soldiers, but these held the red and white banners of Castile and Vilviestre, his uncle's colors.

"Why doesn't Ruy Blásquez honor the word he pledged this morning and come to our aid?" he wondered aloud.

Gustio lifted his head wearily. "I don't think he ever intended to help us."

"We should give him a chance to explain himself," said Rodrigo. "Maybe he doesn't realize we need help."

"How blind would he have to be?" snorted Gustio.

"All the same, shouldn't we try to talk to him?" asked Rodrigo.

"I'll go," said Diego. "I'm the eldest. He's known me the longest."

"No," said Gonzalo. It sounded more like a moan than he intended. He was the least wounded of his brothers: what right had he to complain? "He's high up on the ridge, and something's wrong with your leg. I will go."

"You'll need a sign of peace," said Rodrigo, searching in the folds of his tunic.

Gonzalo staggered up, surprised by the weakness of the legs beneath him. He accepted the bloodied handkerchief on which Muño Salido had wiped Rodrigo's hands what seemed like years before, and started down the hill, holding it high. Moorish soldiers scrambled to their feet to face him.

"Please," said Gonzalo, hoping the fabric square was still white enough to make the statement he needed, "ask your commanders if we may call a truce for a short time, so that I may go to my uncle and demand of him why he refuses to help me and my brothers at this time when we so sorely need it."

Two of the soldiers nodded mutely and ran with the message up the same slope where Gonzalo had seen Ruy Blásquez. For an instant, he thought his uncle must be their commanding general. Soon some words in Arabic pulsed and echoed through the ranks, originating from a hastily raised tent on the same ridge as his uncle. When it seemed that the thousands of warriors must have heard the words, one of the soldiers nodded to Gonzalo that he might approach unhindered.

Gonzalo looked up at the ridge. His uncle sat unperturbed on horseback, banners waving garishly even in the fading light. Gonzalo marched ahead and the troops parted before him. His stomach clenched when he smelled some kind of cooking from a campfire. Through the sweet smoke, he tried to look into the eyes of the cook, but his pace never changed. Under a stoic mask, he changed the pain in his skull into a growing hatred of the soldiers around him and the uncle who'd put him there. Fuelled only by anger, he overcame the hill via the most direct route, not the easiest.

He knew this was no time for formalities. He grabbed the reins of his uncle's white steed and stared grimly into the darkening space where he judged that his uncle's face must be, because of the harsh wheezing. He mustered his force. "Uncle, do you not see how sorely we need your help?"

Ruy Blásquez's mount danced with the agitation he must have felt from his rider, but Gonzalo wouldn't let go of the reins. "Gonzalo González," said Ruy Blásquez in a hollow voice, "neither you nor your brothers could ever rightfully ask for my help."

"My lord," he replied deferentially, "we are your sister's sons. To further strengthen that bond, we were given to you in homage as a sign of friendship by our father, your own brother-in-law. You have responsibilities to us."

"You were given to me in fealty in a legal transaction arbitrated by the Count of Castile in which I never had a chance to make my case. The blood of Álvar Sánchez cries out from the sand in Burgos, telling me I must not help you, as do my broken nose, the blood of Doña Lambra's page, and most lately — because you and your brothers cannot help yourselves from constantly sinning against me — the blood of my knight who died for me."

Gonzalo distinctly remembered the hand of Ruy Blásquez accepting each individual coin of the fifty *sueldos* due for the soldier on the road. It was the same list of offenses Gonzalo had successfully argued against Santiago much earlier in the day under a hail of arrows. He and his brothers were absolved of them in a way he could prove in a court of law, if only he could find one.

"How can I forget any of these offenses?" continued Ruy Blásquez. "The blood of her page wouldn't wash out of Doña Lambra's dress, and as permanent as those stains are, so are your offenses. You and your brothers are fine knights. Defend yourselves, since you'll have no help from me."

Gonzalo's need to refute the claims was not as strong as the helplessness his uncle provoked in him. He released the reins, turned, and regarded the valley, which now gave the impression of an inkwell in its blackness. When he closed his eyes, it was daylight, and he was on the valley floor. Doña Lambra sighed with pleasure under him as he kissed her fiery lips. Even better, he lay on the soft grass and she moaned with delight on top of him. That was what she needed. A few nice thrusts, and she would never complain to Ruy Blásquez again, their uncle would become the kind relative he remembered, and they could go to reconquer Toledo and restore rightness to the world. But when he opened his eyes, she wasn't there, and so the problem had to be solved with swords and daggers and the instruments of rage.

He thought of spooking his uncle's horse, but couldn't summon the force. He let the earth drag him back down the ridge. When he reached the valley bottom, he smacked into another soldier he hadn't seen in the dark. He stumbled toward his brothers, passed among the ranks of enemy soldiers like a drinking goblet to be shared around the table. In the light of a fire, he saw another group taking supper. Another fire let a group of warriors clean and prepare the fallen for burial. Willing himself not to, he recognized his brother Fernando's shoes caked in mud, tunic torn, and hands calloused with the handling of a sword. But the helmet of gleaming polished leather and pewter studs was nowhere to be seen.

"Where's his head?" Gonzalo whispered. The soldiers continued pushing him in the direction of his other brothers. "Where's his head?" he repeated. He would keep asking until he got an answer. By the time Suero took his hand to pull him over the top of the hill, he was screaming, "Where is my brother's head?"

He stopped when he saw the horror on his other brothers' faces as they flickered in the firelight.

"What did our uncle say?" asked Rodrigo.

"He won't listen to reason. He won't acknowledge the ties of blood between us, nor the bonds of the law. I didn't remember about Fernando until... Otherwise, I would have struck him down right there, truce or no truce."

Their silence told Gonzalo that they knew their doom was upon them.

"And you saw Fernando?" asked Martín. The grime was gone from his face, and now Gonzalo could make out a red gash across his cheekbone.

"Yes," Gonzalo responded through a tight throat. Despair and exhaustion nearly felled him in that instant, but he pushed against them. Martín embraced him and together they mourned their brother, shaking with helpless sobs.

Diego's hand was on his shoulder. Gonzalo thought he would join them and the six of them would huddle together to be strengthened in their shared weakness, but Diego said, "Pull yourself together. Something's happening on the crest."

Gonzalo wiped his eyes and stood with them, facing the ridge where their uncle probably still kept watch in the dark. A serpent of lights grew from the top and inched toward the bottom, growing all the time. As it came closer, Gonzalo could tell that it was a group of soldiers, many of them on horseback, wending double file down the path he had cut through the Moors in the valley. Every fifth or tenth warrior carried a torch to light the way.

"Those are Ruy Blásquez's personal troops," said Gonzalo. "Has he become impatient with the Moorish generals? Are these coming to finish us off?"

One of the soldiers waved a piece of white fabric near a torch. Hope blossomed in Gonzalo's heart. His uncle had repented, knew Fernando's death was more than enough to even the score, and wanted to take them back to Barbadillo, where their mother would feed them and give them rest. Even Doña Lambra would kiss them, all six.

The forerunner came up the hill to talk with the brothers face to face. The new soldier couldn't hide his shock at their condition. Their silence encouraged him to speak first.

"We've come to help you. Ruy Blásquez wants to keep us from it, but we're so disgusted with the way he's letting the infidels win that we've decided to risk his wrath in order to do the Christian thing and fight for you."

"Bless you, bless you, brave knights," said Suero.

"If we come out of this alive, we'll defend every last one of you against Ruy Blásquez!" shouted Gonzalo.

The new soldier turned. "Are we starting now?" Martín said.

"There's no reason to wait," he replied.

Each of the six took a last swallow of water from the pool, placed their helmets on their heads, sheathed their daggers, and gripped their swords. With a nod acknowledging the need to fight for one another, they ran down the hill after the new knight into shapeless chaos.

Wielding his sword as if chasing a randomly zooming fly, Gonzalo charged into a mass of soldiers he could barely see. When the Muslims killed or injured one of Ruy Blásquez's knights, they also doused his torch if he had one, so that within an hour, the valley was eclipsed into deepest night. Like demons, the Moorish soldiers seemed to see in the dark, their scimitars aiming true for Gonzalo's vital parts. He deflected every blow even as his arms protested, but hesitated to attack, because if he sent his sword outward, he might strike an ally or a brother.

The dark made him feel swaddled like a baby. Maybe he was already dead: this was the inferno. While the noise of the fight during the daylight hours had ceased only when the knights from Lara had retreated up the hill, the dark was accompanied by an eerie silence. Gonzalo could hear the barest sigh of his opponents, the slightest crunch of their mail as the links rubbed together. "God save us for our mother's sake!" His voice rang out strong, with no noise to oppose it.

Ruy Blásquez's rebel knights made no sound at all. As the sun rose over the valley crest, Gonzalo saw their bodies stacked out of range of the conflict. Every one of three hundred Christian knights had gone to his death soundlessly. Their bodies were contorted and profaned, torn open and covered in blood. Only their honor was intact. The last of the brothers' support had disappeared from one blink of the eye to the next. The Moorish soldiers, however, seemed not to have lost a single man. If they had been fighting ten thousand the previous morning, ten thousand still came at them, in spite of the stacks of Muslim bodies set respectfully distant from the Christian ones.

The six brothers formed a tight circle as they had before, an eye in the middle of the storm of Muslim soldiers.

"They're demons," said Gustio. "They're not human. They'll never stop."

Gonzalo felt his limbs failing him, refusing to obey his wishes, and he saw his brothers struggle, too. With every wild, aimless thrust, their reaction time lengthened twofold. Suero and Martín, fighting side by side, leaned together in order to hold each other up.

"Santiago, save us!" cried Gonzalo.

Another voice fell over the valley as if in response. Gonzalo looked toward the sound, and saw that one of the Moorish generals had stepped out of his tent and shouted a command. The other general joined him and shouted something else.

The Moorish soldiers murmured and laid down their arms. Salvation had emanated from the most unexpected place. When there was no noise but the brothers' labored breathing, the two generals made their way to the center of what had been a storm.

Under his helmet, Gonzalo blinked fiercely, trying to make sense of the images before his eyes. The two men had honey-colored skin and wore turbans so tall they tottered atop their heads, bedecked with multicolored feathers and studded with improbable jewels. They seemed out of place even among the Moorish soldiers, whose only decoration was crimson blood. Gonzalo was sure the generals had come to personally cut them down, but he couldn't lift his sword in self-defense. He could barely lift his own head. Suero and Martín let themselves collapse to the ground with a simultaneous groan. In response, Diego and Gonzalo threw themselves over their brothers to protect them from the generals.

But the first general spoke in a calming tone in Castilian Latin as he approached. "My name is Ghalib, and the other general is Viara. Peace, Christians, peace." Viara corroborated the sentiment, making sweeping gestures.

When they arrived in the inner circle, both generals held out their hands for the brothers to take, and led them through the battlefield back to their tent on the hill. Before they'd stopped fighting, the scene of battle had become so sluggish, Gonzalo noticed every detail of every piece of armor and every slash of blade. Inside the tent, however, there was too much pleasure to experience at once and time sped by. Muslim servants hurried about, removing the brothers' helmets, surcoats, and chain mail so they could breathe more easily. They then administered water to the prostrate brothers' battle-weary faces, wiping away the grime and guts of a thousand deaths. They encouraged them to sit up on piles of silken pillows, wrapped linen around Diego's leg and Suero's arm, dabbed at

Martín's still weeping facial wound, and gave them white bread and red wine.

Gonzalo sniffed at the wine, then thought he had nothing else to lose, and drank it down greedily. It was the most delicious nectar he had ever had the privilege of tasting.

Rodrigo was the first brother to say what they were thinking. "Generals, such generosity was never before seen on a field of battle."

"Eternal gratitude," Gonzalo managed to pronounce around his mouthful of bread.

The others nodded wearily. Ghalib and Viara stood viewing the scene from near the tent flap and smiled, as if they were looking down on a wedding feast.

Out of nowhere, Ruy Blásquez burst into the tent. "Ghalib and Viara, what are you doing? Aren't you my friends? Aren't you pledged to do Almanzor's bidding? Didn't he tell you to exterminate these Christians at all costs?" He kept his gaze away from the brothers, but gestured toward them as if they were deaf, dumb animals.

Gonzalo found the strength to speak out. "Traitor! You brought us here to kill the enemy and now you tell them to kill us. Villain! God will never pardon you for such an offense."

Ghalib spoke in an appeal to the Christian charity Gonzalo doubted Ruy Blásquez possessed. "You've seen everything that's happened. It wasn't honorable to keep attacking them in such conditions. Might we offer them hostage status? We could earn a fair ransom."

"You do very ill to stray from your strict orders," said Ruy Blásquez, without acknowledging either Gonzalo's outburst or Ghalib's reasoning. "If you don't stop what you're doing right now, I'll bring in my troops from Vilviestre and set them on you. And even if you escape them, I'll go to Córdoba and get Almanzor to put a price on your heads so high, you won't have a friend from here to Damascus."

He remained in the entrance for a moment longer, observing the way he had brought the activity in the tent to a halt, and then turned and let the flap fall closed. Once he was gone, Ghalib and Viara conversed in a musical Arabic that nearly lulled Gonzalo to sleep. Then Ghalib turned to Diego, who, as the eldest, represented all of the brothers.

"Please understand how sorry we are. We have no quarrel with you, but I think you know Ruy Blásquez well enough to know that he will carry out his promise and probably more. We think he might go to Córdoba, convert to Islam, and pursue us for the rest of our lives."

"Are you sending us back out there?" asked Diego.

"We have no choice."

Gonzalo rose unsteadily to his feet. "Why don't you just get it over with, right here and now?"

"I'm sorry," insisted Ghalib, making gestures to the servants that they should rearm the Christians.

"Why waste more of your troops on us if this is going to end with our deaths, no matter what?" shouted Gonzalo.

"Please, please," said Ghalib, "finish your bread and wine. You have some chance of surviving. It's the best I can offer you."

Diego shooed the servants away, and the brothers helped each other reassemble their mail, surcoats, and helmets.

The moment they appeared once again at the entrance of the tent, the drummers gave a terrifying crash and the Moorish knights fell on them, surefooted even on the undulating slope. Gonzalo gripped his sword as his only lifeline and thrust outward, cutting and swiping at whatever he could. The Moors in charge of moving the dead and wounded took away a hundred soldiers within two hours. Gonzalo fought on two fronts: the fear rising from his darkest heart had to be beaten back at every turn, and the neverending troops had to be cut down.

The effect of the bread and wine ceased, and still the soldiers kept coming, with fresh horses and undamaged shields. Their prey could hardly move enough to control their own hands, and most of them had broken their shields in half and lost either their swords or their close-range daggers.

At last, Gonzalo permanently defeated his fear. He knew this existence could not continue, and he felt Santiago's hands on him, lifting his dread of death. The pleasures of the flesh were already too far away to be missed. He saw Suero, Martín, and Gustio lay down their arms and hold up their bare hands in the sign of surrender. When Gonzalo did the same, the Moorish knights miraculously left him alone for a precious moment in which he thought he could see the gates of heaven swinging open for him.

Then a Moorish soldier, no longer his enemy, swept him up onto his steed and carried him back up the hill. Gonzalo saw Diego, Martín, Suero, Rodrigo, and Gustio receive the same treatment. Rodrigo must have fainted, because he kept falling from the horse. His rider hoisted him astride again each time.

Chapter X

For two days, Gonzalo Gustioz found solace in sleep during the night and the day in a windowless room. On the third day, he was awakened by Almanzor's slender hand on his shoulder. Gonzalo opened his eyes to discern the chamberlain and the two guards who had brought him to the cell.

"Good morning, Don Gonzalo," said Almanzor.

"Is it?" he replied, painfully reentering a world in which he had been betrayed by his closest friend—a man who planned to have his sons slaughtered.

"We have been unable to verify whether the contents of the letters you carried have any truth in them," Almanzor continued. "I'm moving you to a more comfortable cell."

Having no news of his sons, Don Gonzalo found no comfort in anything. "Did you send your generals to Almenar, as the letter asked?"

"The generals he mentioned are very far north and I've heard nothing of them this month. If they're in Almenar, it isn't because I sent them."

The guards led him into the sunlight, which was so bright he couldn't make out the details about his situation within the palace grounds, but they walked for some time and climbed two sets of stairs. His new room reminded him of the place where he'd eaten the rice dish before meeting Almanzor. It had a bank of tile benches and many pillows. The window had two archways connected by a column and through it, he saw green leaves and heard a fountain's patter and the cooing of the waking doves. His muscles relaxed.

"Thank you, Almanzor. You are merciful indeed," Gonzalo said, but when he turned around, no one was there. The door had been shut and locked, but his senses had been too dazzled to hear. He lay down atop the pillows and expected to lose consciousness quickly, but sleep did not come. He sat up and thought that this impotent imprisonment without knowing what his sons were doing was worse than death. Almanzor's mercy had made Ruy Blásquez's revenge all the more sharp.

He heard the key in the door this time, and responded loudly, "I will not eat or drink anything. It's better to take it away now."

Rather than leaving, the person at the door came through holding a plate and a goblet. "Why will you not eat, my lord?" she asked.

Gonzalo hadn't expected a female, especially not one who spoke his Latin so well. Her body looked wispy under a blue silk blouse that hung loose around her waist like a tunic. Underneath, she wore loose breeches made of the same material, drawn in at the ankle and showing her golden slippers. Though she wore her hair cut in the front like the other servant girl he'd seen, in the back the tresses fell long and loose like the tail of a well-curried black horse. The arms that bloomed out of the elbow-length sleeves looked barely strong enough to support the weight of the items she carried. Gonzalo stood before her, speechless.

"You must eat to keep up your strength, my lord. No one can know what is to come," she said.

"Very well," he said, bewitched. He sat on the bench and waited for her to bring the items to him. "I will eat and drink only enough to keep myself from dying and offending God with my desperation."

"My name is Zaida," she said as she crossed the room. Placing the victuals beside him on the bench, she sat down so that Gonzalo couldn't help but look into her almond-shaped eyes, as green as the leaves outside the window. "I've been personally selected by Almanzor to comfort you in your misfortune. Tell me, what has befallen you that is so terrible that you hardly wish to live?"

"My name is Gonzalo Gustioz of Lara. I'm the lord of many towns. I left my wife Sancha in Salas to seek money in Córdoba, and now I fear I may never see her again."

"Why are you imprisoned?"

"I don't understand it myself. I believed I was carrying some letters demanding repayment of a large debt Almanzor owed my brother-in-law, but instead, they carried betrayal, asking Almanzor to kill me and meet my seven sons on a battlefield."

"You have seven sons, all warriors? Tell me what they're like."

Images of the sons who had been the source of his greatest pride and most profound frustration flooded Gonzalo's mind: Muño Salido teaching Suero archery while Martín talked his way out of the lesson in order

The Iberian Peninsula in the Tenth Century
France
Navarra
County of Barcelona
Kingdom of León
Covadonga
León
Busto de Bureba
Burgos
Barbadillo
Salas
Zamora
Medinaceli
County of Castile
Toledo
Caliphate of Córdoba
Córdoba
Madinat al-Zahra

to finish an epic chess match with Don Leovigildo de Valdavia, who even with his Muslim advisors, could not best the boy; Count Fernán González serving as godfather at Fernando's baptism, the water running over his transparent newborn skin; Gustio and Rodrigo arguing over girls, and Gustio winning through blunt force; Diego's first steps, his first words, his first siege, the first triumph of so many; and young Gonzalo. His lips could hardly keep up with the words clamoring inside of him.

When he at last paused, Zaida said, "I hate Christians because I, too, had seven warrior sons and a fine, handsome husband, and although they were not at fault, and I had never committed a crime, a Christian lord took them all away from me over the course of one day."

"Was the Christian lord called Ruy Blásquez?" Gonzalo said bitterly. He looked up from his plate, from which most of the rice, fish, bread, and eggplant was gone, and studied her, knowing she was too young and too slight to have borne seven sons.

But one surprise followed another when she replied, "Yes, that was the Christian lord. His name makes my heart rot with hatred." A tear appeared in her eye.

He reached up to keep it from falling onto her silk, and felt the shock of his rough hand on her cheek, softer than even his new pillows. The tear glimmered for an instant, then broke over his finger.

"So, you understand my pain?" he whispered.

She nodded, turning her demure gaze back to his face.

"And Ruy Blásquez is an unstoppable demon?"

She mutely stood to avoid the empty plate and goblet and leaned in to embrace him. Her jasmine scent seeped into his clothing and his nose. "I cannot hate all Christians," she said, "now that I know one of you feels the same pain I have carried."

Gonzalo sobbed helplessly. Zaida held him steady with unexpected strength as he shook and coughed. "Yes, my lord, weep. It is your only defense against despair."

More exhausted than he could have imagined, and well fed, Gonzalo slept until the evening hours. Muted light came in the window and with it the trilling, swooping song of a night bird. A crashing sound, and the bird fell silent. He had not fallen back to sleep and was drowsily listening to the doves in the morning again when Zaida came to the door to bring another breakfast of eggplant and leeks with rice, and bread to scoop up the spices.

"You must be hungry, my lord. You didn't wake all day, so I couldn't bring you supper."

He recognized her voice. His eyelids were so swollen that she appeared as a bright blur. "Zaida, do you know what happened to that bird last night?"

She came toward him. "I do. We call that bird nightingale, but in your language it is known as *Ruy Señor*. I cannot bear the sound of its song because I know Ruy Blásquez sent it to torment you and me. I threw a stone at it, intending to kill it, but it flew away."

"Zaida, the bird shouldn't suffer for its name," Gonzalo said. But knowing what the songster was called, a chill passed through him. He wished he had the strength this wisp of a Moorish girl had. She sat down next to him and for moment he thought she wore nothing at all. Focusing through his surprise, he saw that in fact she was covered head to toe with transparent veils made of some fabric like a spider's web, which wasn't much different than being naked. He turned away. "What are you wearing?"

"My lord Don Gonzalo, we are bonded by the betrayal of the demon Ruy Blásquez. I want to comfort you with whatever happiness you can take from me. Perhaps you can replace my fallen husband and seven sons, and I can replace your wife and your seven sons."

She stood and planted her feet before him so he could not help seeing the outline of her body. He held out his hand to stop her, and when her smooth belly met his flesh, he shuddered with pleasure. In his mind, he saw Sancha combing and plaiting her long brown hair the morning after their wedding ceremony. She looked back at him with a coy smile that made his heart leap. He spoke quickly. "Only Sancha can comfort me in the way you suggest. My sons need no replacing. When they hear what's happened to me, they'll come for me, abandoning Ruy Blásquez and Almenar." Predicting a happy outcome brought a grin to his face.

Zaida backed away and held her arms over her breasts. "I understand. Your wife is very lucky." She turned and left, her feet skidding across the smooth floor. Gonzalo ate his breakfast wondering what Sancha must be doing and waiting for his sons to arrive at Medina Azahara and deliver him. It was so like them to keep him waiting. He paced around the chamber, watching the sunbeams fall through the leaves outside his window, wondering if there was something he could do to speed his sons on their way.

Zaida returned about midday when Gonzalo's back was turned to the door. "A midday repast for my lord, who seems to be in much better spirits." He nodded, turning away from the window. She was dressed more modestly in a similar outfit to the one she'd worn the first day. She set down the plate and goblet and joined Gonzalo at the window. "Do you see those trees farther out toward the horizon?"

He could see nothing beyond the green grove outside his window, but he nodded anyway.

"Those are almond trees. They bloom with white petals in the winter. Abd al-Rahman, the father of our present caliph and the great leader who built Madinat al-Zahra, put those trees there so his favorite wife wouldn't miss the snow from the Sierra Nevada so much."

"He did that for his wife?" The sentiment in one so powerful awed Gonzalo.

"Yes. As a matter of fact, her name was Zahra, and all Madinat al-Zahra was built for her."

"What a bewitching place you live in," he exclaimed, taking her hands in his. She leaned toward him, but he released her hands and backed away.

"Do you like to look at the grounds?" she asked, clearing her throat. "Perhaps I can ask Almanzor if we might take walks around the gardens."

"I would like that. This room is spacious and beautiful, but I'm beginning to wonder what I will do until my sons come for me."

Zaida stood and lifted the plate, revealing a chess board. She extracted black and white pieces from pockets hidden under her tunic and began setting them in order. "Do you know how to play, my lord?"

"I know a simple version of this game," he replied. "But my son Martín knows games that take days to complete, and he tells me they come from your people."

"Travelers from Damascus and Baghdad bring us new ways to play and even write treatises on it," she told him. "It's the noblest game and the best way to spend the time you have here."

Gonzalo sat back and ate his midday plate while she finished setting up the pieces and described the rules of her favorite Baghdad version of the game. He couldn't follow it. He noticed she had combed her fringe back and pinned it into the rest of her hair. If she were wearing a tunic, she could've passed for a Christian woman. When she lowered her gaze, intent on one or another of the pieces on the board, it seemed as if time had gone backward and Sancha herself was before him.

Probably sensing his bewilderment, Zaida started the game over with the rules he knew. He won within an hour's time, and suspected she had let him win. Her enigmatic smile would neither confirm nor contradict his protests.

Days later, when he'd finished his morning meal, she took his hand and led him out of the chamber. "You must promise not to try to escape," she said.

His sons thought he was here, so here he would stay. "I can't imagine making it all the way through Andalusia by myself again," he told her by way of promise.

They wended along narrow pathways through shady cypress trees and date palms and paused to look at the fading rose blooms and many flowers he couldn't have named. Most of the time, Zaida held his hand, because the sunlight was so bright Gonzalo could hardly open his eyes to find his way along the paths. She brought blooms close to his face, to smell them, she said, but it was also the only way he could make out their shapes. He didn't admit that he couldn't see, but she took her cue from his stumbles and missteps. The next time they went walking, it went without saying that she should lead, grasping his hand. More than once his foot strayed over the edge of a deeply sunken garden plot, and she pulled him back to prevent his fall.

They passed burbling fountains that displayed bronze sculptures of frogs and deer or extravagantly robed people upon closer inspection. Feeling a cooling breeze on their faces, they crossed over a bridge that ended up on a lower level and stopped in the shade of a wall. Now Gonzalo could see that it spread out before them and then made corners.

"This is the caliph's mosque," Zaida explained. "I can take you inside if you like."

He was curious, but he said, "No, thank you. I don't think it would be right."

Zaida turned back into the glare and led Gonzalo back to his cell. The following day, she brought his meals as usual and they played an hours-long game of chess. She let him win again. She wore a long dress similar to the kinds of frocks the Christian women wore in Castile and León. After she had gathered the pieces and stowed the board, she caressed his shoulders, making him feel warm and accepted. "Rest well, my lord," she said. She kissed his cheek and lit a candle, which filled the room with radiance such that he couldn't see her leave. Misfortune had brought them together. Gonzalo marveled at the close bond they had formed in such a short amount of time. He had never been friends with a woman before, and above all, it was extraordinary that she should understand him so well, being Moorish. He went to sleep thinking he would miss her when he returned to Salas.

It was not Zaida who came to his door in the morning. Silhouetted in a ring of light was a shape so tall and imposing it could only be Almanzor.

Sensing his sons nearby, Gonzalo sat up and said breathlessly, "My lord, have you come to grant me your ultimate mercy and release me from this captivity?"

"It's true, Christian, I have come to grant you that mercy," the great warlord replied. "But first I must ask something of you. One of my generals has brought the heads of eight noblemen he says come from the region of Lara. Will you identify them for me?"

Horror froze his blood and stopped his breath. "Were the heads taken in Almenar?" Gonzalo whispered.

"Come with me," Almanzor said.

As they walked, Gonzalo broke into a cold sweat. He faltered when they entered an open-air palace courtyard shaded by long white strips of cloth hung from eave across to its opposite eave. In the cool shade, Gonzalo saw eight heavily soiled bundles that had been arranged in a row on a white sheet on the tile floor. A large jug of wine stood next to the sacks, waiting to clean what was inside. Ten guards stood around the courtyard, prickling with attention.

Wincing, Don Gonzalo reached for the closest bundle, untied the knot at the top and let the encrusted fabric fall away stiffly. The head was obscured with matted hair, blood, and dust, so he took the jug and dribbled some wine over the top. The lifeless features of the man he had entrusted with his sons' education were revealed: the heavy eyebrows, the eyes, almost as piercing in death as in life. The death of Muño Salido could only mean the death of the charges he had cared for during a quarter of a century. Gonzalo let out a strangled cry and lost consciousness.

In dreams, Sancha came to him and led him to an open field covered in spring blossoms where Muño Salido helped Diego, eleven years old, teach Martín, Suero, and Fernando to march. Rodrigo imitated them, but fell down more often than not, and Gustio babbled to his mother before running off to become tangled in weeds. Sancha held young Gonzalo swaddled at her breast, still perfectly shaped in her husband's eyes. Don Gonzalo awoke under a torrent of water. The guard who was pouring backed away and Gonzalo felt the hot tears in his eyes, knowing the scene he dreamed had never taken place and wondering if it had been a glimpse of heaven. There had been no saints, but as he recognized the space he was in and the task set to him, he knew his sons were all the martyrs he needed.

He looked toward Almanzor, who stood framed by an archway, too far away to distinguish his features. He stole glances at the guards, noting their positions and how they held their weapons.

"I can identify these heads," Gonzalo whispered.

He had no need to see the faces, and yet his hands moved inexorably toward the other bundles, untying and decanting trickles of wine, revealing little by little the full and terrible impact of Ruy Blásquez's betrayal.

When they had proved to be the eight most important men in his life, Gonzalo returned to the head of Muño Salido. He threw the stiff cloth it had been wrapped in as far from himself as possible and picked up the head, arranging its hair and brushing away the impurities, then holding it to his chest as if it were his own heart and he were trying to replace it within his body.

"This was my cohort and friend, Muño Salido, who raised my children and taught them to be knights as fine as he had been," he announced to Almanzor and the guards, showing the head for them to admire as a jewel. "Greetings, my friend. You were always feared in Castile and León while you had these warriors under your care. May God forgive you for going along with Ruy Blásquez, even for a moment. I know you couldn't have imagined his treachery, since you had none in yourself. Forgive me, my friend, for abandoning you in your greatest need."

He placed the head back on the cloth, and then took the head of his eldest son, wiped it off, and held it for all to see before clutching it in a way that made it seem he would never let go. "My son Diego González, I'm a wretched old man because I allowed the lancing of the scaffold at that wedding. I loved you the most, and I had every right to, since you were born first. Count García loved you, as well, because you were his greatest commander. Your deeds in the Vado de Cascajares will never be forgotten. You bravely held the flag. Although the enemy tore it down three times, three times you raised it again. You killed two kings and a commander. Count García was never better served than on that day. Ruy Blásquez would've done well to die rather than keep on living to become such a traitor. He gave you Carazo as an inheritance when it was half populated. Now that you've died, it will be abandoned to the enemy."

Gonzalo then took the head next to Diego, dousing it in the tears that coursed from his eyes. "Oh, my son Martín, I was blessed in my second son as well as in my firstborn. I could speak all day of your virtues and never do you justice. There's no better player of board games than you in all of Hispania, even Andalusia, and your measured speech pleased all who heard it. Now that you're dead, I'm worth nothing. I don't care whether I live or die. I only grieve for the way your mother, Sancha, will feel when she learns of this. Without sons or a husband, she'll be completely destitute.

"This one is Suero, my third son, always so loyal. No one equaled him as a hunter. He could take down any bird with his hawk, and he could train any wild creature as well. Your mother's brother made you attend an evil wedding. It put me in prison and had you beheaded. Everyone alive and yet to be born will call Ruy Blásquez a traitor."

Wiping at his tears, Gonzalo raised his head and noticed that the guard closest to him also wept.

"My most honored son, Fernando, has the same name as the first Count of Castile, his godfather. An emperor would have been well pleased with him. He was the most lordly of all knights but could also kill lynxes and wild boars. No one could find his equal on foot or on horseback. You never loved lowly people, but always fit in with the noblest and most high. Such evil celebrations your uncle made you attend, which put me in prison and killed you!

"Rodrigo, my wisest son, unfortunately named for the uncle who sent him to those evil celebrations that got him killed. A king would be well served by you, such a great friend and so loyal to your lord. I never saw a knight who could handle his weapons better than you. You are no longer in this wretched world, and Ruy Blásquez has lost paradise forever."

Gonzalo rested the head next to its kin, and picked up that of his second youngest son. He brushed away the dirt obscuring his face and kissed his son's eyelids in ineffable grief. "Gustio, named for my father, such wonderful qualities in you. You wouldn't have lied for all the treasure in Hispania. You were great with a sword. You never wounded, but you killed. Vile news about you will travel to your mother in the region of Lara."

Don Gonzalo tried to wipe some of the tears from his eyes as he replaced Gustio's head on the sheet and took up that of his namesake. He was no longer performing for the Muslims around him, but addressed his son as naturally as if he had been alive. "Gonzalico, my little one. Your mother loved you most of all. Who could ever count all your good qualities? You're a good friend to friends and loyal to your lord. You're knowledgeable about the law. Nothing gave you greater pleasure than theorizing about cases. But you're also a strong knight, and no one ever saw a better lancer of the scaffold, as you proved at those evil celebrations. You could speak with men and women and you were ever generous with gifts. Those who feared me because I had you will now become my aggressors. Though I may return to Lara, without you I'm not worth a rotten fig, because I have no friend or relative to avenge me. Death would be better than this life."

He'd identified the heads as he'd been commanded. Gonzalo placed that of his youngest son gingerly next to the others, doing it as much honor as he could while blinded by tears. He'd ensured that the gentle nature of his actions had made the guards sympathetic to him and complacent. They were looking at each other, murmuring in Arabic and wiping stray tears.

Gonzalo leapt up, seized the sword of the nearest guard and gouged his throat. Three had fallen gurgling to the tile floor before the others knocked Gonzalo down and held his arms and legs. One of them kicked him sharply in the eyes with a shout. Blinded, Gonzalo closed up into a ball and sobbed.

"Almanzor, I have done great evil here. You must kill me. Great Almanzor, you cannot tolerate such outrages within your palace. You must behead me, like my sons."

"Christian, you will not die here. I refuse to add to your misfortunes." When Almanzor spoke some commands in Arabic, Gonzalo felt the guards trying to get him to his feet, but a weakness in his legs and the unresponsiveness of his arms made it necessary for them to pick him up and carry him back to his cell.

He writhed upon the pillows, willing his life to leave him, to join his sons and never see this wretched world again.

Chapter XI

Zaida let her serving girls wash her and comb her hair in the style that seemed to please Don Gonzalo.

"Princess," said a blonde girl who had lived in Castile until she was five years of age, "if you really want to look like a Christian, you should have your hair braided and maybe even wound up around your head. Then we'd have to find you some kind of headdress."

Zaida studied her eyes and brows in a hand-held mirror. "I think sweeping away the fringe is enough for now," she murmured. When her brother Muhammad — or, as everyone else called him, Almanzor — had summoned her fewer than fourteen mornings before and told her he had a new Christian nobleman in his prison who needed her comfort, she had resisted.

"No, brother, I will not give myself to any Christian in that way. How could you ask it of me?"

"Dear Zaida," he had answered, "you can watch him more closely than any man ever could and learn his secrets. Besides, the crimes committed against him are intolerable. Have pity on one so innocent and unfortunate."

She looked at him in a way she knew would weaken his resolve. "If he's so pitiable, why don't you just release him?"

He readjusted his stance into the imposing posture he used with underlings and foreign dignitaries. "I cannot let him go because of an alliance I have with his persecutor. I must hold him until I can prove his innocence or safely sever ties with a Christian lord called Ruy Blásquez."

Imitating his official demeanor, she asserted her sisterly rank with him. "As your sister, I expect to be married to a great commander. Would you jeopardize that future for the sake of pity?"

"As my sister, any great commander will be happy to have you in any condition. I risk nothing in granting Gonzalo Gustioz this mercy. A beautiful young woman who can speak his language is his only hope in this world. You will do as I say or suffer an ignominious death."

She knew then that her brother had been generous to hear any of her arguments. There must be some political advantage to treating this prisoner well. She bowed before him as if offering her head for him to cut off at his pleasure, then ran through the gardens on the energy of her frustration. Her knees buckled on the stairs and her veil suffocated her. She pulled it away from her mouth and plodded back to the small garden outside the women's living quarters. She sat down at the central pool, letting the ripples under the fountain calm her. Perhaps she could gain this Christian's trust, poison him, and that would be the end of it. Her mind set, she inhaled the scent of the myrtle bushes in order to brace her senses against whatever unpleasantness she might find in the prison cell. Leaving her maids whispering among the carved stone archways, she headed out again.

Beyond the garden boundary, she saw one of her brother's plumed guards carrying a tray and goblet. Realizing she didn't know where the prison cells were, Zaida asked him, "Do you know of a Christian prisoner Almanzor has recently taken into the prison cells?"

Bowing as well as he could without upsetting the tray, the guard replied, "Yes, my lady. The prisoner was in the cells at first, but he's been moved to this visitor's chamber." He gestured with his head toward the door they stood in front of, some ten paces away from the women's quarters.

"Did my brother say why he was being moved?" Zaida asked, sensing she knew already.

"Almanzor doesn't need to justify himself to us, my lady."

"It was to save me traveling to the prison. I am to care for this prisoner. Give me the tray and goblet and unlock the door."

The weight of the food and drink riveted her to the spot, and she had to screw up her courage again while the door opened. She dismissed the guard wordlessly and focused on the smells of chickpeas, salt, and pepper wafting from the plate. She never expected to feel the way she did when she finally saw the prisoner. His tunic, once red, was faded by the sun and worn at the seams, and Zaida understood that he was far from his home. Although he was older, he stood straight and tall, and above a soft brown beard flecked with white, his eyes glimmered such that she thought she could feel his pain. The strange idea that this Christian had a soul like hers seized her mind. Most surprisingly, he didn't smell bad.

He said he wouldn't eat, but Zaida must feed him if she was to poison him. Or perhaps she wouldn't. Perhaps she would take care of him as she'd told the guard. Whether she gave him her favors in the way her brother suggested remained to be seen. She knew only that she wanted to peer into this Christian soul she'd discovered to see whether it was like hers, and to gain his sympathy, she lied to him. But as the words against his enemy Ruy Blásquez left her mouth, they became true in some way, and the tear that flowed unbidden from her eye at so many emotions seemed to convince the Christian. A bridge of sympathy had sprung up between them in a matter of a single moment.

Zaida closed the door behind her and stared at her feet, concentrating on the swish of her silk slippers against the cobblestone floor so she wouldn't have to admit to herself that she'd found the Christian fascinating. As she returned to the women's quarters, her maids scurried to her, but Zaida felt quiet inside. She told them what she was doing over the course of the next two days in pieces, dropping tidbits like ripe figs to the ground. The maids appeared to have put it together by the third day, when she appeared before him in the transparent garment, and they began to treat their lady with the delicacy required for a woman in love. Zaida appreciated that none dared to use such a word in front of her, but the younger maids offered her sprigs of myrtle to use in divining the man who would be her future husband. When Zaida blushed at the mere scent of that plant, the older maids seized the sprigs and chastised the bold servants.

This day was the most important of all, because she had seen the eight bundles that had arrived in Madinat al-Zahra under the care of General Ghalib. Her beloved Christian's worst fears had come true. Today she would have to comfort him in every way. She would finally make him hers by pretending to be the wife he so fiercely clung to. She took care to leave no trace of Arabian-inspired fringe in the front of her hair, and tolerated her maids' fumbling as they tied a charmed amulet around her neck and dressed her in a plain, greyish wool tunic-type garment one of the eunuchs had ventured into the Christian markets to buy. She beheld her rippling reflection in the central pool. Were these the shapes and colors that would please Don Gonzalo in his hour of need?

"You could pass for a Christian lady, mistress," said the eunuch who'd bought the dress.

Zaida blushed. She hadn't thought she'd said the words aloud. She nodded to acknowledge the compliment and left to find the prisoner.

When she opened the door, Don Gonzalo, or a shapeless mass on the floor that seemed hardly to contain the breath of life, groaned at her.

"No," he rasped without opening his eyes. "Now I truly will not eat."

She said nothing, but crossed the room to the window and opened the shutters. She guessed that with light flooding the room, he wouldn't be able to distinguish her features. He barely protested the brightness, and she took the moment to lie down beside him, pressing her body and Christian dress against his body, which felt more solid and welcoming than it had appeared at first. She made low humming sounds, afraid to speak in her accented Latin, and kissed his face, exploring the creases around his eyes and clearing away the salty wetness as it continued to dribble out. His pupils looked as if someone had poured milk over them, but that did nothing to stem her infatuation. She kissed his lips, lightly but lingering, and when she pulled back, he whispered, "Sancha?"

Zaida murmured and hoped it sounded affirmative. Then, ever so gently, she lay on top of him and, ignoring the sharpness of the floor tiles against her knees, kissed his lips again and again. "Sancha," he sighed. A golden band sparkled on his hand as he drew her to him. Only the amulet came between their heartbeats.

Never hurrying, Zaida coaxed Don Gonzalo's body toward pleasure. Each time he seemed to want to speak, she covered his mouth with kisses. Soon the only sounds were moans of enjoyment as they inhaled each other's scents and tasted each other's skin, cooing like the doves that had taken shelter on the windowsill. Zaida had resolved to stay quiet because she had no idea what a Christian woman would sound like in such a situation, but when the moment came, she cried out loud and long with the ecstasy of new love. Her pleasure seemed to thrill him so much that he climaxed at the same time. Sighing and kissing, she stayed on top of him until she could no longer, then lay on her back on the floor with her knees pulled up.

"I must have died and gone to paradise to find you so quickly, my wife," he said looking vaguely upward. "Your body, it's just like it was before you had Diego." His brows creased, and Zaida knew he was already remembering the unbearable sorrow of his life. Her hand between her legs, she stood and crossed to the window again, this time to close the shutters. She picked the grey dress up from the floor and slid the scratchy fabric over her body.

He sat up. "You. You tricked me into betraying Sancha!"

She hadn't really believed her ruse could deceive him, knew that somewhere deep down he'd wanted to make love to her as much as she'd wanted him. This rejection was worse than the first, so many days before, and her heart broke when she heard the accusation from her lover's mouth. She knelt and sat beside him, trying to take him into her arms, but he pushed at her and wept again.

"I love you," she said. "Marry me. We can start again. I'm Almanzor's sister. You could become a prince of al-Andalus and never have a worry about Castile again."

"No," he moaned. "Sancha is alive. I must return to her."

"Sancha is too old to bear you any more children. I can give you seven more sons and seven daughters besides."

"Sancha will never take me back now. Without Sancha, I have nothing to live for." He went slack and the tears coursed down his squint lines onto the tiles.

Zaida took up his limp body and rocked, showering him with as many tears. "Don't leave me, my love! Stay with me always. We can be happy."

"I want to die."

Zaida felt like dropping his body and breaking it on the tiles, but instead she grasped him tighter and felt his breathing become labored. She whispered into his ear. "Gonzalo Gustioz, I wonder at your dismay. In battle, I'm sure you climbed over bodies just to keep fighting. You're a terrible coward. You remember, I once had warrior sons, like yours. They were the meaning of my life. Then, in a single battle against Christians, I lost all seven of them, and their father as well. I pulled out my hair and scratched my face and suffered greatly, but I never wanted to die. I'm just a woman, so imagine you, a man, a great, strong man, wanting to die! It cannot be. Weep, get it out, because you don't want the sorrow to get stuck inside you and make you sick. But you must understand that all the crying in the world will not bring your sons back to you. You could engender a new family. A son who could avenge you."

He turned away from her, so she let him go. She stood and wiped her face and tried to arrange her hair and dress.

"Think it over," she said, and walked out the door.

Once she removed the key from the lock, her composure fell away. How could he reject her so brutally? How could he not love her? She had told the fantasy about her previous family to make him understand that he must have the strength to face a new and better life here with her, but he was literally too blind to see. She should have poisoned him at the beginning, after all. She turned toward the women's quarters, but had to grasp at the wall to avoid falling. Her sobs echoed off the walls of the guest rooms and the caliph's chambers, and after what seemed like thousands of years, a eunuch and a maid came running to lift her up and carry her back to her bed. She lay there atop the pillows, too weak to move. The embarrassment at appearing weak before her lessers was as a single drop in the sea of her rejection.

One of the oldest maids held her head up and extracted something from under her bolster. Zaida could just make out the tiny green leaves. A tang of piney citrus overwhelmed her nose. "Myrtle," she whispered, and in spite of her exhaustion, she wept again with sobs that wracked her entire body. Now she knew why she had dreamed so vividly of Don Gonzalo for the past few nights. There must be some truth to the old wives' tale about myrtle revealing the man you are destined to marry.

A maid brought water. Zaida grasped her arm, saying, "I'm in love!"

"Should I bring a physician?" asked the maid, widening her eyes at her lady's admission.

"Yes," replied the princess. "It hurts. It hurts!"

"Almanzor and the caliph won't want a man to come into the women's quarters."

"Ask whatever permission you must."

The maid must have asked Zaida's brother and he must have shown concern because within minutes, the women replaced the veils over their faces and Almanzor's best Jewish physician arrived at her bedside with a satchel of the elements he needed most often.

"May I, my lady?" he asked her, sitting on the side of the bed.

She nodded, and he palpated her belly through the rough cloth. She winced at the scratching.

"Headache? Nausea?" he asked.

"Yes," she whispered, "and heartache."

He looked into her eyes, nodded, and searched in his bag. "First, you must rest. Then, a rich diet and much tea, water, and some wine. While you're resting, I'll prepare a regimen of music and games." He leaned in and whispered. "Can you tell me, Princess, whether you've had sexual intercourse recently?"

She nodded. "Not an hour ago, with my beloved."

"Then I can't understand why you're suffering so greatly, my lady. That is the ultimate cure for your disease."

She opened her mouth to speak, but new tears choked her. Suddenly, the activity around them came to a halt. The lower servants genuflected, so Zaida knew Almanzor must be there. He towered over everyone and stood at the head of the bed so Zaida could look up into his face. He said nothing, but studied her. Zaida knew he could see the change in her from beloved little sister to woman possessed, but she couldn't detect sympathy.

"Isaac, what ails my sister?" he asked.

The physician nodded his head in respect. "She is deeply in love, my lord."

Almanzor turned to his sister. "Is this true, Zaida?"

She nodded weakly.

"Who put you in this state?"

"Don Gonzalo is the only man for my heart," she whispered so softly that he had to bend low. "Help me."

His face softened. She couldn't tell why he would smile in such a case. He turned back to the doctor, so that she could see only his ear while he pronounced her fate. "I would not have this love cured."

He sat on the edge of her bed and made a sweeping gesture with his long arms that everyone understood. As everyone else filed out, the physician bowed and said, "My lord, may I make her a tea that she might rest peacefully?" Almanzor nodded, and the doctor hurried away to catch up with the maids. Within moments, the brother and sister were alone.

She clasped his hands. "Muhammad, thank you for the tea. I might never sleep again without it. But why don't you want me cured?"

"I have decided that Gonzalo Gustioz has suffered enough. I'm considering sending him back to Castile."

"No!" More frightening words had never been spoken in Zaida's presence.

"But seeing that there is very little left for him in his homeland, I would also consider letting him stay in Madinat al-Zahra."

"Oh, yes, let him stay with me always," she said in a stronger voice. "Let him marry me and give me children." She fingered the amulet and her slow heartbeat raced again. The emotions gathered in her throat and she choked.

Her brother lifted her head up and held the water goblet to her lips. "I'm glad you've found such love, Zaida. Don Gonzalo is a good man. But does he love you as much? Enough to convert and pledge me loyalty?"

She pursed her lips together, unwilling to tell such a horrible truth. Another tear ran down her cheek and her brother understood.

"You deserve a powerful husband," he said. "Many other men would not reject you or cause you pain, and would follow Islam besides."

"I can win him," she said with conviction. "Make him stay where he is, and I can win him."

He smiled. "We truly come from the same mother and father, Zaida. I will let you win him, but then I will test him."

"I can prepare him for any test," she replied. "Unless it's a test of vision. I think the hardships have stolen his sight. Do you think the physician could do anything for him?"

He stood. "I'll send him in for an examination. Rest now, my sister. You must regain your strength."

She sighed and sank into the pillows. As her brother left, the physician came back in with the tea. She drank down the sour poppy extract and thanked him.

She didn't wake until the following day, feeling purged and restored to health. She bathed luxuriously, well rid of the woolen dress. She put on her favorite green silk tunic and pants, and ignored her maids' knowing looks. She saw the physician coming from Don Gonzalo's cell, so she stopped him.

"Feeling better already, Princess?"

"Yes, doctor. I'm sure I won't need any more of your ministrations now that you've explained the best cure to me," she said with a wink. "Have you seen Don Gonzalo?"

"It is as I was told," he replied. "He is inexorably losing his sight. But he will not consent to surgery. He says his God will restore his vision."

"What do you prescribe?"

"He must stay in the dark, otherwise he can't see at all. With the windows closed, and no lamps lit, he can make out shapes and shades of color, but even that won't last long."

"Thank you, doctor," she said, and turned the key in the lock.

She stepped inside and before her eyes could adjust to the blackness, she heard him whisper, "Zaida."

"Gonzalo," she answered, and just as quickly he embraced her, planting feverish kisses on her lips, eyelids, and neck with a passion to match her own. "You've changed your mind?" she said between gasps. They said no more. She felt lighter than air as he carried her to the bed. They played and adored one another for several hours.

"Do you love me, Gonzalo?" Zaida continued during a break in the passion.

He looked at her, and in the dark she knew he could see her as clearly as he ever had, but he took too long to answer. She turned away, but knew he would hear the tears in her voice if she spoke. "You know," she whispered, "Almanzor won't let you go. But he will give you lands and soldiers if only you marry me."

He turned into the pillows. "I'm already married," came muffled back to her ears.

"You're never leaving al-Andalus. You'll never see her again. You might as well start over. I love you," she insisted.

He turned back to her and held her so that she could see the tears he cried. "You want me to convert to paganism and be a Moor, but I can't do it."

"Why can't you accept my love for you?" She rolled over him and stood. She picked up her clothing and covered herself. "There's nowhere for you to go. You'll admit it sooner or later," she finished, and walked out the door against his protests.

She refused to despair that evening, and her confidence was rewarded with a passion that grew each day. They never spoke of his captivity or the possibility of love, but she took every meal with him in his cell and they spent many hours besides in bed together. Some days, she put a strip of cotton around his head to cover his eyes and they went walking in the gardens again. She guided him by the hand under the cypress trees and held up leaves, blossoms, and fruits to his nose and lips. Without sight, she thought his other senses must be exaggerated, since every fragrance and texture sent him into raptures that translated into even more vigor back in his cell. The lovers lived in a cocoon of sensuality where no sorrows could touch them.

For three weeks she floated on a cloud of such bliss. When Zaida could feel their love taking shape inside of her, she called for the midwife to make certain.

She smiled wryly. "I see your lovesickness has been cured of its own accord, Princess."

Zaida giggled like a girl and barely kept her delight under control as she made her way to Gonzalo's cell. He met her at the door and embraced her, but she held him back. "Wait, my lord. I have something to tell you."

"What is it, Zaida?" he asked eagerly. She led him to sit on the bed and they looked intently at each other in the dark.

She grasped his hands and sighed with contentment. "I've waited to tell you to make sure it's true. Almanzor is delighted. I'm carrying your child."

His surprise was greater than she'd imagined. He stood and paced, looking unsure what to do. Finally, he turned back to her and took her hands again. "Zaida, you've brought hope back into my life. The greatest gift you could ever give me."

They danced around the room in each other's embrace. Zaida felt her entire life fulfilled. She knew she could feel no greater pleasure, even as Gonzalo brought her back to the bed to caress and kiss her over and over. She tried to imagine how they would put together such a complex marriage contract, but in her ecstasy such details hardly mattered.

She closed the door behind her, leaving him asleep. He loved her. She could feel it in his hands, his lips, his moans of pleasure. If his Christian past made him too ashamed to speak the words, so be it. She knew, and that would have to be enough.

Chapter XII

The morning sun stabbed Don Gonzalo's eyes through the window Zaida must have forgotten to close. He groaned upright and felt his way toward the offending radiance. They would say the light had gone from his eyes, but they would be wrong. All he saw when the window was open was a mass of light, shining like the halo of an avenging angel.

In the comforting darkness, he stood and smoothed his hair and ran his fingers over his teeth, his thoughts lingering delightfully over the previous night with Zaida.

He heard the key in the lock and the door thrust open authoritatively.

"Zaida, my darling, back already?" he said before he realized the figure was no woman.

"Christian," Almanzor said, "I have come to express my condolences for your misfortune."

"You are most gracious, my lord," Gonzalo mumbled as he scraped the floor in reverence.

"Have these last few weeks done anything to lessen your sorrow?"

A jumble of memories of Sancha and their seven sons herding goats or learning to fight competed with the scent of jasmine and bergamot, the tactile enchantment of Zaida's skin, and the cooing of the doves in his window over the past weeks, and Gonzalo could say nothing.

Almanzor launched unanswered into the motive of his visit. "Given the obvious treachery practiced upon you by Ruy Blásquez, I can see no reason for me to honor his request to kill you. Neither do I see the benefit in increasing your sorrow by keeping you locked up. In the time you've spent in Córdoba, you've shown yourself to be a loyal and passionate defender of your family. We value these virtues. I would like to send you home, so that you may do something about the grave dishonors you've suffered and live out your days with your wife."

"My Sancha!" If he could be with his lifelong companion again, then hope hadn't left Gonzalo completely.

"Go to her," said Almanzor. "I'll give you provisions for the journey, an escort, and safe passage. You may leave tomorrow if you so desire."

Gonzalo made another bow. "I hope one day to be able to repay such kindness and generosity, my lord."

Only when the man who seemed more powerful than the caliph had swept back out of the cell and locked the door did Gonzalo remember Zaida, the beautiful Mooress who had bewitched him into enjoying life again. Outside the door he heard murmuring. He pressed his ear against it, but it wasn't necessary. Zaida's wail came through clearly. Gonzalo's heart, so full of the news of his journey home, nearly emptied at the sound.

More muffled voices told Gonzalo the scene wasn't over yet. The key turned in the door and Zaida stood before him like a wild creature, her hair making exaggerated silhouettes in the blur of light from the passageway. Gonzalo knew she was looking at him, but couldn't see her expression. Ten of the chamberlain's guards filed in behind Zaida and took places along the wall. Eight of them held satchels and two carried a long wooden case between them.

The door closed, Zaida waved her arms at the guards. "Leave them. Just drop them on the floor. Leave him alone with his dead and rotting past."

Gonzalo realized that the satchels must contain the heads of his sons and Muño Salido, and the case must be a kind of casket for them. When the guards didn't move, Zaida wrenched the closest bundle out of the guard's hands and held it high as if to dash it against the floor tiles.

"My son!" Gonzalo skidded across the space to seize the sack before she could do violence to it. He held it to his chest and sat on the floor to undo the string that bound it together at the top. While Zaida gave orders to the guards in Arabic, Gonzalo ran his fingertips along the face of his middle son, Rodrigo. His dark hair still gleamed in the penumbra of the cell and his skin felt as fresh as the day he'd helped his brothers bring a lynx to the main house. Gonzalo put his nose to the scalp, trying to discern whether there was some magical Arabian oil keeping it so well preserved, but the scent of his living, breathing child filled his senses. Perhaps Rodrigo was a martyr and God had honored his flesh by protecting it from the decay of mortality.

"I'm sorry, my love," said Zaida. She still stood in the doorway, but the guards had gone and Gonzalo could make out that she was smoothing her hair. She knelt beside him and placed the other satchels within his reach. "I haven't given birth to your child yet, but I know I would act the same if any harm ever came to him."

He took her hands in his and held them in acknowledgment, and together they opened the sacks to reveal the faces Gonzalo had known all their lives, looking as if they slept peacefully. Zaida opened the casket, and the fragrance told him it was lined with cedar to keep crawling things away. Sheets of linen and other soft fabrics would cushion the heads on their long journey home. Gonzalo kissed each one and laid it snugly beside its brothers, Muño Salido last of all, to continue to protect them as he had died trying to do. Zaida closed the latch with a click. Gonzalo took her into his lap. Her weight was no more than that of a feather, but she was so warm and alive, he could just believe a new life was quickening inside her.

She sighed. "You're returning to Castile."

"I'm sorry, my dear. I must," he whispered. "Sancha expected me weeks ago."

"Tell me how your son will recognize you as his father."

Gonzalo removed the golden ring from his left hand. Although it had no jewels set into it, unlike his other rings, it was engraved with Latin characters and serpentine beasts, a reminder of his people's Visigothic glory. There would be nothing else like it in Córdoba or even Andalusia. He worked the ring between his hands until it snapped in two. "Tell him my name, and give him this half. When he's ready, he should come looking for me in Salas. I will keep this half of the ring, and he can present the other half to me as proof of his identity. I won't deny him."

Zaida enclosed the metal arc in her hand. "Very well, my lord. And what if you've engendered a girl?"

"In such a case, I will always remember the daughter I never had. You may give her to Almanzor to find a suitable husband for her." He reached for Zaida's chin and turned her face toward his. Her sorrow coursed over her cheeks, so he kissed it away, and yet it renewed with every caress.

"My lord, the deed is accomplished. You don't need to do this with me anymore."

He refused to stop. "You've given me the greatest gift anyone ever could. Let me return some little portion of the joy to you."

Her body silently agreed that yes, she deserved at least that. He hoped she knew without his speaking the love he was leaving behind, and with which she could raise the child. Afterward, he fell asleep, exhausted, and when he woke, Zaida was gone. He shot upright, afraid he might never see her again.

The next morning, someone else brought a breakfast of nuts and dried fruits to his cell and he ate in silence. This new person left the door wide open the whole time and spoke not a single word to him, but took him by the wrist and led him through a maze of bright passageways and out the front archways, which he recognized by the feeling of upward pull when he walked under them.

When he crossed the threshold, the sounds of a gathering expedition swept over him. Knights and squires talked and joked with each other in Arabic, shifting packs into carts and fastening leather and metal buckles while the horses snorted and pawed. His silent guide placed his hand on a horse's flank, and Gonzalo helped himself into the saddle with what he hoped was some measure of dignity. The sensation of freedom was immediate—he saw himself atop a steed that galloped over the plains of Castile between castle and fortress, leading his mighty sons to a new victory.

"Where are my sons?" he asked the bright blur in front of him.

"They're right next to you, my lord," came Zaida's voice from the air beside him. His heart sank. He had been right: he wouldn't have known she was there, and so he would never see her again. He tried to hold back the tears, but they came to the surface so easily now, he knew the entourage would never think him anything more than a sad old man.

"They've set the casket into its own cart," Zaida explained, "and it's right next to you." She took his hand and guided it to the left. "Just beyond your fingertips. You'll be able to see for yourself this evening, I'm certain."

"Thank you, dear Zaida," he said in her direction, hoping she believed he was looking into her eyes. "Can you ever forgive me?"

"We mustn't speak of such things in public, Don Gonzalo." Her lips touched the back of his hand to kiss it goodbye, and her whispers traveled up his arm and calmed his heart. "You can never leave now. I have a part of you with me always." A teardrop stung his skin. He carried it to his lips, where it tasted bittersweet.

A rider made a sound that must have been a word, and the group started down the road toward Córdoba. Gonzalo's eyes watered so much that he kept them closed for most of the day, and when he opened them he wasn't rewarded. The sky poured piercing rays into his skull and made him close down all over again. The horse knew what to do for the most part, but once, Gonzalo didn't hear the telltale signs in time and walked his mount right up against the back of the knight ahead of him.

"Open your eyes, Christian!" Surprised to hear a language he could understand, Gonzalo did as he was told, but could see no more than before. Several of the squires murmured together and at last a knight — likely the first who'd become frustrated with him — said, "Get down. We can't have you riding if you're blind."

He found his way off the saddle and someone took his hand. When he felt the wooden railings of a cart, he climbed up. His hand encountered the smooth wood and latch of the casket, so he lay down next to it and let grief take him over. No one tried to hold a conversation with him. It wasn't until nightfall that he was able to count that he was traveling with twenty men. Gonzalo wondered whether they had other business in Castile or if they would turn around for Córdoba upon their arrival in Salas. And so it went for fourteen mornings. Sometimes he cried until there was no moisture left in his body. Other days he stared into the blazing sun, wondering when autumn would ever arrive in this torrid zone and willing the sun to burn him up from the inside if he arrived in Salas only to find his beloved wife dead, also murdered at the hand of his brother-in-law.

One day, he caught the scent of dry, brown oak and beech leaves drifting coolly on the breeze. The knights stopped and asked, "Salas?"

The reply came in a Latin Gonzalo could recognize, free of southern accents. "Five leagues down that road." He sat up, unable to believe they were so close.

His head darted in every direction, and though it looked the same to him, his body knew this crossroads. There was a small farm to the north, and through the trees one could make out a little wooden hermitage. If one had eyes to see with. "You'll soon see a rocky outcrop through the trees. Then we'll come to the stone church of San Pelayo, and a bridge, and my lands are right after," he said.

"The Christian is risen," said the impatient knight, accompanied by chuckles. Gonzalo couldn't find the energy to explain to them that he would have conversed with them the entire journey if they had only shown some will for it. He was too busy wondering whether Sancha was there waiting for him, or had already abandoned him and gone to her homeland now that her sons were no more, or whether she knew what had happened, or thought he was dead. Perhaps it had been her prayers that had opened Almanzor's heart.

He heard the bells long before the road approached the church, and then the horses' hooves and wagon wheels clattered over the bridge, and his heart was in his throat when the entourage stopped before the grinding and splashing sounds of someone at the well in front of his own house.

Don Gonzalo climbed out of the cart, and thanked the hands that led him through the horses and safely to the source of the sounds. "Who is at the well?" he asked.

The bucket clattered against the stones. A thin voice came out to meet him. "My lord?"

"I am Don Gonzalo Gustioz, Lord of Salas and Lara," he said with as much confidence as he could muster while he still didn't know what had happened to Sancha.

"Are you a ghost?"

"I am flesh." He held out an arm for her to test his assertion. "You're Luz, Sancha's most loyal servant, aren't you?"

A hesitant touch on his forearm drew back instantly. "My lord! My lady was beginning to suspect you had died on your journey. But what's wrong with your eyes?"

"Nothing. Please fetch your lady. I'm back from Córdoba, but…"

The girl ran away from him shouting. "It's Don Gonzalo! Don Gonzalo returned!"

∼

It wasn't that anything was wrong. The harvest tributes had produced enough grain to see Salas through the winter with plenty to spare for seed. Doña Sancha gladly accepted two war horse foals and three traveling fillies, and one especially prosperous vassal had brought a matched pair of oxen, complete with yoke. But it had been so long since Doña Sancha had heard any news from her husband or sons that the silence was crowding her. She missed Suero and his hawk, and Martín's constant board games, Muño Salido's heart-to-heart talks, and the warmth and security of her husband's embrace.

Not long after her husband and sons had abandoned her, a jongleur had appeared on the road, bringing his pointed cap and sack full of music with him.

"Fair lady," he'd said with a sweeping bow out front by the well, "I bring news for the mistress of Salas."

"It is I, Doña Sancha," she'd replied, her heart pounding.

"Great Mistress of Salas, your son Don Gonzalo sent me here to tell you that he and his brothers are well and that, to increase the glory of Castile, they have set out with their knights and many of Ruy Blásquez's number to take Almenar."

That must mean her brother and sons truly had reconciled. The news opened her senses to the blue sky, the singing birds, and the beauty of all God's creation. "In that case, Sir Musician, you are very welcome in this house."

The tributes had already begun, so they set the tables out between the main house and stables and feasted on some of the pledges that had already been made with the vassals who had traveled from the farthest corners of Lara. Sancha seated the minstrel beside her and he cheered her and the rest of the table with gossip and rumors about the King of León, the Caliph of Córdoba, and the princes of France. He always seemed ready for any task, and within a single day he formed an important if ill-defined part of the estate. Each night, he tuned his rebec by the hearth and Sancha, her maids, and the traveling vassals gathered around to enjoy his songs of bravery, treachery, and romance.

On the third night, he cleared his throat at his place near the fire and addressed Sancha. "My lady, there is a very new song I would like to share with this noble company. Would you like to hear about the wedding celebrations of Ruy Blásquez and Doña Lambra?"

Sancha watched his face tense while he waited for her answer. Finally, she put him out of his misery. "We like to listen to all the latest here. But how could there be a song on that subject so quickly?"

"A minstrel who attended and witnessed the events began it. I've added my own flourishes, of course." He tweaked the tuning pegs. "But if it's not agreeable, I have many other songs to share."

Sancha enjoyed pleasing the little man who had made the harvest tributes like a celebration, but hesitated. "Is there anything in it yet about a cucumber?"

"A cucumber, my lady?" The jongleur's eyes were wide.

"Thank God for small mercies," said Sancha. She felt curious how the events would be heard throughout the county and in kingdoms beyond. "Please proceed."

Grinning, the musician played a dancelike melody. Just when some of the vassals were standing up from their benches and pallets to dance, he took the tempo down and sang.

"Leaving Zamora, the great Count García Fernández
Took with him many from León and Portugal
To be present at the wedding of Doña Lambra and Ruy Blásquez.
He rode with his company until he came to Burgos,
To see the great feats and feasting and the lancing of the scaffold.
He ordered a special tent for Doña Lambra along the riverbank.
The first to throw his lance was Count García Fernández,
And then Ruy Blásquez did very good work,
And Muño Salido, who can tell auguries with birds,
And many men from many places, and then Álvar Sánchez."

When he sang the names of her sons, they entered Sancha's ear like a caress. She knew she had been extraordinarily blessed, almost too much so, with every one of her sons growing up strong and talented and her husband both powerful and affectionate. But she also felt weak in their absence. It occurred to her sometimes to take the jongleur with her into the bower, the small chamber off the main hall where she slept alone when there were so many visitors. But she knew that even at her age, such grasping at basic human warmth would not be well viewed. Perhaps Luz and the other girls could join her instead. But again, she knew without trying that their weight on the pallet would not be the same as Don Gonzalo's. Her Gonzalo! When would he come back to her? She couldn't stop the tears. Luz jumped up to get rags out of the trunk near the entrance to the hall, drawing the minstrel's attention.

He stopped playing. "I'm sorry, my lady. The death of Álvar Sánchez is too fresh for you to listen to in this manner."

Sancha mopped at her face. "It's a beautiful and informative song. I was there, too, you understand. Let me help you make it accurate. I hope you'll stay many more days with us in Salas."

So he did. He remained after the tributes were over and the vassals had gone home. Sancha taught him with a gentle manner about the workings of the farm and in return he followed her about and tried to anticipate her needs before even Luz could. He seemed happy among the chickens and geese, so she appointed him their master.

Sancha supervised when he released the geese into the copse of pine trees beyond the pig sty for their daily grazing. Then he and most of the serving girls sat around the hearth sorting lengths of wool cloth from the bags of tribute.

"No, dear boy," Sancha said, "that length is much too rough for that stack. Put it with the material for blankets and pallets."

Luz smacked the door open, spilling her bucket of water. "Doña Sancha!"

"What is it?"

Luz gestured as if she had lost her tongue. Sancha followed her outside and understood why.

A strange retinue of horses and carts and men wearing turbans and armor awaited her. But her eye found the important piece of the puzzle standing alone by the well. She wept with joy and disbelief. "Oh, Gonzalo, my life, I was sure you were dead and buried in pagan lands!"

He wrapped his arms around her and buried his head in her neck, inhaling. "Sancha," he murmured, "my Sancha." He kissed his way up to her lips, where his tongue explored the inside of her mouth with a passion she remembered from their distant past.

She pulled away to look into his eyes. They were closed, and the eyelashes were crusted with dried tears and other bodily humors. "What's wrong, my love? Haven't you brought riches back from Córdoba?"

He opened his eyes for a moment, and Sancha saw milky white orbs where she was accustomed to the mirror of his soul. She gasped.

"There are no words to describe what has happened," he said in a dry, broken voice. "Almanzor took pity on me..."

"Took pity on you?"

"Oh, my beloved wife, and the mother... I'm so sorry I have to be the one to show you what your brother has sent as a gift."

It looked odd when he gestured toward one of the carts with his eyes closed. "Help me, please," he said, and one of the knights, or squires — she was unable to distinguish rank from their bizarre costume — came out to take his hand and lead him to the cart. Another Moorish knight brought a coffin around to where she could see. Her hairs stood on end. Don Gonzalo loosened the latches by feel and Sancha looked on with growing horror as the knight opened the lid to reveal not one but many bundles of cloth inside.

"There are eight of them," she whispered, unable to find her voice.

Gonzalo felt at the first cloth to lift it away from whatever it protected. Sancha recognized the hairline and eyebrows of her youngest son and felt herself floating away.

She stood before a banquet with her sons, each of them sporting necklaces, a ring on each finger, and cloaks of the richest red and purple velvet. Each son sat next to a wife who looked at her husband with adoration. To Sancha's left and right, young men and women of every handsome shape partook of the meats and breads before them with a happiness Sancha wanted to inspect more closely. But try as she might, she couldn't distinguish their features. They were the grandchildren she would never have. Sorrow took her away from the banquet, and soon she stood with her new husband outside the church where they had just spoken their vows, her sons not even as material as a thought except in God's unfathomable plan. Don Gonzalo, his hair raven-black, held her hand aloft in his to show their bond and the crowd threw flowers. More and more flowers, daisies and roses, complete with thorns, came down on her head and pelted her brow and her shoulders.

The water that revived her was cold and cruel. "No, no," she said when she realized she was on the ground in front of the cart that had borne such evil tidings. Gonzalo was kneeling over her, cradling her. She looked at his crusted eyelashes, a terrible reminder of the abundance and health they no longer enjoyed. "I don't want this life," she said. "Send me to be with my sons."

"My darling, my love, I can't protect you from the truth. You're all I have left. Please be strong for me. You must take comfort in my return to you. I will never leave you again."

He stood and, taking his hand for support, she drew herself into a standing position. The water, still cold through her underdress and against her skin, ran down until she felt as if the icy fingers of some evil spirit had hold of her. Young Gonzalo's dark hair still led the grim procession inside the casket.

"All seven, gone?" She wiped her nose.

"With Muño Salido," Don Gonzalo acknowledged.

Sancha wanted to be strong, but she couldn't accept what her husband was telling her. She reached toward the heads, but Luz's hand shot out in front of her. "No, my lady."

Sancha looked back to see her entire household gathered around the carts. At least she wouldn't have to repeat the news for them. "Luz," she said, "I need to see them."

The girl screwed up her mouth, then seemed to understand. "I'll help you."

Together they laid the eight bundles on the lip of the cart and untied the strings to display their contents for all to see. Their hair shone in the autumnal sunlight and their lowered eyelids made them look as if they were taking a nap. "How I've longed to see their faces again," said Sancha. "I never imagined it would be like this."

She put a hand on Martín's brow and buried her hand in Suero's hair. She stroked Rodrigo's cheek, then stood back and, finding Diego, kissed his face with the motherly affection she might have spent on him if he'd lived until the Last Judgment. No one tried to stop her as she went down the row, loving her helpless children and bathing them in her tears. Only yesterday, it seemed, they had crawled along the straw-covered floor to terrorize cats and make conquests over the kingdoms of mice. Such a short time later, they had become men — a house full of men — where had they come from so suddenly? They had been her protectors and her legacy, but none of them had wives, and none had their own children. As quickly as they had arrived, they were gone, leaving her cold and alone. She lifted her head from Gonzalico's face only to be confronted with the neverending row of eyes like her husband's, noses like her father's, and lips like her own. Mercifully, her vision clouded with tears. She stood and let them fall at their will.

Gonzalo's arms wrapped around her and he held her head to his shoulder, where she sobbed and gasped, struggling to undo the terrible event.

"Weep, Sancha," whispered her husband. "I know you must weep. But don't cry too much. Look at what weeks of crying has done to my eyes. Don't let your brother blind both of us."

"I care nothing for my brother or anything else on this Earth. Is there no relief from this pain?" She looked past Don Gonzalo's eyelids, searching out his soul, while she held her breath.

"No," he murmured. "There is no relief." Tears slid out from between his tightly pressed eyelashes to join hers.

Luz's reedy voice entered their small, quaking world. "How long have they...? My lady, it's just that they look so unscathed."

"I believe it's been at least six weeks since they were murdered," said Gonzalo, clearing his throat and looking in not quite the right direction at the girl, who stood like a sentinel by the edge of the cart.

"My lord and lady, have you noticed that there is no decay? Perhaps your children and their tutor are martyrs, and God honors them with everlasting flesh."

"I think that may be true. God knows they are the victims of the worst betrayal since Judas kissed Jesus Christ," said Don Gonzalo.

"My brother did this?"

"It's unbelievable, I know," said her husband.

Sancha was confused by an urge to spring into action. If her brother had truly done this unspeakable thing—and it was becoming evident that he had, that there was no escaping the fact that even the most powerful saint couldn't revive her sons now—then her children could be martyrs, attracting pilgrims from all over Castile and León, and there was a lot to do. It felt better than sitting in Salas for the rest of her days, going blind with grief. She walked out of Gonzalo's embrace to address him and her household together.

"We must call the priest here. We'll have the biggest funeral in the history of Castile and the priest can examine our sons and Muño Salido. Perhaps he'll display the heads near the altar as relics. All our vassals must return and help us mourn. Our Moorish friends here can help, too." She sent her servants and squires in every direction with the news and gestured the Andalusian knights inside to help make more bedrolls for the extra guests.

Luz helped dry Sancha off and replaited her hair. Then Sancha had her bring another bucket and tallow soap and set it before Don Gonzalo where he sat on the bench away from the fire. He squinted as if he could make out the details of the house he hadn't seen for so long while the two women scrubbed away the dirt of his long journey.

Sancha had done her waiting, and her husband was home at last. She would not drive him away with sadness.

Chapter XIII

Justa released the hogs snorting and gamboling into the edge of the forest, as she had done each morning since Ermenegildo Antolínez had abandoned Barbadillo to whatever fate Doña Lambra designed for it. The hogs foraged for acorns, truffles, and whatever else they were pleased to eat. Later, she would collect leftovers from the dinner table into a bucket and toss it into their enclosure, where they would find it added to the previous days' leavings. Justa most enjoyed using a long stick when she returned to the forest to tap the hogs and suggest they return home for the night. They were easier to control than sheep, and she was learning the personalities of each one. One was diminutive, like Little Page, another cried a lot and reminded her of Gotina, one was greedy and bossy like Doña Lambra, another was handsome and gentle like Adalberto, and one always came last, whether leaving the pen or returning to it, and her Justa called Última.

Upon the Lord of Barbadillo's absence with some of his key servants, Justa had watched carefully as Lambra shied away from the hogs and their filth, and volunteered to take care of them. She had glimpsed what life would be like with a kind lady for her mistress when Doña Sancha had allowed Justa to accompany her and her seven sons on the hunting trip that had ended so tragically. She understood for the first time that when she slept or ate needn't depend upon Doña Lambra's whim, and for all their stench, the hogs had come to smell a little bit like freedom.

She gave Última a last friendly tap and returned to the sty, only to see Adalberto closing the gate. In her surprise, Justa was unable to greet him before he said, "So many tons of wild pork for one sweet maiden."

The heat rising in her cheeks, Justa noticed again how brightly his eyes shone when he looked at her. She laughed shakily. "I will welcome the aid of a strong squire when I'm rounding them up again."

"Are you certain you don't need an army of doughty knights?"

"Certainly not. Those hogs are as tame as hounds." She hurried away toward the house so he wouldn't see her face burning with the hundreds of emotions his attention caused her. She spent the day convincing herself he wouldn't be there at sunset.

Before nightfall, Justa went back to the forest to round up the hogs and Adalberto followed her at a respectful distance. Knowing he was behind her, watching over her, made Justa's heart beat faster. How quickly her life had changed once she'd found something she could do without her lady.

She whistled for the hogs with a dry throat. They came at once and followed her toward the buildings, heedless of her confusion. Behind her, Adalberto's voice was soft and deep.

"Justa, have you ever considered leaving Doña Lambra and starting your own family?"

One day long ago, Doña Lambra's parents had taken Justa by the hand and declared her their foster daughter. The world with its possibilities had been open to her until Lambra's parents died on the roads to the south. That was the last day Justa mistook her station. Her lot in life was to serve and obey.

"No," she replied, opening the gate and ushering the hogs inside the sty, where they happily grunted and wallowed.

"But you're so beautiful," he said behind her. "You would make such a good wife."

She turned to look him in the eye. His face was open, with no hidden meanings lurking under the brows. "I'm only a servant, like you. I can't make any plans for my life without Doña Lambra's express permission."

He took her hand between his and a soft heat flushed her skin.

"Perhaps you might ask her."

Her heart pounding, she took back her hand and lowered her gaze. "I dare not." She darted out from between the pen and his body, leaving him to close the gate for the night.

Over the next several days, Adalberto accompanied her during her release and recall of the hogs, maintaining his distance. Even without words, Justa understood his intentions. She came to desire these stolen moments above all other times of day. After a week, he spoke to her again about matters of the estate. She stared at his square jaw in the morning sunlight through the trees and by the glow of a lamp in the evening and began to believe that the possibility might exist for her to marry and start her own family somewhere away from Doña Lambra. Day after day, the thoughts became headier and more elated until the evening Adalberto leaned toward her between the trees where no one could see and kissed her lips.

Her legs weakened and a warmth more pleasant than sitting by the fireside came over her.

"Would you like to be my wife, Justa?" he said. "I don't have land, but perhaps if I can impress Ruy Blásquez whenever he returns, he'll grant me something, or I could save money until we can go away from here. We'll travel through Castile building irrigation systems."

"Yes, please," she breathed. "I'd like that very much."

Unwilling to break the enchantment, they stood with their arms around each other until the hogs found their own way back to the gate and they felt obliged to open it for them. Then she told Adalberto to stay behind as usual. With him, she left her hopes. She thought perhaps she might find a way to broach the subject with Doña Lambra the next day. After all, Lambra was a married lady and could easily find other serving girls to replace simple, quiet Justa.

But when she came around to the main house, she saw her lady standing at the front door in an attitude of blatant appraisal. Before her, Ruy Blásquez with his new crooked, scarred nose and a retinue of twenty soldiers appeared to be recounting what had happened to them. Justa froze in place and watched her lady's exaggerated gestures and her lord's diminutive nods and small advances toward his wife in the fading light. He stopped talking and the soldiers stood stiffly. Suddenly, Doña Lambra threw her arms around her husband and kissed him even more fervently than the way Justa had shown her affection to Adalberto.

Relieved, Justa continued forward when the knights headed to the stable with the horses and her lady released Ruy Blásquez. Doña Lambra turned her face toward Justa, remaining in her husband's embrace. "Justa, dear maid, rejoice with me. Revenge is ours!"

"Is it?" she said. What did that mean?

"Gather the household in the hall," said Doña Lambra. "We're going to make a grand announcement."

It wasn't hard to find everyone because they were about their assigned duties or already in the main building for the evening meal. Doña Lambra and Ruy Blásquez stood atop the wide bench at the table in the center of the hall, surrounded by the servants, squires, and knights, with women on the right and men on the left, keeping to the strict segregation Doña Lambra had enforced since the first night. Justa looked across at Adalberto, who was beaming back at her. It could be that whatever was so wonderful would permit gifts to the household. Maybe Doña Lambra would feel generous and allow Justa to find an appropriate husband and a new home.

Doña Lambra spread her arms as if laying a blanket of silence over the hall. "My faithful servants," she began, "prepare for great festivities."

Gotina, standing next to Justa, whispered in her ear. "How can we ever have proper entertainment here again after she dismissed that jongleur? Her memory is short, but his isn't, and he'll have told all the other entertainers he's met. I knew our lives were over that day."

"Hush," said Justa.

"There is no longer any stain on the honor of either of our united families," Lambra pronounced. Her husband looked at her with an expression Justa couldn't interpret.

"Tell us what happened, Don Ruy," said Adalberto below him, betraying none of the impatience Justa thought he must feel.

Their lord cleared his throat. "The González family is finished."

Above the confused murmurs, Justa heard one of his knights say, "They need to hear the details."

"What has happened?" asked one of the pages.

"Not a single one of the seven so-called noble knights of Lara survives, and their father was beheaded in Córdoba," said Doña Lambra, clasping her hands as if she held a treasure. "Go on, my love, tell them how you led them onto the battlefield in Almenar, and they could barely defend themselves against Moorish soldiers." She shoved him as if to launch him into the story.

He appeared to think his words over. He wiped his forehead, sending his eyebrow hairs in all directions. "I led the seven knights González to Almenar. They were eager to sack it."

"And they didn't even last an hour, did they?" said Doña Lambra. "And how many Moorish soldiers were there? Only seven!"

"Yes," said Ruy Blásquez, "that's right."

"And then what profane thing did the Moorish knights do?" encouraged Lambra. She took his arm.

"Oh, yes," said her lord, a bit more loudly, "it was passing strange. Once each brother was dead, they beheaded him and wrapped the head up to send to Almanzor in Córdoba."

"That's because Almanzor hates Christians, isn't it?" said Doña Lambra. She leaned in and kissed him on the cheek, a gesture that astounded Justa, there amidst the servants, who gave voice to their own surprise.

With more confidence, Ruy Blásquez explained, "That's right. There is nothing Almanzor hates more than Christians, and he was afraid of Castile while those brothers were alive, but now he can remain in Córdoba without fear, since they're dead." Justa thought his reasoning folded in on itself, but there was no time to think it over.

"What wonderful news it is," said Lambra. She circled her husband, doing a round dance atop the table. "Rejoice with me, those from Bureba! We are now the most powerful family in Castile. My horrible nephews are dead. They killed my cousin and my page—one of you—and now they're dead."

"Little Page never saw Bureba in his life," whispered Gotina.

"I know," said Justa. She didn't dare take her eyes off her lady.

"And their father is dead, too. There can never be another knight González of Lara to dishonor Ruy Blásquez or my house of Bureba," Doña Lambra was saying. "Let's all get a good night's rest. Tomorrow we must prepare feasts and games."

The people dispersed in anticipation of laying out the pallets for the night.

Justa was almost convinced she was in the clear when she heard it: "Justa, come here." She followed her lord and lady obediently, carrying a beeswax candle to light their way around the stables to the slaughterhouse. Doña Lambra took her arm with too much exuberance. "I'm hoping to give ten children to my lord, now that he's proven what a great man he is." Ruy Blásquez turned to her with a grin, his teeth glinting in the candlelight.

Justa's face got hot. She had no idea what an appropriate response would be. "Of course, my lady."

"We'd like to get started now, but we want privacy. There's no bower apart from the great hall, so stand guard at this door."

Justa opened the slaughterhouse door and let her lord and lady enter. She closed it and stood with the candle, staring into the forest. A tear fell from her eye, and many others followed. She couldn't keep from imagining what was happening as the moans and grunts surged behind her. Were they kneeling in the straw? Was she doubled over the filthy table? How long had it been since the last slaughter? What did it smell like in there? This was the place where Little Page had swirled a cucumber in a bucket before he died. How could Lambra do this in such a space?

The tears were still flowing when Ruy Blásquez and Doña Lambra reemerged, holding hands.

"Don't cry, Justa." It was a command, not sympathy. In reply, Justa sniffed and wiped her eyes as quietly as possible. "It's not exactly a burden to lie with such a good husband."

"Of course, my lady."

A shrill whistle came from Ruy Blásquez's contorted nose. "Lambra, you've made me so happy."

Justa escorted them back to the hall, where they arranged their pallets near the fire with her lord on one side of Doña Lambra and Justa on the other.

The next day they slaughtered one of Justa's hogs and roasted the parts over a crackling bonfire. But the feast took place in near silence. No one, not even Ruy Blásquez, let the death of those seven talented knights move them to joy the way Doña Lambra had. Gotina looked across at Justa, making faces. With no music or other distractions, Justa noticed that even the knights who had been with Ruy Blásquez were sullen and restless. The brothers had duly paid for the deaths of Álvar Sánchez and Little Page, and although she missed them both, Justa didn't think the gracious Doña Sancha should have to suffer such a loss for them.

She had no real reason to doubt the news, but felt in her heart that the strange story their lord had told them about Diego, Martín, Rodrigo, Fernando, Suero, Gustio, and Gonzalo being overcome and beheaded by only seven anonymous Moorish knights couldn't be true. Perhaps they weren't truly dead. She took courage in that hope and looked down the table at Adalberto, who was making a show of lustily biting into a chop of meat to the tepid amusement of the pages around him. Justa knew the tenuous balance of Lambra's delight and the servants' obedience wouldn't last long. She wondered if whatever change was coming would permit her to become Adalberto's wife. A knot of dread in her stomach prevented her from tasting her food. Her dear friend, the hog like Adalberto, had sacrificed his life for nothing.

Ruy Blásquez's soldiers slipped back to their own towns or estates one by one without fanfare. In the same stealthy manner, Justa found time to tend to her hogs, but saw Adalberto less and less often. Morning and nightfall became her lord and lady's preferred times for escaping to some secluded nook in the forest or one of the outbuildings for the private consummation of their newfound passion. Justa prayed they would understand that they didn't need her to stand guard every time, but God never granted her selfish wish. She took to staring at Adalberto across the table at meals, attempting to speak without words, and purposefully reaching for the goblet or dipping her finger in the sauce at the same time he did in the hope of some brief brush with his hand.

She had felt much happier in ignorance of love.

One afternoon, Gotina came upon her standing sentry at the slaughterhouse door. A wicked smile crossed her face. "Are the lord and lady in there?"

"Yes. It will only be a few minutes now if you need something," Justa replied.

"I don't know why they bother you looking for private spaces when all of us can hear them going at it all night long."

"Gotina! Keep your voice down."

"Well really, shouldn't she keep her voice down? What has it been, two or three months? Is she not pregnant yet, after all this?"

"No, but that's hardly your concern."

"If I have to listen to it every night, it becomes my concern. Perhaps she isn't mature enough to conceive?"

"Oh, no. Lambra started her monthly courses two summers ago, right after I did. Now they're as regular as the full moon. She may control everything I do, but she doesn't have any secrets from me." Realizing she'd spoken aloud, Justa blushed. The heat flowed from the top of her head into her neck.

"My, my," said Gotina. "Do I detect dissatisfaction with your lot in life?"

Visions of Adalberto, their own parcel of land teeming with vegetables, and their own children appeared before Justa's eyes. "Of course not. I would never argue with what God has planned for me." She tried to deflect Gotina's interest. "Those aren't the sounds of someone avoiding a baby. She'll have some good news soon enough." Her blushing would not subside. She would have to make sure Gotina never found her standing guard for one of these trysts again.

Doña Lambra sauntered out the guarded door, her hair disheveled. "Gotina, shouldn't you be in the kitchen?"

Gotina bowed her head and returned to the main house so silently, one might have assumed she was mute.

Doña Lambra slipped her arm through Justa's and walked with her as if the past ten years had never happened. "Justa, I'll need you to brush out my hair before the evening meal," she said.

"Of course, my lady."

"I think my lord likes to see my golden hair shimmering in the candlelight."

As they passed the stable, a strange movement caught Justa's eye. All at once, her heart was in her throat. She'd glimpsed Adalberto's back as he stood up from a kneeling position, facing southeast, his hands cupping his ears. What was he doing out there by himself? She'd heard about some of the strange rituals of the pagan religions, of the movements they made as the demons traveled through their bodies. Was Adalberto a Moor? He'd made a big show of biting into the pork at the banquet, but she couldn't be sure she had seen him swallow. That was the mark of both Jews and Moors, according to the priests. Priests were incapable of lies, but obviously Adalberto was not.

She wanted to stand still and let the earth swallow her, but she kept pace with Doña Lambra. If he was a Moor and Lambra found out.... She shuddered.

Doña Lambra blithely entered the main house, perched herself on a settle, and handed Justa her brush. Justa unclasped the metal tips that held the braids together and shook them out with hands that trembled. She tried to ignore her unsteady heart and pay attention to the latest praises of Ruy Blásquez that issued from her lady's mouth.

"Wasn't he the greatest knight at our wedding, knocking over that part of the scaffold before anyone else?"

"Of course, my lady."

"I suppose Álvar Sánchez would've been the best there, if he hadn't been so brutally murdered."

"Of course, my lady."

"But in avenging Álvar Sánchez, my husband becomes as great as he was."

"Certainly, my lady."

"And in defeating all seven of our nephews, my husband becomes as good as they were evil."

"We are all most fortunate to have him as our lord." Justa sighed.

Justa never knew what was atop her bread charger at the evening meal. She picked at the stale bread itself and felt it scrape the inside of her throat. She did not reach for the goblet or the sauce, and when the pallets were laid out, she stared into the blackness and wondered if Adalberto had been sent by the Devil to entice her. Or perhaps he was Satan himself, creating such uncommon ambition in her. But this desire for a different life didn't feel like ambition. It felt like love. No, this evil, suffering, rotting love was the Devil's temptation toward envy and lust. Justa wished there was a church much closer so that she could slip away to it without her lady, or that a traveling priest or a novice monk would happen by in search of souls to save.

She didn't close her eyes all night. When a sliver of light made its way between the shutters, Adalberto's voice was at her ear.

"Darling, come and meet me at the stables. I can't live like this, seeing you and never speaking with you."

She rolled over with a groan and hid her face under her hands, determined not to fall into the Devil's snare. But if the Devil was in Adalberto, he surely was in Justa, too, because her love for him, and now her desire to protect him from their lady, hadn't waned. When she moved her hands, Adalberto was gone, but the light hadn't increased or moved along the windowsill. Perhaps God was prolonging this moment for her to confront her tempter.

Shifting about the hall as quietly as possible, she pulled a tunic over her underdress without bothering with a belt and wrapped a fur around her shoulders. Something stronger than Justa transported her to the stable, where she saw Adalberto waiting with a burning taper. Her resolve from the previous night was like a leaf in the autumn wind. Adalberto was no demon, only a kind and handsome man.

"Adalberto," she said in quick, hushed tones, "the moment Lambra finds out you're a Muslim, she'll have you whipped and exiled, or worse. And if she finds out about us...."

"But I'm not..." he began, then started again. "We may have to run away from here, darling." He took her wrist to pull her inside the warm stable. Some of the mares whinnied at the human intrusion so early.

His touch made her decision. Justa said nothing more, but kissed his lips hungrily. He responded with equal passion and traced the shape of her body through the layers of fabric with his hands. She thought that as long as the straw was clean, the stable would be almost as comfortable as lying on a pallet in the main hall, and wondered why her lord and lady had never thought of it. If Justa and Adalberto were quiet, as they had been up to now, even the horses wouldn't notice. She looked into his eyes and saw devotion.

"Do you love me, Adalberto?"

"For all time, Justa," he said breathily.

She inspected the stable wall in the candlelight, took a pitchfork she found leaning against it, and shoveled new straw into the pathway in front of the stalls. He watched, apparently too confused to help, as bawling mice dispersed into different burrows in the wall. By the time she set the pitchfork down and returned to him, he seemed to have understood.

"Are you sure you want this, here?" He tenderly brushed a long golden strand away from her brow.

"Yes."

He bent to lift both of her skirts and placed his hand between her thighs. She felt such a rush of pleasure and excitement, she might not have noticed if the stable caught fire. The interruption they did have was the only one that could have kept her from her purpose.

Doña Lambra's head, then the rest of her body in only a gauzy underdress, came through the door. "Justa, I've been sick. Come and tell me the other signs. I think a baby is finally in my belly."

Justa's skirts fell back into place, rustling the hay, but Doña Lambra didn't acknowledge Adalberto's presence or ask what Justa was doing in the stable. Justa never knew how her lady had found her or who had cleaned up her morning vomit. They returned to the hall and Doña Lambra sat daintily on the settle, waiting for the information she sought, while the household put away the bedding and set up the table for the day's first meal. She seemed warmed from within, so that her early foray into the autumn air hadn't raised a single patch of gooseflesh.

Justa thought Lambra had probably been sick, plain and simple, and that everyday vomit had taken away the only moment that had ever truly belonged to Justa. She began brushing Lambra's hair to avoid looking her in the eye. "I'm sorry, my lady, but I don't know very much about pregnancy," said Justa.

Gotina, bringing their lady's tunic, belt, and jewelry, muttered, "Neither the symptoms nor the way it comes about."

Loneliness and frustration took hold of Justa and she raised the hairbrush, ready to strike Gotina with it. Only Lambra's decision to ask a question at that moment stopped Justa from venting her pent up energy.

"Perhaps there's a midwife in town who could tell me whether I'm expecting?"

"Yes," said Justa. "Why don't I take a couple of maids or a servant with me and go looking for her? We could bring her back to you before the morning meal is over."

Doña Lambra nodded. Justa readied herself to leave Gotina to finish dressing her lady and fetch Adalberto from the stable to accompany her to town — and possibly much farther — but her lord Ruy Blásquez barged in the front door. If his expression had been inscrutable upon his return more than two months earlier, now he was unmistakably apprehensive. He kept his head low and his gaze never alit on any one object. A knight, armored with mail and a leather breastplate, followed Ruy Blásquez indoors and waited while the lord kissed his wife on the cheek and she returned the greeting full on the lips.

"Who do you have with you, dear husband?" she asked. "Does he bring news?"

"Indeed. This is Don Fulgencio Benítez." He paused as if he didn't want the next moment to arrive. "He has some news." Ruy Blásquez backed away and let the new knight kneel before Doña Lambra. He looked at Ruy Blásquez, apparently doubting whether to speak.

"Please tell me what you have to say, Don Fulgencio," Doña Lambra said.

"My lady, Don Gonzalo Gustioz is alive and has returned to Salas."

Doña Lambra's posture became erect, her arms stiff at her sides. "That's impossible. Someone lied to you."

"I was there, my lady, and saw him with my own eyes."

Lambra shifted her gaze with the barest movement of her neck to bore into the top of her husband's head. "You told me Almanzor had him beheaded."

He shook his head but did not look up. "That pagan has severely betrayed my friendship."

"Faithless traitor!" Justa wasn't sure whether her lady referred to Almanzor or to Ruy Blásquez. "Didn't you tell him the offenses his family has committed against us, against you?"

"I don't think the letters could have been any clearer."

"You can never tell what a Moor will do," she said disdainfully, and Justa wondered whether she could rely on her Muslim.

"Those rampant blasphemers have no sense of loyalty," Don Fulgencio confirmed. "But there is more to tell."

Doña Lambra stood and held herself as if she were carved out of wood. "What else?"

"Don Gonzalo and Doña Sancha invited the noble families of Lara, like those from Los Cameros, and from all over Castile, León, and even Navarra, and had great celebrations in honor of their seven sons."

"They're not alive, too?"

"No. Although the celebrations rivaled your wedding in Burgos, which I attended, this was a funeral."

"What kind of celebrations? They ... they didn't lance a scaffold, did they?" she asked.

"No, but there were musicians, dancing, tournaments and skills demonstrations, and so much feasting. The count himself brought ten calves to be slaughtered."

Doña Lambra didn't look at the knight, but spoke to the air. "García Fernández is my cousin. Why is he indulging in such unchristian activities with my blood enemies?"

"Gonzalo Gustioz has spent too much time absorbing Andalusian customs, and now he's converting others. . . ." Ruy Blásquez advanced toward Doña Lambra, but she took an equal number of steps away from him.

"Do you intend to stay here indefinitely?"

Ruy Blásquez looked at her, beseeching. "Should I be somewhere else, dear wife?"

"I think this would be an opportune time for you to start a campaign against Salas."

"Of course," he said. "I'll rouse the troops."

"My lord," said Don Fulgencio, "I wouldn't set out for Salas so quickly. You see, Don Gonzalo brought back the heads of his seven sons and their tutor. After the funeral celebrations, the Bishop of Burgos blessed the heads and declared them relics because they haven't decayed or deteriorated. They've placed the heads in a chapel to the side of the main altar of the Church of San Pelayo and leave it open for contemplation and prayers at all times. Some of the eyes are open, and some are closed, and sometimes I think they blink. If I hadn't known better, I'd have sworn they were still alive. People leave candles and gifts for their parents and pray for revenge. No one who is not a friend can approach within seven miles of that place without being struck down."

The silence continued for such a long time that Justa looked to Gotina to break it. At last, Ruy Blásquez managed to put his hand on Doña Lambra's shoulder. "Let me take you to Vilviestre. There we can safely plan our revenge." If possible, she stiffened even further.

"My people need me in Bureba." She spun around to relieve herself of his hand and held out her arms. Justa recognized the signal to put her belt on her and stepped toward the storage chest, but Gotina placed it in her hands. The men dissipated like clouds on a hot day. "Justa, get everyone from Bureba together and start packing the carts. I'd like to leave tomorrow."

Quiet descended over Justa's ears, leaving her with an elusive buzzing sound that insulated her from the tasks and speeches she was expected to perform. She grabbed Gotina's arm and held on while the maid gave instructions to the Bureba folk that Justa couldn't hear. She followed Adalberto into the stable and watched him saddle and harness a black stallion. His lips moved continually, but Justa never knew whether he was asking her to go with him, and could offer no reply. His face was serious and hers, covered in tears. He mounted the grim horse and offered his hand to her. She moved through the air with ease and alighted on the horse's rump, safely behind her love. When no one was looking, in the confusion of trunks and supplies and carts, they galloped away south, toward freedom.

The cold wind whipped through her hair and she squeezed his waist to make sure she never let go of him. Behind them, a woman was screaming, shouting at Adalberto to return with the horse at once.

"Come back! Come back, Adalberto!"

It wasn't until Gotina lifted Justa off the hard ground outside the stable that she realized she was the woman screaming. She held not onto Adalberto's muscular trunk, but to crumbling clods of parched earth.

Part Two

990 A.D.

Chapter I

Mudarra ran through the gardens. The branches of trees and floral bushes, leafing green in February, reached for him as his slippers skidded along the pathway to his favorite spot on the hill across from Madinat al-Zahra among the almond trees. He tapped one of the grey trunks to make the white petals flutter into his palm like snowflakes. It was something he'd loved to do since he was a child, ever since his mother, Zaida, had first told him how Abd al-Rahman's favorite wife had longed for the snow on the Sierra Nevada in Granada.

He blew the wispy petals from his palm and sat under the tree, letting it tower above him. He faced Córdoba and breathed deeply. It calmed him to contemplate the road between the capital city and the administrative palace. Not an hour before, Mudarra had ridden along the road with Hisham, the caliph, after prayers in the Great Mosque. He had accompanied Hisham to the most secluded place on the top terrace, the garden the caliph's rooms shared with the women's quarters. Mudarra still lived there, mostly because everyone knew his mother wouldn't permit him to be separated from her. But when he arrived in the archway, his mother's voice had carried and he had stopped and listened. He idly watched the rainbows refract on the walls from a series of crystals that hung from the entrance arch while he tried to make out the serious-sounding conversation.

"I don't know what I'll do. He's already completed fifteen years. The day is coming soon."

The other voice belonged to old General Ghalib, who had been Mudarra's teacher and friend for as long as he could remember. "The boy is well prepared."

"But I'm not!"

Mudarra loved Zaida as much as any son loved his mother, but he couldn't help but bristle when she held him back. He puffed his chest out, ready to take on whatever challenge they might be talking about. But what day was coming?

"Princess, you've been preparing him for this his whole life. His destiny is written on his face. Sometimes when he's training, I see a flash in his eye and he looks just like Gonzalo González in Almenar, all those years ago."

Something about the name he'd never heard before made his heart race, and he fled to the almond grove even though he knew his trainers were waiting for him for lance practice.

Gonzalo González sounded like a Christian name. Perhaps this man had something to do with why his mother had insisted he learn to speak the Christian language and had always taught him to respect, or failing that, to tolerate, the Christian emissaries who filed through Madinat al-Zahra. It was never easy because they seemed so stupid, mouths invariably agape and eyes always as big as honeyed buns. Many of them appeared to be unacquainted with the manner of taking a bath, they were ignorant of proper poetry, and they eternally called Almanzor the caliph when he was only the chamberlain. Although, perhaps they were more astute than he gave them credit for: Caliph Hisham had never taken on a governing role since his father's death when he was eleven, and spent most of his time sequestered in the library or traveling to the Great Mosque to be "among his people." In reality, Hisham, and by extension Mudarra, spent their worship time in Córdoba in a niche off the mihrab, with lobed arches and Byzantine tile craftsmanship, separate from the other faithful. All were somehow equal before God in spite of the differentiating setup.

How could Mudarra look like a Christian he'd never heard of who'd been in some place called Almenar who knew how many years before? In spite of his favorite view, Mudarra's pulse accelerated. He closed his eyes and listened to the music of a nearby waterfall. The high-pitched call of a peacock wasn't enough to break his meditation, but when he heard silk slippers against the ground, he opened his eyes to see General Ghalib in a posture of interrupted stealth.

He ran his hand through his thin grey hair. "Mudarra, why aren't you practicing the lance? Your trainers are waiting."

"I'm a bit tired from my outing with the caliph," said Mudarra. "And haven't I vanquished Ruy Blásquez enough times?"

They were most likely setting up another scaffold for him to throw against and try to dismantle. Such scaffolds and other opponents in training unfailingly had the name "Ruy Blásquez." Mudarra had once been talking with an emissary from Navarra and referred to their common enemies as "Ruy Blásquez," causing the diplomat to frown—whether from lack of understanding or some other offense, Mudarra never learned. Although General Ghalib had clarified that the name could not stand in for all that was evil in the world, this went against everything Mudarra's mother had taught him. It was the only Christian name he was permitted to categorically hate and it loomed in his imagination like a mythic beast. Suddenly he wondered if it was the name of a real person. He doubted it because he couldn't fathom that a real human being, created by God and blessed as a member of the *dhimma*, the people of the Book, could be so evil.

"You still need to beat him a few more times, I'm afraid," said Ghalib. "It won't surprise you to know that I think you're the most accomplished warrior who ever lived, Muslim, Christian, or Jewish. But that doesn't mean you don't need to keep improving."

Mudarra stood up by Ghalib's side and they started back to the palace. They passed through the army barracks to walk among trees that would bloom fragrant later in the springtime, marble statues of Roman gods and goddesses, and chuckling fountains bedecked with stone rabbits, frogs, turtles, stags, and lions. Cooing doves darted through the shade, seeking crumbs and seeds. Mudarra couldn't argue with the logic of someone he regarded so highly. But he needed to know more about these Christian names that haunted him.

He opened his mouth to ask a question, but Ghalib began speaking. "I've been wondering, Mudarra, how you feel about living at Madinat al-Zahra. Do you ever feel lonely?"

It had never before occurred to him that he should spend time in the company of other boys his age. His mother, his tutors, the caliph, and Almanzor kept him constant, instructive company. The other women had always comforted his heart, and lately, they'd provided other comforts as well. But now that Ghalib pronounced the word *lonely*, he knew it described his state of mind.

"Yes, teacher. All the time."

Ghalib nodded at the confirmation of his suspicion. "There aren't many children in Madinat al-Zahra, but Almanzor always kept you away from boys your own age because he wouldn't have you associating with lessers, and in his eyes, there is no one to equal you. Almanzor returned this afternoon from the campaign in the region of Zamora. Perhaps I should speak with him about changing that."

"Do you think he would welcome the idea, General? Perhaps I should do the speaking, to show him I'm no longer a child who can be so easily influenced by persons of a different class." If Mudarra could talk with the chamberlain and lord of al-Andalus alone, with sincerity and honesty, perhaps he could get answers to the questions he was unable to formulate now.

"Of course," said Ghalib.

They passed through an archway on the middle terrace and entered the courtyard where his trainers had set up a scaffold against which to practice with the lance. "What shape is Ruy Blásquez taking today?" Mudarra asked the two men, but saw for himself. "Ah, a dragon." The wooden beast reared up on two legs and a tail and the head balanced on a preposterously thin neck. They made it too easy, Mudarra thought. That was the only reason he excelled at these activities.

He marched to the opposite end of the courtyard, picked up the first lance within reach, held it at throwing height, and tossed it toward the dragon. The wooden spear smacked in the middle of the dragon's neck and the head clattered to the tile floor. Mudarra picked up the second lance and shot it into the dragon's tail, weakening its entire structure. The final blow landed in the middle, perhaps where the dragon's heart would have been, and brought the scaffold tottering into a pile of timbers. "Thank you, teachers," Mudarra said. "This has been entertaining."

"Sir Mudarra, we constructed the scaffold so that it would be especially hard to break," said the first trainer.

"Not really," replied Mudarra. "It was a simple question of geometry."

"But how did you make the lances aim so well?" asked the second trainer. Turning to Ghalib, he continued, "This boy astounds us every time."

"You'll have to try harder. He's not even challenged anymore." Ghalib chuckled. "Come, Mudarra, let's get you fed and rested. The Governor of Segura is coming tomorrow, at your invitation."

"Ah, I'd forgotten." Mudarra abandoned his efforts to help clear the wreckage. His chess master, Walid, had said that the Governor of Segura's reputation as a player reached back to Baghdad, and so Mudarra had written to him, challenging him to a friendly game. If he played well, Mudarra could expect to amass a fair number of coins or silks. He donated his winnings to the poor because his needs were seen to before he was aware of them.

He took his leave of his tutors and made his way through the winding corridors back to the women's quarters, where servants were distributing mashed chickpeas fragranced with saffron on green and white ceramic bowls to the women and eunuchs seated on pillows around the central pool. Mudarra took his usual seat next to his mother, kissing her on the cheek and taking bread from the stack.

"Layla's lucky tonight. She's dining with Almanzor and they've brought back sherbet from the Pyrenees," said Aysha, one of Almanzor's less favored concubines. She waved at Mudarra, who visited her in Almanzor's absence with the other women their silent accomplices.

"Oh, what flavor?" asked Fatima.

"Please, my brother has fooled you again. It's barely warm enough to think about eating such cold food," said Mudarra's mother. "It must still be the cold season up north, so the ice won't have melted much on the way here. That must be the cheapest sherbet in the world." Everyone sniggered at what Mudarra had always interpreted as sibling teasing. No one else was permitted to speak of the chamberlain in such a fashion. Zaida turned to her son. "But tell us, my love, what did you learn today?"

These questions had begun when he first left the women's quarters for his training and tutoring. As the years went on, he became more creative with his responses.

"Today I learned about generosity, and how we should never be selfish, like Ruy Blásquez."

"Well done," said Zaida, and the others around the pool put down their bread and plates in order to applaud.

After a second course of eggplant, peas, and rice, the party broke up into different sleeping quarters. Aysha waited at the pool for Mudarra, so he went to her and twisted the ends of her long walnut-brown hair between his fingers. Her hazel eyes gazed at him longingly. "Will you lie with me tonight, Mudarra?"

"I'm sorry, Aysha. I must be well rested tomorrow. The Governor of Segura will be here to play chess."

"I'll let you sleep. I get so lonesome when Layla's away."

"Tomorrow night." He kissed her on the mouth as a promise, and when he looked up, everyone else was studying the corners of the courtyard. "Here's Fareed." Mudarra grasped the robe of one of the eunuchs. "Let him comfort you tonight."

Aysha stood looking indecisively at Fareed, but another lady reached for her hand instead. "Come, Aysha, we're not tired. Fatima has a new scroll of poetry from Córdoba and we're going to read to each other through the night."

She looked back at Mudarra. "Tomorrow," she whispered, then let herself be led down the corridor beyond another lobed archway.

Mudarra loped into his mother's chamber, where she already slept under several blankets against the February temperatures, her greying hair veiling her nose and mouth. Maids scurried about in preparation for the night, dousing lamp flames. He wet his hands in a basin where rose petals floated and washed his face.

"Your bed awaits you here as always, Lord Mudarra," said a maid. His mother's eyes fluttered open at the sound.

"My baby, my true love," she cooed.

The other women in the quarters were for Almanzor, the caliph, and other military commanders and administrators, but Zaida belonged to herself. She was the one who made Mudarra feel as if he were the only man in the world. He knelt atop his blankets. "Mother, why does no man ever visit you here in your chamber?"

"Because I love no man but you," she said, and settled back to sleep.

Mudarra snuggled between the blankets and the silken pillows. Perhaps he was the product of a virgin birth, or was pulled full-fledged like Minerva from a piece of stone. These ideas, unlike other thoughts that had passed through his mind that day, fit in with his mother's and Almanzor's teachings and his own experience of a calm, ornamented life in which the only thing he had to do was learn from the wonderful things he tasted, smelled, and touched. He fell asleep.

In the morning, Mudarra dressed in a blue silk tunic with verses from the Quran embroidered on the sleeves and neckline in silver thread, but neglected to put on a turban, since he was most accustomed to wrapping one as a helmet in battle practice. After ablutions, prayer in the congregational mosque at Madinat al-Zahra, and a filling breakfast of flatbread and freshwater fish in spiced sauce, Mudarra made his way to the caliph's private reception hall, where he would match wits with the man who was reputed to be the finest chess player in al-Andalus. He brushed past myrtle branches and stood for a moment, entranced by the way the light came in through the garden archways and refracted off the quicksilver pool at the hall's center, which in turn created a sparkling frenzy in the gold and silver tiles on the ceiling. He'd heard that one of the caliphs in the past had slept atop the gentle undulations of the ankle-high pool on an inflated leather mattress.

He noticed a lutist in the corner strumming his instrument atmospherically. Many of the viziers were in attendance, including Rabbi Samuel, and most of his tutors—Jewish linguists and mathematicians, and Muslim combat, religion, and poetry instructors. Some of them had set up a plain slate and laid out the carved stone pieces in two rows of eight on each side according to the rules of the most basic version of the game. His chess master, Walid, stooped over the board, tweaking the pieces' angles as if fractions of a degree at the outset would decide the result. His concentration was so great that his turban kept sliding down over his eyes, and that was the main reason Mudarra objected to wearing the headgear for intellectual pursuits. General Ghalib and many other commanders and warriors sat cross-legged on pillows and tiled benches along the walls, discussing and pointing at the different pieces.

"Don't get too excited," said Mudarra. "If the Governor of Segura is as much of a master as they say, this game won't last long."

"Laugh all you want," said Walid, "but we believe you're going to put that governor in his place."

A man with such commanding presence that he must be the Governor of Segura walked to the garden archway and stopped, his retinue of fifty unsmiling turbaned warriors fanning out behind him like a peacock's tail feathers. Three such feathers stuck out from his high turban, and the rings on his fingers sparkled in the rainbows cast by the quicksilver pool, further dazzling Mudarra.

"And what, in your opinion, is my place?" asked the Governor as he strode toward Walid.

General Ghalib stood next to Mudarra while the courtiers bowed before the governor, especially Walid. "Governor of Segura," Ghalib said, "my friend and ally, this is your opponent in chess or whatever game you desire. His name is Mudarra and you must not be led astray by his youthful appearance." He joined the other spectators along the wall, who were readying themselves for a drawn-out battle worthy of an epic poem.

Mudarra nodded his head as low as he could without breaking eye contact with the steely governor. The governor made a gesture with his right hand and men from his retinue brought a chest and laid it next to the pool for all to see. "I'll wager one hundred gold dinars," he said.

"Let that be my wager also," replied Mudarra. The governor eyed the hall as if seeking proof that the boy had such an amount at his disposal.

"Almanzor will guarantee any wager Mudarra makes," said Ghalib.

The governor sat and surveyed the board and pushed it tentatively. "I cannot accept playing the black pieces. Someone come and turn the board."

But Mudarra sat at the opposite side and swiveled the entire board with one hand without upsetting any of the pieces.

"You won't mind playing the black side?" the governor asked.

"They're only colors, my lord. They cannot have any effect on who we are, nor on our abilities as players. Will you be so good as to make the first move?" said Mudarra with what courtesy he could muster. The governor had a shapeless mole under his left eye that seemed to move, but Mudarra fixed his gaze on the board and refused to be distracted.

Within half an hour, Mudarra had captured all the governor's pawns, one horse, and one castle, placing them with utmost respect on the table alongside the board. The governor was in check, and the game lasted another few minutes only because he considered his options so long before making his move. When Mudarra made his coup de grace with the swiftness of a goshawk, the observers from Madinat al-Zahra and a few of those from Segura applauded.

"The only reason this boy can best me is because I'm so distracted by that racket," said the governor. He turned to the lutist. "Stop playing this instant. In fact, gather your instruments and leave this hall."

Walid helped the lutist carry his bows and lute through the garden archways.

"Governor, I'm willing to play another game with you for the same wager, now that the distraction is gone," said Mudarra. "In fact, why don't we reset the board for a more difficult game? What's the most difficult version of chess you know?"

The governor stroked his mole and considered. "Celestial chess."

"I've read of it," said Mudarra. "Please help me set the pieces correctly, though. I've never played it or learned how the pieces move."

A servant placed a flat ceramic serving platter over the slate to serve as the circular playing board.

"If it's true you've never played before," said the governor, moving his defeated pieces into their arcane positions, "then I wager all the coins in the trunk."

Mudarra considered. "And if I lose, we'll count the coins in the trunk and I will pay you the same amount in coins, cloths, swords, or horses until you're satisfied."

"Very well," replied the governor. "The king is the sun, and moves in a circle around the rim. The counselor is the moon, which also follows a circular movement. These other pieces are Mercury, Venus, Mars, Jupiter, and Saturn, and move at different diagonal angles across the sphere," the governor explained hastily, as if to speak faster than Mudarra could hear. "The pawns are stars, and move only one piece-width at a time, in any direction." Several of the observers gasped, unable to follow the instructions, but Mudarra wasn't worried, because the pieces logically corresponded to their counterparts in the sky. He could almost see lines drawn across the platter to illustrate his strategy.

The governor moved first, and Walid returned to the hall. He whispered in Ghalib's ear, and when the general whispered back, the chess master shouted, "What?" Everyone, including the players, turned their attention to the disturbance. "That's the most complex game ever imagined, and Mudarra's never played it. What kind of cheat is taking place here?"

Some of the governor's guards assumed an aggressive position around Walid. The chess master seemed to realize too late that he had insulted the noble emissary from the eastern part of the caliphate. He held his arms over his face as if accepting punishment.

"My lord, please excuse my chess master," said Mudarra. "He always expounds on the difficulty of a game before I learn it to prepare me for an arduous journey. But he meant no harm against a reputation that has spread all the way back to Baghdad."

"Stand down," the governor instructed his warriors. "No more distractions." He hunkered down and put his arm to the side of his face, shielding himself from the sparkles and rainbows that continually danced around the quicksilver pool.

"As the sun travels higher in the sky, the archways will block the sun's rays, my lord," said Mudarra, offering the hope of future comfort to his agitated opponent.

"Make your move," the governor grunted.

Mudarra kept his sun out of danger by spinning around the attacks from the governor's Venus and Mars, and then Mercury and Jupiter. He used his stars to set up a barrier around the governor's sun and moon, which his opponent didn't notice until it was too late. Within twenty minutes, and well before the true sun in the sky stopped inflaming the quicksilver pool, Mudarra's Mars had put the governor's sun into a position of no escape.

He stood to declare victory. He strode to the treasure chest to open it and distributed handfuls of coins among the lower-ranking warriors and less wealthy lords from Madinat al-Zahra, reserving nothing for himself. They happily collected and stashed coins and jewels about their persons, but the Governor of Segura stood up in order to tower over Mudarra with his full height, his turban, and its three feathers.

"You would be a generous lord, if only you had your own wealth to give."

Mudarra's patience with his opponent's petulance and skills that didn't live up to his reputation vanished. He faced the governor and leaned forward. Even though he lacked a turban and did not match the governor in height, he witnessed the other man's miniscule retreat before the threat.

"I will always have wealth to give as generously as I please, whether you wish it or not." Both Ghalib and Walid stood by him, but Mudarra wasn't sure whether it was in support or in an attempt to restrain him.

The governor's cheeks turned bright red and the mole seemed to crawl in circles under his eye. He made a dismissive gesture. "Rather than wasting your time giving away other people's wealth, you would do better to go looking for your father."

The cut at the lineage he had so recently begun to question was more than he could bear. "You may be a governor, but you will not speak to me that way," threatened Mudarra.

"Leave my sight, son of no one!"

Mudarra looked around for a weapon. He didn't want to seize a scimitar from the hip of a lord or a guest, so he picked up the chessboard platter and slammed it alongside the governor's head. Ceramic pieces flew through the air and plopped into the pool of quicksilver, and the ripples sent slow-motion rainbows in so many directions, Mudarra felt that he was inside a soap bubble, floating in the afternoon sunlight. The governor fell back, unconscious, and blood ran from his nostrils.

"I do not know who my father may have been. I know only that I am not no one's son," Mudarra announced. "All of you, wait right here and I will come back and tell you who he was."

He made for the garden archways, knowing his mother wouldn't lie to him, but the governor's companions drew their swords as one man and bore down upon him before he knew what was happening. First the poorer knights who had received the bounty, and then the other members of Almanzor's court, also drew their weapons and fell upon the governor's retinue in Mudarra's defense. The hall became a giant crystal that shone and refracted sunlight off quicksilver, steel blades, and gemstones on hilts.

Mudarra fell to the floor, his legs pinned by friends and foes alike, and closed his eyes against the glare. He could hear each discrete swipe of a blade, each time a hand caught a body before it fell to the tile floor, and the unearthly sloshing of footsteps chasing other footsteps across the quicksilver pool. It was a tremendous clamor, and he knew help must be on the way.

He opened his eyes in time to see the elevated turban of Almanzor in the archway, accompanied by a dozen courtiers.

"Clear them out! Beat them down, my soldiers," said the de facto ruler of al-Andalus.

The pressure on Mudarra's legs lifted and he was able to stand again, miraculously unscathed. The Governor of Segura's people fled the courtyard and went running through the garden, abandoning their leader to his fate. Before Almanzor could ask what had caused the fray, Mudarra said, "Excuse me, but I must speak with my mother." Someone else would tell his uncle what had happened. Mudarra could wait no longer.

He found Zaida sitting before the central pool in the small garden next to the women's quarters. She contemplated the water, whispering with golden fish, while one of the eunuchs read poetry to the other appreciative women. Mudarra wondered whether they were the same scrolls Aysha had listened to the previous night.

"Mother." He went to her, throwing his arms around her. She kissed his face. "We need to have a conversation. It can't wait any longer." He stood and held his hand out for her to take so they could retire to her chamber, but her green eyes gazed into his with so much clarity, he knew she understood what he wanted to talk about.

"Nearly everyone here knows the story. Sit down next to me, son."

He did, crossing his legs and sitting erect in anticipation, but instead of speaking, she cried silent tears. The maids and eunuchs moved from their spots around the pool to comfort her with their embraces and murmurs, and Mudarra felt alone in the mass of people he'd known all his life. So many of them couldn't keep the secret, so he decided to prompt them.

"Mother, I've just ruined diplomatic relations with Segura defending myself against the governor's claim that I am the son of no one. I know I must be someone's son, but you've never told me whose."

Zaida buried her face in her hands.

"Mother, why do you fear to tell me? Is he of lowly birth? Was he violent to you? It wasn't the beast, Ruy Blásquez?"

"Oh, no, you mustn't think that," she said, taking his hands in hers as the comforting arms parted for them. "I hesitate only because you've brought me so much joy all these years, and once you have knowledge of your father, your nobility of spirit won't allow you to stay here with me. I knew this day would come, but I could never prepare for it."

"Mother, you must tell me. He came from far away?"

"Your father is a great lord. He holds large tracts of land and has many vassals, but he resides in a noble city called Salas, far to the north of Córdoba, beyond the border of al-Andalus. When he was your age, he must've looked a lot like you. He had the same wavy hair, the strong brow and jaw, and the most open and earnest eyes. But I gave you your eye color. His beard must be white by now. His greatest fame is that he had seven warrior sons, your brothers."

"Is that why Almanzor gave me not one or two, but seven nursemaids?" He had always wondered about the excessive figure.

"Yes. He wanted you to have the strength, wisdom, and abilities of seven men so that you would be the equal of all seven of your brothers. I wanted it for you, too, but it's only led to this evil day when you're going to leave me."

"But why did my father leave Madinat al-Zahra? How did he come here in the first place?"

"He came here to Almanzor as a prisoner of Ruy Blásquez."

"So this Ruy Blásquez is a real person? And he still lives?" The story was becoming less believable than the tales of genies and talking animals Mudarra had studied as a child.

"Yes. I've told you every day of your life how evil he is because of the terrible things he did to your father, his own brother-in-law. Ruy Blásquez sent your father here, believing he would be killed. Fortunately, your uncle could find no just cause for such a request, and your father lived in the cell down the corridor from the women's quarters for some months. He made me fall in love with him for his noble bearing, his open demeanor, and his handsome face." As the tears ran down her face, the years since the events fell away and Mudarra could see his mother the way his father must have: a sincere, beautiful girl in love.

"Then, Ruy Blásquez forced all seven of your father's sons into a terrible battle alone against thousands, where they were mercilessly beheaded. General Ghalib brought the heads wrapped in cloth for your father to identify. Your father must have loved them as much as I love you, because when he recognized them, he cried his eyes out and wanted to die. I told him all was not lost, because he could still have a child who could avenge those seven sons."

Mudarra's hairs stood on end. He had been conceived as a replacement for not just one, but seven mythic warriors. Christian warriors. It was harder to accept than a virgin birth. His mouth dry, he whispered to the eunuch. "Fareed, could you get me some wine?"

He took hold of his mother's shoulders to steady her for what was probably the saddest question. "Why didn't my father stay here?"

"Christians can take only one wife, and he already had a wife he loved more than himself. She must be quite a lady," she whispered, then descended into sobs.

One of the older ladies took over the role of storyteller to allow Zaida her tears. "Almanzor let him go, so he returned to Castile and left your mother expecting you. He hoped that when you came of age, you would go to Castile and help him exact revenge on Ruy Blásquez."

Mudarra looked across the rippling pool, but instead of calming him, it gave him visions: the tilework fell into the water piece by tiny piece, the myrtle bushes dried up, and cats and dogs devoured the doves and then fought amongst themselves. His world crumbled under the stress of this new knowledge.

"I can't stay here," he said with not a little astonishment.

"Go to your father," Zaida said in a newly even tone. "He's expecting you."

"But how will he know me?"

She pulled a small golden arc from under her tunic, where it was loosely sewn into the hem, as if it had always been there. Mudarra realized it must have hidden inside every garment his mother had worn since before he was born. He received it as if it might be burning hot, and inspected the identifying whorls and what could have been the eye or tooth of a beast. He had only seen similar designs before on the pins of the cloaks of Christian emissaries.

"I know in my heart that your father has kept his word and still guards the other half of this ring. Go to Salas, my son, and seek out your father, and identify yourself with this ring. Serve your father by taking revenge on Ruy Blásquez in whatever way he tells you to. It is what you were born to do."

Holding the half-ring awkwardly in his sweating palm, he marveled at his mother's acceptance of such a strange fate. "I'll have to ask Almanzor for permission."

His mother nodded.

Aysha emerged from an archway and handed Mudarra a silken bag that pulled closed with a long string. He thanked her, but didn't have the presence of mind to understand what she intended with it. She took the half-ring from him, slipped it inside the sack, and tied it around his neck. Then he thanked her more sincerely, clasping her hands and kissing her. Feeling more lucid, he said, "But, mother, you haven't told me my father's name."

"Your father is Gonzalo, son of Gustio, and the most respected lord in the region of Lara."

"So in Christian lands, I should call myself Mudarra ibn Gonzalo?"

"The Christian form would be González. And perhaps, would you do me the honor of calling yourself Mudarra González ibn Zaida?"

"Of course, dear mother."

She stood and they embraced. Zaida sighed. She fastened her veil over the lower half of her face, then took her son's muscular hand and walked with him through the administrative levels and down to the gardens, where doves and peacocks lined their path between the orange trees, which still smelled tangy with the last fruit of the season. When the two of them appeared in the ambassadors' hall and stood under the giant pearl, Almanzor's attendant darted into the throne room. The emissaries waiting to see the chamberlain made obeisance when his tall form appeared in the archway, but he ignored them, embracing the nephew he hadn't seen for several months. The three of them walked out to the gardens where they could speak in relative privacy. They made a circuit around the mosque and Zaida stayed a few paces behind.

"What brings you to see me, dear boy?" Almanzor said.

"Welcome back to Madinat al-Zahra from your successful campaign, uncle," said Mudarra, easing into the issue through formalities. His mouth was dry. Fareed hadn't brought the wine before he left the women's quarters. "And thank you for coming to my aid when the Governor of Segura's men attacked me this morning. Tell me, has the Governor woken up? Is he well?"

"Yes, the physicians have had a look at him and believe he'll be able to travel back to Segura in a few days. Don't worry. I've got enough Berber soldiers in Segura to quash any thought of revolt. Is that why you've visited me?"

"In a way, it came about because of the Governor of Segura. He said I had no father, and I knew it couldn't be true, so I've spoken with my mother."

"I see." Almanzor reached up to grasp an almond blossom.

Mudarra looked at Zaida, who was running her fingers lightly over the thorns of a rose bush. Growing up among so many pleasures, it shocked him that her inner life had so much pain. By extension, so did his, which was even more difficult to comprehend. Almanzor neither encouraged nor discouraged him, so he surged forward under his own impetus.

"She says my father is expecting me. I've come to ask your permission to leave al-Andalus and cross the border into Castile."

"What is this?" said Almanzor. "You're only a boy. I don't send children to the frontier."

"I'm disappointed to hear you say that when you've provided my training and witnessed my mastery of every task set to me."

"Well, your confidence belies your youth," Almanzor said with some surprise. "I haven't stopped to consider that you are getting older all the time and will soon no longer be a child."

"I'm confident because I know where to seek my true father."

"Ah!" said the victorious ruler. "I've loved you all these years even better than my own sons. I had forgotten that this day would come. I dread nothing more than seeing you go."

"My mother feels much the same." Mudarra glanced again at Zaida, who seemed unsteady on her feet. "If you'll allow me to go, and if my father is good and respectable, I will bring great honor to you by serving him and return to serve you. If he isn't, you'll never have to see me again or endure the shame of being associated with me."

"You have a good and honorable father. He's known all over Hispania. No one can tell you differently without suffering my wrath. You will always be welcome here, and you don't have to leave now if you don't truly wish it." Almanzor went to Zaida, lifted her chin and kissed her forehead. She leaned on him for support.

"You both know I love you and respect you more than anything," said Mudarra. "You also know that I have to go. There is no other task worthy of the excellent education you've given me."

He had never felt so purposeful before. Finally, a reason for the mock battles, chess games, and military strategy lessons. A reason to love Christians as much as Muslims, for he was both in one person.

Almanzor cleared his throat and nodded his head but didn't leave his sister's side. "Mudarra González, from this moment on, your primary duty will be to defend our great western land from anyone who would wish it harm, especially that most gruesome beast of Castile, Ruy Blásquez. To that end, I grant you two hundred knights and their squires and servants to use in any military maneuver you deem appropriate."

Mudarra was surprised to have convinced him so easily, and the generosity came unexpected. Mudarra had imagined setting out north on a lone pony to wander until someone told him he was in Castile. "Thank you, my lord. I never imagined such a gift."

"You'll need a lot of men to defeat Ruy Blásquez, whose castles I've been sacking in the north. He has an incredible amount of military support, no doubt obtained by threats. I'll pay your troops seven years' wages, although I hope with your training, you can defeat him once and for all much more quickly. No, it would be even better to give you the captives I hold prisoner in Córdoba. There will be more of them than the free knights, and they will be in service to you for life."

"Thank you, great Almanzor." Mudarra knelt painfully on the gravel and kissed his uncle's hand, glittering with rings. Almanzor and Zaida each laid a hand on one of Mudarra's shoulders in blessing.

"I will return to the ambassadors' hall," said Almanzor. "You must bring the caliph's jailer to me so that I may set him to the task of inspecting the prisoners. After that, you must accompany your mother wherever she wishes and do whatever she asks, because I don't believe it will take many days to assemble your army."

Mudarra bowed before them.

"Return for me here, son," said Zaida. "I would wander for a few hours with you under these almond trees."

When the task was finished, Mudarra ran back to his mother like a child, his feet slapping the pathways and his body tingling with the urgency of spending time with her while he could.

He took her by the hand and hesitated before he asked about what had most disturbed him of the information about his father. "You say my father cried his eyes out?"

"The sorrow of the death of his sons had washed over his eyes and made it impossible for him to distinguish any details in bright light. Perhaps his grief has lessened with time, but the damage seemed permanent."

"Do they have doctors in Castile? Perhaps my uncle could send a willing surgeon with me who could cure him?"

Zaida's eyes smiled softly above the veil. "Nothing would make me happier than to know that your father could see your face. I will mention it to my brother."

Mudarra bowed his head in meditative attention while Zaida led him through the gardens, around the administrative buildings, down and back up the different levels and from the mosque to the barracks. His back ached and his feet felt as if he walked across knife blades with no slippers, but as long as she appeared energetic, he listened while she told him again the stories about Abd al-Rahman III and the building of Madinat al-Zahra as if for the first time. Ten thousand workers and one thousand five hundred mules had created the city out of rocks and mud. They started in the beginning of the caliph's reign and never stopped embellishing lest the caliph reprimand them. Craftsmen came from Syria and Constantinople with their tiles and gems. The caliph had named it the radiant city after his beloved concubine and planted the almond trees to show her it could also snow in Córdoba.

It slowly dawned on Mudarra that he had grown up in the most astonishing place in the world. His home had been the pearl, and now he was headed for the unrefined meat of the oyster.

Mudarra and his mother sat next to a fountain, and when the light was fading, General Ghalib appeared before them. He took Mudarra's hands.

"I was there, at Almenar, when your brothers died," he said.

"I don't need to hear it," said Zaida, and headed to the women's quarters.

Bracing himself against whatever Ghalib might say, Mudarra invited the old general to sit next to him so he wouldn't have to look into his eyes.

"They fought bravely for two days and two nights. It was the seven of them against an army, the likes of which hasn't been seen again — all my soldiers, as well as General Viara's, and mercenaries from all over al-Andalus. Even though your brothers couldn't have had any strength left, Ruy Blásquez was so afraid of them that he had thirty soldiers line them up with their hands and feet bound. They lay belly down in the order they had been born and each lost his head to an executioner's ax. Gonzalo, the youngest, and the one you bear most resemblance to, was last, and he resisted until the thirty soldiers fell on him, all at once."

The scene unfolded in Mudarra's mind. The lack of mercy, even from Ruy Blásquez, rendered him speechless.

"Viara and I waited until it was over before we came out of our tents and saw the bodies while they wrapped the heads in sacks. Ruy Blásquez demanded we take the heads to Almanzor to hang in the archways of Córdoba as some kind of warning to whoever wanted to cross him, but neither of us wanted such a shameful mission. Viara talked his way out of it, and I was left to carry out the task. That's why your father found out about the deaths of his sons while he was in prison. I regretted my part in that business so much that I never returned to Medinaceli. When I knew you were on the way, I stayed here to help your mother."

Mudarra wanted to make some gesture of thanks to the man who had acted as his father when Almanzor couldn't, but the gruesome history made his body feel heavy and unresponsive.

"My burden is great," he whispered.

"I'm sorry," Ghalib said, embracing him for the last time.

That night, Mudarra's mother pushed him into Aysha's arms, and the concubine happily took him to her bed. He looked into her eyes and ran his fingers through her hair, but couldn't return her kisses with such melancholy growing inside him. When she fell asleep, he wrapped himself in a blanket and laid his bare feet on the cold marble and tile to wander out of the women's quarters and around the complex, searching in the corners of the places his mother had shown him for the peace he lacked inside.

He breathed the leafy scents and gazed at the unfathomable almond trees, ghostly under a full moon. Everything else was quiet, but the waters still whispered in the dark. He contemplated the road into Córdoba from his favorite spot. At dusk, they had lit the lamps along the path, and in the dark, it looked like a string of pearls holding the two places together. A stray thought that no city in Christian territory would provide such an elegant solution to nighttime threats sent him pacing back through the complex again. He was making his second circuit of the menagerie, listening for the slumber sounds of the exotic creatures that rested within, when suddenly the caliph stood before him, unguarded. He wore the simple white robes of a scholar and held a rolled piece of parchment and a pen in his hands as if he expected to find a place to sit in the moonlight and compose poetry.

"Ah, Mudarra," said Hisham as if the hour of their meeting were normal. "They tell me you're going to Jilliqiyya?"

"Yes, my lord. More specifically, to Castile, to Salas, where my father is a great lord."

"What is great there is likely different from what is great here. In fact, I must advise you not to go. I've read an account of this Jilliqiyya that Ibrahim al-Turtushi gave to my father. The land is flat and covered in sand and the food is very poor, just grains. Even the drinks are made from grains. The inhabitants are treacherous and depraved. Once they put on their clothes, they never change them, just let them disintegrate on their bodies."

"What, doesn't this Jew of your father's think the Castilians ever wash?"

"Maybe once or twice a year in cold water. They claim the filth that covers them is healthy for their bodies. What did I tell you? Depraved."

Mudarra silently admitted that these reports matched his suspicions of the Christians who came to Madinat al-Zahra. "Tell me, did he make mention of what the Castilians are like in war?"

"According to Ibrahim al-Turtushi, they are courageous, and once a battle is started, they won't contemplate fleeing. They would consider death a lesser evil."

"I'm fully prepared to meet such honorable foes in combat. Don't worry, my lord. I will emerge from Castile victorious and return to you safely." He kissed the caliph's hand with the reverence of a goodbye, but his real motive was to end the conversation and get as far from Hisham as he could, for the caliph with his doubts embodied Mudarra's emotional state all too accurately.

He returned to the women's quarters, but left Aysha to rest, favoring his bed near his mother to wait out the night. In the morning, he was drained of life force. His mother looked on him with love that blinded her to his discomfort, and all day he accompanied her to the mosque and ate with her and read to her and played chess with her and did everything he could think of to please her.

Near the end of the day, a strange notion took hold of her. They had finished a game of backgammon by the central pool with the women in attendance when she said, "Mudarra, since you won't have any more chances to study wisdom and culture from the East, you must prove to everyone here what you've learned so far. Please recite for us."

"Right now?" Mudarra had imagined that since he hadn't seen his tutors, he was finished with school.

"Right now. Stand up," Zaida said lightly, but Mudarra believed these women would demand even more of him than General Ghalib.

He stood by the edge of the pool, cleared his throat, and recited an easy poem about the moonlight. As he finished, the women ululated their approval. He was planning his next piece when he saw a small man without a turban in the entrance archway.

"He doesn't belong here," Mudarra said to Fareed, who made a straight line for the archway. Contrary to what Mudarra expected, the man and the eunuch conversed, then Fareed took the man's left hand while he covered his eyes with his right. Mudarra noted that there were sizeable gaps between the man's fingers and his eyes darted everywhere. The women prudently veiled their faces.

Mudarra lifted the man's hand away from his face. "What do you want here?"

"Lord Mudarra, Almanzor sends me to tell you to ready yourself. The prisoner-soldiers will assemble and leave tomorrow."

"That was even faster than I thought it could be," said Mudarra. "Are there many?"

"One hundred on horseback, and twice that on foot."

Aghast, Mudarra stepped backwards, nearly losing his footing into the reflecting pool. He laughed. "If I can keep my balance, we'll be an impressive sight parading on the plains."

"Ruy Blásquez's rotten, black heart will kill him on sight of you," said Zaida. Her eyes above the veil were stony. "Come, my son. We will go to prayer and then straight to sleep. It's my request of you in these last hours, when I can demand anything of you as mine and mine alone."

In the mosque, separated from his mother, Mudarra's mind raced. He knelt and recited in unison with the other men, but the words held no meaning for him. He wondered if the God of Islam was the same as the God of the Christians. He looked surreptitiously to his sides and recognized each of the Muslims alongside him. When he thought that this was the last time he would feel such security and brotherhood, it was almost as if a genie had passed through his body and stolen his spirit.

He met his mother outside the orange grove after the prayers and walked hand in hand with her in silence. They each shed bitter tears before they looked at each other and made a wordless pact to never again show that sorrow. As the maids doused the lamp in Zaida's chamber and settled into their beds, he curled up against his mother. He dreamed he was back inside her womb.

Chapter II

In the morning, Mudarra set off for the main gate with his mother's kiss still warm on his forehead and the pouch string around his neck. The noise, motion, and colors he found there under the red and white archways stopped him in his tracks. The mass of soldiers resembled a herd of the striped horses in the caliph's menagerie. They wore black and white striped robes over mail or boiled leather armor. Each had wrapped an identical white turban around his head, so it wasn't possible to distinguish the origin of each man, but Mudarra knew quite a few of them must be Christian warriors captured in raids while they were defending their land or their religion. They must know what waited on the other side of al-Andalus, and so they had an advantage over him, lacking his sickening uncertainty as he tried to imagine the land of his father.

A man held out his hand and Mudarra blocked it, convinced he was about to be punched in the gut. The man looked startled. Mudarra took a deep breath and tried to see the man through the confusion of thoughts and sensations. He wore a black striped robe like the other soldiers, but it didn't cover an armored bulk. His light brown hair swept over blue eyes that sparkled with youth.

"Lord Mudarra, I am Yusuf ibn Iksandarani. Almanzor has appointed me your guide to Salas." He smiled warmly, and Mudarra understood this man was going to be his ally.

"Ah, of course, Yusuf. I look forward to pleasant travels with you."

Almanzor appeared abruptly from the direction of the administrative buildings, flanked by four court officers with jewels and feathers atop their turbans. The army quieted as each man realized their captor had arrived.

"Soldiers," said Almanzor, "this is Mudarra González ibn Zaida. You owe your undying loyalty to his person and his cause. You will take your orders from him and never abandon him, no matter what he tells you to do, until you die or he releases you. If you do not uphold this obligation, my Berber armies will hunt you wherever you hide and send you to your God's judgment."

Leaving them to murmur amongst themselves, Almanzor turned to his nephew. "Lord Mudarra, your horse, the finest long-distance traveler I could find in Córdoba, awaits you at the head of these ranks. You will find the carts supplied for the journey with furs, velvets, and plenty of flint to help keep you warm. Reserve the money to bargain for more food in Castile and to pay the faithful soldiers." One of the officers scribbled down everything Almanzor said.

"How many of the soldiers do you think will be faithful to my cause?" asked Mudarra with some urgency.

"Ruy Blásquez is strong, but if these men are anything like my heart, they will stay with you forever."

The warrior chamberlain's long face softened and he became the uncle Mudarra recognized. They embraced, and Mudarra couldn't tell whether it was he or Almanzor shaking with emotion. Perhaps both.

"Go with God, son. Bring honor and fame to your father and al-Andalus."

A ball of hot wax in his throat kept Mudarra from replying. He made his way through the mass of soldiers with Yusuf ibn Iksandarani already leading him.

Mudarra mounted the tall black horse at the head of them all, the only one without a rider and closest to the archway through which his father must have passed a generation earlier. As he turned to address his men, he studied the expressions of several blue-eyed Castilians and discovered joy. They must be thrilled to go home. Suddenly, he thought of the way to motivate them.

"Gentlemen, thank you for joining me on this long and dangerous journey. I've never travelled so far north and know little of the customs of Castile, but I think many of you must have been born in Castile or León and have families there. If you serve me loyally and help me defeat my enemy, I pledge to allow you to return to your homes freely and with only the most pleasant memories of al-Andalus in your hearts."

The crowd hardly reacted to the speech, and Mudarra was disappointed until he was inspired to repeat it in the language of the Christians. Then he heard the shouts and saw the waving arms and jumping legs he'd expected.

"There's no reason to wait, then. Yusuf, lead us, and knights, follow!" A bank of drummers he hadn't noticed in the crowd blasted a fanfare and slowly the mass of human beings and animals moved through the arches, officially on their way.

He felt his horse plod beneath him in a regular rhythm. Occasionally it whinnied, as if giving voice to Mudarra's busy mind. He barely noticed as they passed the golden walls of Córdoba and headed into wild terrain, the dark sierra an ever-receding goal.

For his mother to have fallen so deeply in love that she accepted never marrying, but instead devoted her life to a child who was destined to leave her, and for the undefeated Almanzor to have been so impressed, this Gonzalo Gustioz must be a truly great man. But he was also blind and, to Mudarra, that meant his body must be infirm. He wondered if his mother was holding onto an image of a perfect man that had faded from the world of action. Wouldn't a perfect man have been Muslim? How could a Christian from this lawless place he was headed toward seem perfect to anyone, let alone Zaida, sister of the great Almanzor?

At his side, he noticed Yusuf waving, trying to catch his attention. Only then did he realize it was already growing dark. He had no idea how far they'd come.

"It may be time to stop for the night, light some campfires, and cook and rest, Lord Mudarra," said Yusuf diplomatically.

"Of course," said Mudarra.

He welcomed Yusuf and several of the nobler members of his army to his tent. They lay upon pillows and wrapped themselves in enough layers of blankets to feel comforted against the chilly night after a meal of bread, beans, chickpeas, and cheese.

Mudarra whispered across to Yusuf in the dark, unsure whether the others would hear. "I didn't intend to make the men ride all day without resting."

"But we did rest, my lord. Not often, but enough."

Blushing in the dark, Mudarra promised himself that he would never become so distracted again. He thought of the years of his childhood, when he had felt beloved by the adults in his life but never really known anyone his own age he asked, "How long have you lived at Madinat al-Zahra?"

"I was born and raised in Mérida, and came to the radiant city when I was twelve."

"How come I've never met you before? I feel we could've been friends."

"I was apprenticed to an emissary to Jilliqiyya who traveled back and forth all the time, so while I know León, Navarra, and France very well, I haven't had the privilege of spending much time in al-Andalus. But I think we will be friends now, Lord Mudarra."

"It gladdens my heart to hear you say so, Yusuf." He spoke with more force now that someone else in the tent was snoring. "What can you tell me about Castile? How is it different from al-Andalus?"

"They have little appreciation for poetry," mused Yusuf. "Everything is less refined than you're accustomed to."

"I expected that."

"I also perceive a great deal of confusion concerning the feud you're going to put an end to. Even though Almanzor's last raids have been exclusively against castles and towns Ruy Blásquez holds unlawfully, and he hasn't harried the Count of Castile or bothered your father's loyal lands, Christians still draw an alliance between Córdoba and Ruy Blásquez in their minds."

"Probably because of the way my brothers died and my father was taken prisoner."

"Indeed, and I think we can use the confusion to our advantage, moving through Ruy Blásquez's territories without resistance. We can imply that we've been sent by Almanzor. We may not even have to lie to gain the confidence of the populace."

"What about Ruy Blásquez himself?"

"I've never met him. We'll have to wait and see what the best strategy is. But in the meantime, we should enjoy these travels into hostile territory during the winter months, when there's sure to be snow in the sierras and on the northern plains."

Mudarra chuckled, and, comforted by his ally, settled in to sleep. Before he slipped away, Yusuf whispered, "But since we're going into Christian lands, I need to warn you that you're going to have to eat pork."

Mudarra snapped awake, more alert than he had been all day. "The caliph told me they only eat grain."

"They do eat a lot of grain and vegetables and fish, because meat is expensive and because they maintain a complex calendar of days when they're allowed to feast and fast. But when it's available and permitted, you can be sure pork will appear on your plate. They don't take no for an answer."

"Have you had it?" asked Mudarra incredulously. "They say it tastes like human flesh. I can't imagine a more disgusting meal."

"I've never eaten human flesh," Yusuf said chuckling, "but it does have an unclean texture and flavor." At his lord's silence, he continued, "Allah will forgive you in such a case of necessity, and it's no cause for worry now. With any luck, we'll only encounter it once before we return to al-Andalus."

After a night of such bizarre concerns, Mudarra was anxious to keep moving. They rose into the Sierra Morena during the morning hours. Mudarra's horse was so surefooted that he found he often had to stop and wait while the troops snaked the cumbersome carts and pack animals through narrow passes full of freezing puddles and clumps of real snow. He recognized it from the occasional sherbet serving in Madinat al-Zahra and thought that if it was going to be so rocky and cluttered with mud and dead leaves, he much preferred the false snow provided by the almond blossoms.

During these waiting periods, if Yusuf hadn't joined him, he would dismount and pat his horse's neck or search out tidbits for treats. In just two days, he had come to feel a bond with the animal, who could bear his weight all day without flagging and now proved to be as skilled as a mountain goat as well. When the train caught up, Yusuf sometimes had to remind Mudarra that they still needed to rest, so he couldn't continue on yet. Mudarra was glad for the advice, which was offered with kindness. The only formality that remained between them was Yusuf's insistence on addressing him as "lord."

Later in the day, after they had taken a meal from the carts under a bright sun, Mudarra had run ahead yet again. While he navigated a complex series of switchbacks he couldn't imagine getting the carts through, he heard the strangest sounds. He couldn't fathom the cries echoing off the rocky walls until he turned around a boulder and witnessed what must have previously been a gentle stream, now running rapidly with new ice melt over a confused mass of sheep while they bleated, and a couple of shepherds shrieked, and their dogs barked frantically from the opposite bank.

A ewe, her fright apparent in her eyes and frenzied muscles, was swept apart from the group and began floating helplessly downstream. Mudarra judged that the water wouldn't come much higher than his knees, dismounted and leapt in to seize the sheep and bring her across to the shepherds.

He hardly felt the icy water rushing into his clothes, he was so focused on the struggling, sodden creature in his arms. She was panicked enough for a dozen sheep, and Mudarra nearly dropped her when he distinguished the bodies of her unborn lambs in her abdomen. He tripped over a stone and flung the ewe onto the dry bank, where she righted herself with help from the shepherds and wriggled to free herself from the icy dripping.

When he looked back, he saw the vanguard of his troops standing startled over the scene between the boulders.

"There are more than three hundred of us and less than a hundred of them," Mudarra shouted across the raging watercourse. "Each man, take one across."

Looks of skepticism were replaced by imitations of Yusuf's unhesitating example as more and more of the knights appeared at the opening.

When he saw the operation progressing as planned, Mudarra addressed the shepherds through chattering teeth. "What are you doing in the sierra? It's still winter here."

"I thought it was time to take them to my pastures close to Córdoba. It was a terrible mistake," said the elder one. Mudarra thought the younger man must be his son. The troops landed on the shore and set down their sheep, shaking from the dousing. The shepherd wiped a tear from his eye. "I should've lost every last one of them."

"You can show your thanks by building a fire on this bank so my soldiers can dry off and warm up before they have to wet themselves again to help the others get our carts and horses across," replied Mudarra more regally than he intended.

"Of course, my lord," the shepherd said, already running to gather sticks that weren't soaked with river water or melting snow.

By the time Mudarra was dry, the rescued sheep were vying with the dogs for space near the fire and the shepherds were busy keeping their wool from burning on their backs. Mudarra's horse quietly waded through the water and nudged him with a whinny.

"How calm you are." Mudarra patted the steed and rubbed his legs down with cloths from the shepherds' packs. "I think I'll call you Tranquilo."

Yusuf stood smiling. "I can't say I expected to do this today, Lord Mudarra."

"I couldn't let those innocent animals go to their deaths for no reason other than their shepherds'..."

"I don't condemn you. I would have tried to do the same. You see the kinds of unexpected things that happen on the road."

The shepherds helped the knights bring the carts and more excitable mounts across the water, which was already abating. When the last soldiers were warming themselves by the fire, Mudarra had his men check the provisions in the carts to see whether anything had been damaged. In the small space between the water and more boulders, they laid out flatbreads, dried meats, cheeses, and legume spreads that were no worse for fording the stream.

The men stood close together and ate hungrily after the exertion while the sheep milled about. The father shepherd said, "I can never express our gratitude for your acts of valor and now your liberality with your provisions. Who may I say has been so generous with me and my son?"

"I am Mudarra González ibn Zaida," he said, relishing the name, "and it has been our duty and our pleasure to help you."

Beside him, Yusuf calmly passed the bread to the shepherd. "My lord, perhaps it would be a better idea to travel in secret until we know what we're facing in Castile."

"Are you Mudarra, son of the wronged Christian and the princess?" the shepherd asked in a hushed voice.

Mudarra felt himself blush. He was entering dangerous territory. He should keep his wits about him.

"You are," exclaimed the shepherd. "Everyone in al-Andalus knows your story. Anyone will be happy to take you in, give you provisions, anything you need, and all the more when they see how generous your heart is."

"That's very kind of you to say." But even as everyone in Madinat al-Zahra knew him and loved him in some way, Mudarra couldn't believe his story would be important to others in the wide world.

They packed up and moved north through the few remaining crags, and the shepherds herded their flock behind them. They bade them farewell as they exited the sierra, and, consulting with Yusuf, Mudarra cautiously informed the lord and lady at the estate where they hoped to camp of his name and direction of travel. As the shepherd had said, his identity became cause for celebrations and banquets. Al-Andalus opened out before him like an extension of the caliph's palace, where he was not only accepted but adored. In spite of the travel hardships they experienced, such as having to sleep in their tents some nights, Mudarra enjoyed the rhythm of the journey and the possibility of anything turning up around the next bend.

As they went farther north, however, they found fewer cities and noble estates. After nearly fourteen mornings on the road, Yusuf told Mudarra they had arrived at that place in between, where General Ghalib used to send his patrols to keep order, the no man's land. It seemed more immense and open to the sky than the rest of al-Andalus, but there were still plenty of castles well stocked and full of welcoming people, in spite of their lonely appearance. Before they set out from the castle at Alcocero, Mudarra noted that their provisions still appeared to be untouched, in spite of all they had eaten and given away to the needy people they'd met on the road, because the reserves had been replenished and more each time they'd stopped at an estate or fortress. He was filled with gratitude, but he wasn't sure where to direct it until he joined the castellans on his prayer rug.

Here he was, at the edge of the world he knew. He should be frightened or at least a little daunted and perhaps ill from the journey, but he felt healthy and wealthy and ready to face whatever his enemy could think up. God truly was great.

That morning, they met the first people they had seen coming from the north for days. At first, Mudarra wondered if his eyes tricked him, or whether they were elves or little spirits. The three of them plodded along on two-toned leather slippers with jingle bells attached to the toes. The jangling sounds spread out weirdly into the pine trees along the path. They wore pointed caps with wilting feathers and they hunched under the pressure of the oddly shaped packs they carried on their shoulders.

"These are certainly from Castile. We must keep the secret of your name and mission now," said Yusuf.

"Where do you travel without even a mule, men?" Mudarra said as they drew near.

They stopped and the leader doffed his faded green cap with a flourish that might have seemed jaunty if performed by a younger man. "We are humble musicians on our way to lighten the hearts in Andalusia, brave knights," he said with a formality and an accent Mudarra had never heard before. The other two made more conservative reverences in greeting.

"You're from Castile, are you not? Do you know a lord called Ruy Blásquez?"

"Is this a jest? He's the reason we're leaving Castile," said the head jongleur.

"What do you mean?"

"When he finished taking all the lands except Salas for himself, that mad wife of his started telling him the count's castles belong to her, so he went to each one, annexing them or besieging them when he met resistance. He's left the González family with no lands or money to speak of, even though they have pockets of silenced supporters throughout Castile and León, and now the count is practically destitute, as well. And since Ruy Blásquez doesn't know how to have a good time unless his wife tells him to, and I once had a run-in with her personally that did away with my chances of ever entertaining her again, I've joined up with these gentlemen to seek better fortunes in Andalusia."

"Is it truly so bad?"

"It's terrible. I had to leave Salas years ago, when they were first unable to support their servants, and now none of the landowners who oppose Ruy Blásquez are even allowed to give them charity. I think they survive on root vegetables and God-given determination."

"How can Ruy Blásquez treat his sister so ill?" asked Mudarra.

"If you'll forgive my honesty, I don't think things would have reached these heights if it weren't for his wife. She has sworn to keep Don Gonzalo and Doña Sancha down, as low as the worms. And whatever she says, Ruy Blásquez does. You'll see the results for yourself if you continue on that road."

Mudarra turned to Yusuf. "I want to meet my father and tell him we're here to avenge him and bring him prosperity, but I hesitate to go up that road."

Yusuf nodded. "Let's find Ruy Blásquez's home territory and get some information so we can bring a solid plan before your father."

The jongleur squinted at Mudarra and looked him up and down. Mudarra was afraid he had figured out what they were doing in Castile, but the entertainer said only, "Vilviestre is off the northeastern road," pointing. "If I may impose a little, my lords, could you tell me whether my companions and I will be welcome in Andalusia now?"

"Of course," said Mudarra, thankful for the information but also happy to see the clever little man leave the territory. "Our nobles are always excited by exotic entertainments such as you can provide. Go to Toledo or another big city and find yourselves noble patrons."

"You are gracious, my lords, and we are most grateful." He made another sweeping bow, which his companions imitated as best they could under their packs.

"For pity's sake," said Mudarra. "Give these men one of our mules." A Christian soldier released one of the mules from its train and presented it to the musicians with a satchel of bread and cheese. Amid profuse thanks and lines of jubilant song, the jongleurs loaded the animal with their packs and continued southward around the regiment while it veered east.

"Yusuf, I'm still a little confused," Mudarra said to calm his heart. "You said Almanzor had raided in León, but not Castile. What's the difference?"

Yusuf chuckled. "I suppose it seems unnecessarily complex to someone who grew up in a unified caliphate. Castile is a county, or government division of the Kingdom of León, but it's become independent enough that neither the Leonese struggles over succession to the throne nor Almanzor's raids make much impact beyond a general fear."

"He truly hasn't attacked my father's lands since I was born?"

"No. He knew your destiny, even if you didn't, my lord."

"When did Almanzor sack León?"

"He began as soon as Caliph Al-Hakam passed. You must have been very young. He razed the capital city to the ground two years ago and seized Osma last year. And he's just returned from yet another successful raid."

"I well know about that one. My mother made fun of the sherbet he brought back." Memories of Zaida and the girls weighed him down, but when he thought about what awaited him at their destination, he tried to take refuge in the burden again, only to bounce back and forth in his mind until he felt unwell and unsure why he was on this journey.

Mudarra would almost have preferred the sickening uncertainty of those few hours of approach to Vilviestre to the strange clearing they found at the end of the road as night fell. He'd never seen such dark, closed-off buildings, so closely huddled together. All built of stones and thatched roofs, building after building he couldn't imagine the purpose of. Most of them looked new and scarcely used, as if they had been raised in order to employ more wealth than their lord knew what to do with. Mudarra shook his head at the waste. All of it had been gained at his father's expense.

A few people in expensively decorated clothing shuffled between the buildings, going about their business with no urgency, chatting amongst themselves with no concern for the cost while their torches or lamps illuminated and warmed them. A child servant spied them with astonishment and ran inside the largest and what looked like the oldest edifice.

Mudarra's heart jumped when a balding man came out the door and toward them with quick steps and no visible surprise or fear, flanked by two torch bearers. Could this be Ruy Blásquez? He stopped before them and rested his meaty hands on the rounded sides of his flawless cerulean velvet tunic. His squinting gaze traveled up and down, encompassing the ranks, carts, horses, and mules. "Who are you?"

"We seek a place to rest," said Mudarra. He knew what the animals in the caliph's menagerie felt like under such scrutiny.

"You've not been sent by the count or Gonzalo Gustioz?"

"No, we're from al-Andalus, as it's plain to see," said Yusuf, flicking the feather on his turban. "We have no quarrel with you."

The man leaned back as if to take in the scene one more time. "Ah, very well then. Welcome to Vilviestre. I am Don Ramiro Mendoza, your host while my lord Ruy Blásquez is away."

"Is Don Ruy often away?" Mudarra asked as if casually curious.

"Yes, this is his ancestral home, but he usually has to patrol his other holdings, or that wife of his — excuse me." Ramiro looked up at the starry sky and then at the ground. "He's often gaining new territories to please his wife."

Yusuf shot a look at Mudarra, then asked Ramiro, "And what is his wife's name?"

"You really are strangers here," said Ramiro. "Doña Lambra, of course. But come, I've got soap and buckets for you to wash after your journey."

The soldiers set up a few tents in the clearing behind the cluster of buildings near the trees and Mudarra elected fifty eager Christian volunteers to sleep in the main house with him and his hosts. He and Yusuf followed Ramiro to the stables, where they immersed their arms in buckets of icy water that made Mudarra want to scream and applied a soap that felt as scratchy as sandstone to the bared patches of their bodies. The other knights took turns with the buckets and scrubbed the soap on themselves so hard, Mudarra couldn't watch, so he and Yusuf went into the main house.

The atmosphere was thick with what might be evil spirits, so they whispered under their breath the formulas for greeting good djinn and keeping the dark ones at bay. Nonetheless, Mudarra couldn't shake the feeling that he was entering a snare that would collapse around him the instant anyone found out who he was. They found three long tables set up with benches, a burning torch in each of some thirty sconces on the wall, and five or six lamps at every table so that the indoors shone as brightly as midday.

The kitchen area was ablaze with activity. Maids and pages scurried in and out, bringing buckets of water or bags of spices from other buildings, and cooks chopped vegetables and fish heads and stirred large cauldrons over the fire, which spit at the workers. A boy ran about waving a wet cloth to keep the heating element under control.

When Don Ramiro approached them with open arms, Mudarra said, "We don't mean to impose."

"Nonsense, Don ... I didn't get your name?"

Though his heart fluttered, Mudarra replied with a mixture of the names of the important men in his life, knowing the Christian would never assign meaning to them. "Hisham ibn Abi Amir. And my companion, Yusuf ibn Iksandarani."

"Yes. ... Well anyway, we want for nothing here and always look for excuses to use the wealth we have, so you're doing us a favor. I'm only sorry it's a fast day and we can't serve some kind of meat, as at a proper feast."

So, he would still not be subjected to eating the pork so favored by the Christians when it was permitted and available. Mudarra smiled with relief. He sat with Yusuf on a bench that Ramiro showed him was the proper place for foreign guests, and a maid set stale bread trenchers before them and a goblet full of apple cider that gave off an aged alcoholic fragrance.

"I wonder if you have any tea?" Mudarra asked her.

She stared at him blankly.

"Perhaps some water?" he tried.

"Of course, it flows down clean and cold from the mountains. But we have anything you could ask for — cider, wine, beer...."

Mudarra imagined the alcohol burning through his system and dulling his senses. No, in this nest of potential vipers, he would stay alert. "Water is the only thing I could ask for."

She shrugged, and while the rest of the selected troops settled at the tables, Mudarra and Yusuf had set before them water, roasted apples from the previous harvest, white bread made from refined wheat, and a thick fish stew laden with anonymous vegetables and only a little garlic, paprika, salt, and pepper. Mudarra watched the large numbers of servants scurrying from the kitchen to the tables to serve the sudden guests, and many of them disappeared to serve the knights who had to stay outside in the tents.

Yusuf had to whisper into Mudarra's ear to be heard over the conversations and clattering utensils, but he still spoke in Arabic to ensure privacy. "It may look rough to you, Lord Mudarra, but this is some of the finest lodging and food Castile has to offer. Ruy Blásquez has no shame living like this when the Lara family has come to ruin and the Count of Castile can't maintain control of his castles."

"I can hardly bear to look upon it. But do you get the sense that the blame for what happened to my brothers doesn't belong entirely to Ruy Blásquez?" asked Mudarra.

"Yes, I was going to say something. We mustn't miss this opportunity to learn what we can about this Lambra."

After the supper, the troops helped the servants move the tables and benches and lay out enough pallets for everyone. Mudarra joined Don Ramiro at the hearth and Ramiro's wife brought them each a goblet of wine.

Mudarra's face already felt grimy again under the torches and soot. He wiped it with his hands, much missing the basins of warm water fragranced with oils and flower petals he used to wash up at night in Madinat al-Zahra. The wine emanated an enticing fragrance, but Mudarra set it back down far from himself.

"Is Ruy Blásquez's wife with us this evening?" asked Mudarra. "I would like to meet her."

"No, she's lived in her ancestral home, Bureba, these past fifteen years. And most of the ones before that," replied Ramiro between hearty swigs. "Ruy Blásquez goes there to receive instructions for battle and the occasional reward, if you know what I mean, so like I said, he's rarely here."

To Mudarra it sounded like the behavior of a European queen using her vassals to increase her own power. Ramiro had no reason Mudarra could imagine to concoct a negative story about his lord, and it coincided with everything the honest jongleur had let them know.

Mudarra wondered if he was seeing visions of his enemy while the firelight threw ghoulish shadows down the hall and on Ramiro's face. "So, what is Andalusia like?" the host asked.

The words flowed over Mudarra's tongue like warm honey over a ripe fig. "It's a land of plentiful rivers, springs, and stone wells. It grows the best grains, produces the finest wines and purest oils. It is a paradise of every sort of sweet, full of gardens and orchards, and fruit trees that blossom with silkworms busy in their leaves. The mines bring forth silver, gold, copper, iron, tin, lead, kohl, marble, and crystal. Almanzor has an army the likes of which has never before been amassed on Earth. Noble people from lands overseas hear of the glory of our caliphate, bring gifts, and are generously recompensed."

"Truly?" said Ramiro. "I wonder that such a large party of you elects to leave such a place."

"We have important business in Castile," Mudarra said. He realized too late the risks of speaking from his heart in the house of his enemy.

"You must be here to help Ruy Blásquez take more castles," said Ramiro with a nod. "That Caliph Almanzor is a good friend of his."

Mudarra felt his throat close and the heat rise in his cheeks at these suggestions, but couldn't correct them and expect to stay the night. "Yes, well, we're all very tired. Perhaps we can talk more tomorrow?"

Although his skin crawled when he thought about the traitorous actions that had provided the comfortable beds, he slept as if under the influence of opium in so much warmth. He wondered whether his troops in their tents were as well tended.

He woke to an overwhelming feeling that everything was wrong. The thought of sitting across from Ramiro over the day's first meal brought forth harsh judgments, both that he was ungrateful and that he might be sullying himself and his troops by partaking of his enemy's wealth. He consulted with Yusuf, who agreed the place could not remain so prosperous at the cost of Mudarra's honor. Then he woke his soldiers to help the others pack and hitch up the carts without a thought of first breaking fast.

He sent the majority of the soldiers ahead on the road west toward Salas with the supplies. With Yusuf's encouragement and a heavy heart, Mudarra commanded the last ten to enter the buildings and wake the women and children and make them stand in the clearing, then take one of the omnipresent torches and light each thatched roof.

Mudarra heard the first screams, then he ran under the influence of what he thought must be fear. He mounted his horse, which carried him to the center of the moving army for cover in case the people of Vilviestre shot arrows. No such retaliation occurred. No doubt they were too busy trying to save their loved ones and homes. Though he was tempted by the sounds of crackling flames, shouting men, screaming children, and water sloshing out of buckets, Mudarra never looked back. A nervous excitement he couldn't identify coursed through his body, so he focused on Tranquilo, who maintained an awe-inspiring calm. He leaned forward and whispered to his mount, "Dear Tranquilo, you are the steadiest horse I ever rode." Even in a whisper, he heard his own voice trembling, so he pushed ahead, looking for Yusuf.

He found his friend at the head of the troops, faithfully leading them toward Salas, but also looking back at Vilviestre with fear.

"So it begins," said Mudarra. He felt relieved, and realized his greatest fear had been that the victims would find him and ask why he made them homeless after their generosity. He reminded himself that they were the enemy. With as much bravado as he could muster, he continued, "This is the start of my revenge."

The village in flames receded into the distance behind them, reflected in Yusuf's eyes. He tore his gaze away and gave a firm nod. "This is what you were born to do, Lord Mudarra. This is what your destiny looks like."

Chapter III

Doña Sancha awoke with a start in the darkness of Sunday morning and felt the weight of the blanket oppressing her. She reached out and touched Luz's shoulder without meaning to. The three of them slept huddled together in the bower, ever since the last of the servants who weren't willing to stay for the sake of loyalty had abandoned the González family and their once wondrous estate, Salas. Sancha patted Luz in absentminded appreciation, and the maid sat up with a groan.

"I didn't mean to wake you, Luz. You can stay in bed," Sancha whispered.

"Day's coming eventually. It always does," she replied with the forbearance that had served her so well since the death of her seven young lords. Sancha was relieved to think that Luz would be the one trying to get the cooking fire going without even a flint to make a spark.

As Luz stumbled through the door into the great hall, Sancha turned over and touched the original object of her urgency.

"Sancha?" Gonzalo said.

"Yes, my love," she whispered. She had become so accustomed to deciphering his features in the dark for lack of candles that she could hear his smile. "Listen, darling, it's too early to get up. I've just dreamed something strange."

"Tell me."

"You and I were in the peaks of the high sierra. I saw a hawk come flying toward us from Córdoba, slowly, as if it had all the time in the world. It landed so gently on my hand and opened its wings and cast a shadow so large it covered us both. Then, it flew away and landed on my brother's shoulder. It grabbed with its talons so hard, his arm came away from his body. There were rivers of blood running from the wound, and I . . . I knelt and drank his blood. Why would I do that?"

He breathed deeply, considering. "How long has it been since our sons were murdered?"

"More than fifteen years." In all that time, her prayers for another son, or any other miracle, had gone unanswered.

"Your dream is the symbol of our revenge. I think it may come true soon."

"Our revenge will come from Córdoba, the very place where you were affronted? It doesn't make sense."

"Muño Salido could tell auguries, and now it seems you can, too. Take hope from your vision."

Hope had left Sancha the day her boys followed her traitorous brother to Almenar. She hadn't even heard the word except in the occasional stilted Church Latin phrase for all those years. No one had been dim-witted enough to use it in her presence. After a reflex urge to slap her husband's face passed, she held the word in her mind, and as it grew in meaning, an unfamiliar sensation took control of her. She remembered its name: joy.

Ignoring the aches and pains that called at her fifty-five-year-old joints, she kissed her husband's lips, and he responded with tenderness. It wasn't long before she woke his passion. Over the years, she had found that with so little sight, he was even more sensitive to touch. They explored each other until insistent rays of light slid through the shutters. Their love was all that was left to them.

In the hall, Luz had warmed the previous evening's flavorless gruel over the meager fire that was all the light they could ever permit themselves indoors. They stood at the cook pot, guarding their threadbare clothes from the flames and taking turns sipping out of the ladle. Two years before, after a blight that took their vegetable patch as well, they had been obliged to trade their last bowls for grain. Luz wrapped a cloth around Don Gonzalo's head so that no one would have to see his dead eyes and took him by the arm to church. Normally Sancha went with them, but this day she felt a need to stay behind.

At first, they had kept the hall dark because the brightness bothered Don Gonzalo, but by the time it hardly mattered whether his lids were open or closed, there was no more money for beeswax candles, for bees, or for animals whose fat they could render for tallow. Sancha opened the shutters to let in the light she thought she needed, but it only made the hall appear before her as a vast empty chasm. The sunlight glittered through hundreds of tiny holes in the front door, because they had sold the metal studs more than five years earlier. They had provided the last payment to the Jewish lenders. Although they were more lenient than Sancha expected from non-Christians, eventually even the lenders' patience ran out. By the grace of God, Don Gonzalo had been spared being sold as a slave because of his blindness.

Ignoring the sluggish tears in her eyes, she raked the straw on the floor to freshen it, thinking that this used to be only one of hundreds of tasks she had assigned to a hundred servants. The last time the hall had been crowded was during the great funeral ceremonies, when the bishop arrived and the tributes came, and that silly jongleur entertained them with songs and stories. He had managed a solemn dirge on his rebec as the vassals processed with the caskets on their shoulders to the same church where her husband was worshiping now. Every time they went to mass, they could visit their sons and light a candle at the altar where their heads rested in a state of blessed nondecay. If it hadn't been for the way everyone had eventually abandoned them — even that darling, foolish jongleur — Sancha would have thought time had stopped all together in Salas.

She rested her hands atop the rake handle and sighed. Time had been their enemy, and now they were moments away from starvation. But this morning, Gonzalo had explained that their redemption had required that much time to come about simply because the betrayal had been unfathomable. She looked into the water bucket. Time to go to the well.

She lifted from its place at the hearth the lynx fur her sons had so proudly shown her before she'd entrusted them to her brother. The edges were blacker than the spots from the remains of soot and sparks, and parts were worn through from years of sitting on it atop the stones. But Gonzalo and Luz had taken their only other furs, so she wrapped it around her shoulders and headed toward the well.

When she opened the door, instead of the usual snow-glazed ground and the solitary well, Sancha's eyes met two other brown ones, smoldering under a turban. She gasped and dropped the bucket, and the fur slid from her shoulders. The unexpected visitor dismounted from his roan steed, which seemed even taller because of its plumes and glossy armor. The hidden items in the pack hanging from the horse's saddle responded to the movement with a jangling sound. The visitor gallantly picked up the bucket by the handle and presented it to her as if it were the most important tribute in an entire cartful.

"Thank you, Don. . ." she whispered, trying to banish the loose threads and faded wool of her garments from her consciousness.

He lifted the cloth that came from his turban to protect his face from the cold, revealing a young brown beard and angular cheekbones below the intense gaze. Plumes of warm breath rose from his mouth and nose. "My name is Yusuf ibn Iksandarani, but perhaps you would be comforted to call me José Alejandro."

"Don José," she said with a bow that was as deep as her aching back permitted, "you're most welcome in Salas, but can you have meant to come here?"

"Yes, Salas is my precise destination. Where are the lord and lady?"

Her face burned with shame for her appearance and more tears followed the ones that had begun flowing inside the hall. "I am the wretched Doña Sancha, who should never have been born only to come to such shame."

He set the bucket on the ground with a snowy crunch and took both of her hands to kiss them. "Dear lady," he said, ignoring her sobs, "accept these gifts in the name of making a good impression. An important guest is coming to see you on the third day from today."

He pulled a pack from the opposite side of his horse, which was snorting and stamping to keep warm. Sancha wanted to offer him grain or hay, but had none. The stables were too dilapidated for such a fine mount. She hoped he had a good place to stay somewhere, and these thoughts distracted her until Don José held out lengths of silk before her. Embroidered in the Moorish style with gold and silver thread and covered with translucent beads at the ends, in every color, they left Sancha no option but to stand stunned.

"Your visitor will be a great comfort to you," Don José was saying.

"May the Lord grant that he is the avenging hawk I dreamed of," Sancha whispered, accepting the slippery cloth into her arms with a smaller pack on top.

When she looked up, the apparition had disappeared into the trees with his steed and his turban. She had but two days until the important visitor would arrive, so she abandoned the bucket and carried her gifts inside to the carved settle that was their only remaining furniture and where Don Gonzalo spent much of his waking time. She buried her face in the silks, savoring the healthy, fibrous smell of fabrics free of moths. She lifted the black silk from the rainbow-colored pile, thinking it would be the most noble as well as the closest color to her continued grief. The smaller pack, nothing more than a leather envelope, slid to the floor with a smack. She picked it up and opened it to find more coins than she had ever seen together in her life. Moorish gold, valued and accepted in every kingdom and county. There were also gold bracelets and a long gold chain. Her heart fluttering, she slipped the chain over her neck and adorned her arms with the bracelets. She remembered being a great lady.

The front door opened behind her. "Why are the windows open, Doña Sancha?" asked Luz. "What is all this?"

"We're having a visitor," Sancha began. "I've already had a surprising visit, and he left these silks and jewelry and gold pieces for us so we can make a good impression on the important visitor. He's coming on the third day, and we've got to put together at least one dress for me, and one for you, and a tunic and leggings for Don Gonzalo."

Luz held Sancha's arm still so that she could inspect the gold. "But we don't even have thread."

Sancha held out one of the coins. "We'll buy some." Luz gasped and clasped the coin to her breast as if it were her long lost child.

Don Gonzalo had remained in the doorway and removed the wrapping from his eyes. "I think your dream is coming true," he said.

"Yes, Jesus grant that it is," Sancha replied.

She sent Luz wrapped in both of the furs and with most of the coins into town for the supplies, and while Gonzalo sat on the dirty hearth, bewildered by the light, Sancha finally got the water from the well and set it to warm in the cook pot. She scrounged up a clove of garlic from the corner of an otherwise empty larder and tossed in a dry apple slice for texture. She hoped Luz would bring cheese and bread or meat, because otherwise, this was their meal for the next two days, and it would not do for an important guest.

When she had done all she could until Luz came back, she stood stirring at the cook pot.

"Sancha," said Gonzalo with unmistakable seriousness, reaching for her.

"Yes, darling?" She knelt and patted his beard, which always seemed to calm him.

"You know I've never loved anyone but you, and I've never been unfaithful."

"Just as I've always been true to you." The assurance came with more difficulty than she let him hear.

"I've loved none other than you. Is there anything that will part you from me?"

Now Sancha was sure he knew something about the visitor. "Only death could part me from you, Gonzalo. I made a vow forty years ago, and I make it again now."

"You won't leave me in my old age? You won't go back to your people, as you could have done all along?" He crushed her against his chest with a frenzy Sancha understood as devotion.

"Do you doubt me, my lord? Do you know something about this visitor that you should tell me?"

"I don't know who it will be, but we'll serve him in Salas for as long as he wishes."

He let her go back to the cook pot and she stirred the unsavory concoction while suspicions revolved in her heart. "I've stayed with you when we were the most prosperous family in Castile, and I've stayed with you when we've been on the edge of starvation. Nothing could be worse than what's already happened to us."

"In that, you're right, of course."

A knock at the front door sent Sancha scurrying across the empty floor. Luz was at the head of ten men and women, some of whom had worked at the estate before. Each one carried a bulging pack of something that must be sorely missed and longed for, since in Salas they had been lacking everything.

"What is this?" asked Sancha.

"My lady, they were so happy to see me in town that they wouldn't let me leave with only thread, but kept asking what else we needed. Finally I realized the visitor had left us enough money to employ several of them for an entire year."

"Clever girl," Sancha said embracing her, although Luz was far from girlhood now. One of the men pulled two cured ham hocks out of his sack, bringing tears of joy to Sancha's eyes. "Praise God it's not yet Lent! We've sacrificed enough for any martyr. And can the women sew?"

Sew they did, for two days straight, while the men repaired the obvious decay in the main house and built two long dining tables with matching benches with mature wood from the mountain that still felt as cold as snow to the touch on the third day, despite the constant warming at the hearth. Bread, both coarse and fine, baked in the ovens out back and created the best aromas Sancha had smelled in a decade. She looked outside and saw that there was no time to fix the stables, much less to fill them with horses worthy of their status. But whenever she worried how it would look to the visitor, she looked at her husband, who sat peaceably in the bright light flooding through the windows while Luz told him stories and described what happened around them. He had never seen the houses falling down around them, but he must have sensed it, and yet he always maintained dignity worthy of a king, or for all Sancha knew, an emperor.

And so, on the third day, Luz dressed her in a bell-sleeve tunic of deepest black embroidered with silver that Sancha hoped the visitor wouldn't be able to tell had been so hastily stitched together. The maid then coiled her hair, which matched the embroidery's color, around her head in what Luz said looked like a hundred different braids to make up for the lack of a headdress. After they'd eaten and cleared away the new pallets in the hall, Sancha sat next to her husband on their old settle and tried to project the same serenity. But when she grasped his hand, it fluttered like a moth.

"I don't know who will come through the door," said Sancha, "but perhaps you do."

He turned his face toward her with so much delicacy she almost forgot he couldn't see. He shook his head.

"Well, anyway, this visitor has already brought wonderful improvements to our lives, so there can be no cause for worry." She only wished she believed herself.

They hadn't been waiting long, with the kitchen noises and the servants rushing in and out of side doors to access the new food stores behind them, when Luz came and announced a name that would have been unknown to her, except that the surname was González. The girl kept talking about how many men he'd brought with him, or some nonsense Sancha couldn't pay attention to because her youngest son had just walked through her front door as if not a single day had passed since she'd last kissed him.

"Gonzalico!" she cried, her heart racing, and, astonishingly, the apparition kept walking toward her, becoming clearer instead of fading away.

She compared the monstrous being, obviously some kind of trick on her aching heart, to the image she still held as fresh in her mind as her last visit to church. It must be her last son, how could it be anyone else, with the same cowlick in the front of his dark, almost black hair that pointed in every direction before curling tamely under his ears? His eyes were shaded under the same wild brows, and his long, straight nose was exactly like his father's. His square chin supported the same half-grown stubble of a child on the verge of becoming a man. His mouth was pursed in seriousness, but Sancha recognized its shape, always ready to burst into laughter. Every one of the distinguishable characteristics matched those of her most bewildering and most beloved son with no variance.

Where had her son been all this time? He'd been doing well. As he knelt before them, his long cloak opened to reveal that it was lined in a fur as fine as silk and much warmer than the hole-ridden lynx pelt. The tunic he wore underneath, made of a soft-looking, fuzzy fabric, seemed to create its own heat with its bright red color and golden embroidery. The hand he held out to her and her husband had golden rings embedded with shimmering carbuncles on each finger. Even his boots were studded with beads that sparkled as much as rubies. The only detail that seemed out of place for a well-landed lord somewhere in Andalusia or in the borderlands was the length of rough string that secured a small pouch around his neck.

He kissed both of their hands as if pledging his fealty. Her husband sat impassive before his longed-for son, unable to be moved by the vision. "You must not kneel before us, welcome visitor," said Sancha. "I'm sorry, what is your name, Don...."

"Mudarra González ibn Zaida, but I'm not a knight and do not merit standing before you, who are my lord and lady."

With his face tipped into the light, Sancha saw that the apparition's eyes were much lighter than her Gonzalico's had been. In fact, she would say they were as green as the emeralds on his belt. So this was not some forbidden magic, but the very thing her husband had known he couldn't hide from her any longer. This was Don Gonzalo's son by some other woman.

Tears broke free from her eyes. She felt so confused she wished she could faint and be relieved of so many questions and emotions.

"My servants are preparing a feast to welcome you and return the respect you've shown us," said Don Gonzalo. "While we wait for them, please tell us where you've come from and where you're going."

Mudarra González settled on his haunches. "I've come from Córdoba, the capital of the caliphate of al-Andalus. I have been raised by Almanzor, my uncle, and the princess Zaida, my mother. I come here today because my mother tells me you engendered me, and I am your son."

Don Gonzalo shook his head. "Since I married Doña Sancha, I've had nothing to do with any other woman, Christian or Moor. The people of Salas will serve you for as long as you stay here, but there is nothing else I can give you." Sancha watched the lies fall from his lips like gobbets of scum. His mouth pursed around them as if they tasted as vile as they sounded. She almost said something so as not to drive their potential savior away, but he was already standing up, about to turn back out the door.

"If you don't want me for a son, then I won't have you for a father, since my mother's family is much nobler than this one." He paused and breathed deeply. "But I have been raised for only one purpose. Let me avenge the seven noble knights of Lara, who I'm told were my brothers. I care nothing for any inheritance."

Sancha stood and held Mudarra by the arm, which was as stiff with strength as the arms of all of her sons. She made an effort to keep her words level so her husband wouldn't know the conflict she was suffering. "If you could see, dear husband, you would say that he looks just like our Gonzalico. There can be no doubt that you engendered the man who now stands before us. Don't reject him because you fear me, and don't disinherit him for my sake, because that would be an even greater sin than having lain with his mother when we're so in need of someone who can avenge us, and he's so willing. If this man represents your sin, then you sinned seven other times with me." Her head felt light, and she thought the longed-for faint might come at last, but she needed to hear his response.

Gonzalo bowed his head and clutched his hands to his heart. "If he's the son of the princess, he'll be able to give me a sign."

"I have no reason to satisfy you in that regard," said Mudarra in a voice Sancha wondered whether she was meant to hear. He strode forward, extracted a small piece of metal from the odd pouch around his neck, and threw it into his father's cupped hands. "This is the half-ring you left with my mother."

Sancha studied the intricate patterns and recognized a ring she'd assumed Gonzalo had lost during his imprisonment. It was just as well he'd given it away, or they would have had to sell it for grain in the meantime. Even more astonishing, her husband stood and reached into a pocket in the bottom of his tunic she never knew he'd had and pulled out the matching half. He worked them together by feel and the patterns fit perfectly.

"I acknowledge you, Mudarra González, son of Zaida, as my rightful son," he said, holding the ring between his fingers and reaching toward Mudarra to embrace him. "We'll have the ring forged together and nothing will separate the parts again."

It was at once the best and worst answer to Sancha's long prayers. A son and a savior in one person, and in the same person, the evidence of her only love's infidelity. She would have to erase his past — adopt him and make him fully hers in the eyes of God.

"Thank you. I have an ocular surgeon with me. We should make arrangements as soon as possible to restore your sight," Mudarra said.

Sancha let the tears fall as she joined the men's hug and Don Gonzalo kept asking if such a miracle as seeing again were really possible. She beckoned her new, God-sent son to her table that still had the fragrance of the forest about it, but he refused to sit while his troops waited outside. Sancha held the door open a crack after he exited and saw that Mudarra had backed up his promise to revenge them with some three hundred soldiers, horses, mules, and carts still laden with supplies even after the journey.

"We'll have to feed them in shifts," Sancha said to no one in particular, glad to have such a large crowd to occupy her busy mind. Most of the soldiers could sleep in the hall, but they set up tents to shelter the horses and mules and lit a fire to make sure they wouldn't catch cold. Sancha glimpsed Don José at work amongst the carts and smiled at his pleasant demeanor. When she found Mudarra in the midst of the movement and wisps of visible breath, she knew what she had to do before anything else.

"Mudarra," she whispered at his side, "I want you to meet your brothers."

He gave her his fur cloak and took for himself a furry hide from the carts Sancha imagined could have been from a bear they'd killed on their way. She slipped her arms into the sleeve of the cloak and, as she'd suspected, it was as soft as immersing herself in freshly churned cream. They set out for the church of San Pelayo. She put her hand in his and felt transported to a long-ago time when she had strolled with one of her sons, all of whom had also been at least a head taller than she. They walked slowly in spite of the cold because Sancha didn't want to break the spell by entering the church and seeing the true condition of the sons she had carried inside her and raised to adulthood.

She told Mudarra about the wedding ceremony turned violent, and how Gonzalo had been prideful in attacking the man who claimed—claimed only—to be a better lancer than he. "But that was no reason for his uncle to attack him, even at the urging of his new wife, and the count settled the entire matter right there."

"And his uncle's name is. . ." interjected Mudarra.

"Ruy Blásquez, my only brother."

As she continued speaking, she noted the calm concentration with which he listened to her. Although none of her sons would have done it the same way, she loved Mudarra for it. She felt sympathy with him in spite of their not sharing any blood. She recounted as best she could the way Doña Lambra had coaxed them to stay in Barbadillo and then sent her page at Gonzalo with that bloody cucumber. "I know, it's so strange. I still don't fully understand it." The page had been faultless, but his rank didn't merit a homicide fee. Knowing Doña Lambra harbored such bizarre sentiments, they fled, only to be lulled into a false sense of camaraderie again by her incomprehensible brother.

Mudarra supported Sancha to make sure she wouldn't fall while they made their way across the icy bridge and again she wanted to express gratitude for his existence, before he'd even promised to do anything specific to remedy their situation. "He took them away to Almenar and no one knows what they suffered, but I never saw any of them again. I suppose you know something about the way my brother further betrayed us, sending my husband—your father—to be killed in the court of Almanzor."

"Yes, my mother only recently explained to me exactly why she had taught me all my life that the name of my enemy is Ruy Blásquez," said Mudarra. Sancha detected no hate in his voice.

They stopped outside the church door. "Since your father came home with what remained of your brothers, we've passed a very long, cold winter, year after year, waiting for you. But now you're here and bring the promise of springtime."

Mudarra looked down into her eyes. His cheeks were red with the cold. "Salas will bloom again. I'll make sure of it."

She nodded and smiled from deep within. "We'll call upon our vassals to join us in Burgos, where the Count of Castile will knight you and you can be baptized, reborn as my son." She watched his face and it seemed to her that his half-smile indicated agreement. She pushed the wooden door inward.

Sancha and Mudarra crossed the flagstone floor, empty except for a few bits of straw. A couple of beeswax candles as long as an arm illuminated the main altar. It consisted of a podium with open-looped vegetable carvings, an altar cloth, and a large painting covered with unadorned shutters that Sancha knew to be a breathtaking depiction of San Pelayo making his stand at Covadonga. Sancha knelt before the altar and crossed herself, then took Mudarra's sleeve and tugged at him to imitate her. She separated his fingers properly and touched them to his warm forehead, his broad chest, and across to each square shoulder. Then she tried to stand, but her knees wouldn't permit it, so Mudarra took her hand this time and helped her back up. To their right was a niche hidden by a heavy red curtain, and Sancha held onto Mudarra's arm and guided him toward it.

A tonsured priest came out from behind a door opposite, saying, "Doña Sancha, come to light the candles for the noble knights of Lara?" She nodded, so he handed his candle to her and worked the ropes that opened the curtain with a grinding that echoed off the walls. Sancha lit the first candle so Mudarra could better make out the red and blue painting on the back wall of a haloed Santiago slaying Moors from his towering white horse, but more importantly, the pediment that supported the row of sacred orbs.

"They haven't decayed," said Sancha. Mudarra's face was expressionless, and she wasn't sure what to do next.

The priest stepped in to explain to the new visitor. "It's a sign of divine grace, the lack of decay. God was with the brothers and their tutor on their final day. And with all respect for Doña Sancha, that makes Ruy Blásquez the instrument of Satan."

"I have long known that he is the very embodiment of evil," responded Mudarra, not separating his gaze from the saintly row. "God, with all his mercy, would still be obliged to send Ruy Blásquez to Hell as one of the few permanent inhabitants."

"And God in all His wisdom will certainly condemn him, won't He?" Sancha asked the priest, who nodded wholeheartedly.

"Is this first one their tutor?" asked Mudarra.

"Muño Salido was with them until the very end. He was so wise and taught them everything he knew. No one alive today was present there except my brother, but I would venture to guess that he must have done all he could to protect them." Sancha lit the next candle. "Beside him is my eldest son, Diego. His brothers would have looked to him to direct them." Two more candles caught fire. "Martín probably used the power of his words to plead with my brother, and Suero, I know, would have much rather been hunting, but his loyalty to his brothers would not permit him to part from them." The heads' eyelids danced in the light as Sancha lit another. "My middle son, Fernando, was the most honored of them, and so I know that he protected all his brothers from ignominy in their final moments." Her hand was shaking and the priest removed the taper from her hands to light the remaining candles himself. Sancha was blinded by the way the blaze as bright as any daylight mixed with her tears. "Rodrigo was the most diplomatic. Perhaps he made my brother hesitate in his ruthless slaughter with his reason, but when the final blows came, Rodrigo would have defended them with his skill with the sword. Gustio! A more tactless and witty boy I never saw. I can imagine him perfectly, taunting his uncle until there was nothing left to be said. And the littlest brother, Gonzalico. He was only as old as you are now when he died, and yet he had mastered every skill. He was the most impetuous, but if I had to choose, I loved him the most."

She wiped away her tears and saw the two young men staring at each other, as if in a reflection, making it impossible to accept that one of them was no longer alive. Mudarra's hand, glistening with jewels, stopped before it touched his brother's face.

"You look just like him," said Sancha. "It doesn't seem possible that with all seven brothers and their wise tutor together to protect each other, this could have happened. I've tried to imagine over the years what that army must have been." She looked away from Gonzalo and his brothers in time to glimpse Mudarra's teardrops gleaming amber-colored in the candlelight. He was shaking his head as if he could still change his brothers' fate.

"I pledge now to the Christian God," he said so quietly that the sound barely reached Sancha's ears. She knew God would hear them nonetheless. "I promise the Lord of the World that my life will be worth nothing if I don't avenge the tragedy that befell my brothers and their tutor."

Sancha pressed his body tight against hers, as if she could compress his spirit and make it part of hers. She knew that even if that were possible, he could not become more dear to her than he already was.

Chapter IIII

There were so many different dishes at the welcoming feast Salas presented to Mudarra and his retinue that his fear of consuming pork waned long enough for him to pick and taste a slice of ham soaked in wine and spices before asking Yusuf, who sat at his right side, what it was.

"How was it, my lord?" he asked in reply. "Your first taste of forbidden meat."

Mudarra felt himself blush while the bile rose in his throat. He swallowed hard and paid attention to his stomach. Perhaps he was more Christian than he'd thought. The flavor had delighted his mouth, although he did feel dirty with that bite of flesh inside. "Well, I can see why they eat it. It's not bad."

He and Yusuf laughed at their private joke and Mudarra forced down the bile, strengthening his resolve, until Doña Sancha touched his arm. "Speak Christian so everyone can understand you in this, your home."

The word "home" suggested something different to Mudarra than this place where he needed Yusuf to interpret not the words, but the meanings behind every phrase and gesture. He ate no more for fear of being overcome by the different cuisine. Instead, he cast his gaze about the estate, taking in the pine trees and unidentifiable greenery, and lingered over the stacks of timber and piles of stones obviously intended to become a slaughterhouse and other outbuildings. The stable was so new it still smelled of wet mortar and lacked a roof. All of it must have been purchased with the money he'd sent ahead—he'd have to ask Yusuf what the place had been like only days earlier. There was a crumbling well near the house, but not a single fountain, no flower gardens, no sweeping vistas of the mountains or the town, no musicians to sweeten the feast, and the serving girls were so bundled up against the elements that he couldn't tell how old they were. Their only perfume was the wafting scent of the stews and sauces. In Madinat al-Zahra, he'd felt himself in the center of the world. Here, the space spread out before him, but didn't connect him with anything. If Yusuf had said this was just an extension of the no-man's-land, he might have believed that more easily than that this was his ancestral home. He knew for certain that when his mother had described his father's grand estates, she hadn't imagined anything as poor as this. He clasped his friend's hand to signal that he wasn't turning away forever and twisted toward the small woman to his left who would tell him everything he needed to know, if not from a perspective he could understand.

He watched Doña Sancha's tiny hand swiping some sauce for her meat or fussing over Don Gonzalo's trencher. She was covered in a cloak of wool she must have bought with his gift money, because it was so new the threads still stuck up, sharp like tiny spikes. Underneath, she wore a dress made from the black silk he'd sent, but the shape of it baffled him. The sleeves dipped onto her food and caught along the edge of the table, so she held each one back with one hand while the other performed a task, revealing wrists about width of his scimitar's blade. Mudarra had thought his mother was the smallest a woman could be after having borne children, but obviously he was mistaken. He wondered how such a slight woman could've carried even one of his half-brothers inside her belly, although there was no doubt she was old enough to have seven children. Her silvery hair, twisted into many strands atop her head, overwhelmed her face instead of making her look more regal, as he was sure she'd intended. Perhaps at some time her skin had been softened with soaked flower petals, but the years of poverty had brought out wrinkles around her eyes, mouth, and forehead, and dried and cracked her fingertips. Why had his father chosen her over his mother?

He contemplated the man at the head of the table, who had to wait until the servant or his wife cut up his food to receive his nourishment in this new environment where his gnarled hands fluttered about in confusion, free of rings or other adornments. He could see the affinity to his own face in the line of the jaw and curve of the brows, although not in their overgrown, ragged appearance. This was not the strong, exemplary Christian Zaida had described with such rapture. His eyes showed no trace of liveliness, his snowy hair none of the vigor she'd recalled. He wondered whether the attractiveness had ever existed, and if it had, whether it would have deteriorated quite so much if he had stayed with Zaida.

Without thinking, he sighed.

"What is it?" Doña Sancha asked with alarm.

"I apologize, dear lady," he said. He decided to take the opportunity to ask a question that would help him gauge this new place. "I was wondering, where is the nearest library to here?"

A deafening silence followed the question. Mudarra didn't understand the hesitation until Doña Sancha answered proudly, "I think the church of San Pelayo might have as many as five books."

In spite of their captive status, Mudarra was sure his knights carried more books than that among their supplies—spiritual treatises, medical reference for the physician, a few chess treasuries and many personal copies of the Quran. Mudarra kept his securely in a tunic pocket. He fingered it now and couldn't help musing to Yusuf in Arabic, "If these Christians are People of the Book, where are the books?"

Everyone within earshot who could understand him burst out laughing. He hadn't meant it as a joke.

He must have shown his frustration, because Doña Sancha abruptly took his hand and he rose from the bench under her surprising power. Together they walked without a word past the revelers and the tents Mudarra's soldiers had already set up. "They can take care of themselves for an hour," she said. She pointed to the ground under a tree that would give forth some unknown fruit in the spring or summer but was now the only bare thing in such weather. Mudarra could see only Doña Sancha's nose, red with the cold, and puffs of warm breath billowing from under her hood.

"Let me show you Salas as it's meant to be," she said.

Mudarra gazed at the estate from this new vantage point and felt as if Doña Sancha were his general, explaining her plan of attack on the eve of battle.

"Of course, we'll start by replacing the roof of the main house. As you can see, they've already made a start on the stables because I knew you would bring many horses. I'm sorry you have to shelter them in tents, but when they're finished, our new stables will be twice the size the old one ever was, because Salas will become a center for travelers, merchants, and vassals once again."

Her hand gestured under her cloak as if she were drawing him a picture over this too empty parchment.

"Those shorter trees will be cut and used for firewood, for they've overtaken the area where there used to be a slaughterhouse, hogs, and chickens. Farther back, we'll make a place for geese and goats. We'll have grain silos as high as the pines, one each for wheat, millet, flax, and oats."

"And the doors will be capped with horseshoe arches," Mudarra murmured.

Doña Sancha paused to look at him, puzzled. "Of course. Whatever will show the new magnificence of Salas."

"And we'll repair the well, of course," he continued. "What about fountains?"

"I don't think there's enough high water to flow into a fountain," she said, her enthusiasm unabated. "But we can embellish the well with anything you like."

Mudarra could see the grandeur she spoke of as if it were laid out before him, so solid he could almost touch it. As a visitor approached, he would gasp in amazement at the flourishes and animal reliefs around the well, and would then be overwhelmed with the plenty represented by building after building and archway after archway and fat, lazy animals everywhere. It would be like Vilviestre, but better.

"But who will see it, Doña Sancha? No one can be openly loyal to Salas with the monster Ruy Blásquez rampaging." He said it before he remembered the monster was this kind woman's brother.

"What you say is true. The first thing to do is to send letters to everyone who might sympathize with us in the region of Lara, like the people of Los Cameros and Piedra Lada. We'll tell them about the army you've assembled, so it's safe to support us, and call them to travel with our entire household to Burgos to see the Count of Castile. My brother has offended him, too, so I'm sure he'll want to help us. He can knight you."

"And I'll be baptized and initiated into the Christian Church?"

"Of course, that's most the important. You can't restore Christian Castile without first becoming a Christian. The count himself will sponsor your journey into Christianity."

Mudarra felt as if he were losing his footing. Although the pristine state of his brothers' heads had almost won him over, he knew his mother and Almanzor would never accept him as a Christian. He hadn't agreed to leave his faith, but Doña Sancha didn't seem to need consent. At the very least, he needed a lot more schooling in Christian doctrine if he was to accept baptism and take what was apparently a Christian revenge on someone he'd never met, for all the stories he'd heard about his evil. Doña Sancha took his arm and walked him back to the table, pointing out patches of ice as if they were what was making him unsteady.

While the servants were clearing the table, Doña Sancha asked Mudarra to bring a scribe. "I've waited some fifteen years, and I'm ready to start," she explained. Yusuf, whom Sancha inexplicably referred to as "Don José," brought the scribe who knew Latin to the table and helped as the four of them navigated the three languages of Arabic, spoken Latin, and written Latin. They worked long into the afternoon, nibbling at bread, letting busy servants, soldiers and builders pass them by. Then Mudarra, Yusuf, and Sancha left to allow the scribe to make ten copies, which Sancha then sent with ten of the builders, regretful that the letters would slow down the rebuilding.

"Never mind," said Mudarra. "By the time we return to Salas, our vision for it will be practically complete."

Yusuf preferred to sleep outside in the tents with the majority of the soldiers. Mudarra gathered them together and instructed them to draw as little attention to their prayers as possible. If he was to employ these soldiers in this predestined war, he must avoid clashing with Christian beliefs, the outlines of which were still murky for him. He then retired on a pallet in the main house with his father, Doña Sancha, their servants, and his Christian mercenaries. Those soldiers' spirits had lifted when they'd crossed into Castile and they seemed to find the sleeping arrangements comforting, somehow — Mudarra thought he would never understand how that could be. He listened to rats patrolling the floor, mice making nests, and innumerable snores, sure he would never fall asleep with so many things to consider, until he did.

After a breakfast of mushy grains he had to show to and discuss with Yusuf in the tents before swallowing, Mudarra found his father standing outside in bright sunlight. The physician Almanzor had sent with the caravan stared into Don Gonzalo's eyes and felt his neck for the pulse. The physician's assistant stood helpless while the doctor feverishly articulated his diagnosis in Arabic, neither of them able to speak Latin. Don Gonzalo stood like a statue, a portrait of calm, not even flinching while the physician pulled at his eyelids.

"Can you help him?" Mudarra asked.

The physician turned his attention to the man he knew could interpret for him. "The cataracts are very advanced. The only hope is to cut them out."

Mudarra flinched at the idea of inserting a knife into a human eye. "Will he be able to see again after the surgery?"

"I don't think there's anything to risk." He gestured at Don Gonzalo, who didn't react to what he couldn't see. "He can't see anything now, so if the operation fails, he'll be no worse off. We might as well try."

Don Gonzalo remained still, blinking. Mudarra understood that he needed to add some hope to the doctor's words. "Father," he said, laying his hand on his father's shoulder. "Good morning. The doctor thinks he can improve your sight with surgery. It's wonderful news."

"It would be a miracle to see you for even a moment," said Don Gonzalo. He leaned in close to Mudarra and whispered, "The last thing I remember seeing was your mother's face."

It pierced Mudarra's heart like a dart and his knees went weak, but he held them firm. For the first time he understood his debt to this man, the man who had left Córdoba, taking his mother's heart with him. He stared, bewildered, into Don Gonzalo's face — not at the expressionless eyes, but at the soft grey beard whose earlier version his mother had so evocatively described, and at the lips that had just made the low-voiced confession to Mudarra alone, in the hopes that Doña Sancha would never hear. Mudarra embraced him and felt the same strength in his father's muscles as stirred within his own. He saw himself obliged to make this man as elegant as his mother remembered.

"When can the surgery take place?" Mudarra asked the physician.

"As soon as we set up a table with clean linens and clean water out here in the light and find enough strong men to hold down his arms and legs and keep his eyelids open," he replied with his customary matter-of-factness. "We shouldn't wait for the afternoon. The best light is now."

"Father," said Mudarra, "the physician says there's nothing stopping us from doing the surgery right now."

"What about tomorrow or another day?" Don Gonzalo said.

"It could be cloudy tomorrow," said Mudarra. "Stay right here. We'll bring everything out to you."

He coordinated the effort, and in less than an hour, ten of Mudarra's soldiers had brought the dining table from inside the hall and positioned it at the angle the physician specified, checking the light and setting his assistant to work washing some tiny knives. All the soldiers and servants came to witness, murmuring out of reach of the table and out of the doctor's light. Mudarra stood next to Yusuf and Doña Sancha after she laid the linen over the table with nervous precision and helped Don Gonzalo climb atop and lie face up. She held her husband's hand and patted it obsessively, trying to provide comfort when she had none to give.

"Are you sure you want to watch?" Mudarra asked her.

"I must stay by my husband's side when he needs me."

Mudarra admired her fortitude. He doubted his own mother would've stood by during surgery, no matter who the patient was.

A strong man stood at each of Don Gonzalo's feet and right hand, Christian knights from Mudarra's retinue, ready to hold the limbs down upon the physician's command. Another soldier came to Doña Sancha's side and said, "Pardon me, my lady. I can hold this hand down for you."

"No, Sancha," said Don Gonzalo, "don't let go."

"Thank you, Sir Knight," said Sancha, "but this hand is taken."

"I need someone to hold his eyelid open," said the physician.

After a silence during which Mudarra thought everyone must be watching with as much dread as fascination, he said, "I will do it," in both Arabic and Latin. He raised his hand as if someone had protested. "It is my duty."

"Time to begin," said the physician, gesturing toward the water bucket. Mudarra rinsed his hands in water he was sure must be on the verge of forming ice and dried them on a folded piece of linen that lay on the far end of the table. Then he took up his position at Don Gonzalo's head.

"You won't feel any pain, father," said Mudarra, hoping it was true.

"Thank you, son," he said. Mudarra touched the flesh of Don Gonzalo's forehead, wrinkled and warmer at least than the air around them. Thinking of his mother waiting for his return by the reflecting pool in Madinat al-Zahra, Mudarra gently pressed down on Don Gonzalo's eyelids, one set of fingers for each side, and tried his best to stay out of the physician's way. When the physician came close with the point of that odd, tiny knife, Don Gonzalo's body tensed and each assistant grunted with the effort of holding his hand and feet down. Doña Sancha visibly returned the pressure on the hand she held, but Mudarra let the lids slip from under his fingers and shut tight.

"I know it seems like a threat, father," said Mudarra, "but God can't perform this miracle without your consent." Yusuf behind him chuckled, but Mudarra had impressed himself with his Christian-sounding encouragement.

When Don Gonzalo opened his lids again, Mudarra pressed down harder, fighting the new moisture and careful not to insert fingers into the socket. When the physician approached this time, Don Gonzalo sucked in his breath to steel himself and Mudarra couldn't help it, he closed his own eyes, even while maintaining his position as if he were one of those old Roman statues in the gardens in Madinat al-Zahra, even through the various cries from the spectators and the physician's commands of "Silence!"

"Silence," repeated Mudarra in Latin without shifting.

The miracle occurred when the physician's voice penetrated Mudarra's closed world. "The incision has been successful." He hadn't had to witness the cutting.

Mudarra opened his eyes to see that the surgeon had traded his tiny knife for an even smaller one, which was as slim and sharp as a needle, and through the incision, was attempting to spear the milky disc that obscured his father's sight. Some people in the crowd moaned and shuffled away. Another small miracle allowed Mudarra to maintain his delicate hold on Don Gonzalo's eyelids while he averted his gaze from the disturbing sight. Doña Sancha was looking into the distance, and her long braid almost swung into the surgery site.

Mudarra concentrated on his father's shallow breathing. The moment extended until the physician said, "Close his eye. We'll cover both of them when we've finished, and he shouldn't open them for seven days."

"What's happening?" asked Don Gonzalo, his tears flowing in spite of his exemplary stillness.

"Keep both of your eyes closed for a moment, father," said Mudarra. He reached in the direction of the clean linens and Doña Sancha handed him one. Mudarra wiped at his father's tears, with especially gentle pats around the operated eye. He noticed shallow channels that ran down Don Gonzalo's cheeks — the tracks of old tears.

When the surgeon held the clean knife at the ready, Mudarra opened his father's other eye and said, "We're halfway through. This will be just like the first."

He looked away again for the incision and trusted the doctor when he changed instruments, but looked back when the man said, "I can't extract this one. I'm going to have to push it to the side and hope it doesn't float back over the apple." Mudarra watched with horror as the needle nudged the milky disk imperceptibly away from the pupil and iris. He fought Don Gonzalo's eyelids, which strained to squeeze themselves shut.

"Why is it taking so long?" Don Gonzalo demanded.

"This one is more difficult," murmured Mudarra. "Patience, father."

Mudarra wasn't sure how much longer he could hold on and appear unmoved by the unspeakable visions before him. He squeezed his own eyes shut and felt the muffled movements of the surgeon as he battled the stubborn disc.

"Sancha!" Don Gonzalo shouted.

Mudarra looked up and saw she had turned away and must have relaxed her grip on his father's hand. She turned to face him and patted his hand, but kept her gaze directed at the sky. "I'm here, my love. I won't leave." Mudarra decided his mother would have behaved as well as Doña Sancha if it had come to this.

"Just think, father, soon you'll be able to see again. You'll be as strong as you were when you went to Córdoba. You'll be able to ride with me."

"Mudarra, you've brought us so much, so quickly," said Doña Sancha. Her brown eyes regarded him with what he recognized as gratitude, but so profound he would never have imagined witnessing such a force on Earth. In that frank stare, Mudarra could feel some of the power that must have drawn his father back to her from a life of essential leisure. Doña Sancha dared not take one of her hands away from Don Gonzalo's in order to wipe away her tears.

When the ordeal was finished, the sun had already passed its zenith. The surgeon tied a length of linen over Don Gonzalo's eyes. "He should remove the bandage in six or eight days, and then we'll know whether the surgery has worked. Thank you," he said to Mudarra, "and thank your mother. Your help was invaluable."

Mudarra smiled and weakly patted the physician on the back, unsure whether he was meant to write a letter to Zaida for sending the physician or to verbally acknowledge Doña Sancha's stamina. He could put no words together to ask. He and Doña Sancha helped Don Gonzalo off the table and walked him to the waiting pallet in the bower. The serving girl who seemed especially close to Doña Sancha brought some kind of broth and spooned it into the patient's mouth.

"There's plenty of this for everyone," she said.

"Thank you, Luz," said Doña Sancha. "I know I won't have the stomach for anything stronger today."

"Perhaps no one will," said Mudarra. He walked outside with Doña Sancha into the cold but fresh air, where some men were already maneuvering the table and others feebly inspected the stones for the stables. The surgery had distracted him from his original purpose of setting out to stay ahead of any news that might come from Vilviestre. Now he felt strange, trying to leave when his father was so weakened and there was so much to do. But then he caught Yusuf's eye, and the guide strode over to be with them, a stalwart reminder of Mudarra's single purpose. Yusuf nodded, and Mudarra turned to Doña Sancha and recited the speech they had practiced, replete with evocations of his brothers' history.

"Before we all go to Burgos, I would like to ride ahead to Barbadillo, where Doña Lambra attempted her symbolic revenge, and Ruy Blásquez made the traitorous letters that caused my father's imprisonment and my brothers' deaths."

He emphasized Doña Lambra's name and watched Sancha's reaction, but she seemed unmoved by the role her brother's wife had played in the troubles. Perhaps the trauma of watching her brother so swiftly become a traitor had clouded her judgment. Mudarra could see that if Ruy Blásquez had never married Doña Lambra, he might still be playing the part of doting uncle to the seven noble knights, who would by now have burgeoning families of their own and far too many new accomplishments to count. Instead, it appeared to be Doña Lambra's ambition that sent Ruy Blásquez to overrun Castile and take what didn't belong to him.

"I'd rather we traveled together," said Sancha.

"I'm sorry to leave you like this, but it's a matter of military strategy. I'd love to stay and help rebuild Salas, but it will all be for nothing if I can't stop Ruy Blásquez."

"You've just come to us. It's the evil of the world that takes you so quickly from me," she said, quietly wiping away a tear.

"I'm not leaving you, really," he said, holding her to him as if he were truly her son.

"We'll meet in Burgos in three weeks' time," she replied, muffled in his tunic.

Chapter V

They packed up the carts and left the next morning amidst the cheers and songs of the entire city. Yusuf remained at his side.

"You know," said Mudarra, "even though no one has acknowledged Doña Lambra's part in the deaths of my brothers, I can't help but think…"

"I agree, my lord," replied Yusuf. "The revenge for which you were born wouldn't be complete if we didn't take her into account."

"I thought I might leave Barbadillo to you and the troops. Take it and destroy it as you see fit, and then move quickly on to Burgos, where Doña Sancha says we'll be well protected."

"And you would seek out Doña Lambra?" said Yusuf, scrutinizing him.

"Yes, to observe by myself with no army to draw attention. To try to figure out what would be an appropriate revenge, because I'm not sure what action I can take against a woman. It's puzzling."

Yusuf nodded. "You should ride with us to Barbadillo and strike out under the protection of secrecy from there. I'll sketch you a map to Busto de Bureba, where you're certain to see the lady herself."

"Thank you, Yusuf. I'll meet you in Burgos." Mudarra rode the rest of the day sharing his mount's sense of calm.

They rested the night in the forest outside Barbadillo, and in the light of dawn Yusuf led the troops to the estate and asked for the lord of the place. Mudarra felt drawn toward Bureba, or perhaps simply away from this place with its evil history, and slipped out onto the road after Yusuf had asked the fellow's name: Ermenegildo Antolínez.

Tranquilo stepped lightly through shaded, snowy woods and between rocky crags for three more days while Mudarra held Yusuf's scrap of parchment before him, turning it to match the terrain. He dared not follow roads for lack of knowing who might be his enemy in this wild place, and hoped only that the thieves and robbers had somewhere warmer to stay over the winter. Finally, chilled to the bone despite his nightly fires, Mudarra rode into a clearing of farmland that stretched as far as the mountains at each horizon. An estate, more modest than Salas but better maintained, lined the river with stone houses, stables, and pens full of hogs, chickens, and geese.

Behind the largest building, the river ran fast and playful over stones and rushes and Mudarra felt it as a current of nostalgia through his heart. The splashing and trickling sounds were so similar to his fountain-filled home. They were sounds he hadn't thought he would ever hear again. A lone apple tree had sent out shoots that struggled to bloom, as if it believed it was already springtime. Beneath it, Mudarra stopped and dismounted so Tranquilo could drink the icy water. He wondered whether he had erred the way, and whether this place was void of humans. The silence told him it was so. Even the geese regarded him with a quiet unnatural to them. The low chatter of the river, the only appreciable sound, lulled him, but his guard went up when he heard someone or something open the front door of the main house.

He ducked behind the tree trunk, from where he observed a being who radiated so much brightness he hardly dared to keep watching her, and yet he couldn't look away. As he stared, he distinguished two long braids the color of gold thread that pulled the hood from her head and whipped from side to side and front to back as the girl-woman changed her gait to suit her mood. Her mantle flew away from her body with each step, like the wings of a bird taking flight. At her neck, an underdress of an almost transparent fabric protected her fair skin from her tunic's blue wool. The skirt, covered in embroidered whorls, danced stiffly atop soft leather boots. Somewhere below the rapturous feelings the female caused in him, Mudarra thought he would visit a cobbler and have similar boots made for himself. She passed the empty bucket from one soft-looking mitten to the other as she meandered toward the riverbank. He had never laid eyes on anything like her. He stepped out from behind the tree.

When her clear blue eyes alighted on him, her face darkened into a frown. "Who are you?"

Her curiosity encouraged him not to hold back. "I'm a traveler from Madinat al-Zahra, in Castile to be knighted in the cathedral in Burgos."

"Muddy Net. . . ." An innate sadness Mudarra detected in her downcast gaze and colorless cheeks in contradiction to her demeanor couldn't permit her plump red lips to pronounce words of such rampant beauty. She shook her head. "They don't knight non-Christians."

"You're right. The Count of Castile is going to be the godfather at my baptism, and then he's going to knight me."

She looked him up and down. "It's strange you aren't a Christian. You don't look evil."

"Do you know what's even more strange? You don't look evil, either." He couldn't believe the things he was saying to her. The absurdity sent him into a fit of laughter.

"Why would I look evil?" she asked with genuine curiosity, then growing panic. "Your laugh is too loud. Hush, be quiet! I don't think my mother would want me talking to you."

"Who is your mother?" Mudarra asked, although he already guessed.

"Doña Lambra, Lady of Bureba and most of Castile. She's the count's cousin. If the count's going to knight you, it's strange I haven't heard of you."

Mudarra's heart raced. He thought he should leave and never speak to this half-woman again, but the idea made him feel even more ill. "And what is your name, my forbidden maiden?"

"Blanca Flor."

The name evoked the beauty of the place Mudarra had left behind. "So you're a white flower. What kind? Are you a rose? Or a lily? Perhaps an almond blossom?" He only meant to tease her in a way her gentle frankness invited, but as he pronounced the words, a dull pain came over his body, as old as creation. It crept into his mind and enveloped it.

"No, just Blanca Flor," she said with a half smile that made Mudarra feel he had no heart in his chest, only the ache she had replaced it with.

She turned and knelt to dip her bucket into the river, where the clean water filled it up. "The water's flowing swift because the snow is melting in the mountains," she said into the silence left by Mudarra's staring.

He momentarily forgot the warmth the maiden's presence had caused to spring up inside him, and remembered that his fingertips had never felt the pricking of such chill as they had in this strange place. "How can the snow melt when it's so cold?" he asked.

"Cold?" the girl said, pulling the bucket out of the water and sloshing the element on her mittens. Mudarra cringed at the thought of it clawing such delicate skin. "It's not cold now. Summer will be here before long." She looked at Tranquilo, who shivered with his cold drink. "You and your horse must be from a torrid place. I hope you have a warm place to stay tonight."

Mudarra patted and rubbed Tranquilo to warm the both of them. "I wonder, would your mother notice if I slept in the stable with my horse?"

"The stable boys would tell her. Would you like to come inside and meet my mother? She isn't the best hostess, but perhaps she would let you stay with us as a proper guest, and your horse in the stable besides."

Mudarra watched her expression and came to the conclusion that there wasn't much possibility of the scenario coming true. And how could he sleep in the same hall as Doña Lambra, even with a false name? Such a night would bring no rest.

"It's probably better that you don't," Blanca Flor murmured. "Well, they're waiting for this water."

Everything inside Mudarra rejected the thought of her going away. "Will you come back here tomorrow?"

She nodded vigorously. "My mother hardly ever goes outside, so she'd never suspect.... She'd never keep me from fetching the water." She bowed in farewell, pulled her hood back up over her head, and returned to the far side of the building in a more stately manner, weighed down by the full bucket. Mudarra willed the moment never to end, for that white flower never to disappear around the corner, and that was when she turned her face back toward him. The hood partially covered her expression, and so Mudarra was left with an image he could try to reconstruct all night long.

He crossed the fields with Tranquilo and set up a campsite in the trees. "Sorry I couldn't get a stable for us," said Mudarra. "But we're strong. We can withstand these temperatures as long as we need to." As long as he could go each day and be warmed by the smiles and sweet words from Blanca Flor's mouth, he thought, unwilling to admit this detail even to his trustworthy mount. He ate some cheese and bread out of his pack, flattened by the journey, then pulled out a long blanket and held it to himself while he stood next to Tranquilo for his body heat. Mudarra dared not light a fire until he could be sure no one in the estate would come looking for its source.

When he fell asleep at last, he smelled roses and almond petals. He watched the petals fall as they had always done, and felt compelled to catch a certain one. In his hand, it was the most perfect white bloom he had ever seen. He knew if he breathed on it, that would be enough to wilt it, and if he clasped it to himself, it would be crushed and killed, and yet he needed to hold it to him, to touch the silken petals and smell the delicate perfumes. If he didn't, he was sure someone else, a monstrous presence in the distance, would seize the flower and murder it more quickly than his devotion to it would. He decided to hold it gently and run, but his legs didn't work, and the monster was coming closer. When it was nearly close enough to see who it was, the dream started over again with the falling petals and his need to catch only that one.

He awoke feeling as if a cart had driven over him, digging its wheels into his spine and neck. He lifted his head to look at Tranquilo, his only companion in this strange new world in which his body resisted the harsh conditions, but his heart felt right at home.

"Good morning, Tranquilo." He took out a brush and deliberately curried his friend, who showed his appreciation with shudders and quiet whinnies. Mudarra would have given almost anything to have spent the night atop the silken pillows in his mother's chamber, soothed by her liquid-smooth lullabies. What would she say if he could tell her he had found love? Could she accept that it was possible to love the daughter of the demon Ruy Blásquez? Her stern face, recounting the way the Lara family she had loved through his father's stories had been betrayed, planted itself in the front of his mind.

He packed up some essentials in case he had to leave without visiting the camp again and rode Tranquilo to the river to wait for Blanca Flor, but only to question her about her parents and decide on a strategy. That was the reason he had come here, and he would fulfill it and return to Burgos to begin his transformation into the Christian knight who would bring the house of Gonzalo Gustioz out of poverty and humiliation.

The church bells tolled, echoing strangely off the open fields and the buildings. He sensed stirring inside the buildings and glimpsed several servants heading toward the stable, henhouse, and other animal pens, so he hid behind the main house and tried to keep an eye on the activities from the shadows. The angles were wrong, so he moved around the back corner, but found many small windows open to the morning light. He returned as quietly as he could to what was obviously going to be his post for the next several hours. People came and went all over the estate, but no one noticed the black horse and frozen rider in the shadows. The church bells tolled again and again. He prayed as best he could, although he had left his Quran at the forest camp and southeast confronted him with the stone wall. The movement and spiritual contemplations helped him ignore his circumstances, but he had pressed up so close against the wall to avoid being seen that it couldn't bring him the concentration or the sense of community he had become accustomed to. Even his mother's face, his inspiration for this patience and the questions he was going to ask, faded as he huddled next to Tranquilo for warmth. He focused instead on the cramps in his muscles and the sheen of cold on his skin despite his furry cloak. What kind of awful person would grow up in such an unforgiving environment?

Blanca Flor answered his question, coming out of the house and pausing at the river as if looking for something. Mudarra's muscles relaxed and Tranquilo responded to the change in tension with a nicker. Blanca Flor turned toward them and grinned. Mudarra took in the rows of neat white teeth, like the petals in his dream, and witnessed the material world, with its grass and trees and anger and sorrow, fade away. He felt no hunger or cold, but only joy. For a short moment, Mudarra glimpsed paradise. He returned to Earth in time to keep his body from falling over in a dead faint.

Blanca Flor approached, looking even more like a beacon of light than she had the day before. She brought her mittened hand to his cheek. It was so warm and soft, he couldn't tolerate imagining what her bare hand must be like. "How long have you waited here?" She took her hand away. Some of the fibers in her mitten caught briefly on his whiskers like the legs of a fly in a spider's web. It was all he could manage to keep from grasping her hand and holding her to him.

"Since before sunrise," he answered.

"It's after midday now. You're not used to the weather. You must be hungry and cold."

"It's not so bad," he said, his teeth chattering.

"I'll try to bring you some food tomorrow. If you're coming tomorrow." She gazed demurely at the ground as if his answer didn't matter to her.

He grinned, knowing he would return as many days as she would have him. "Yes, I'll be back. What will you bring me?"

"Do you like cheese? We've got a nice hard block of goat cheese we'll be cutting into tomorrow. Maybe I can fit some bread in my pockets without anyone noticing, either."

"Anything from your hands would be as sweet as honey," he replied. In his daze he was committing bad poetry. She turned to the river and bent to dip her bucket in with light, carefree movements. He followed and stood behind her, watching the sun glint off her golden hair and water splash off the bucket, always missing her clothing by some magic.

But if her surreptitious food gathering became known, their little idyll would be over. He couldn't risk punishment for her, not to mention what they might do to him if he couldn't keep his motives quiet. And even if they were never discovered here, how much would he have to stand about, hiding in the cold? Were a few words with a girl worth so much discomfort? His muscles ached anew and his head was bursting. He decided he would leave as soon as he gathered the information he needed.

"Why aren't there more people out and about here?" he asked before she turned around.

"These fields are to lie fallow this year. The ploughmen and other serfs are working the fields and pruning vines beyond the churchyard."

So there were many people somewhere he hadn't yet seen. "Is your father ever here?"

"Not often. I'd like to know him better, to see if what my mother says about him is true, but the longest I can remember he's ever stayed with us is a week." She set the bucket on a flat patch of ground and turned to him. "Do you need to speak with my father?"

Mudarra felt his cheeks redden before the simplicity of her question. No, he did not need to speak with her father. How could he murder the man who had created such a lovely creature? Without thinking, he reached to the side of her face to stroke her hair and her white skin blushed, all the way to her hairline and even along the part. They stood, both with cheeks flushed, until he said, "Not today," in answer to the long-forgotten question.

"Until tomorrow," she whispered, then staggered away, struggling with the bucket's weight.

Pangs of loneliness added themselves to Mudarra's woes. He waited for one of the servants to finish a journey between the main house and the stables, then slipped unseen back into the trees. He surveyed his pathetic campsite and wondered what he would do until the next day's meeting. He got as far as packing everything up into the two packs across Tranquilo's hindquarters, determined to find Burgos, where he would be welcomed and wanted and wouldn't have to hide. There were probably many beautiful maidens in the city, if that was what he was so concerned about.

But he felt he owed Blanca Flor some kind of debt, not least because she was innocent of the crimes against his family, and yet his revenge would do her great harm. He should at least tell her goodbye. After all, he had promised to return and eat whatever she managed to smuggle out of the kitchen. Muttering and cursing himself, he unbound the packs and set up his tiny tent on the rocky terrain, threw a blanket and both empty packs over Tranquilo for warmth, and settled down for another long night of the same recurring dream.

The following day, he ate his dry provisions, curried Tranquilo, and read his Quran while he waited until after the sun was high in the sky to dart behind the main building and wait for the girl he was resolved to say farewell to. To his delight, as he came around the stone structure, he saw that Blanca Flor was already waiting for him by the river, throwing stones into the swift water.

"Thank goodness you're here," she cried, pushing crushed white bread and cheese that was melting from her body heat into his hands. "Take it, and eat well. I have to get back inside."

"So soon?"

"I've been waiting for some time. My mother might suspect!"

"What would she do to you?" Mudarra asked in alarm.

She paused. "I'm not sure. We never talk about it, but everyone's so afraid of my mother that I am, too, a little bit. So I try to stay quiet." She picked up the bucket by the handle and made as if to leave. "Have you noticed how silent it is here? My mother won't tolerate any noise but the church bells. She's hit me before, and I don't like that, and then Justa has to wait until she goes somewhere to look me over or cure me. I think her coldness is why my father doesn't stay long, but she's like that with everyone, and most of us can't escape. Oh, say you'll come tomorrow, a bit earlier."

He stood speechless at the riverbank as she scurried back to the house, looking back at him with hope in her sapphire eyes. When he was safely under the cover of trees, he stood watch, absently chewing the ruined food. He waited until the sun no longer illuminated the fields, yet saw no one who might have been Blanca Flor's mother. Servants went about various jobs, and a poorly dressed woman dumped a bucket of refuse around the back, but he couldn't imagine what Blanca Flor, her mother, and whoever the woman was who cured her after a beating, were doing inside all day long. What kind of seclusion was this? It was worse than the women's quarters in the caliph's palace, because Blanca Flor never emerged, even with a veil, and she had no visitors. Mudarra gained a sense that his new duty was to rescue Blanca Flor from such imprisonment.

Most days he arrived just in time, and she gave him whatever victuals she could stash on her person. Mudarra ate any dried meat she presented and considered it part of his Christian training to become an indiscriminate eater. They stood in the shadow of the building or, if no one was about, they sat at the riverbank and spoke of things that under other circumstances would have been without consequence. However, in that short, stolen time, with the glint in her eyes and those prized moments when she laughed, each word became more precious than gold. They never touched. In every corner of his body, Mudarra needed to hold Blanca Flor, kiss her, undress her, and thrill her for days on end, but he understood it was not yet time. The corners of his soul were satisfied with the gazes they shared and the way she stood or sat imperceptibly closer to him each day. Her presence was more intoxicating than the small amounts of wine she sometimes brought him inside tiny medicinal flasks. If he ever doubted whether he should stay in Bureba one more day, Blanca Flor entered his thoughts like a scythe, cutting down all argument.

On a day when Mudarra felt the weather warming, he dismounted Tranquilo by the tree at the appointed time and sat on the riverbank poking stones with a stick in idle wait. To his surprise, when Tranquilo nickered, he looked up to see not his beloved lady, but his friend, the guide, approaching on his roan horse.

"My lord," Yusuf said. "When so much time had passed, we had to come looking for you. We found most of your supplies in the trees back there. I decided to leave the troops there so as not to reveal our secret purpose."

"I've been camped out there this whole time," admitted Mudarra.

"Have you discovered anything about our enemy?"

"Yes," said Mudarra, hoping he wouldn't pursue. "But I think I need to spend a few more weeks here, Yusuf."

"My lord, we have to get you to Burgos."

The strange circumstances of his life and how he had ended up spending his nights in vigil in some prosperous but forgotten corner of Jiliquiyya rushed back to him, as unstoppable as the rushing river before them. "Must I return to that?" he muttered.

"You have no other purpose than to return to that life," said Yusuf, whose ears must have been more sensitive than Mudarra remembered. "Has something happened here? You haven't asked what happened in Barbadillo."

Something wondrous had happened here in Bureba, but Mudarra knew Yusuf wouldn't compare the importance of it favorably with whatever news he must have.

"Please tell me what happened in Barbadillo."

"We gave them fair warning, as you probably saw before you departed. They admitted loyalty to Ruy Blásquez, and they had few men equipped to defend them, so we dispatched them and burned the buildings. We took much of the livestock, and left most of it in Burgos for the feasts. We killed everyone who resisted and left only those who would carry our message to their lord."

He regretted asking. "Women and children?"

"Some of them fell defending him whose actions cannot be defended."

Mudarra imagined the women and children as different-sized versions of his Blanca Flor and could not conscience their destruction, whether deliberate or accidental. "Was it necess... Were you obliged... Do you think God, whether the Muslim or the Christian one, looked on those actions with a smile?"

"You forget that there is only one God. You seem much more like a Christian now, with their three gods, which is just as well, since we're going to Burgos to baptize you."

Mudarra tried to visualize the ritual from what people had told him, but it was so convoluted, it seemed that his ride into Burgos would be even more mysterious than the voyage to Salas.

"But yes," continued Yusuf, "God smiled on our actions to the same degree that he wept over your brothers. That's the way some of our Christian mercenaries have explained it to me, and I think Doña Sancha would second them. I followed the orders you left with me."

Mudarra noted that Yusuf had no time for his philosophical musings. His horse danced, agitated, under him. Mudarra felt so devastated, pulled by his pleasure in the presence of Blanca Flor, and uncertain whether he should take responsibility for the destruction his own orders had caused, that he merely stood on the riverbank, unresolved.

"My lord, you can't start something like this and then stop. Did the women and children in Barbadillo fulfill your purpose? Do you want them to be the only ones who suffer? Take the suffering of Salas to its source, Ruy Blásquez."

Mudarra imagined sending Yusuf away and seeking employment with Doña Lambra so he would never have to leave Blanca Flor, or perhaps he could sweep her up behind him on Tranquilo and they could ride away to al-Andalus before anyone inside the house could raise the alarm. Both of these sounded more attractive than following this stern Yusuf. He wished Yusuf would at least display some of his good humor again.

"Mount your horse, my lord. We must go back to Burgos."

Memories of Zaida describing his duties toward his father made him step toward Tranquilo, but then Blanca Flor appeared around the corner of the main building. Mudarra's heart leaped. He told himself he was being childish, but his heart cared nothing for reason.

She approached hesitantly at the sight of the new skittish horse and his turbaned rider.

"So that's what's happened," said Yusuf. Much lower, so that only Mudarra could hear, he continued, "We can attack Doña Lambra's estate right now, or we can turn back to Burgos today."

Mudarra was outraged at the ultimatum, but knew Yusuf would carry out the threat, so he tried not to let it show. When Blanca Flor came near, he took her hand, covered as usual in a soft white mitten. "Today I must say farewell, my forbidden maiden," he said through gritted teeth.

She inhaled, a question forming.

"This is my friend," explained Mudarra, putting emphasis on "friend" so Yusuf would understand the betrayal he so suavely committed. "He's come to take me back to Burgos to be knighted."

"I suppose I knew this day would come," she murmured. She startled him with the blueness of her eyes, then cast them down. He placed his finger under her delicately pointed chin and lifted so they were eye to eye again.

"Don't be afraid," he said, both to Blanca Flor and to himself. "I'll come back for you, and when you see me again, I'll be a Christian." Making himself worthy in her eyes was the best argument Mudarra could think of for converting. She threw her arms around him and held him, quaking. Mudarra knew God, whether Muslim or Christian, wouldn't take away such a love, now that it had been granted them. For love it was, full of longing and hope, unlike any other fancies he'd taken with other girls. If some other girl had shown this much distress at his departure, he would have puzzled over it for a few moments, and then forgotten her name. But Blanca Flor had taken his heart that first day, and now, with this embrace, he was almost certain she was giving her heart to him in exchange.

"I'll come back for you when I deserve you, I swear it."

"What if I said you deserve me now?" she said into his ear, but somehow Yusuf must have heard it, because he rode forward and made his horse nip at Mudarra's hair.

"For the love of..." Mudarra started, the moment lost. He mounted Tranquilo more abruptly than the steed deserved, but reached down for Blanca Flor's hand again.

Instead of resting her hand in his, she slipped off the fuzzy mitten the weather no longer called for. "I'll tell my mother this fell into the river and she'll have another one made so my hands don't get rough," she said. "This is the only token I can give you to remind you that you said you'd return."

Mudarra held the gift to his chest and felt his throat closing. "I will honor it," he choked out. "I will honor this mitten equally with my promise."

Yusuf turned and rode back to the trees where the camp was hidden. Mudarra waved as Tranquilo followed, and Blanca Flor waved back, but soon turned away toward the river. He knew she must collect herself and not appear flustered or risk the secret of their love. With a sigh, he looked for Yusuf to find he had ridden far ahead. Mudarra enlivened Tranquilo's pace, but barely caught up with Yusuf before they arrived in the camp with twenty warriors who had been waiting.

When Yusuf dismounted and made himself busy in the cart without saying a word, Mudarra stood beside him. "Yusuf! How dare you give me an ultimatum and then act as if I were one of your lowliest servants?"

With an expressionless face, Yusuf turned to look Mudarra in the eye. "I have committed acts for you that I would not have otherwise done in my life. Your revenge is begun. You must complete it, or your life will be worth nothing."

Mudarra recognized the words of his pledge to Doña Sancha before the heads of his brothers, and his immutable fate stared down at him. "You're right, Yusuf. The words you've spoken have bound me to carry out this fate for the sake of my father and his wife. I can't blame any of this on you."

"Blame it on Ruy Blásquez. It will make things much simpler."

Mudarra wasn't sure how simple it was to focus his murderous energy on Blanca Flor's father. A hot tear sped down his cheek and he wiped it away. "I'm sorry I caused you to do things you were never meant to do, Yusuf, when it's not your destiny, but mine. Only be my friend again."

"Of course." The men sealed their reconciliation with an embrace. When Yusuf smiled, Mudarra was almost convinced he could go through with all of it.

Chapter VI

The first signs of Burgos appeared grandly over the treetops as Mudarra and Yusuf approached with their cohort. The castle brooded atop the city with its impenetrable-looking stones. When he brought Tranquilo through the woodland and saw that the entire city was walled, Mudarra wondered at the need for so much strength. The people here spoke suspiciously about the Kingdom of León, but as they approached the guarded gate and Yusuf gave the password, Mudarra realized that the greatest fear of the people of this fortified hinterland consisted of people like him, who came from al-Andalus to wreak havoc. Almanzor himself had just returned from such an incursion when Mudarra had learned about his past and true destiny. He felt strange: at the same time an outsider and inexorably drawn deeper into the labyrinth of one- and two-story wooden buildings, as if Yusuf had been guiding him all this time not merely to his father, but to his fate. He put his hand over his heart and felt the soft mitten he had hidden under his tunic, calming him with its promise.

So this was a Christian city. Córdoba's pathways were as twisted, but perhaps because of their whitewashed brilliance, the walls seemed cleaner and more welcoming than this rabbit warren of brown bricks and greying wood. Perhaps it was because he'd gone into the Andalusian capital only at times of prayer, but he didn't remember ever seeing anyone trying to usher an entire flock of geese through its corridors in spite of cross traffic and a herd of hogs coming the other direction. After pulling the soldiers through the streets of Burgos like a tangled thread, Yusuf stopped them in a more open space Mudarra soon comprehended as the cathedral square. Across from the bakery and inns, the monument to Christianity reached as far skyward as its smooth grey stone would allow, which was not much beyond the two-story structures encircling it. The double row of windows that ran up the side of the bell tower — he caught himself before thinking of it as a minaret — looked like a set of fussy eyelets, ready for lacing.

He was studying the portico, festooned with enigmatic human figures, when Yusuf drew his attention to a group of live humans approaching from behind the cathedral. At their head walked a man a bit younger than his father, but as richly dressed, and perhaps more weary with the concerns his natural authority attracted. Next to him were Don Gonzalo and Doña Sancha. She held his arm as if leading him as usual, but his stance was much more confident. He regarded Mudarra with open-mouthed astonishment. The silk cloth around his head only covered one eye.

"Father, you can see!" said Mudarra, running toward him and catching him in an embrace.

"Yes... son," he responded. "Your doctor worked a miracle."

Mudarra pulled back and looked at the exposed left eye. The lid was inflamed around the edges, but where the milky disk had once disabled him, now a clear black pupil sent Mudarra's reflection back to him. "Allah — God be praised. What about the other eye?"

Doña Sancha took Mudarra's hand and formed a bridge between her husband and his son. "Three days after the surgery, I pulled the bandage off, and he could see perfectly. But it was too much for the right eye. It went dark again within a few minutes."

"I can see well enough, my son. Thank your doctor and his assistants. I have, but I want him to understand the full depth of my gratitude in his own language."

"I will, father," he answered. His astonishment that the grotesque proceedings had had such a good result distracted him until Don Gonzalo took a ring Doña Sancha proffered him and held it up for Mudarra to see.

"The ring that led you back to me," Don Gonzalo said. "We had it reforged."

Mudarra held it in his palm to study the detail. Although the decorative whorls were missing in two opposite places where the halves must have been joined, those areas didn't appear to be weaker than the parts of the arcs that preserved every curve of the ancient beast. "It will never come apart again," Mudarra said, more because he could tell it was true than because he thought it would please his father. He offered it back, but Don Gonzalo pushed his hand away gently.

"It's yours to keep now, son," he said, tears coming from his exposed eye and out from under the wrapping.

"We would be honored if you would wear it always," said Doña Sancha. She took the emerald ring he had already been wearing on the third finger of his left hand and in its place, she slid the inherited band, hesitating over his knuckle. "A perfect fit," she said. "On that finger, your true family will always be connected to your heart."

"Oh," Mudarra said. "Now that I know him, my father is never far from my mind, and I won't forget you, ever." As he embraced her, he couldn't help thinking that she was about the same size as Blanca Flor, though not the same shape. Warmth and comfort spread over his body not from the golden band, but from the concealed white mitten.

"We're forgetting the count," said Doña Sancha. She stepped back and allowed the important man to approach him. Now that he looked, Mudarra understood that the commanding air came from a height taller than his father and well over Doña Sancha, a wide stance, and an expensive tunic as well as four tough-looking attendants.

"So at last I meet Castile's savior, sent by God from the most godless place in Hispania. You look like Gonzalo González himself. This is his body and his face."

Don Gonzalo nodded in firm agreement with the count.

Unsure how to respond, Mudarra began to bow, but the count grasped his hand to stop him and gave him a rough embrace. He grinned, revealing a gap where one of his eye teeth ought to have been.

"Ah, yes, I still forget about that. I lost that tooth fighting our enemy, Ruy Blásquez, a few years ago. My hands are still intact!" He held them up to show Mudarra fingerless gloves of soft brown leather and slim, white digits. "I haven't met him in battle since, because most of my vassals are too afraid of him to send their soldiers against him, though he's provided us no lack of provocation."

Mudarra had listened to tales of the havoc of Ruy Blásquez from the mouths of estate owners and even a jongleur, but the missing tooth in the face of the highest secular authority in Castile impacted him the most. He still hadn't said anything to the count, and couldn't come up with any words before the vastness of the problem opening out on all sides. This monster had gone far beyond ruining his father's family and had seeped into the highest levels of the nobility of this strange land with his destruction. What could a single man do against such overwhelming force, no matter whose son he was or how talented his mercenaries were? And could that monster really have engendered the song he carried always in his heart in the person of Blanca Flor?

Yusuf punched him in the shoulder blade and Doña Sancha said, "Mudarra," as if he had been drifting to sleep under their gaze.

"I will serve you against Ruy Blásquez with all my loyalty once I'm a Christian knight," he said, imagining that day comfortably far away.

"Then you'll be able to start tomorrow," the count replied.

Mudarra stood stunned. Doña Sancha grasped his hand and pulled him toward an entrance to the cathedral, shaking him from his lax state. "So soon?" he asked her.

"We'll complete the first step right now," she said smiling. "Don José sent a messenger ahead, so we've had time to prepare your baptism."

Mudarra looked back at Yusuf, who nodded. "I'm taking good care of you, my lord," he said in Arabic. They stopped outside the door.

"My baptism? Don't I need to learn more about Christianity first?"

One of the men who followed the count approached him. "Repeat after me: *Credo in unum deum.*"

"*Credo in unum Deum.*" That was easy enough to understand, *I believe in one God*. But for Mudarra, that God was called Allah and he was sure there must be some other name for the Christian God. Or was it the same God?

"That's plenty to know for now. If you have questions later, you can ask," said the man, who must be a priest because of his embroidered robes, his strange haircut, and his cross pendant. The man stepped back to allow the ceremony to begin.

"This way, dear boy," said Doña Sancha. She beckoned him inside a circle of women, each of them grinning. One of them handed Doña Sancha a folded piece of fabric Mudarra recognized as the red silk he'd given Yusuf to bring to Salas. One of the women had come up behind him and begun undoing his belt, then lifted his tunic over his head. He caught Blanca Flor's white mitten as it flipped through the air, but it was whisked away from him, too, making him feel exposed. Another woman removed his leggings, but he felt naked enough and held the knots in his linen underpants, deflecting prying fingers. They gave up, and he had no time to register the cold or embarrassment because the red silk had already been unfolded.

Doña Sancha accepted no help from anyone, and Mudarra puzzled out that the fabric had been sewn such that it made a large sleeve, not because he had the time to inspect it, but because it tightly encased his head and shoulders and then the rest of his body. He dared not breathe in, but the long journey north and his last days in Madinat al-Zahra passed before his eyes as he waited helplessly, his arms pressed to his sides, in the dark cocoon.

Gentle hands on the other side of the silk guided him to the cold ground, and then Doña Sancha was rolling the silk away from his head. He could breathe again, and while Sancha worked the silk down his shoulders, Don Gonzalo held his head off the ground, almost as if he were receiving Mudarra from Sancha. He imagined the silk was meant to stand in for the birth canal. He was being reborn, with just as little intention on his part as the first time. He lifted his body from the ground by clenching different muscles to help the process and watched Doña Sancha pulling and tugging, past his chest and catching a little over the rings on his fingers. His knuckles retained them in their place and he let his arms flop to the ground when she delicately moved the fabric over the undergarment. He was glad the symbolic tube was made of silk, because if it had been wool, he might have suffocated inside a scratchy sleeve they would have had to cut him out of.

Doña Sancha swept the sleeve off his feet and folded it hastily into her dress.

"Now you are truly my son as well as Don Gonzalo's. Now you may truly call yourself Mudarra González."

"...ibn Zaida..." Mudarra whispered, although in his mind, an image of his mother flaked away as if it were being studiously erased with a knife.

"Now you must take revenge not only for my sake, but also for Doña Sancha's. She is your mother by Castilian law," Don Gonzalo said.

Mudarra wanted to say something, to say goodbye to his real mother or to thank Doña Sancha for accepting him, but he was pulled inside the church door as if he were a grain of sand in the great tidal winds. Yusuf stayed outside somewhere, and had probably abandoned him and ridden back to Andalusia, so Mudarra bowed to his parents, acknowledging the words spoken.

He turned and saw that the cathedral was filled with men and women standing shoulder to shoulder, with no separation inherent in the architecture, except for the area in front of what must be the main altar. He hadn't realized women would be allowed into such a sacred space. The windows, tiny compared with the grand archways of even the smallest mosques Mudarra had entered, had pieces of colored glass in them, but didn't let in much light. Paintings of what he supposed were saints or scenes from the Bible in lurid reds and yellows loomed over the flickering candles, which were positioned at every possible height. Before the main altar rested a large stone basin full of water. He looked back to the hundreds of people, but found no friendly face, only curiosity.

Doña Sancha took his hand once again and led him to the basin, where the count and the priest waited. Doña Sancha and Don Gonzalo stood on either side of him, and the priest recited in Latin. At a certain point Mudarra couldn't have distinguished from the others, Doña Sancha told him to step up into the basin. He stood shin-deep in the water, shivering a little. He covered his erecting nipples with his palms and had plenty of time to feel embarrassed, not only because he was almost nude but also because things were expected of him, but he knew not what.

"Kneel, my son," said Doña Sancha.

He lowered himself into the basin, careful not to splash the water out onto the floor. He winced as it covered his knees and soaked into his linen. Don Gonzalo moved, and Mudarra faced the congregation. Every man, woman, and child stared back at him with an improbable mixture of distrust and joy, their eyes glinting in the candlelight. The priest, who hadn't ceased reciting in Latin, picked up a flat white seashell and scooped some of the water into it, only to pour it back over Mudarra's head. He shivered violently as the cold liquid found its way down over his goosebumped geography. Regaining his self-control, he wiped the water away from his eyes and was rewarded with his first sight as a Christian: long golden braids, a delicate pink mouth, and blue eyes that studied him with unabashed wonder. He could see Blanca Flor as if the noon sun shone upon her, the only recognizable face in the crowd.

For a moment he thought he'd died, or perhaps was having a mystic Christian vision, but the image lingered and seemed to speak to the person next to her, and he was convinced that she was truly there. She would've had to take a different road, since no one in his band had seen her, and ridden hard to be there so quickly. It must mean she loved him as much as he loved her. Her eyes met his like a dart finding its target. He became obsessed with an outlandish idea that razed all the plans of his father, mother, the count, and these other extraneous people. Love had simplified everything.

He barely heard the rest of the ceremony, but thanked whoever it was who put his clothes back on him, and held onto the white mitten in one of the folds of his tunic. When the priests retreated to the chambers behind the altar, the crowd began to disperse. A drop of water splattered his nose, so he ran his hand through his sopping hair and directed the water backward, where it crawled down his neck with the deliberation of a portent. He knew he would have little time before his father and Doña Sancha—his new mother—collected him to fulfill yet another obligation, so he strode toward Blanca Flor, ignoring anyone and anything between them.

Her smile was as wide and striking as he remembered, but she said nothing. He took her hands in his and carried out his plan. "Blanca Flor, I'm a Christian now. Will you marry me?"

Her face locked into an expression of surprise. Mudarra could no longer resist: he embraced her, holding her to him and shielding her from the commotion of too many people around them. He felt her relax against his chest as if it were the only place she ever wished to be, and the emotion overcame him. He reached up to wipe a tear from his eye, and only then did he notice the woman nearby who watched them. She had the same blonde braids and style of blue wool dress as Blanca Flor. His blood turned to ice, but he didn't let go of his beloved. "Doña Lambra?"

"My name is Justa. I was Lambra's foster sister, and now I'm Blanca Flor's nanny."

Mudarra noticed with relief that Justa's dress didn't have as much embroidery as Blanca Flor's, and she wore no jewelry. She couldn't have been Doña Lambra.

"Thank you for bringing Blanca Flor here."

"I know what it's like to love someone. I couldn't say no," said Justa so quietly Mudarra strained to hear. She glanced about as if she were a hind pursued by hunters. "We've taken a risk coming here. Lambra thinks we've gone on a pilgrimage to Santa Olalla, and that isn't very far from Busto de Bureba. We need to leave right now."

Blanca Flor turned her face up to Mudarra's. Tears flowed down her cheeks. He didn't want to think about anything else; he only wanted to hold her into eternity. His lips found hers under their own will.

It was unlike any kiss he'd had before. They entered a space without noise, in which time didn't pass. They must have crossed the veil separating the earthly realm from spirit, because the only thing that existed in that space was pleasure. It wasn't the basic bodily pleasure he'd experienced in the women's quarters, but the pleasure one feels when nothing is out of place, when one is in the right spot at the right time doing the right thing with the right person. Blanca Flor was his other half, and he rejoiced in having found her. Suddenly, he wasn't sure she was aware they shared this destiny. He pulled away, and the sounds of people chattering all around whooshed into his ears.

"You can't kiss in the cathedral!" someone shouted.

Blanca Flor placed her soft hands on either side of his face and drew him closer to her. He took it as a signal that she loved him the same way, and prepared to enter that state of bliss again, in spite of what people were saying. But she merely brought him close enough to hear what she asked. "Are you going to kill my father?"

Why would he want to do such thing? Mudarra sighed as the world's meaningless details came back to him. "Your father is Ruy Blásquez. If he were anyone else, I would protect him with my own life, simply because he's your father. But...."

"But...?" Blanca Flor's face was a contorted portrait of pain Mudarra couldn't bear to think he had caused.

The figure of Yusuf entered Mudarra's field of vision. He had taken off his turban in order to enter the cathedral, but its lack did nothing to lessen the didactic value of his presence as he took a place beside Justa.

Mudarra shook his head in disbelief. "I don't have a choice," he told Blanca Flor.

She shuddered and collapsed onto his chest, wetting the front of his tunic with her tears. "I don't know my father very well," he felt more than heard. "My mother isn't very fond of him. Justa and I will return to Bureba and never say anything about this to my mother..."

At these words, Justa seized Blanca Flor's shoulders. She stared at Mudarra so intensely that it made him even more leery than Yusuf's gaze. "You're planning to take revenge on Doña Lambra, too, aren't you?" she demanded. "Promise you won't kill her."

Mudarra felt as if he were a mouse cornered by three indignant cats. He looked earnestly at Justa and opened his mouth, trying to form words that would satisfy all three of them, but Justa cut him off. "Don't promise me. Promise Blanca Flor. Tell her you won't kill her mother."

He tried to look into her eyes, but they were downcast and flooded with tears. In his confusion he said the most cowardly thing that came to mind. "But you said you were afraid of your mother."

"She's all I have," Blanca Flor whimpered.

"No, darling, you have me. I can take care of you always." She leaned away, and Justa took the opportunity to pull her away.

"How can I accept someone who's planning to kill my father?" Blanca Flor said in a voice that would have echoed off the archways if it hadn't been so hollow.

Mudarra clutched her arms over Justa's hands and pulled her back toward him. "I won't do anything to harm you. I'll only do exactly what I have to," he whispered, but knew Yusuf could hear him, anyway.

Suddenly Blanca Flor let out a piercing scream. Mudarra let go, realizing they'd been tugging at her as if she were a piece of rope. Her face was ashen, wilting before his eyes, and she looked ever backward while Justa escorted her through the doorway. He made as if to follow, but Yusuf had unsheathed his scimitar and now lowered it in front of Mudarra as a symbolic portcullis. Outraged, he put his hand to his hilt, but of course there was no weapon there, only a mateless white mitten. He'd just been baptized and was barely beginning to dry, while the only meaning he'd found in his life was transported far away.

"I'm sorry, my lord," Yusuf said. "You seemed distracted."

"Mudarra, what's going on here?" Don Gonzalo asked. He and Doña Sancha had made their way through the thinning crowd and appeared as if by magic to help Yusuf return Mudarra to the path he'd come to Castile to follow. "Who was that girl?"

Yusuf had replaced his weapon at his side. "No one," he said in the absence of a response from Mudarra. "An old acquaintance of mine."

"She seemed awfully upset," said Doña Sancha.

Mudarra felt the tears rising. To fight them back, he pronounced the words that described the only reality that would bring him happiness. "She's a good Christian lady I would like to marry once all of this is over."

"Oh," said Doña Sancha.

"None of our other sons showed such a readiness for marriage." Don Gonzalo chuckled. "We can talk to her family when Lara is once again the most powerful region in Castile."

"Yes, for now we have to ready you to be knighted tomorrow," explained Doña Sancha.

"Ready me?" Mudarra was baffled. They hadn't had to prepare him in any way for the baptism, but now they were going to take great pains to explain knighthood to him? "I've trained and studied my whole life."

"Don't worry, my son. We've taken care of everything."

Chapter VII

The scholar had a long grey beard that would've reminded Mudarra of the fakirs in the court of Hisham and Almanzor if he had accompanied it with a simple turban. He had been talking nonstop for what might've been days. After the baptism, Mudarra had attended a feast in the great hall of the castle as guest of honor. They had stuffed him full of pork, and he'd felt slow and stupid when they'd brought him into the cloister of the cathedral. At the bottom of the swirling sensations caused by so much food and drink, he'd been grateful his senses were dulled and his thinking and memory impaired.

Someone, probably Doña Sancha, had shown him the quiet, arched space and said that before his ceremony, any knight-to-be must keep watch through the hours of darkness and prepare himself mentally for the responsibilities of knighthood. Normally, the vigil was a solitary process, but in this case, they'd been fortunate to have in Burgos with them the man who'd written the definitive treatise on Christian knighthood.

They sat facing each other on a bench wrapped in cloaks and furs, and with only a sliver of moonlight to see by, the man began to tell Mudarra the things he ought to know. Mudarra felt a glimmer of hope that at last he could resolve what this revenge had to do with him and whether he could maintain his Christian honor if he killed his bride's parents. When it became clear that there was to be no instruction on how to conduct himself in his specific case—there wasn't even a mention of knights who were new converts to Christianity—Mudarra suspended himself in the comfort of his drunkenness.

Now that the learned man had gone on for so long, the stupor had begun to wear off, and panging thoughts of Blanca Flor and what he had to do to her family crossed between his ears with terrible regularity. He fingered the mitten and sighed.

"I'm doing this as a special favor for Count García," the teacher said. "If you're bored, I can return to my home and leave you here to contemplate what it means to be a knight on your own."

"I might fall asleep."

"I'll send in servants to prod you awake every hour."

"I'd rather have the benefit of your wisdom, teacher," said Mudarra. He thought he might be able to get a kind of half-waking rest if the man continued droning until daylight.

"Very well," said the scholar. "No more sighing."

"No, my master," replied Mudarra, opening his eyes wide to appear alert. How did they expect a man to enter knighthood with a clear mind and pure heart if they kept him awake all night? Mudarra knew when the moment arrived, his only desire would be for sleep.

When the sky was brightening from black to blue, the droning tapered off. Mudarra snapped to attention. "Am I ready?" he asked.

"Only you know when you're ready," the scholar said. "But it's dawn now, and I've told you everything I've written in my book." Mudarra imagined how the night would've been different if he'd been permitted to read the book himself and search its pages for meaning. "Do you have any questions?"

"Questions?" said Mudarra, surprised. He felt suddenly more alert than he had been since before he'd left his mother. "Yes. How is a Christian knight different from a Muslim one? Principally, is it Christian to carry out the kind of revenge I'm destined for?"

The learned man looked surprised now. He narrowed his eyes and cocked his eyebrow in consideration. Shaking his head, he seemed ready to speak when one of the priests or priest helpers entered the cloister.

"Don Mudarra, it's time," he said.

"It's time? What do you mean, it's time? I'm about to get some important answers here," he answered feverishly.

"Go ahead," said the teacher. "You've been an excellent pupil and must be ready." He patted Mudarra's arm as if that put an end to any doubts he could have.

Mudarra stood stiffly and followed the priest, dragging the cloaks with him. The teacher followed him and picked up the ends of his garments when they went out into the street. In the cathedral square, more than five hundred people jostled for position, and when Mudarra emerged, they all cheered. There was none of the previous doubt in their expressions, and for the first time, Mudarra felt as if he belonged in Castile. He smiled when he distinguished the knights from the retinue Almanzor had granted him, and even those who had pushed and shoved their comrades for a view moved out of his way. He needed no one to lead him, but headed for Count García, who waited on a platform they must have built the night before, while Mudarra had imagined everyone asleep.

His head high and his knees aching with cold, he ascended the steps to the high-backed wooden chair, where the count sat regally. Mudarra knelt before him as he thought he remembered the teacher saying he should do, and looked up at the red and gold painted castles that covered the chair, the banners held by some twenty pages, and even the count's robes.

"Mudarra González, do you present yourself this day to me, your lord, as a good Christian and with a pure heart?" the count declaimed above the roar of cheering.

"I do."

"And do you pledge homage and promise loyalty to the County of Castile, and to defend it against enemies, winter or summer, day or night?"

"I do."

"And will you hunt down the traitor Ruy Blásquez and stop him from ever betraying Castile again?"

Buoyed by the constant rumble of approval from the crowd, Mudarra replied, "With all my heart, I will."

The crowd became deafening until the count stood, his robes falling into stiff waves around his ankles. He waited, smiling widely enough to reveal the missing tooth, until he was sure to be heard. "Then I hereby dub you knight, Don Mudarra González. Additionally, I have brought together one hundred salaried knights to aid you against our enemy today."

That made approximately four hundred troops under Mudarra's command. While the trumpets blared and the crowd roared and stamped their feet, he wondered whether any of them were Christian generals who could instruct him in predicting Ruy Blásquez's strategy, but the count was speaking again.

"I declare you *alcaide mayor* of all the land. No other knight shall rank above you and all shall be called into your service whenever you have need of them. The traitor Ruy Blásquez once held this highest honor, before he took my castles, and before him, your brother Diego González."

A chill went through Mudarra, in spite of the people's warm reception of the news. He wondered at the declaration. How could he represent Castile as its highest military power when he could barely grasp its customs, and that with a lot of help? He sensed someone standing behind him, a solid, reassuring presence, and couldn't resist the urge to look back to see who it might be. All he saw was the empty edge of the platform and the steps leading down. He faced the count again while another chill passed through his heart and bones. He'd never known anyone who had died, not before his mother had told him about his brothers. Could it be Diego González visiting in the form of a *shebah*, summoned at the mention of his name and rank to complete his unfinished business? Mudarra wiped away a tear of pity, but the count appeared not to notice.

"I regret that I cannot grant you fortresses, since the traitor has taken them from me, but I do grant you the open lands without cities or castles on them to begin with, and any castles you can win from Ruy Blásquez will be yours to govern as you wish."

"I thank you, my lord, for so much generosity," said Mudarra as loudly as he could. The crowd quieted as the knights strained to hear what he would say. He kissed the count's white hands. "I will serve Castile with my strength, intelligence, and vassals, but I cannot accept the castles I'm sure I will take from Ruy Blásquez. I intend to win them for you, Lord of Castile, for my ambitions do not venture so high."

Several cries of "He's right" and "How just" emerged above the vigorous cheering.

"Very well," the count said. "I have many other gifts to give you at the palace inside the castle. There will be feasting, bullfights, and jousting in your honor."

A band of fife and drum players led the way out of the square and most of the crowd followed, taking with them the manner in which Mudarra had kept his spirits afloat. He dreaded more feasting, more cheering and cajoling, especially if he had a ghost following him with a single-minded goal. Truly, he wanted only to return to a bed full of pillows and think about Blanca Flor, to see whether he could dream up a way to honor her request and maintain the promises he'd just sworn to.

Several people worked against the tide of revelers and headed toward the platform. The first to show themselves were Don Gonzalo and Doña Sancha, whom he could not refer to in his mind as his parents, as tenderly as he felt toward them.

Mudarra held out his hand and Doña Sancha took it as she climbed the steps. She embraced him and put her whole body into the effort. Don Gonzalo joined them on the platform and said, "We're so proud of you."

"Thank you, father," said Mudarra, using what air Doña Sancha hadn't pressed out of him.

Yusuf ascended the steps and clapped Mudarra on the shoulder. "You've done very well."

The words gave Mudarra something of a foundation to stand on. He nodded and smiled. "I guess I have."

"Of course you have, my new *alcaide mayor*," said the count.

There remained one more person who had not followed the musicians to the castle. He ascended each step one at a time, laboring so that only the top of his grey head was visible to the others. His cloak was embroidered with leaf patterns and castles and the hand that held the knob of his walking stick was embellished with sparkling rings, so it was strange that no servant or squire helped him on his way.

"Who are you?" asked the count.

The man looked up from his place on the steps and said, "Count García, I am one of Ruy Blásquez's retainers. He sent me with a message. Pity an old man and do not harm me."

"Of course not, Sir Knight. Come and deliver your message."

Mudarra was so anxious to hear some evidence that Ruy Blásquez was a living human being that he went down and took the man by the waist to ease his progress. On the platform, he leaned on the knotty stick that served as his crutch and caught his breath inside a tight circle of people that included the count's banner holders.

"Ruy Blásquez has sent me to tell you he's heard of this Moor come from Andalusia to avenge the house of Lara and that he holds him in no regard. He says before the year is out, he will meet him in battle and, just as he sent the heads of the seven noble knights to their father, so will he do with this child, God willing."

Mudarra heard a gasp beside him and turned to see Doña Sancha limp in Don Gonzalo's arms. Mudarra cupped her face in his hands. "Don't worry, Doña San . . . mother. That coward may send as many messengers and say anything he likes, but my head isn't going to be separated from my shoulders. I will find him and stop him long before the year is over, or else my life has meant nothing."

She blinked, breathed in, and exhaled with a nod as Mudarra pulled her out of her husband's arms to stand on her own. Seeing that she was stable, he turned to the old man. "Have you come from Ruy Blásquez himself?"

"Yes."

"Has he instructed you to keep his location secret?"

"No," the old man said, shaking his head. "I was with him in Amaya."

Mudarra turned to Yusuf. "Is it far?"

"It's not far to the northwest. We could be there by nightfall tomorrow if we left now," said Yusuf with his characteristic seriousness.

"But I doubt he'll stay in Amaya, now that he's sent a message to you," the old man said.

"So, he's the sort who would flee rather than hold to the threat he's made?" Mudarra asked.

The old man chuckled. "Doña Lambra doesn't know about you, so she can't order him to face you. He'll keep running for as long as he can."

Mudarra couldn't help but bark a laugh at the spinelessness of the traitor who'd wreaked such destruction and loomed so powerfully evil in his childhood imagination. He preferred chasing his phantom enemy and meeting him head-on to attending another feast that only represented a delay to the destiny he couldn't escape.

"All the more reason to get started." Mudarra caught Yusuf's eye. His friend bowed to the count and sped down the platform steps to rouse the troops away from the festivities. "Count García, where may I find the salaried soldiers you've granted me today?"

"Wait right here, Don Mudarra. We'll bring them to you," the count said.

He gestured, and one of the banner carriers scrambled down the steps behind Yusuf. Another pair of trumpeters escorted the messenger off the platform, in the direction of the castle, perhaps to share some of the feast with him. Mudarra's stomach ached with emptiness and he envied the old man, who could hardly walk, but would at least be comfortable today. "We'll take some of the food for the feasts with us as our provisions."

Mudarra's traveling retinue returned to fill the square in short order with their carts. They helped each other don their chain mail and then turned to those who had leather plates to fasten their ties and buckles. Yusuf ascended the steps with Mudarra's armor and fitted him as efficiently as if he were a squire.

"When we're chasing that traitor, we must be armed and prepared at all times, because we can never tell when he might ambush us," Mudarra said.

"It's a very good idea," said Doña Sancha. "Much as I wish it were not so, everyone knows I have the strongest possible blood tie to Ruy Blásquez, but since he married Lambra, I haven't been able to predict or comprehend his actions."

"This is a fine army you're assembling," said the count, his gaze fixed on the activity in the square. "I will send my own troops to Urcejo and Urbel, not only to take them back from the traitor, but also to try and distract him and divide his army."

"Thank you," said Mudarra smiling. Between them, they would create an infallible strategy. Yusuf fastened the last stay and Mudarra felt impenetrable. "Where is your armor, Yusuf?"

His friend wore cloaks that would only keep out the cold. "I need to stay flexible if I'm to guide the army to Amaya, where roads may not exist, if we even wanted to travel by them."

"And what would you have me do?" Don Gonzalo asked the count.

"You'll come home to Salas with me and wait for news." Doña Sancha spoke the plans Mudarra had assumed.

"But I can see to ride now. I can keep up with Mudarra and his soldiers, I'm sure of it. I have even more interest in bringing Ruy Blásquez to justice than Mudarra, since he betrayed me and tried to have me killed. Please, Don García, I have been the father of two of your *alcaides mayores*. Let me join my son on his important mission."

The count smiled. "Such decisions are up to my *alcaide mayor*."

"No, Mudarra. Don't take him away from me," said Doña Sancha.

"Everything will be fine," said Don Gonzalo, holding her close. "I'll be back in Salas before you know it, delivering the good news to you myself."

"You said very similar words before you left with my brother, all those years ago."

"No harm can come to me now that our savior is here."

Don Gonzalo held out his hand to Mudarra, who disliked being called a savior. He had been catching almond blossoms without a care in the world a month before. Now he was not only a Christian, but the designated savior of what should be a powerful group of Christians. His life was too strange to make any decisions. But Yusuf nodded vigorously, so Mudarra took his father's hand and said, "Of course, it will be an honor to have you by my side, advising me as we defeat our enemy together."

"You will defeat him and come home safely," said Doña Sancha, between a question and a command.

When Mudarra hesitated, Yusuf stepped in. "He will, or his life will have no meaning." He gestured toward the square, where the additional hundred knights had arrived to stand with the other three hundred, their swords shining in the morning light, their targes and roundels polished to a sheen.

Mudarra felt as if no time had passed since he was nine years old, running through the maze-like corridors of Madinat al-Zahra, escaping the chastisement of his mother, General Ghalib, and even the visiting dignitaries. How had he arrived at the head of this glittering army when all he ever wanted to do was run? It occurred to him to run now, to push past his father and adoptive mother, and the count, and even his friend Yusuf and run in the direction of Bureba until he found Blanca Flor or exhaustion overcame him.

"The fulfillment of your life's purpose," Yusuf whispered in his ear. "See how much your father wants to help you. Look what good soldiers support you."

When the last word ended, a swath of dust or a fine mist obscured the front line. Before Mudarra's eyes, the chaotic material coalesced into human forms. At first, they were transparent and colorless, but with the passing seconds, they took on colors and became nearly solid. He wondered if they were shadow beings, trickster djinn come to cause chaos in the ranks. Each man had dark brown hair and was armed with the red and gold emblems of Castile. He recognized all seven faces. He'd beheld them before, in the candlelight at the church in Salas. Mudarra, his stomach still aching, cast his gaze around the square to test whether he were having visions brought on by the lack of sleep and sustenance. Perhaps he would see Blanca Flor again. But there were no other unusual signs in the plaza. The ghostly *shebahs* fixed their grim expressions on Mudarra and would not look away. He knew they must linger on Earth until their souls judged that their bodies' lives had not passed in vain.

The count, Yusuf, Don Gonzalo, and Doña Sancha didn't appear to have noticed the new additions to Mudarra's dedicated fighters, who now brought the total to four hundred seven besides himself, Yusuf, and Don Gonzalo. The living people seemed to be waiting for some words.

"The count assures me that this is the finest gathering of knights to ever take place on Castilian soil. We will soon face an enemy who has wrought all manner of destruction and untold pain upon our greatest families. But that enemy is cowardly, and has few to support him, now that we have decided to set things right. We cannot fail. Are you with me?"

The living troops raised their swords or clubs or shields. "For Castile, for Santiago, and for the *alcaide mayor*!"

The seven knights remained still, their hands at their sides, unblinking, although the diaphanous material that made them flickered with the living soldiers' movements. Mudarra knelt at the edge of the platform so his lips would be closer to their ears.

"You'll be able to rest soon."

The seven brothers turned and disappeared like so much smoke.

Chapter VIII

No sooner had they exited the city gate than Mudarra halted at the head of the column. The signal to stop traveled backward until each one of the four hundred awaited instructions.

"I haven't eaten for more than half a day," said Mudarra. "Let's make use of some of these provisions."

The feast from the night before should have tided him over for several days, but there was no arguing with what his stomach told him. They sat on the carts or atop their shields, blocking the road, and devoured some of the ex-feast meats. Some of the bread was still warm.

The food cheered Mudarra, and he realized what good company he was in. Following Yusuf's lead blindly, he listened to Don Gonzalo's stories of life before Ruy Blásquez's second marriage, always looking to make sure his father didn't steer his mount into a tree or a rock. With only one eye, he wasn't as aware of the space around him as a good rider needed to be. Mudarra heard his soldiers assuring the new recruits of his magnanimity, and by the end of the day it was no easy job to distinguish between the two groups. They often broke into song to ease the traveling, and after he'd heard them a few times, he found himself singing along, about rotten provisions, cold campsites, battle wounds, and easy women.

Though he studied his surroundings in order to acquaint himself with this Castile he represented, he caught himself abandoning the trees and bushes that all looked alike in order to retreat into his mind and contemplate Blanca Flor's golden hair or intense blue eyes. Would she have reached Bureba by now? What was she doing at that moment? Did she cower before her mother, only to slide under her blanket and think about Mudarra and the earth-moving kiss they'd shared?

If he wasn't careful, he'd lick his own lips, savoring the memory. There was only ever half a chance Don Gonzalo would see his distraction, but even riding ahead and examining the trail for traces of those who might have gone before, Yusuf had a supernatural talent for noting when Mudarra was forgetting the purpose of his life.

"Do you need to stop and rest, my lord?"

"No, thank you, my friend. We should forge ahead while conditions are good and the enemy can't be sure we're coming. Say, friend, do you think these songs are appropriate for a band of Christian warriors?"

"I've never especially liked the songs about camp whores, but they help set the rhythm of the march. There's no real harm in them."

Mudarra was relieved to have company in his discomfort with the subject matter at the same time that he enjoyed the spirit of camaraderie they created. He looked back to find his father handling his mount with surprising agility over fallen branches and continued uninterrupted, joining the warriors in a rendition of "Our Phalanx is the Best Phalanx."

He thought they must have made good progress when they stopped for the night near a river, an excellently appointed place for the four hundred of them to set up tents, dig into the unfailing food stores, and water their horses. He was sure they had made good time when he heard Yusuf whistling along with the rest of the men.

Don Gonzalo's eyelid drooped while he sat by the fire, doing his best to follow the conversation. He fidgeted with the linen over his bad eye, as if he wanted to shutter the other eye, too.

"There is no shame in going to sleep, father," said Mudarra. "Allah — God knows, we've had a long day."

He helped Don Gonzalo get settled on a pallet in the tent where he and Yusuf would retire for the night. Mudarra kissed him on the forehead before he removed the linen around his head and replaced it with a clean one, fastened loosely over both eyes. It must have felt somewhat comfortable, as his father was snoring before he returned to the fire, where Yusuf stared into the flames and idly poked the embers with a green stick.

"When this is over, what will you do?" Mudarra had a vague notion that he wished his friend's answer to include abandoning his life of constant travel and staying with him wherever he and Blanca Flor found a home.

"I'll return to al-Andalus and join another expedition to Jilliqiyya." The flames threw deep hollows into his young face. "But I do wonder when it will be time to stop. You have a defined end to your mission, but when can I say that my stints as a guide through Christian territory have completed my life's purpose? Perhaps my life's meaning is waiting for me in some other occupation or among other people. Perhaps Almanzor will send emissaries to France or Germany and I can meet their learned men. I don't know, but Allah will provide in the end."

"Of course," said Mudarra, confused. He badly wanted the mission to come to an end so he could search for Blanca Flor and find the way to her forgiveness. But if fulfilling this preordained revenge meant that the first friend he'd ever had and upon whom he'd come to rely would wander off into the wilds of Europe without a second thought, he asked himself whether he was enthusiastic for their time together to be over.

"I think I'm as exhausted as my father," said Mudarra.

"Go to sleep, my lord. More good progress tomorrow."

He never knew whether Yusuf had come to sleep, and in the morning they were off, fully armored again, as if they had been practicing such speediness for months. When night was about to fall, they came upon the castle at Amaya, on a rise in the middle of an empty field that was big enough for an army three times the size of Mudarra's to make camp.

The four hundred of them strode to the main castle gate and displayed their swords and drawn bows. When the door remained sealed and the ramparts silent, Mudarra began knocking his sword against his shield boss, and when the others joined him, the racket echoed off the stone walls. Soon after, Yusuf spotted a woman between the crenellations atop the wall who waved her arms to attract their attention, so Mudarra gave the command for silence.

"There's no one here," she said. "Only me, my husband the castellan, and our son, and daughter, and servants."

"Was the traitor Ruy Blásquez here?" Don Gonzalo shouted up to her.

"He was, but he left two days ago, taking his knights with him."

"I hereby claim this fortress for Castile and Count García," said Mudarra in remembrance of his knighting ceremony. "If you accept, and if you let us in, we can give you food and supplies to last until the count can see to you."

When the woman failed to react, Don Gonzalo said, "This is Don Mudarra González, the new *alcaide mayor*. He has the count's ear and will follow through with his promise."

The woman disappeared. Mudarra looked at Yusuf.

"She's probably discussing it with her husband. They'll open soon."

While they waited, Mudarra felt something akin to shame for his thoughts the previous night. Had his reluctance to bid farewell to Yusuf stalled the ending of his duties? Was his useless confusion over friendship to blame for Ruy Blásquez's flight? Was this what the Christians called guilt?

At last, the gate cranked open. The first inhabitant to appear was a small girl in a grey woolen dress with bare feet. Mudarra's heart reached out to her because her auburn hair was the same shade he thought his children with Blanca Flor would have. An older boy emerged to throw his arms around her protectively. She threw him off and advanced toward what could have been an average sight for her: four hundred armed men and nearly as many horses.

"Mama and papa have to open the gate together," she said. "Come in."

Enchanted, Mudarra followed the girl and her brother into the castle's outer courtyard and waited for the men, beasts, and carts to join him, walking Tranquilo around overturned buckets and wet straw. The children busied themselves with discarded chain mail and saddle parts that lined the walls. It was as if Ruy Blásquez had left in a hurry moments before.

The castellan and his wife met him as he dismounted. "We must apologize for the state of the place, my lord. Ruy Blásquez isn't accustomed to leaving a place so quickly, and he took all the able-bodied men except my husband. We haven't had the labor to tidy up properly," said the woman.

"No matter," said Mudarra. "Now that we're here, we'll help you."

"Are you the Moor come from Córdoba to redeem your father's inheritance?" asked the castellan.

"Of course he is," said his wife. "Just look at him. He's the very image of Gonzalo González."

Mudarra blushed, thinking of the handsome ghost he'd seen. Everyone else was seeing that ghost in his own face.

"He's also the new *alcaide mayor*. We can't stay long," said Yusuf. "We have to follow Ruy Blásquez and meet him in combat. You say he left two days ago. Do you know what direction he headed?"

"I'm almost certain he headed for Castro, Sir Knight," said the castellan. The boy left his sister with a bucket and came to stand by his father's side.

"Then we're off to Castro in the morning," said Mudarra, eying Yusuf. His friend nodded in answer to the tacit question of whether he knew how to get to the place.

"I know how to get to Castro," said Don Gonzalo.

"Father, may I go with them?" said the boy.

"Of course not," said his mother.

"You didn't want to go with Ruy Blásquez," said the castellan.

"But these men are going to defeat Ruy Blásquez. I want to go with them."

"Have you attained your age of majority?" asked Don Gonzalo.

"Have you trained in the military arts?" asked Mudarra, astonished at the ambition in such a gawky youngster.

"No, but a lot of knights have come through here and taught me how to handle a sword. Just three days ago, Ruy Blásquez himself taught me to swing a mace."

Mudarra laughed, though he wasn't sure why.

"We can't take you with us on such a dangerous mission," said Yusuf.

"Thank you," said the castellan's wife.

"Please?" begged the boy. "I could assist the archers. I could tend the horses. Anything to help win back castles for Count García."

"Your patriotism is inspiring," said Mudarra. "I'm sorry we can't take you, but it puts my mind at ease, knowing the people of Castile want to restore legitimate power to the count as much as I do."

It turned out that Ruy Blásquez hadn't left the castellan's family destitute, so when Mudarra left Yusuf to oversee the distribution of provisions, he returned to the chamber within the hour. Mudarra no longer felt guilty about having wished the mission wouldn't end. He understood that Ruy Blásquez had escaped that night so God could send him the castle with no casualties and the boy's message of support for his mission. He was so comforted that he nodded off before he and the knights received an invitation to join the castellan's family in the great hall for supper and whatever entertainment they could dream up.

Don Gonzalo sat close to the castellan, so Mudarra took the opportunity to speak in Arabic with Yusuf. He had decided his confusion was unnecessary. Yusuf had seemed frustrated with the constant traveling. All Mudarra had to do was tell Yusuf what he wanted and ask if he'd join him.

"Yusuf, if you're not sure what to do when this is over, please consider staying with me as my friend and retainer."

"Will you continue to fight battles for the count?" His friend took a swig from the goblet. "Would you expect me to guide you through terrain that will inevitably become part of al-Andalus sooner or later?"

Mudarra looked down into his potage, which wasn't as murky as his thoughts. "I would never expect you to betray the caliph or Almanzor," he murmured.

"What do you think your life will be if you continue to be the count's *alcaide mayor*? You won't get to choose your friends. The count will decide whom you attack and with whom you make peace."

"Perhaps the count will let me live my life in peace with a wife and children and vassals."

"When will you forget that girl? What would I be in your little household? Your stable boy?"

"That girl? Her name is Blanca Flor, and she will be your mistress." Mudarra threw down his spoon and they stared at each other. The other diners looked for the source of the tension.

"Gentlemen, do you have some argument? Why not settle it with a game?" said the castellan.

"Do you have a chess board?" Mudarra didn't care whether Yusuf had ever played before. He would win the match, Blanca Flor would be his, and Yusuf would faithfully serve them wherever they went.

"I'm sorry, we don't," replied the castellan. "You could throw dice or darts."

"I will not risk my lord's future on a game of chance," said Yusuf. He stood and bowed to the castellan's wife. "I am very sleepy. I hope you won't mind if I retire." He walked in the direction of the chambers without waiting for anyone's response, the turban he had never given up wearing casting bulbous shadows on the wall. Mudarra appreciated Yusuf's principles, but was saddened he couldn't make his friend understand that love was more important than war. He stayed up most of the evening throwing darts with his troops in the hall, then lay down on a pallet there and spent the rest of the night stroking the white mitten and wishing it were morning so they could be on their way.

They departed Amaya armed and Yusuf led them over streams and hillsides to arrive at Castro to a familiar scene: a castle on a hilltop populated only by the castellan and his least able-bodied retainers. Ruy

Blásquez had taken the knights and added them to his army and left for Saldaña the previous day. And so Mudarra gained the castle at Castro for Count García peacefully. He left a few more provisions with them so they could hold out until the count came to see to their needs or sent someone in his place.

Blanca Flor haunted Mudarra. It seemed at all hours she was telling him to convince Yusuf to stay with them. He imagined overseeing the workings of a productive farm, perhaps the estate at Busto de Bureba so Blanca Flor would never have to leave her home, his only worry whether the wheat would be blighted that year or whether the oats would be enough to feed the livestock. Yusuf would enjoy such a settled life, but Mudarra could barely get his friend to look at him, much less think of the right words to say. They arrived in Saldaña in the evening of their seventh morning on the road without having settled the matter, and found an empty village with a few sickly chickens and an ass too stubborn to leave.

"Where has he gone now?" Mudarra asked no one in particular.

"I'm not surprised. That traitor is fleeing all over the countryside, bringing every place he stops to ruin," said Don Gonzalo.

"My lord," said Yusuf, "I think we should stay here tonight. I'll be able to follow the trail in the morning."

"Very well," said Mudarra. "I suppose we can stay in these abandoned buildings."

"My lord," said Yusuf. He gestured toward the army, who, in spite of the frantic pace and frequent disappointments, had never ceased laughing and singing all the week. "This appears to be more of a chase than a battle for now. The knights would never say it, but they must be exhausted with carting their armor and supplies. Why don't you send them back to Burgos? You and I and your father can continue the search unencumbered, and send for them when we finally find Ruy Blásquez."

Mudarra looked at his troops and understood the wisdom of the idea. None of the knights had the strength to pull on their horses' reins to keep their heads up and the slumping shoulders belied the smiles on their faces.

"It's an admirable idea, Yusuf, one that shows unity with the cause," said Mudarra. His friend appeared to be about to speak, but he turned and addressed the soldiers. "Men, you have followed me faithfully and with good cheer, not to mention some very nice singing. Because this mission has become a chase or hunt instead of a battle, my advisor suggests we will be better able to search out our prey if there are fewer of us. We'll stay here tonight, and you may all return to Burgos in the morning."

When they threw up a great "Hurrah," Mudarra looked back at Yusuf. "Thank you. I think this will help. Can you truly pick up Ruy Blásquez's trail?"

"Of course. He and his troops have left telltale signs all over the roads they've followed. We may find him as soon as tomorrow if we move quickly enough."

In the morning, after they'd moved provisions from the carts into the saddlebags of Don Gonzalo's, Yusuf's, and Mudarra's horses, each of the four hundred warriors clasped Mudarra's hand to renew their pledge of support. Most also gave their thanks for allowing them to return to Burgos until they were needed. Yusuf inspected the signs their enemy had left, mounted his horse, and faced his chosen direction, impatient as his horse pawed the ground. At last, Mudarra watched the backs of his soldiers disappear around a bend, and he was alone with the men who had become the most important in his life since he'd left Madinat al-Zahra.

"Let's find the traitor," he said. Don Gonzalo raised a whoop and trotted in the direction Yusuf had been pointing. Mudarra and Yusuf galloped to catch up, and throughout the day, they maintained a faster pace than they would have been capable of with the rest of the army in tow.

Each time Mudarra caught the look on his father's or Yusuf's face, it was a smile. They laughed with the sensation of shared freedom and of a well-completed destiny. When they slowed to step through a rocky creek, Mudarra addressed Yusuf in Arabic.

"Have any of your other lords been such a loyal friend to you? Have any of them ever offered you a permanent position before?"

"No, Don Mudarra. That is why I'm taking your proposal into consideration."

"You are?" Mudarra's disbelief turned to relief when his serious friend smiled at him again. "When Blanca Flor and I get settled, you'll be the first person we bring to the estate. You can have your pick of any duties — or powers, for that matter."

"Perhaps I could be overseer of the harem?" said Yusuf, his smile turning wry.

Mudarra chuckled, then thought it over. He had been raised in the women's quarters, so he'd had more contact with women than the average man in Córdoba. On the other hand, he'd seen women absolutely everywhere in Castile. There was hardly any separation of the sexes. He tried to remember the layout of the estates and castles he'd already visited. "I don't think Christians in Castile have harems."

Yusuf laughed.

"You really must speak Christian, my son, now that you're the *alcaide mayor*," said Don Gonzalo.

"Of course, father. I have no secrets from you."

Yusuf struck out ahead into the trees and the other two followed as quickly as the obstacles allowed, laughing as if it were a game of skill. Mudarra had plenty of time during the day to contemplate what his life in Castile might be like without his friend and guide. Without Yusuf, Mudarra would never understand much of anything. He would be obliged to go back to al-Andalus, regardless of the high rank he had with the Count of Castile.

They dismounted when they came to the bank of a river Yusuf told them was called Carrión. Holes in the ground where tent pegs had been, patches of ground scorched under cook fires, discarded animal bones, and a broken wagon wheel indicated that the area had recently been occupied and even more recently abandoned.

"Yusuf, was it Ruy Blásquez?" asked Mudarra.

The guide scratched under his turban and took a long view of the riverbank. "It had to have been. What other army is moving so quickly without an obvious destination at this time of year?"

"The longer it takes for us to find him, the less respect I have for him," said Mudarra. "What kind of coward would keep up this pace after threatening to meet me in battle? He doesn't sleep the night in the same spot where he eats supper!"

"I lost any respect I had for him as my brother-in-law long ago," said Don Gonzalo. "The only thing keeping him so powerful for so long was fear."

Yusuf spat. "I don't know how we'll ever face him in combat. He is no worthy enemy of the *alcaide mayor* of Castile."

Mudarra was moved by Yusuf's loyalty. "Thank you for saying so. But he is the enemy I must face. How many knights do you think he has with him?"

"Given the space they occupied, and the mound of bones over there, either Ruy Blásquez is skilled at hiding his numbers, or he has no more than two hundred soldiers."

"That matches my estimate," said Don Gonzalo, squinting in the sunlight.

"So he has half the number we sent back to Burgos," said Mudarra, watching his father pick up stones to throw into the river. "God is truly on our side."

When they passed through Monzón finding similar evidence of Ruy Blásquez's passage, and when the castellan at the tower of Morojón indicated that he thought the traitor had left in the direction of Dueñas, Mudarra's sanguine outlook faded.

When the trail from Dueñas led them back to a freshly abandoned camp site at the Carrión, Mudarra cursed under his breath.

He followed Yusuf through Pisuerga, Tariego, Cabezón, and Serrato, smiling and accepting the praise, encouragement, and hospitality of the citizens they met. They showed their grateful support for his cause with fresh food and bedding, the finest they could offer, but his frustration prevented enjoyment. He wore his disappointment like a sickness that gave him an inability to stay awake longer than a few hours and an acute sensitivity to light.

He took it into his mind that was being sent through some kind of Christian purging process in order to clear the Moorishness out of him. When he prayed to God and Jesus and the Holy Spirit, he asked for this Sisyphean labor to end. Blanca Flor appeared to him as the promised reward, if only he could suffer adequately.

Yusuf took his arm and dragged him from his bedroll at their campsite on the Esgueva River, and Don Gonzalo had to help with the task to get Mudarra to rise from his slumber in Aranda del Duero.

Finally, one afternoon at Coruña, a little girl told Don Gonzalo that Ruy Blásquez and his soldiers had departed that same morning. Her mother indicated it was likely they'd headed for Espeja because they'd taken the southern road. All at once, Mudarra's illness lifted. He dismounted Tranquilo and snatched the little girl into his arms, not neglecting to embrace her mother. He hopped back onto his faithful horse and said to his father and Yusuf, "Let's keep going. We can probably catch them tonight, can't we, Yusuf?"

Yusuf was nodding a qualified agreement when several other adults came running out to see who this man was who ravaged women and children.

"It's all right," announced Mudarra. "I'm the *alcaide mayor* of Castile, and I will defeat Ruy Blásquez."

They departed Coruña with cheers Mudarra hoped the enemy army couldn't hear, wherever they were. After dusk, they spotted the lamps of a town through the trees. Keeping cover, they approached and observed some twenty buildings that lined either side of a crooked street that wove upward along foothills. At the lower end, well-dressed men reveled outside what must have been a tavern, and beyond that building, carts and enough tents for two hundred soldiers surrounded several campfires.

"They'll never catch us!" one of the drinkers shouted over the roars of his companions. "Ruy Blásquez is the most elusive prey in Christendom."

"I think we've found Ruy Blásquez," Yusuf whispered.

"If anyone's found him, you have, Yusuf," said Mudarra. Hope's seed had been planted, and he cared for the new growth by following his friend's wise directions. Yusuf sent Mudarra and Don Gonzalo with their horses and supplies to different vantage points, which they pledged not to abandon until one of them could verify that their enemy was among the army assembled there. Mudarra employed the energy his disappointment had conserved in watching everything each man did in the town, never pausing to sleep in the hidden bower among the trees Yusuf had set up for him near the spot where they had first stopped. He strained to listen and disdained blinking while he observed the older gentlemen and the way the soldiers behaved in their presence. No one had ever described his enemy for him, so any of them could be their infamous leader.

On the second day at noon, Yusuf and Don Gonzalo approached Mudarra's hiding place with so much stealth, they didn't even disturb the sparrows until they reached out for him, and he jumped in surprise.

"I've seen the traitor, son," said Don Gonzalo, so low that Mudarra was obliged to read his lips. "He's had the audacity to take his goshawk hunting in the valley beyond the town."

"Are you sure it's Ruy Blásquez? How can he go hunting when he could be captured at any moment?" mused Mudarra.

"He must think we've lost the trail," whispered Yusuf. "I wouldn't have guessed such a coward could show so much pride, but your father has identified him beyond a doubt."

"It's my brother-in-law, pride and all," confirmed Don Gonzalo. "It's time to send Yusuf for your knights."

"Yes," said Mudarra, "but how will we prevent Ruy Blásquez from fleeing while we wait for them?"

"Follow him," replied Yusuf. "Leave signs for me to find. He won't get very far, because I'll bring your army with all speed."

Mudarra watched Yusuf leave as secretly as he had arrived, then turned to his father.

"You look exhausted, son. Why don't you rest? I'll keep watch and make sure he doesn't get away."

Mudarra must have been more tired than he'd realized, because he lost consciousness while thanking Don Gonzalo. When he woke in the middle of the night, they continued to keep watch, but this time in shifts, and with breaks for the food and drink in their saddlebags. When there was no sign of Ruy Blásquez among the soldiers for two more days, Don Gonzalo returned to his vantage point in the valley and reported back the following evening that the traitor had been hunting again.

"He sent his goshawk after a heron," said Don Gonzalo. "I think he goes every morning, but I don't know where he must be sleeping and eating."

"Did he seem pleased with the results of his hunt?" asked Mudarra, stretching out his arms and rubbing his neck, tense with the wait.

"No. The birds disappeared into the trees and he never saw either of them again. I think it's a sign that our time draws near."

"I hope you're right, father. There's nothing worse than waiting." He couldn't help but think how strange it was to lie in wait for Ruy Blásquez when all he wanted to do was present him with gifts and ask for his daughter's hand.

Yusuf shook Mudarra out of a deep slumber. There was no light anywhere, but Mudarra recognized his friend's voice. "I've left the army a few leagues back so as not to attract attention."

"Good thinking," Mudarra said while he tried to remember where he was and what he was doing. "What hour is it?"

"I think it's about three hours before sunrise."

"Can we move the troops into the valley in silence? Don Gonzalo thinks Ruy Blásquez goes hunting every morning. It would be an ideal place to present our ranks and our readiness to fight."

The sun came up to reveal not an empty valley ripe for hunting, but four hundred three warriors, most on horseback, prepared for whatever enemy they might meet on that field. Petting Tranquilo's neck in appreciation, Mudarra headed up the formation, with Yusuf on his right and Don Gonzalo on his left. To either side, a single row of archers equipped with roundel shields extended all the way to the trees. Behind them, footmen and cavalry stood ready in their separate sections, each with a sword and shield and a multitude of other weapons stowed in various places in their or their mounts' armor.

With the arrival of the light, the knights stopped taking pains to keep silent, and soon were talking, singing, and clanging their weapons as much as possible. Mudarra knew they would be heard, and Ruy Blásquez's army must come out to meet them, but when? As the sun intensified its rays in the valley, he felt the quilting under his reinforced leather waistcoat wicking hot moisture away from his skin. He hadn't had time to check on his father or Yusuf, but saw that Don Gonzalo rode covered with mail and stiff pieces of armor, while Yusuf's extravagant robes could have been covering anything. He decided not to disturb the high-spirited composure they'd achieved by asking about such a trivial detail. He wondered whether the seven ghosts he'd seen in Burgos would make an appearance on the field. From what he knew of ghosts, they would emerge to see their business completed, so they might be his only signal that he was going to avenge his brothers.

On the far side of the valley, warriors emerged from the tree-lined hills and took their places single-file under shouted commands. Try as he might, Mudarra couldn't find the source of the shouts. In what seemed like minutes, the enemy army had assembled in a similar formation to Mudarra's, although the lines were half as long and not as deep. Their estimate of two hundred soldiers had been accurate. A clear gutter, filled only with grass and a few early butterflies, had formed in the space between the companies, wide enough to make the faces indistinct. Once every man was in place, a last command rang out and the archers nocked and drew their bows taut.

The threat was too obvious to ignore, although the army remained anonymous. Would Ruy Blásquez reveal himself? Mudarra addressed his warriors.

"Friends, stand your ground and make no move. I want to see if that traitor will come out from hiding among his knights. If he does, the world will talk about what happens. If they begin to flee, you should follow them because I will not rest in my pursuit. Today my brothers will be avenged, or I will die upon this field."

The men showed their approval by clashing their weapons against their shield bosses, but Mudarra raised and lowered his arms several times. Although he held his shield and sword, it was the signal for quiet.

The two groups stared at each other during a silence in which Mudarra thought he could detect the movement of the sun across the sky. The archers in the front enemy line began to quiver under the strain, but Mudarra wouldn't give his command to shoot. Finally, the voice traveled unimpeded across the grasses. "Who are you?"

"I am Don Mudarra González, *alcaide mayor* of Castile," said Mudarra, confident they could hear him as distinctly as he'd heard the question.

"That cannot be. I am *alcaide mayor* of Castile."

So the speaker was Ruy Blásquez. He was mounted, near the front of the formation, but surrounded by horsemen on all sides and well behind the archers. Mudarra had to overcome considerable surprise that his mythic enemy was a mere man, and not a very big one at that. His grey hair stuck out under a brown leather cap helmet and his grey beard put Mudarra in mind of a wise man, someone who should command his respect, not meet him on the battlefield. It frustrated him not to be able to look the legendary beast in the eye.

"Count García Fernández dubbed me knight and made me his highest ranking protector in Burgos before every one of the men behind me. I represent Castile and you represent your own interests."

The knight in the middle of his protective cushion hesitated, and another to his side whispered in his ear. "What are you doing here? Since you came to Lara you've greatly offended me, killing my men and burning my villages. But now that you're here, you'll pay for those offenses with your own body."

"You lie, traitor. I have committed no offense, but only defended Castile against your pillaging and usurpation. But today you will right all the wrongs you've ever conceived of."

"It will be you who pays today. These are my most loyal vassals. They won't leave me, and if you advance your army, we'll have you out of that saddle, and no one else will ever dare attack me. We'll send sad news of you back to my old sister this evening."

The mention of Doña Sancha startled Mudarra, but also reminded him why he was in this valley in the middle of nowhere instead of safe in Madinat al-Zahra with his true mother. He considered the ill he would cause Don Gonzalo and his dear wife if this ended badly and weighed the risk he was taking with the soldiers' lives, not to mention the life of his own father. He cleared his throat.

"Let's put an end to this. Instruct your cavalry, and I'll instruct mine as well, to stand aside and let us fight each other one on one."

At that moment, one of the archers nearest Ruy Blásquez could withstand the tension no longer. His bow snapped the arrow into a spinning line headed straight for Mudarra. Time slowed. The knights behind him moved their shields into position, and Mudarra raised his own targe to catch the projectile. He knew exactly where it would leap to, and put the boss in its path so the point would bounce off and fall harmlessly to the ground. But when time sped back up to its normal pace, the arrow erred and set itself into Yusuf's left arm, accompanied by inhalations of surprise and horror from both armies. Yusuf let out a strangled cry and only avoided falling from his mount because the bowman who stood on his other side caught him. Evidently, Yusuf had not worn any armor. His turban tumbled to the ground.

"Yusuf!" cried Mudarra. "Why didn't you have someone dress you in mail at the very least?"

The injured guide gave a weary chuckle while three soldiers held him up. "If I'd worn mail, the arrow would surely have gone into one of the holes. We can't avoid what's meant to be." His hands were empty of weapons and his flowing white sleeve had already become a garish red from the point of entry downward. "You must finish this business. It's meant to be."

"Take him to the physician and cure him," Mudarra shouted. "Clean him and bandage him. I have need of him." He looked back at the enemy lines and saw that the archers had lowered their weapons.

While the ranks parted so the three knights could carry Yusuf behind them into the trees where their carts and supplies were stowed, Ruy Blásquez shouted across the grassy line. "Is your man injured?"

"Yes, and badly," said Mudarra.

"We expect full reparation," said Don Gonzalo.

Ruy Blásquez ignored his brother-in-law. "It will please me to fight you, Mudarra, one on one, with no interference from either of our armies."

"Very well," said Mudarra. "Instruct your soldiers not to move no matter what they see, and I'll do the same."

The knights met his gaze expectantly, although they must have known what he was about to say.

"Thank you all for defending Castile so faithfully. I've made an agreement with our enemy to meet him in single combat, and this will be to the benefit of your entire nation. The actions of only two men will settle this matter once and for all. No matter what happens, do not intervene. If I fail, my father may retrieve my body."

"Long live Don Mudarra! Long live Castile!" the warriors shouted, and applauded.

Mudarra turned to run out and meet his fate, but Don Gonzalo held his arm out to stop him.

"Son, that traitor has been a coward up to now, but he's a strong knight. None in Hispania is his equal in armed combat, but I know him well. Let me fight him so that I may avenge my sons and myself and spare you."

Mudarra wanted to dismount and beat the ground in frustration. Had he come so far only to have his father take over at the crucial moment? No, Yusuf would not stand for it.

"I can't allow it. It would falsify the agreement I've just made with our enemy and the pledges I made to the count. I will not take on that traitor's evil customs merely to defeat him." He stared at his father in wonder and recited the pledge. "I must take revenge for my brothers, or my life is worth nothing."

Don Gonzalo's gloved hand brushed away a teardrop that could have been the result of sorrow or his recent surgery.

"Godspeed."

Mudarra received the blessing gratefully and kissed his father's hand through the glove, then faced the open green area and waited for Ruy Blásquez to finish haranguing his soldiers. He rode up and down the front of the formation.

"Those of you who came here squires, I made knights, and those who were already knights, I increased your wealth and shared what I had with you. You're all my vassals. Be warned what will happen to any one of you who abandons me in this field. I will defeat the son of the renegade princess by myself, and once his body is carted away, I will hunt down every last man I find missing and make him regret his disloyalty. Stay right here until I call for you."

Perhaps he had been generous with his knights at some point, but Mudarra was amused to note that none of Ruy Blásquez's warriors shouted their agreement or wished him well. He ceased his chuckling when, without preamble, his enemy charged toward him, lance lowered. Mudarra urged Tranquilo onward and aimed his lance, as well. In the next instant, he was flat on his back on the soft grass.

Spots of dew wetted his hands and the back of his head, letting him know his helmet had fallen off. He sat up and inspected his left arm, which ached from what must have been a spectacular blow. A gaping hole in the mail and the quilted padding on the front side had a twin on the back side, but he could find no blood, even as he patted up and down his arm. The lance, miraculously, had not touched his flesh. As best he could reckon, the lance had hooked into his sleeve and pulled him off Tranquilo, who stood a few strides away, just a little shaken. The lance lay broken on the ground next to him. But where was Ruy Blásquez?

The only man he had ever been trained to fight lay on his back a few paces behind Mudarra. Mudarra stood, checking his legs to make sure they were steady, and walked over to where his enemy's horse was nuzzling his face.

Mudarra pushed the animal away and inspected the bloody gash where his lance had connected with the man's chest. His helmet had flown off, as well, leaving his hair a grey spray on the grass. Mudarra looked Ruy Blásquez in the face for the first time while the crooked-nosed traitor whispered to him, wheezing.

"Don Mudarra, for the love of God, don't hit me again. I'm already dying from the first blow. And please don't harm my vassals. They have no guilt for what I've done."

Mudarra's attention wasn't on whether his enemy's words were sincere, for he could barely hear them. He had assumed Blanca Flor looked just like her mother, but now he found that the sweet mouth he wanted to kiss until it could kiss no more was an exact copy of the presumed gaping maw of the supposed monster Ruy Blásquez. He could not hit the person attached to that mouth even though that person had wounded his friend just now and killed his brothers many years before. He stood dazed for a moment, then collapsed into a kneeling position as if he were tending to Ruy Blásquez's wound instead of contemplating giving him another.

"Finish the traitor! End it now!" Don Gonzalo's voice came at a gallop behind him.

But Blanca Flor's lips spoke with a masculine voice. "Have mercy." The dew rose up from the grass in eight man-sized whorls. Mudarra waited for the figures to emerge: Muño Salido, Diego, Martín, Suero, Fernando, Rodrigo, Gustio, and Gonzalo, all recognizable from the chapel. Despite their insubstantial material, whether it was a gossamer fabric or a collection of wisps of sand, all were armed and as vigorous as if they had never died. The handsomest one, Gonzalo, handed his transparent sword to Gustio and lifted Ruy Blásquez's solid, shining blade from its place on the ground. The ghost set it into Mudarra's waiting hands.

"Must I?" Mudarra asked.

"Yes," said Don Gonzalo, who had dismounted, panting. But Mudarra had wanted the ghosts to answer, and didn't turn back toward his enemy until each of them in turn had given their silent nod. He stood and faced the prostrate man, holding the hilt in both hands. He tried to focus on the twisted nose, surely a sign of evil. But it was the result of Mudarra's brother's blow, and it was a worse offense than the count's missing tooth.

If it had been anyone else, he could have listened to Don Gonzalo and plunged the blade into the traitor's neck, providing a swift and merciful demise. But even at standing distance, the shape of the man's mouth proclaimed his close relationship to Blanca Flor. It seemed as if she begged him in the name of love not to harm her father again. He wondered whether his two tallying angels would record this deed as good or ill, then realized they had probably left him when the priest had poured the chilly water over his bare skin.

"*Ana assif,* Blanca Flor," said Mudarra. He turned his body, holding the hilt in his right hand, and caught a glimpse of the ghosts before he squeezed his eyes shut. The ring that had brought him to his father guided his hand as he swiped the sword randomly downward and let go when it stuck in something. The first thing he saw when he opened his eyes was that the ghosts had disappeared, so he knew he'd done well in their estimation. The surprise in his father's face made him look back at Ruy Blásquez.

The sword had fallen to his enemy's side and was covered in blood. The gash in Ruy Blásquez's left shoulder was so deep that his upper arm appeared to be an indistinguishable clump of gore. Blood had splattered his beard and lips, so Mudarra was no longer reminded of his Blanca Flor, though the wound did remind him of Yusuf, who had been injured because of this weeping soul that clung to its dying body in desperation. Even as Mudarra judged that Ruy Blásquez could bleed no more, he wondered how Yusuf must be recovering and whether he would be proud of what Mudarra had done. The skin under the layer of blood was white, drained of life. And yet he spoke.

"Let me die of these wounds. Don't hit me again."

"Do you think he'll die on his own?" Mudarra asked Don Gonzalo. He knew he couldn't continue to stab this helpless man, although he had once been the terror of Castile.

"I'm glad he still lives," said his father. "We'll take him to Sancha in Burgos. She dreamed of drinking his blood, but perhaps his sister will have mercy on him when she sees what he's come to."

"Do you accept becoming our prisoner?" Mudarra asked, leaning toward the spattered face.

The monstrous traitor, barely holding his arm to his body in the tight grip of his right hand, managed to say, "Yes." He fainted. While Mudarra's soldiers brought a board and transferred Ruy Blásquez to one of their carts, one of the enemy knights approached. Mudarra visually inspected the ranks from afar and could tell that there were no longer two hundred warriors in the group. Many must have fled after their leader fell from his horse.

"Don Mudarra, please don't blame us for Ruy Blásquez's acts. We followed his orders, that's all. If you want us to serve you now, we'll do it gladly," said the soldier, on his knees before Mudarra as if expecting a religious blessing.

"Those of you who haven't fled, you mean," said Mudarra.

"No, we've stayed to face whatever justice you see fit to mete out to us," the knight said.

"It won't be necessary to serve me. Only uphold the count's possession of Castro and Amaya. In fact, now all the count's inheritance must belong to him to dispose of as he sees fit. Always know who is your lord."

"Well said, my son," said Don Gonzalo, "but we'll have to take these knights prisoner until the count is assured of every last one of his castles."

Mudarra left Don Gonzalo to supervise the manner in which the prisoners would be transported to wade through the confusion of activity in the ranks to the place they had set aside for curing the injured. A pair of warriors worked together to stanch the flow of blood from Ruy Blásquez's shoulder. He had regained a semblance of consciousness and was mumbling nonsense as if the men dressing his wounds heard his confession. Yusuf was resting peacefully atop a blanket. Mudarra might have forgotten his injury if his skin hadn't appeared so blanched.

"Wake up, Yusuf! Don't you want to know how the combat turned out?"

A warrior Mudarra failed to recognize stepped between the friends. "I'm sorry, my lord. He bled out. We tried to save him."

"No," said Mudarra. "No." Yusuf was still a Muslim, so he had a succession of angels ahead and behind, protecting him by God's orders. It was not possible for him to have died so uselessly.

He took Yusuf's face in his hands and tried to comprehend the meaning of his friend's lack of expression. He opened the eyelids with his thumbs and they stayed open, offering no resistance. They revealed dull blue irises and clear black pupils that reflected his own raised brows and wide eyes back to him.

"No, come back, Yusuf. You must come back. What will I do without you? If you come back, I'll give you a harem to oversee, just like you said. It will be the only harem in all of Castile, and you will be in charge of it."

When his friend didn't awake even to tell him how stupid the joke was, Mudarra dropped the useless head back onto the blanket and turned away while the soldier measured out lengths of linen to wrap the body in. Ruy Blásquez's babbling harassed Mudarra's ears like the wings of a persistent fly.

His accomplishments lay spread out chaotically before him. The copious blood the traitor had shed to pay for his crimes stained the grass. His father employed his eyesight to direct the prisoners who would help to restore the Castilian fortresses to the count. Four hundred of his knights were alive and well. These details illustrated that he had achieved everything he'd set out to do because Yusuf had told him it would bring meaning to his life. But Yusuf could no longer reassure him that it had been the right thing to do, or that it had been worth the effort. He must've imagined the ghosts of his brothers and their tutor with their unfinished business, because according to his new religion, their spirits must be sitting at the right hand of God, partaking of the banquet of the holy. They could have no interest in these meaningless worldly affairs. But Yusuf's last words to him had implied that all events were somehow preordained. Did that give them meaning? How would he ever find out? What would he do in this strange country, in this strange world, without his friend?

Chapter VIIII

Doña Sancha finished her prayer and turned to look at Luz in the flickering orange light. The count had granted Sancha five other ladies to accompany her everywhere, to dress her and anticipate her needs, but Luz was the only one who knelt before the figures in each chapel and prayed with her after each mass she had paid for to ensure Mudarra's success. Luz was no longer some skinny girl Sancha had taken on in an act of charity, but a woman who had endured every hardship and sorrow by her side, and her youth and beauty had suffered for it. Sancha knew the genuflecting must hurt Luz as much as it did her own old bones, and yet there she was, her muscles tense, her hands clasped, her eyes shut tight, and her lips rapidly moving with whispered supplications that consistently lasted longer than Sancha's heartfelt pleas.

They had come to the cathedral every day at least three times to hear the regular masses and the midday ceremonies she'd exchanged for Mudarra's gifts since her husband and son had left so suddenly. The count had arranged to continue the feasting and games, but Sancha could take no comfort until they returned triumphant. After fourteen mornings and middays, her energy flagged while a devil planted doubts in her mind about what could be taking so long, but Luz had provided a perfect example of constancy. The girl—would Sancha ever see her as anything else?—deserved the grandest reward she could dream of, and so Sancha redoubled her prayers for Mudarra's victory. She would pray as long as God wanted her to, but today, as they crossed themselves and stood up from their places in front of the Santiago chapel, she had a strong feeling that the moment was drawing close.

Sancha and Luz filed out of the cathedral, the serving ladies following after. Most days, they started back to the count's palace within the castle in solemn silence, but as they passed the baker, who was closing up his shop for the day, Sancha said, "Luz, I think the time when I will be able to reward you is near. If I could grant you anything, what would you ask for?"

"You've rewarded me through the years with your kindness, my lady, and more recently with these rich clothes. I couldn't ask more."

"Truly? Wouldn't you rather get married?"

"I would prefer to serve you for always if my other choice was to go with a husband who would accept a wife as old as I am. But now that you say it, perhaps you wouldn't mind hearing my impossible wish?"

"Of course, girl, tell me."

"I'd like to spend the rest of my years in the seclusion of the convent, if I were certain beyond a doubt that you and Don Gonzalo were well cared for."

Doña Sancha halted in the street and embraced Luz while the other ladies did what they could to avoid running right into them. "Whatever you wish." In Luz, God had provided Sancha a sort of daughter, and it wasn't much to ask. She was sure they could find an abbey or convent with a reasonable dowry. It was all the better to give such a faithful girl to the church to pray for them in seclusion. How much more powerful would her prayers be then!

Sancha took Luz's hand and they climbed the crooked path. When they reached the castle gate, guards, pages, and retainers saluted them with as much respect as might have befitted the cortege of the countess. "The count is hearing the end of Doña Elvira's case," said one of the old knights, who had been a close advisor of the count's father, and who reminded her of Muño Salido.

"Thank you," said Sancha, and she and her ladies slipped into the great hall and found their seats to the side of the proceedings, as they had every day since Mudarra's soldiers had left, except feast days. Across the space, Count García sat regally in the center of a dais, his son, Sancho, sullen beside him.

Doña Elvira de Amaya, a window younger than Doña Sancha, was bringing an accusation against her neighbor for the death of her husband. Her brother represented her before the count, and Sancha imagined with sorrow that she would have had no man to protect her if her brother had succeeded in murdering her husband fifteen years earlier. She shuddered, and Luz offered to fetch her a cloak, but Sancha warmed to witness that though the brother argued his sister's case competently, the lady often hissed or snapped her fingers at him from her seat among the spectators and whispered what appeared to be instructions. Count García caught Sancha's eye and chuckled into his hand. Perhaps this woman wasn't as helpless as the Visigothic lawgivers had made her out to be. The previous day, Elvira had held her boy and girl close to her, likely to show the count how destitute they were without her husband, but the children had made such headsplitting wails that the count had sent them out of the hall with one of Elvira's maids.

The brother made his closing arguments with a confidence he could only have derived from Elvira's prompting. The neighbor roundly denied any wrongdoing. The count sat up and declared, "This case is very serious, and likely has consequences for both parties. I will pass judgment tomorrow morning. Reconvene at terce."

Because of the commotion of defendant, accuser, and spectators getting up to quit the chamber for the day, at first Sancha didn't notice that more people were entering than departing. All of a sudden, she was looking into the eyes of her brother, the little Ruy whom she'd helped raise and who later betrayed her so treacherously, for the first time in fifteen years. They were bluer than she recalled, bloodshot, and waterlogged. The siblings shared an instant of surprise before he turned his head away with a groan. A moment or two passed before she understood what was happening.

Ruy Blásquez lay strapped to a board on the floor in front of her, dried blood in his beard and stiffened linen bandages around his torso, leaving him unable to move his left arm. Two soldiers stepped away from the board, drawing Sancha's attention upward, where she found her husband smiling at her. She stood and embraced him, noticing that he was accompanied by many knights, and that when the court spectators had seen who had arrived, none of them had left. The room was far too crowded. She looked back and could no longer see the count on his dais over the multitude of heads.

"You've been successful, my dear husband," she whispered in Don Gonzalo's ear.

"At long last, my darling," he said. "We couldn't fail, not with God on our side, but this coward fled like a hunted rabbit, and it took us some time to find him."

Doña Sancha searched out her brother in his place on the floor and strode through the knights and maids so that she was in a position directly over him. He studiously avoided looking back at her, no matter where she moved. "Where is Mudarra?" she asked her husband.

Don Gonzalo gestured to his son beside him. His posture was so poor, and he looked so unlike the strong and confident *alcaide mayor* she'd seen off all those weeks before that she might never have noticed him in the crowd.

"Mudarra, welcome back to Burgos, and praise God for your success," she said to him. He did not look as if he welcomed an embrace.

"Doña Sancha, I bring you the traitor. Let him be sentenced for his crimes in the manner that best pleases you," he said as he might have to a foreign prince.

She considered her response, inspecting the blood stains on Ruy Blásquez's bandages. She spoke before the sight of the blood could overwhelm her imagination. "God be praised, and thanks be to Him for the mercy he has shown me, for now my dream has come true." The end of the vision she had dreamed before Mudarra's arrival pressed upon her memory. She felt compelled to carry it out to the letter. The saliva built up in her mouth. She knelt next to the broken figure who had once been her brother. She touched the bandage at his shoulder and tested its tautness. When it wouldn't budge, she found Luz standing beside her and said, "Bring me a knife, dear girl."

"What for?" asked Ruy Blásquez with terror in his voice, although he fixed his gaze somewhere beyond Don Gonzalo's hand.

"Mudarra's arrival and protection of Salas was revealed to me in a dream," Sancha said, willing her words to force her brother to look at her. "And in the end of the dream, you were defeated, and I drank your blood."

"My lady . . . my mother," Mudarra said, taking her arm and pulling her away from Ruy Blásquez. "God would never want a traitor's blood to enter the body of one as loyal and good as you."

She looked at Don Gonzalo, and he nodded. "Mudarra's right, as he so often is. Don't commit such a vile act, dear Sancha, but maintain your blood loyal and pure."

She understood in her heart that the dream wasn't a commandment for her to carry out, but she wanted more assurance, and missed the presence of Mudarra's Moorish friend and guide, who had always seemed so calm and judicious. "Where is Don José?" she asked.

Mudarra seized a lock of his own hair and made as if to pull it out. "When all the soldiers were met on the field of battle, one of Ruy

Blásquez's knights killed Yusuf. We buried him in the Valley of Espeja as well as we could, according to the Islamic rite. The road was his home in life, and now in death." He let go his hair and rubbed at his eyes, but the tears wet his tunic anyway.

She wiped away the moisture on his cheek. "Our triumph has come at a steep price, my poor son. I'm only sorry this traitor has a single life to pay in exchange for his long list of crimes."

Mudarra swallowed and wiped his nose. "You hold his fate in your hands at last. Command his sentence, and we will carry it out."

"This is the count's court," said Sancha. "I wouldn't sit in judgment in his place."

"It is your place to judge this traitor and no one else's," said the count, forcing his way through numerous bystanders. Sancha couldn't understand why he didn't send at least some of them away. "He killed Don Mudarra's friend, and he took my castles...."

"The castles belong to me through my marriage to Doña Lambra." Ruy Blásquez's voice rose from the floor with surprising vigor. "I admit no wrong in claiming them."

"We've taken many of his knights prisoner," explained Mudarra, "and will not release them until we are assured all the castles have returned to you, my lord."

"We'll see to it as soon as this traitor's fate is carried out." The count straightened his tunic and started again. Although he looked at Sancha, she sensed his message going out to everyone in the chamber, and by extension, to all Castile. "He has wronged Mudarra and me and most of the people in this chamber. He tried to have Don Gonzalo Gustioz killed, but his greatest crime took place in Almenar when he killed all seven of the noble knights González of Lara, his sister's sons. Doña Sancha, you are the person most victimized by his treachery. As you command, so be it."

Sancha studied the clumped blood in the traitor's beard. "Why won't you look at me?" she demanded. He didn't seem to understand that if she could only look into his eyes, there was a chance she might find whatever vestige remained of the boy she had been so happy to help her mother and nanny care for. They might recall the bond forged by blood and shared experience, and she might remember the fraternal love they shared for many more years than they had been apart. If he begged her forgiveness, or if he acted a little bit sorry for the grief he'd caused her, she might be able to take him back to Salas and nurse his body and their kinship ties back to health. With enough penance before the altar where her sons' heads rested, forgiveness was a possibility. Sancha considered herself Christian enough to give the man who had betrayed her affection and destroyed her family a second chance. She waited patiently, but the moment never arrived. All the people in the chamber knew, and Sancha herself could no longer deny, that Ruy Blásquez, murderer of the seven finest knights in the history of Hispania, must be put to death.

Tears blurred her vision as she searched out her husband's hand. When he clasped it and held on tightly to transmit the strength she lacked, people in the crowd assisted her decision.

"He should be dismembered!"

"Torn into a thousand pieces by dogs!"

"Burn him! Boil his traitorous blood!"

"Traitors must be stoned to death!"

Sancha imagined the projectiles pummeling her brother's already weak body. She dropped her husband's hand in surprise at the inspiration that flooded her mind. She raised her hands to try and silence the mob, who continued to roar more and more violent punishments.

"Quiet!" shouted Mudarra.

"I'm pleased by what you all say," said Sancha gently. "It has fallen to me to pass this sentence, and if God and Mudarra are willing, I would have a great celebration and a scaffold mounted. The treachery had its origin when the knights lanced the scaffold at this traitor's wedding to Doña Lambra. Upon that structure, he raised the betrayal by which my husband became a captive and my sons murdered, and upon a similar structure he must meet his fate."

A great cheer echoed about the ceiling, and no one waited another moment to leave the hall in an impromptu procession to the riverbank. A knight smiled at Sancha and hoisted her onto his shoulders. When she wouldn't stop reaching for Gonzalo, a burly warrior raised him up, too, and they held hands and ducked under the archways together. She glimpsed two of Mudarra's soldiers carrying Ruy Blásquez, moaning, on the board, almost as an afterthought and certainly without any of the honor and fuss the others made over her. One soldier took on the role of crier and ran ahead to shout, "Come to the riverbank to see the traitor Ruy Blásquez meet his end!" Sancha witnessed the street and the people on it below her as if she were a bird flying over, without a care for the matters of men.

How quickly fortune changed! This strange parade, which people dropped baskets and abandoned geese in order to join, seemed even less real than the prophetic dream had been. Outside the city wall, her soldier set Sancha down in what she thought must be the spot where the scaffold had stood fifteen years earlier. Several men and women brought planks from unknown locations and placed them and hammered them together according to the direction of a knight who seemed to have done something like this before. Sancha stood next to Gonzalo and heard the applications of each one of the bystanders. If the person had had a relative who'd perished in Almenar, she directed them to their deserved place at the front of the mob. Others who claimed Ruy Blásquez had robbed them of their castles, their knights, or their livestock were sent to stand behind the first group. Those who had no claim to direct damages by the traitor were sent to retrieve darts, lances, and any other weapons the others could throw. Sancha thought there must be at least one hundred fifty she'd allowed in the main group, and she suspected the others, who must have totaled three hundred or more, would throw whatever they could find.

When the scaffold had been knocked together, Sancha had them lay two crossbeams on the ground in the form of an X. They lay the traitor upon the beams, securing his wrists and ankles to the wood with rope. With Don Gonzalo standing over her, Sancha used the architect knight's knife to open the bandages and reveal Ruy Blásquez's warm skin, leaving only his undergarments, the better to witness the blows he would receive. The gash on his shoulder, while long and red, appeared to be nicely on the mend.

"You've been faking, you coward," said Don Gonzalo when he understood that his enemy couldn't have died from the wound. "Did you think our knights would show mercy to someone gravely wounded?"

"Why do you not beg me for mercy, your sister, the one who loved you most in this world after our parents passed away?" Sancha's hot tears landed on the side of Ruy Blásquez's face, but he would not turn to see her.

Sancha gritted her teeth and stood back. "Raise him up," she commanded.

They heaved the wooden X until it rested upright upon the scaffold. Sancha contemplated the sagging form until he screeched as if he were pierced with a hundred arrows. If he was asking for confession, as he ought, the words failed.

"Shall we give him something to scream about?" said Don Gonzalo.

"Throw," Sancha ordered.

Hundreds of lances bounced off the scaffold or broke and fell below. Even the smallest pieces were handed back to the people in the crowd, and they threw them again and again. Some of the smaller darts landed in muscle. Blood blossomed on the rough skin and slid over and under the linen undergarment, accompanied by continuous grunts and groans. Was this red substance the fetid poison of a monster, or the life force of a mere man? Sancha looked away from the figure on the scaffold and studied the victims of his crimes as they exercised their hatred and pain with neverending casting, catching, and relancing.

A short line of knights appeared in front of the foremost throwers, the eight of them armed with glittering swords and decked out in breastplates with a puncture pattern in the shape of wings. The sight of them filled Sancha with mortal dread. Each man aimed and threw a lance that shimmered with a ghostly glow until it pierced Ruy Blásquez between the ribs, in the heart. With these wounds as with no others, the traitor shrieked with true agony.

When the last of the new lancers had thrown and struck his target, they turned with military precision and made ceremonious bows before Doña Sancha. They stood one at a time so that Sancha could take in the knowing smile of Muño Salido, Diego's warm grin, a blown kiss from Martín's lips, a loving salute from Suero, Fernando's dignified nod, Rodrigo's hands folded as if in prayer for her, Gustio's wink, and a facial expression so wry and self-satisfied Sancha could hardly describe it as a smile from her troublemaker Gonzalico. When next she blinked, they had gone. Sancha felt a tremendous weight lift from her, so that all she was left with were tears of gratitude.

"The thing is done," she said through sobs before she noticed that the crowd had no more objects worth throwing. A great cracking resounded off the city walls and the scaffold collapsed backward into the mud of the riverbank. Sancha hurried to the crossbeams, but found only a mass of blood and innards with hands and feet, but no humanity left. There was nothing over which they could say a prayer. There were no more decisions to be made. There could be no mercy for the man who had once been her brother. Don Gonzalo was by her side, and Sancha grasped him, saying, "Perhaps my brother died long ago, and the thing that died just now wasn't him at all."

"Perhaps," he whispered.

But the crowd didn't realize her seven sons had been avenged and there was no more that needed to be done.

"I still say traitors must be stoned!" shouted someone.

"He cannot be buried as a Christian!" shrieked another.

Two knights approached Doña Sancha with questions on their faces. She nodded, and they untied the ropes and lifted the identity-less bulk from the crossbeams and placed it among the reeds next to the rushing water. Pandemonium broke out anew as men, women, and children seized all the stones they could find and pummeled their bloody target. Sancha watched the stones pile so high, they almost looked like a deliberate monument.

"If it has one, may the soul of that monster be forever damned," said Sancha.

"May he be forever damned!" five hundred people shouted in response.

Sancha put her arms around Don Gonzalo's trunk so that his arms sheltered her. "Where is Mudarra?" she suddenly wondered.

"Do you know, I don't think he left the castle," said her husband, his voice rumbling pleasantly in her ear. She imagined herself on a comfortable bed with a purring cat, and she understood her adopted son's reluctance to continue in the crowd.

"Take me somewhere I can rest," she said.

Sancha slept well next to her husband in her customary chamber in the count's castle in spite of the plotless images of gore, blood, and lances that plagued her. She woke in the dark and reached for Gonzalo, remembering how she had seen her sons the day before. "I have something to tell you," she whispered, so they felt their way out the door and into the courtyard. They looked over the parapet, far down into the cathedral square, where the sunrise cast orange-colored shadows on the walls.

"How beautifully the sun dawns on the first day of our reward," Gonzalo said, yawning.

"Indeed," she said, nuzzling into the crook of his arm, "yesterday was more terrible than I imagined, but today, for the first time since our sons passed into the next world, all is right with us."

"Do you not feel the matter incomplete still, with Doña Lambra unpunished? You sent Mudarra to find her before he came to Burgos."

"No, I think we may rejoice now and find comfort in what Mudarra has already done."

"How can you be so certain?"

"That's what I have to tell you, my love. Yesterday, during the lancing, well, did you see anything unexpected?"

"Nothing. But I was looking away during the stoning."

"But during the lancing, did you not see. . .? They returned to us, all seven of our sons and Muño Salido, for a few moments, to witness their uncle's punishment, and then they turned to me and showed me how content they were."

He held her face and studied her eyes with his single good one. "In all these years, I never saw them like I'd hoped. It wasn't some dust or the slant of the light?"

"No, it was eight spirits, as alive as you and me, but without flesh."

"And you're sure it was them?"

"You don't think I can recognize the flesh of my bones?" Sancha laughed. "I have no doubt, God sent them to show me that the thing is done."

Don Gonzalo grinned, then kissed her heartily. "Then we don't have to worry about damaging the count's honor. Lambra is his cousin, after all. We can enjoy the tournaments and roasts the count is going to provide for us and his *alcaide mayor*."

"Those celebrations are another thing I have no doubt about," Sancha chuckled.

After breakfast in the great hall, the count sent some of his vassals to bring together enough of his knights to see to the restoration of his castles. Several of the count's soldiers brought the captive knights to the head of the table to see the count. He stood from his chair and didn't let them speak.

"Because you rose up against me with the traitor and consented to the deaths of the seven noble knights of Lara, which was a great crime, I cannot let you go free. Once you have each guaranteed a castle for me, you must go into exile in Navarra or Andalusia or France."

Ruy Blásquez's foremost knight raised his hand and opened his mouth, but Count García cut him off. "There is no argument that will hold against my decision."

The prisoners shuffled off, still under guard, and Doña Sancha felt sorry for them, for they had only been following orders, even if the orders had been the most evil ever commanded. Mudarra shifted anxiously on the bench next to her, and she thought he must be more fair-minded than the count.

"My sons are at peace now," she said to the count. "There's no need to mete out more punishment than those knights have already received at the hand of the traitor."

Mudarra looked at Sancha and she got the distinct sensation he knew she had seen her sons the day before, or that he had seen them, too. But he hadn't even been present. How could he know?

The next to appear at the head of the table were Doña Elvira, her brother, and her children. It must already be terce. How lazy the morning had been! Sancha had forgotten about the poor woman and her court case.

"I regret to inform you, Doña Elvira," said the count, "that in the confusion yesterday your defendant fled. I cannot pass judgment if he is not present."

"What other proof of his guilt do you need?" she insisted, lifting her daughter into her arms with some effort.

"Given your situation, you and your family are welcome to stay here in the castle with me until we can track him down. And you may enjoy the revels I've planned because of the death of the traitor Ruy Blásquez."

Doña Elvira accepted his generosity. What else could she do? Sancha approved, but Mudarra gave a sigh.

"What troubles you, my son?" asked Doña Sancha.

"I think I should probably return to Bureba and see about completing your revenge against Doña Lambra."

"The revenge is over. You've done very well, sweet boy."

"How can you be so sure?"

"I saw them, Mudarra. Their spirits came to the lancing, and their spears did the most damage to Ruy Blásquez's body."

She wasn't sure what Moors believed about life after death, so his nod of acceptance surprised her.

"What about the stoning?"

"They were gone by the time the scaffold fell. The stoning was necessary only to appease the crowd's judgment."

"Is the crowd a better judge than the count? Or you, who have been most dishonored by these betrayals?"

"Forget about Doña Lambra and enjoy the celebrations you've caused."

He accompanied her everywhere there was jousting, skills contests, or feasting, but he remained quiet and perpetually agitated. He leaned forward with pursed lips to watch the jousting match the count had designed to commemorate his battle against Ruy Blásquez. They had erected the stands and posts outside the city walls, not near the riverbank, but against the forest. Although it was the largest jousting arena Sancha had ever seen, it was soon filled with quantities of knights and horses she couldn't estimate in the commotion as they took their assigned places.

"My comrades and I represent one thousand knights," shouted one of the warriors on the right side of the arena. "The thousand loyal followers of Don Mudarra!" Hundreds of spectators cheered for the men decked out in red and gold with castles on their banners.

"We represent the two thousand knights of the cowardly traitor," said a knight on the left side, more quietly than his predecessor. The spectators provided grimaces and groans at the announcement. When one of the knights, dressed in blue so as to stand out from the rightful Castilians, identified himself as Ruy Blásquez, the crowd roared, and a few who happened to have stones or bread rolls threw them into the arena, where they bounced off standards and shields and rolled underfoot.

Sancha laughed, but Count García shouted a warning. "There was no one to throw bread rolls on the field of battle!"

Mudarra rolled his eyes. When the air was clear of projectiles, one of the Castilians identified himself as Don Gonzalo, and her true husband beside her clapped and hooted his approval.

"I am Don José," said one of the Castilians, wearing a turban to distinguish himself. Saddened, Sancha put her hand to her mouth and looked at Mudarra, but he wore the same serious expression he'd begun the afternoon with.

The man next to him declared that he represented Don Mudarra, *alcaide mayor*, and Sancha thought the game might never commence, the cheering continued for so long. At last, Ruy Blásquez made his move and foully murdered Don José with a short sword. When the knight representing the dead man got up and walked away, the battle was joined, with the Castilians outnumbered but more valiant, and of course they had God on their side. Sancha relished the thought of the magnificent songs the jongleurs would sing about her heroic husband and adopted son. Each one of Mudarra's soldiers killed two of the traitor's and then set two of them aside to represent the warriors who would ensure the return of the count's castles.

At last, Mudarra knocked Ruy Blásquez from his horse and then engaged in a sword fight that brought Sancha's heart to her throat. She clasped her hands as if in prayer, fretting about the way it would end.

Don Gonzalo put his hand on her knee. "Don't worry, dear wife. Both Mudarra and I made it out alive."

She laughed at her own silliness at the exact moment the Mudarra jouster brought the Ruy Blásquez impersonator to the ground with a heavy blow to the shoulder. The other members of the crowd joined her laughter and cheered even more than they had at the beginning of the representation.

"That isn't how it happened at all," was the only comment Mudarra made.

After three days of festivities, a part of Mudarra's sullenness had made its way into Doña Sancha's mind. In spite of her solicitousness and the love the count and his vassals heaped upon their *alcaide mayor*, he seemed to only withdraw. Sancha wondered whether he wanted to remain in Castile. At breakfast on the fifth day, she was considering sending him to Bureba after Doña Lambra the way he'd requested, when none other than the woman herself made the trip unnecessary.

She burst into the great hall with two other blonde women behind her while the servants were clearing away the bowls and crumbs. Her hair hung wild about her waist, uncombed, and she had torn her clothing to show her grief, but Sancha would have recognized those fiery-icy blue eyes in the head of any creature. On closer inspection, the slits in her flowing, beltless tunic seemed to have been placed purposefully to show the delicate fabric of her chainse and the still youthful figure beneath to their best advantage.

She gave the impression of being every man's dream instead of a bereaved widow.

She broke past the guards in the doorway and dashed to the head of the table, where she stooped and reached for the count's hand, without a thought for the two women who filed in behind her and stood with grave expressions, their faces downcast. Mudarra drew an audible breath at the intrusion, but Doña Sancha was too curious to hear what Lambra would say to attend to him.

"When I heard the terrible news, I came to throw myself upon your mercy. Ruy Blásquez, my only protector in all this world, is dead. I know it's true because I've seen the pile of stones on the riverbank. Only you can protect me from the dreadful vengeance of the Moor who slew my husband, your favored vassal who received me from you as a gift because he had served you so well in Zamora and at other times."

It was quite a mouthful for someone in distress, and Sancha didn't believe she meant a word of it. Sancha recognized the source of the ambition that had changed her brother. She couldn't detect any sorrow to accompany the torn clothing, and something about her posture indicated a self-assurance that gave the lie to the pitiful pleas for help.

When the count stared at Doña Lambra and didn't move, the lady dropped to her knees without releasing his hand, giving a gasp of authentic pain as her bones hit the tile. Both of the women behind her hurried to clasp Doña Lambra's shoulders with a concern that went beyond the relationship between a servant and lady. One of them was an older, wearier Justa, the maid Sancha remembered from the wedding and Barbadillo, but the other girl looked too young to have witnessed those primordial events. She regarded Doña Lambra with a mixture of respect and fear more intense than that of the exhausted maid. Something about the way the girl tilted her head or pursed her mouth seemed familiar to Sancha. "Who is the third lady?"

"This poor orphan is Blanca Flor, the daughter I gave Ruy Blásquez, or that he gave me," replied the lady from Bureba, who still didn't seem humiliated, even on the hard floor.

Sancha brought her hand to her heart. The girl, who looked back at her with authentic sorrow, pain, and desperation, was her niece.

"Beginning yesterday, and from now down through the centuries, no one wants to be of that infernal lineage. The girl is poor indeed." The count rose from his high-backed settle and flicked Doña Lambra's hand away. The lady sank lower and put her hands together as if in prayer.

"Have mercy on me, Count García. I've lost my husband. What is left to me? I'm destitute! I'm the daughter of your cousin, your own blood! Pity me. If Ruy Blásquez did something wrong, then he is well punished, but I have no guilt for what he did. Don't abandon me, for if you do, my days will be few."

Her eyes remained dry, defying the moaning and squealing sounds she made. Sancha knew this to be the woman who sent her sons into the trap at Almenar, and had witnessed her bizarre attempt at revenge with the bloody cucumber. Her desire to rank higher than the seven noble knights had made her insane and more dangerous than a warrior armed to the teeth. And yet, Sancha couldn't bring herself to speak against her, for the sake of her newfound niece, who behaved as her father had done before her, bowing to her mother's every whim. To Sancha's relief, the count had taken control of the situation.

"You lie. I have never seen a more treacherous woman." The count looked down upon her crouching form as if he would tread upon her until she was no more than a flourish in the tile pattern. "You baptized all the betrayals and evil acts your husband performed, and you were lady and queen of my fortresses. You are the cause of the internal conflict in Castile, because you wanted more power than you deserved and wouldn't share it with a worthy family, even for the sake of their relationship to you. From the moment you advised Ruy Blásquez to murder his own nephews, I have no responsibility toward you."

Doña Lambra stood with the helping hands of Justa and Blanca Flor, a look of bewilderment overtaking her features. If she had been thinking of a retort, she was never allowed to voice it, because the count hadn't finished.

"I hereby command Don Mudarra, my *alcaide mayor*, to bring you to your execution, and for your soul to be damned forever, if it is God's will. I grant you the mercy of being allowed to leave here in peace. It is the last mercy you can expect from me or my inheritors."

Now, at last, Doña Lambra's eyes were wet. She stood, stuck in place in spite of Justa and Blanca Flor pulling at her dress, and wept, no doubt because the exaggerated destitution she had claimed before the count had at last come true. It was no worse than what Sancha, Gonzalo, and Luz had had to suffer for the past fifteen years, and Sancha couldn't fault the count's justice. But Blanca Flor looked as if she were a delicate blossom that would wilt under the strain. Sancha stood, thinking to reach out to her niece, but next to her, Mudarra had also stood. He lifted one leg and then the other over the bench, making as if to approach the new object of his revenge. Sancha held him back.

"What are you doing?" she asked.

"I have my orders from the count," he said gruffly.

Doña Lambra gasped, apparently realizing for the first time that the Moor she had professed so much fear of was present and ready.

"Go on," said Mudarra, almost pleading with her. He folded his arms with resolve. Sancha was glad to witness his listlessness disappear, at least. "Get a head start. The count granted you that."

The three ladies joined hands and ran between the guards with surprising swiftness. Sancha couldn't be sure, but it seemed as though Blanca Flor lingered a moment longer than the other two, gazing at Mudarra. No doubt, she had hardly seen a knight besides her father before, much less a Moorish one with so much power. The power to kill her parents, her protectors.

Mudarra had followed the women to the threshold, where he stopped to watch them escape the castle. He turned and bowed toward the count, then moved beyond the doorway and into the courtyard.

"Stop!" shouted Sancha, hurrying after him. "Where are you going?"

"I'm going to get my horse and follow them."

"Won't you need to assemble an army?" Sancha asked, knowing how absurd it sounded. They passed through the courtyard and looked down from the main outer gate. The two women helped Doña Lambra down the steep path, like mice fleeing a cat, but too slowly.

"Honestly, I won't need any soldiers to arrest her and bring her back here to you."

Sancha saw the wisdom in it, and had been present for the count's sentencing, but couldn't gather the strength to see her last son leave her yet again for who knew how long. "I'll talk to the count and maybe he'll relieve you of this duty. Let them die of starvation in the sierra where no one will ever find them. There's no need to bring them back here for burning or being torn apart by dogs."

Mudarra looked away from his escaping prey and revealed a perplexed expression. "I don't mind if Doña Lambra starves in the mountains, but Blanca Flor and the servant. . . ."

"You're right. They're even less guilty than my brother was. And Lambra may be what she is — a minion of Satan, perhaps — but Blanca Flor is my flesh and blood. Did you see how beautiful she is?"

"That did not escape my notice," he said blushing.

Sancha steeled herself against his departure. At least this time her husband was with her. "Bring her to justice, since you must. But don't harm Justa or Blanca Flor."

"I swear that no harm will ever come to Blanca Flor or to her faithful servant if I can prevent it." He clasped her hand and held it to his heart so that she felt it beating strong and steady. His word was true.

"Find your horse, my son. I'll bring provisions for your journey. But don't be gone long. We need you now to complete our home."

He kissed her on the cheek and lunged down the path toward the stables, at the point below the castle at which the horses could navigate the rocky terrain.

Sancha wiped away a tear and turned back into the courtyard, where Don Gonzalo met her with an embrace.

"He won't be long. He learned tracking skills from Yusuf, and she's only a woman, after all," he said.

"I'm not so sure," she said into his chest. "Would a simple woman become the cause of the destruction we suffered these many years? My brother is dead. We had to kill him because she turned him into a monster. All I want is to take our new son back to Salas and live out the rest of our days in peace."

"There can be no peace while Lambra lives," said Gonzalo. "Or didn't you agree with the count? Besides, you should know better than to think a son of yours would consider living quietly in Salas as if he were no more than a babe."

"I had so many sons. Why is none of them gentle and calm?"

"Well, you remember, Martín could be pretty quiet when he was concentrating on his next chess move."

"Chess is nothing more than a simulation of war, and Martín was more competitive at it than anyone else."

"That's right. If there had been need for him, he could have been *alcaide mayor*. But he's not here, and Mudarra is. And now he's the *alcaide mayor*. God wanted you to have many sons and more honor than anyone else."

"So He could test me by taking it away?"

"And reward you by restoring it. Mudarra will come back, and then the count will send him on many other missions sure to gain him castles, lands, and accolades."

Sancha thought back to Salas, how they had left it while workers had been carrying out her plans. Even now, the new and repaired buildings might already be in place, waiting for them to give the stones and planks a purpose.

"Do you miss Salas, dear husband?" she asked him.

"More even than when I was in Córdoba, sweet darling." She looked up and, through her tears, studied his left eye, now as brilliant and brown as it had been before he'd gone blind. Beloved crinkles appeared at its side when he gave a smile to her alone. "Let me take you home."

Chapter X

At times, Mudarra watched Blanca Flor so intensely, he forgot to hide. He'd caught up to the three women within an hour of mounting Tranquilo, after a frank talk with the count. Doña Sancha had laden the faithful horse with food, wine, and weapons and kissed Mudarra farewell even more anxiously than his true mother had done. He amazed himself with the effect he had on motherly women — could he also cause that devotion in Blanca Flor?

During the first day, he followed them at a distance such that any soldier would have sensed him, but Doña Lambra appeared not to realize she was being chased. He watched over them from afar while they lay sleeping under a waning moon, ensuring that no bandit took it in mind to harm Blanca Flor. No one disturbed them. Perhaps the best protection was to travel with a condemned woman.

The second day, they walked on without taking food or drink, and Mudarra thought it strange, but they seemed to be moving into the region of Lara. When they stopped the second night in some patch of woodland foothills Yusuf would have been able to name, but Mudarra could not, he brushed Tranquilo down and left him to graze in a clearing far enough away from the women that not even a trained warrior would suspect his presence. Then he took the bags of supplies and nestled them into the ferns and undergrowth, keeping the pines as his cover, and continued watching them.

He half expected Doña Lambra to emerge from a colorful, bejeweled tent wearing silks and gold, but there were no such things to be had. During the time he watched the women, they slept on the bare ground and never changed their clothes. Mudarra didn't know how they had arrived in Burgos, but if they had brought animals, carts, and supplies, their driver and other companions had abandoned them to their fate. Doña Lambra never showed a sign that she thought she might be pursued, and they stayed in that spot for several days without moving on or even making a plan. They sat on stones or piles of leaves or stood and murmured with each other. Twice a day, Justa left the group through the bushes and returned with a forest salad or berries and water in a wineskin she must have had tucked into her belt. Unlike her lady, Justa's clothes hadn't been ceremoniously torn, and she took pains to avoid thorns and sap as she walked to preserve what was left of her appearance.

At times, Doña Lambra paced in a circle, revolving like the sun around the Earth, shredding the gashes in her dress as if grieving for the first time. She said nothing, but shook her fists at the treetops and, once exhaustion claimed her, collapsed before the cowering figure of her daughter. Blanca Flor sat wordlessly for days on end, making no move to help herself or her mother. Mudarra sympathized with her confusion. He was unsure what he would do in such a situation, himself. He always sought a position from which he could see her face, and every day detected more complex thoughts passing through her mind. He must have appeared similar to anyone observing him in Burgos after Ruy Blásquez's capture.

Was she waiting for Mudarra to make a move? For that matter, was Doña Lambra waiting for him to come and meet her, face to face? He wouldn't do it. Mudarra had spent the festive days in Burgos coming up with his plan, and he had committed to it. There was no place in it for Doña Lambra. He rejected everything that came from her except Blanca Flor. In contrast, he accepted Blanca Flor as his entire destiny. Being with her was the only way to give his time in Castile — no, his time on Earth — any meaning at all.

On the fourth morning, Justa had gone to fetch water and Doña Lambra lay asleep, as peaceful as she ever was. Mudarra was crouched behind a thick pine when Blanca Flor stood and walked as silently as the leaves, rocks, and beetles would permit. Mudarra's instincts abandoned him. He froze in place when he realized Blanca Flor had seen him and was coming near. Was this the right moment? It would have to be.

"I thought it was you," she murmured when she towered over him, leaning on his tree.

"And so you weren't afraid, were you?" He cleared his throat nervously.

"Shouldn't I be afraid?" Her voice was absent from the whisper. "Have you come to kill my mother?"

"No, I came to be with you, and to take you away from here if you want me to." He stood and caught her in his arms, only to feel her struggle against him.

"I can't leave my mother and Justa like this. We have nothing to eat. My mother's doing what she can...."

"I've seen what she does," muttered Mudarra.

Blanca Flor continued undeterred. "But tomorrow we'll have to find a town and go begging in the street. Otherwise, we'll starve out here in the sierra."

He thought about the abundant bread, cheeses, and dried meats Sancha had placed in his saddlebags, but knew he couldn't give them to Blanca Flor without raising suspicions. He took her hands in his. They were blue-tinged and so cold he couldn't detect their softness.

"I'm so sorry I've brought you this low, Blanca Flor. You're everything that matters to me. Let me make it up to you. I've got my horse in a meadow nearby. We'll leave here and marry, and live in al-Andalus, or perhaps France if you want to stay among Christians, wherever you like. No one need know whose daughter you are and no one will find out whose son I am. We'll make up our own little kingdom."

"I suppose I would be your queen?"

"You are already my queen. Look, I keep your mitten with me always," he said, holding the prize out to her. "Marry me, and I'll give you everything I have."

She leaned in toward him, and Mudarra thought her resolve was faltering.

"I have a lot to give. Even if I abandon Salas, Almanzor will see to my wellbeing," he said.

She pushed away, and the mitten fell into the confusion of leaves and twigs.

"No. What about my mother and Justa?"

"We can take Justa with us. I would save your mother if she were anyone else in the world, darling, but you know I can't help Doña Lambra de Bureba. My blood prevents it."

She sobbed, a sudden gushing that caused Doña Lambra to stir in her dreams. "Go away," Blanca Flor managed to pronounce, too clearly for Mudarra to ignore it. She returned to sit silently weeping on a stone. His heart broke.

He turned away clutching his chest, breathing painfully around the gash he felt opening inside him. He stumbled through the bracken and pushed off the tree trunks to propel himself toward the clearing where Tranquilo waited for him.

"My only friend in the world," he mumbled into the horse's neck.

Tranquilo nickered, as if telling Mudarra some comforting words. He accepted the sounds greedily as he looked inside his tunic to verify that there was no gash in his chest. Then he realized the mitten had been left behind. He thought to go after it, but hesitated.

"Am I doing the right thing?" he asked Tranquilo. "I don't imagine spending the rest of my life in Castile, running off to do the count's bidding. I want the life I described to Blanca Flor, and I have nothing to lose by going after it."

Patting Tranquilo and scratching behind his ears, Mudarra worked up his courage. "Perhaps she needs more time to see that she wants me, too. What do you think, my quiet boy? If it's time she wants, I will give it to her. Thank you for staying so faithfully in this meadow. Are you bored? Let's go for a ride."

He mounted the stallion and, shying away from the roads, they wended their way into the town Blanca Flor had mentioned she would visit that day. He found them in the main square and backed away into a side street to watch from a distance, as he had become accustomed. Blanca Flor had mentioned "begging in the street" so casually that Mudarra hadn't comprehended her meaning, and his delicate heart, so recently buoyed by the determination granted only to those with patient horses, sank. The three women sat on the ground much as they had in the forest, but now people passed them by, stirring up dust, and stared at them in their need. Justa, her eyes sunken into dark holes, held her hand out and recited, over and over, "For God's sake, for the love of all that is holy, take pity on us."

Blanca Flor also held out her shaking hand and said, "For God's sake." In the stark light of the plaza, Mudarra could see that both of them were hungrier than their lady. They had sacrificed their paltry share of wild berries for her.

Doña Lambra sat between them, letting her hair cover her face, and said nothing. None appeared to have yet obtained a single coin.

Many people were passing by Mudarra's side street in order to access the main square. Children stared at him, women smiled and nodded, and, seeing the Castilian insignia on Tranquilo's gear, the men waved or greeted him.

From the satchel under Tranquilo's saddle, Mudarra extracted two *óbolos*, parchment-thin silver-plated coins of so little value it hadn't seemed worth lining the pouch with them. But now that he hoped one of them might provide a crust of bread to his beloved, they were more precious to him than the most glittering sword.

When a boy who looked about ten years of age approached the bend where Mudarra waited, he pushed the coins into his waiting palm.

"You may keep one of those if you give one to the young lady begging in the square."

But the boy's father told him to give the coins back, and when the boy hesitated, the father squeezed his hand until he dropped them in the street.

"I'm sorry, Sir Knight, but do you know who those ladies are? The count sent a messenger with an edict he read in the inn three days ago. We aren't to help or aid them, but Don Mudarra, the *alcaide mayor.*"

"I am Don Mudarra González, son of Gonzalo Gustioz and *alcaide mayor* of Castile. Your son commits no crime in taking my coins to those ladies."

"She's Doña Lambra. If you truly are Don Mudarra, you shouldn't want to help her, because she visited the wrath of Hell on the house of Lara, your inheritance."

"But Blanca Flor, the youngest of those beggars in the plaza, wasn't even born when that happened. Should she have to suffer for the sins of her mother?"

"I don't know, Don Mudarra. I only know that my son cannot be seen giving coins to anyone with Doña Lambra." The father nodded his head somberly and ushered his child into the square.

Mudarra knew that not many Christian knights would have tolerated so much discussion and lack of obedience from someone who obviously worked a trade, and that it was within his rights to arrest the man or even strike him down. The boy looked back at Mudarra with eyes that took in everything around them, even what could not be seen, so Mudarra sighed to release his anger and bent to pick up the coins. When no one was coming along his side street, and he was certain neither Justa nor Doña Lambra could see him, he ducked into the plaza and tossed the coins toward the center, hoping they would roll toward the ladies.

Before he was able to dash around the corner, he saw Blanca Flor darting toward the coins.

Mudarra's pounding heart was a sign that it had not been broken forever that morning. He mounted Tranquilo and left the town, following the river and letting Tranquilo drink as much as he liked. Some spot along this river must be where Justa brought the water from, the water that had kept his beloved from dying of thirst. Until he'd seen them begging for the barest necessities, relying on charity that the count had prohibited for their basic survival, he hadn't understood how alone and helpless Blanca Flor had become. He made the day as pleasant as he could for Tranquilo, wandering about, breaking into a run wherever there was room, but his mind's eye retained the image of his love humiliated in the dirt, surrounded by people who could but would not help her, scurrying for the worthless coins thrown by the one protector she had in the world. Would she accept him as her protector, or die because of a grim attachment to the mother who brought her into this flawed world?

The next morning, Mudarra made sure to stand in the same place as before. Justa went for water, and Doña Lambra kept sleeping. Mudarra understood that her exhaustion must come from lack of food, but how much more weary must Justa be, who sacrificed most of the food she scrounged up to her lady and still had to trudge through the forest, while Doña Lambra remained in the sweet oblivion of sleep?

When Blanca Flor approached him this time, his heart pounded and his hands shook.

"Thank you for the coins. It was enough for us to share a loaf of bread yesterday." She smiled weakly, and the hollows under her eyes told him that if she had eaten any of the fruits of his *óbolos*, it hadn't been enough to sustain a sparrow.

"You need much more food, my love. How can you continue like this?" He wanted to hold her, but he knew better than to reach before she was ready.

"We'll go into the town again. Perhaps you'll throw us another few coins? No one else will."

"I have more than enough food, more than bread, in my saddlebags. Come and take some. If you think it's all right to let Justa know I'm here in the woods with you, you can share it with her, but giving any to your mother would cause too much suspicion. I don't think any of you would survive long if you fled from here. You're so weak already. . ." His voice cracked and he held his hand out to her.

She regarded him as if he were a chess puzzle for a few moments, but Mudarra saw the pendulum swing in his favor when she took his hand. He gratefully led her between the trees to his provisional camp site, where he had stashed his food, wine, blankets, and weapons. Quickly, because she looked like a rabbit with its senses on alert, he pulled out a hard cheese, some dried ham, and a wineskin, and handed them to her. He spread out one of his blankets and she sat, thanking him before she gnawed ravenously at the cheese. Fascinated, he studied the mottled patterns the sunlight made in her golden hair as she moved.

After a moment or two, she said, "I feel better already. I think I will take a package for Justa, as long as it's small enough to hide so my mother never sees it."

"Anything for you, sweet lady." He busied himself selecting items and wrapping them in linen and it seemed as if they were any man and his wife stopping for a rest on any journey. Contentment spread through Mudarra, and it must have touched Blanca Flor as well, because she began to make conversation the way they had done in Busto de Bureba. He sat down beside her, not too close.

"They tell me Doña Sancha adopted you," She picked at the ham and placed it on her tongue in an innocent but sensual way.

Mudarra nodded, remembering the suffocating silk sleeve. "It's true."

She gave him a wry smile. "Doña Sancha is my aunt. If she's your mother, we're too closely related to get married."

"Look at me, my white flower. You know I'm not your cousin."

She dropped the ham. She opened her mouth as if to reply, but the words were snatched away from her as the distance between them closed. They kissed languidly, savoring each other as if they were planning to spend the whole day in that single instant.

"I've got to get back," Blanca Flor said, shattering the illusion. She reached for a frond and used the dew to rinse the grease from her fingers.

"I'll be here with you all day," said Mudarra.

"I don't think we'll be in the forest today," she said.

"Don't go into the town and humiliate yourself. It's not worth it."

"We do what we have to. I don't know what else to do."

He held her face between his hands and kissed her farewell. She hid the linen package between her tunic and chainse near her hip and surged in the direction of her mother. Mudarra stayed behind to slow his breathing and his heartbeat. He intended to stay where he was and catch a glimpse of Blanca Flor when she returned from the town, but his concern made him ride Tranquilo into the place where he was welcomed and his beloved was not. It was as bad as the first day. Although no one bothered the three mendicants, they didn't provide any charity, either. It was a matter of time before someone called in an *alcaide* to force them out of the town. They couldn't stay where they were much longer. He would tell her that the next morning.

Back in his hiding place between the trees, Mudarra lay atop and under a blanket, more for the padding and to keep the moisture off than because the weather felt cold. Spring had finally arrived in Castile. Mudarra could tolerate a few bugs if it meant green plants would sprout and bloom. He drowsed, content to be near Blanca Flor and to have the chance to talk with her again the next day. And perhaps one day soon, convince her to come away with him.

A great snapping of twigs roused him. Blanca Flor grunted delicately as she pushed past the branches and ferns that sheltered his hiding place.

He couldn't see her in the scant light projected from the stars, which also hid behind branches, but hearing her voice, he sat upright. "Blanca Flor?"

"Ah, I've found you," she intoned.

"Why have you come here?"

"I've come to... Justa knows...."

"But what about your mother? Does she know?"

"She's asleep, and if she wakes, Justa will make some excuse for me. I don't have to go back until daylight." She located him on the forest floor, and as her warm, soft voice drew near, his muscles tensed and his hairs stood on end. A dainty foot tripped a little over his legs, but she caught her balance and sat down, using her hands to feel where he lay.

"Take the bolster, darling," he said, moving the rough excuse for a pillow behind her. He felt her shoulder through the fabric of her dress and pressed ever so gently toward the ground, and her head found the resting place willingly. She loosed a sigh of relief. He tried to imagine how good such a simple comfort must feel after four days of sleeping without the merest amenity.

"Justa was grateful for the package. She was able to give my mother all the berries she found today."

"Didn't your mother notice you and Justa ate nothing?"

"That's not the kind of thing my mother notices."

He lay next to her, supporting his head on his hand, close enough to feel the heat from her skin, but was careful not to brush against her. "Are you like your mother?"

She chuckled. "You've seen me in the daylight, and now you've seen her. What do you think?"

Mudarra remembered her sweet mouth incongruously set into her father's face when the man was mortally wounded and sent up a prayer of thanks that Blanca Flor had not asked about him. "But on the inside, your character, are you like her?"

"Oh, Mudarra, you said you love me. I don't think you would love a woman who was so selfish and commanding. Now you've made me speak ill of my mother." He heard the forest crunch under the blanket as she turned away from him.

He reached for her shoulder, but found the delicate skin of her neck. Her hair must still have been braided. With the unexpected touch, all his doubts fled. "I'm sorry, Blanca Flor. When I'm not near you, I have too much time to think."

"Is love about thinking?" she asked.

He sensed no recrimination in the question, only the curiosity of someone so sheltered she would have to ask her first lover about every detail. "No," he replied.

He found her lips in the dark, and entered that delicious trance in which they seemed to be the only people in the world. She responded by first holding his head so that he wouldn't pull back, and then she sat up a little and reached down. He waited for her to tell him what she was doing, but after a moment, she placed his hand on her bare ankle. He stroked the downy hairs as if he were trying not to bruise a rose petal, but as he moved his hands up her calf, he found that she had raised her skirts to reveal herself to him. His mouth flooded. He wasn't sure whether Christian women wore anything beneath their underdresses, but when his fingertips grazed the taut flesh over her hips, he knew that Blanca Flor, in that moment, was not.

He kissed her face, and it was wet with tears.

"Am I hurting you?"

"No, Mudarra. I... Justa knows, but I haven't told you. I love you."

It was the realization of his dream, his only objective in life. He wept with the happiness of a condemned man who receives a last-minute reprieve. At last Mudarra tasted the beginnings of a life blessed with meaning. In spite of his initial objections, Yusuf would be proud that Mudarra had achieved his true goal, and so quickly.

"Thank you, Blanca Flor, for the magnificent gift of your love. You are everything to me. I promise here and now to take care of you for the rest of your life and to do everything in my power to please you."

They sighed and giggled and moaned, loud enough to frighten off any curious woodland creatures, but not so loud that the sound would carry back to Justa and Doña Lambra. It seemed a few minutes, but for hours they explored each other, always touching or kissing. Now that he had her, Mudarra would never let her go.

"Does this mean you'll come away with me?" he asked at last, his final doubt still burdening him.

He listened to her breathing and brushed his fingertips over her eyelashes. She was asleep.

When Mudarra woke from a luscious, dreamless slumber, he saw that Blanca Flor was not beside him. He felt at the blanket with his hands to find nothing inside it, not even her warmth. His mind told him she'd returned to say goodbye to Justa and to provide for her mother for another day, but his heart knew this was something different.

A scream pierced the forest, echoing off every tree trunk, startling birds large and small out of the branches, and matching his rising desperation. "Justa! Don't leave me!" he heard. "Blanca Flor, where have you gone?"

Mudarra scrambled through the undergrowth, disregarding what sounds he made, and witnessed Doña Lambra turned away from him in the center of her little campsite, shaking her fists at the sky. There was no trace of Justa or Blanca Flor anywhere.

Mudarra slowly turned his head up and regarded the sky the lady cursed with her arms. Was that sky also Heaven? Were God and Jesus and all those saints looking down and watching him in that moment? If they were, they knew where his beloved had gone. He clasped his hands in prayer and asked all the saints to tell him.

No answer came. Perhaps Santiago Moorslayer, so high up and looking so far down, couldn't see Mudarra clearly, and still considered him a Moor, and felt obliged to slay not his body, but his heart. This certainly was a vengeful saint. How could God allow that kind of aggression up there at His right side? He hoped they would take him back at the mosque. This retaliatory religion was not for him, unless his beloved maintained her loyalty to it.

Doña Lambra's throat sounded dry. She ceased her shouting and darted between the trees. Mudarra made to follow her, but realized she was headed for the town, so he turned back and found Tranquilo in his meadow. The stallion showed his gratitude for the light brushing Mudarra gave him by standing still until his coat shone. Then he danced about, eager for another ride. "I think we'll be doing a lot of riding from now on," Mudarra told him as he mounted.

He didn't need Yusuf to tell him, but read the signs for himself: his beloved's disappearance, her mother's flight, Doña Sancha waiting in Salas to deliver the lady to the justice of the people. Capturing Doña Lambra was a part of his destiny he could no longer ignore. No doubt remained in his mind that he would somehow relieve himself of his duties to the count. Then he would be free to live with his love. If he couldn't find Blanca Flor while he was on the journey to Salas with her mother, he would go in search of her, perhaps toward France. It seemed like a logical place for Justa to take Blanca Flor. Without Yusuf, he couldn't be certain how far that country was, but he had the notion it was several days' travel, with one or two mountains to pass. He would climb the tallest and coldest mountain in the world if that was where his white flower had fled to.

When he arrived in the town square, a crowd of some twenty people had gathered, shouting and gesturing. Children flitted between the crowd and the buildings, screaming confused sentences and throwing twigs and stones at each other. Mudarra dismounted, leaving Tranquilo in the corner he was accustomed to, and pushed through the people to find Doña Lambra in the center of the crowd on the ground, shaking and sobbing with a rage that reddened her fair face. The people pushed in close to her, nearly treading on her, but for all their shouting, they didn't touch her. She looked like nothing more than a trapped animal. Mudarra tried to control the pity he felt for her and ignore the resemblance she bore to his beloved.

"She-demon!"

"Whore!"

"She's alone now. We should stone her!"

Mudarra felt crushed by their pushing and panicked. At long last, the man who had refused Mudarra's coins for his son two days before said, "Where is the *alcaide*? We can't harm her outside the law."

"I'm the *alcaide mayor* of Castile. I'm to deliver her to justice in Salas," said Mudarra.

He did not know where she found the energy after going hungry, then all the walking and the shaking in anger, but when Doña Lambra recognized Mudarra, her voice became as loud as all twenty of the mob. "No! No!"

Those closest to her laid their hands on her while she flailed, and forced her to her feet.

"My horse is over here," Mudarra said, allowing his training to rule his actions. "He's very gentle, but we'd best tie her down." He would not tolerate this thrashing, twitching bundle of muscles kicking Tranquilo.

Between three men and a strong hemp rope, Doña Lambra was secured lying on her belly across the saddle such that she wouldn't be able to raise her head and see where they were going. The position, added to her incessant moaning, hardly befitted someone who had been such a high-ranking lady, but Mudarra couldn't think of another way to accomplish the deed. He turned to address the townspeople, to thank them and be on his way, but their faces were so expectant that he ended up saying, "Can anyone tell me the fastest way to Salas?"

They all raised their hands, as he'd known they would. He invited them to accompany him. Some of them had horses, and from the inn they took a cart and several packs of provisions to replace what Mudarra had left at his campsite. Without fuss, they left their town, which Mudarra learned was called Neila, and processed along the road Doña Lambra, Justa, and Blanca Flor had traversed in the opposite direction six or seven mornings earlier.

He walked alongside Tranquilo and his burden at a pace he knew must frustrate the swift horse. Discomfort came over Mudarra, so he took refuge in addressing the townsfolk. "See how she struggles even now? She will not accept her fate. We won't be able to stop anywhere along the road. If you must eat or drink, do it walking, and if you must piss, run to catch up with us."

The lady wasn't struggling, and while he spoke, she had recovered much of her dignity despite the holes in her tunic, but the men obeyed his whim, whether because they had never met an *alcaide mayor* or been on an important mission before, or wanted as much as he to be rid of the prisoner forever, he did not know. All that mattered was that they advanced as far as possible before nightfall.

They set up several tents and extracted Doña Lambra from Tranquilo limp and pliable. Mudarra didn't trust the attitude of surrender she displayed, and bound her in a tent where five men at a time watched her in shifts all night. He listened to her whine and moan and thought about Count García's parting words to him.

"I've granted your mother the exclusive right to oversee Doña Lambra's punishment. When you capture her, you should meet your parents in Salas."

Mudarra's muddled mind had produced an image of his true mother, Zaida, and General Ghalib, and a few of his tutors waiting for him in Salas's ruined buildings.

"Very well, my lord," he said.

"I won't be able to travel to Salas. I have to attend to matters in Burgos, but more importantly, I can't punish Doña Lambra and retain my family honor."

"But you've disowned her," Mudarra absently protested, looking down the path where Blanca Flor had fled.

"The bonds of blood are even stronger than the law," the count had said.

Mudarra understood. After all, he was obliged to enforce these severest of punishments on people who did their evil before he had even been born, simply because they had offended his father. He still wondered how Ruy Blásquez could kill his own nephews, and wished Yusuf could tell him. Kneeling before the count and kissing his white hands, Mudarra had bidden him farewell, then headed down the path toward Tranquilo's stable and Doña Sancha's preparations.

The rest of the night, he thought of Blanca Flor escaping ever farther north and barely refrained from joining in her mother's moans.

In the morning, they secured the prisoner in the cart. She lay on her back, the sun burning her pale face, with each hand and foot tied to an opposite railing. It occurred to Mudarra that she might be killed by drawing if the cart sped over a rough road, so he checked the bonds.

They were tight around her wrists and ankles, but the rope was loose enough to allow her some movement and to prevent her body being ripped apart before Doña Sancha commanded it so. They must have provided her with plenty to drink, because the moment Doña Lambra caught sight of Mudarra, she began to weep. The salty water wet her hair, but the rope prevented her from brushing it away. Mudarra wondered whether his father had sobbed like that for his sons, and whether Lambra was in danger of going blind for the sake of her self-love.

The sobbing tormented the travelers all day, even when they gave her food and drink. Mudarra could find no peace, but listened to the weeping that turned into moaning and then a low-pitched groan almost like the rutting of a bear. He doubted any of the other men could tolerate it, either, and wasn't surprised when one of them shouted at Doña Lambra.

"You should have thought twice before you killed your nephews!"

"What kind of woman would do that?" A second knight joined the first.

"You aren't suffering as much as they did!" said another.

The groaning became a labored hiccup and then a series of prolonged sighs. Mudarra thought he would have to physically prevent the men from attacking Doña Lambra, but they remained true to the count's command to leave her unharmed for Doña Sancha.

And still the sobbing continued through the morning and the afternoon while they made steady progress.

They came to a fork in the road and one of the knights told Mudarra Salas was near, but the sobbing had not ceased yet. Mudarra dropped back a little so he could look down into the prisoner's face from atop Tranquilo.

"My lady, if you cooperate and we complete this task quickly, I'll be able to find your daughter and keep her safe."

"And Justa?" she asked, regaining her self-control. "And bring them back to me, where they belong?"

Mudarra shook his head. "What do you think is going to happen in Salas? Do you think you're immortal?"

Mudarra had to ride ahead to escape the unadulterated terror that filled the mother of his beloved. When he looked back, she was pulling at the ropes, trying with all her might to bring her hands together and her knees far enough up to reach the binding at her ankles. The ropes would cut through her wrists before she ever untied them, but Mudarra didn't think he could bear the ungodly shrieking for another moment.

"Gag her," he said to the rider next to him, and he did so willingly, climbing into the cart and throwing a blanket over her face for good measure. The muffled sounds might have grated at Mudarra's heart if it had not already been terminally ill, insensible to the suffering of others in the intensity of its own pain.

At last they passed the church of San Pelayo, which Mudarra would have recognized anywhere. Every man crossed himself. One of the men leaned over the cart rail and lifted the blanket from the prisoner's face. "That church harbors the heads of your nephews, the greatest knights Castile has ever seen."

The warrior pursed his mouth and spit on Doña Lambra's cheek.

"Enough!" cried Mudarra. The knight jumped back and the procession continued over the wooden bridge, the clattering horses' hooves and grinding wheels blotting out any other sound.

Soon, one of the maids Mudarra recognized from his first time in Salas came running out to the road. She studied Mudarra for a moment, then took in the cart with Doña Lambra and went scampering ahead of the procession to prepare her lord and lady for their guests.

Mudarra stopped Tranquilo at the well, but nothing looked the same. Instead of the half-built stables and crumbling outbuildings he'd left behind, before him unfolded the Salas Doña Sancha had described for him, as if she had painted over the landscape and brought her dream into the world. The stables were complete and large enough to accommodate several armies' mounts. A sty brimmed with hogs and several other pens sported flocks of pecking chickens and geese. A billy goat stood watch over the door of what must be his mates' evening residence. Other arched buildings and a new reflecting pool displayed marble sculptures of demure ladies and poised warriors. The main house sported a second story with wide windows and a horseshoe arch over the doorway with columns and leafy capitals suitable for the caliphs' quarters in Madinat al-Zahra. Mudarra imagined they'd brought in craftsmen from al-Andalus, and a good number of them to have accomplished so much, so quickly. Even the well sported a polylobed arch with vegetal carvings.

He dismounted Tranquilo and a porter took the horse away to the stables. Don Gonzalo stepped out the front door of the main house and Doña Sancha strode toward Mudarra with a proud grin.

"Mudarra, my boy! At last." She held him so tightly he thought he would suffocate.

"I see you've had success again, of course," said Don Gonzalo, taking his hand to shake it. He still wore a bandage over his right eye, but no humors were in evidence.

As soon as he broke free of his Christian, adopted parents' greetings, Mudarra held his arm out wearily toward the cart that was empty except for a clump of torn fabric that had been moaning mournfully since they'd crossed the bridge. He hid his own turmoil with legal language while one of the men from Neila whipped the blanket away.

"Behold the traitoress," Mudarra said so that all the workers and vassals who had gathered behind his parents could hear. Some hundred people, who Mudarra imagined had to be the entire staff and the guests of the estate, had come away from their tasks to find out whether he had delivered their lord and lady from shame and misery. "I bring her to Doña Sancha under the orders of Count García Fernández so that she may meet her sentencing at the hands of the people she offended most, the people of Salas."

A great hurrah surged up from the crowd and some of the laborers jumped into the air with joy.

Doña Sancha walked to the cart and peered tentatively over the edge of the rail. She met Doña Lambra's gaze, then looked back at Mudarra, the puzzlement plain on her face. He could offer her no comfort for what she might be feeling. Don Gonzalo went to stand next to her, and together they looked down without saying anything.

It wasn't enough for the people of Salas.

"Tell us how she offended you!"

"Tell us about your seven warrior sons, the pride of Castile, before she cut them down without mercy!"

Doña Sancha's eyes watered, but the sorrow was quickly replaced with anger. No one else made a sound as they strained to hear what she said.

"May she never escape the torments of Hell, which are not more than the torment she gave me in this world, without cause. There is no earthly punishment equal to her crime. May she be forever damned."

Another grand hurrah rose up, splintering into cheers and whistles and echoes of "May she be forever damned" that died down as Doña Sancha prepared to speak again. Don Gonzalo held her protectively.

"Count García has already passed judgment on this woman and has entrusted me with carrying out her sentence. First, I wish a marker to be made of solid stone for the place where she is buried. We must find a place where many travelers will pass by. I command a stonemason to carve into the marker the words, 'Here lies one who must be forever damned.'"

"Forever damned! Amen!" the crowd replied. Mudarra watched Doña Lambra's last tenuous hope dissolve. The mother of his beloved Blanca Flor tensed her limbs against the ropes one last time, then exhaled and shuddered into a rest that resembled death.

"The count has already dictated the manner of this traitoress's execution," Doña Sancha continued. "Her parents named her Little Flame when she came into this world. It is fitting that she should leave it also accompanied by flames."

The cheering began and did not cease. Some of the men of Salas brought a tall, solid plank, likely left over from the construction, which they stood upright, not far enough from the well for Mudarra's taste, and buried partially so it wouldn't collapse if the victim struggled. One of the workers gathered kindling. He set it at the base of the stake while five of the strongest of the men from Neila untied the prisoner and lifted her out of the wagon, her clothing soiled and her hair soaked in drool. The number of men seemed excessive at first, when she flopped about as if she were unconscious, but quickly became necessary when her feet touched the ground and she darted away from them. They caught her before she strode two awkward paces. One man each held her limbs and the last, her head, while a sixth wrapped rope about her neck, wrists, and ankles and attached her stiffly to the stake, her final captor.

The men were already rubbing sticks together, but given the time of year, everything was too green to ever light. One of the housemaids provided a flint, and a knight struck it against his sword, but the spark didn't light the kindling. They passed the flint among the soldiers, and each attempted to create a flame while Doña Lambra watched the proceedings with eyes that reflected undying hope, too choked by the rope to plead for her life. By the time the tenth knight struck, the spark took hold near the prisoner's bare feet. Several of them blew on it and created a tiny flame that leapt from twig to branch, increasing in size.

Some of the cheering turned into an ominous chant. "May she be forever damned!"

Smoke rose away from the kindling and billowed out. Doña Lambra made a strangled cough. "What's the matter? Can't take the heat?" called one of the bystanders, but the lady had gone quiet. She had fainted and now hung slumped and crooked to the side of the stake.

A bright orange flame bloomed at the hem of her dress. A snapping sound and a new, acrid odor told Mudarra that the fire had reached her flesh.

The chanting became louder. "Damned forever! Forever damned!"

The flames charred though the tunic and melted the creamy white skin of her legs, ever hungry for fuel to burn.

Mudarra couldn't witness the gruesome scene any longer. He backed away, stumbling over the feet of people behind him who were too busy chanting to note that they had nearly been knocked over. Outside the tight circle of chanters, the space was wide open, so he strode to the stable and fetched Tranquilo, keeping both their heads down in an attempt to flee the rotten stench. Perhaps that was the odor of a demon burning. He paused, watching the flames leap over the heads of the people in the crowd and climb to the top of the stake, licking and crackling.

"Damned forever! Forever damned!"

Was this Christian charity? Where was their pity? The Jesus he knew from Islamic tradition recommended turning the other cheek. How did this additional wrong change the wrong that had been done to the seven noble knights? He remembered meeting his brothers on the battlefield. If they approved of this burning, they would show themselves somewhere in the crowd.

He circled the mass of people around the stake several times, but no ghosts appeared, even when he asked them to in a voice that could not have been heard above the cursing shouts except by someone from another world. He would have an answer.

He mounted Tranquilo, and no human called to him. He galloped to the church beyond the bridge and no ghost stood in his way. He dismounted and pushed the door open, but there was no one inside the sooty darkness. The priests had probably joined the crowd at the burning.

A candle burned low at the main altar. He crossed the black space to grasp the flickering light and carried it to the altar on the right side, where Santiago Moorslayer presided over Mudarra's brothers and their tutor. He brought the tiny flame as close as he dared to each head in their line along the ledge, expecting movement, or murmuring, or even the regeneration of their bodies and resuscitation of their souls, if their Christian relatives' behavior could possibly have that effect. But as he drew near, his nostrils filled with a sickening smell he had never encountered before, as if meat had gone rancid and someone had sprinkled oriental perfume over it. He held his nose shut and brought the candle as near as he dared. Under inspection, the hair atop each of the heads was matted into brittle masses like birds' nests. Where clear brown eyes should have shined, empty sockets led into infinite darkness. Most of the skin on each face had wasted away, leaving behind unnaturally toothy grins, and beards had fallen into ruin under the chins.

Mudarra wondered when Doña Sancha had last looked upon the remains of her sons. Here was nothing of beauty, nothing for which she needed to claim justice, only decay and oblivion.

He dropped the candle when a rat jumped onto the ledge, knocking over the skull in the place where Mudarra had seen young Gonzalo's head more than a month before. It tottered and fell to the hard floor. Mudarra unsheathed his sword slowly, waiting for the right moment, then slashed at the rat. It ran and leapt off the opposite edge, upsetting the other skulls. Mudarra moved to prevent their fall, but balked at the thought of touching the rot. All seven crashed to the floor, leaving teeth and hair in unworkable knots.

He knew the priests would return and think someone had disrespected the seven brothers and their tutor. But Mudarra didn't think it possible to disrespect people who had died years before, leaving the Earth without making a single mark upon it.

He was still alive. He could still find his purpose.

He walked out of the church. The sunlight was too bright, and Tranquilo appeared almost brown. When Mudarra's eyes adjusted, he mounted, and at the fork in the road, they turned north.

Historical Note

The Story of the Seven Noble Knights Through the Ages

While working toward my Ph.D., I became fascinated with the story of *Los siete infantes de Lara*, a dramatic saga of family allegiance and revenge, which scholars believe may have circulated as an epic poem before medieval historians wrote it down.

None of the poetry of the hypothetical epic has survived. In the thirteenth century, King Alfonso X, *el Sabio*, had his scholars compile a history of Spain from Biblical times to their present day, and they recorded the episode of *Los siete infantes de Lara* in several chapters during the rule of the second Count of Castile, García Fernández, in the late tenth century. Twentieth-century scholars noticed that in several places, the historical text rhymed and presented meter and repetition typical of epic poetry. Some of the stanzas have been reconstructed, but the most complete version of the original story comes to us through Alfonso X's version and later medieval histories.

In all versions, it's a story full of violence and old-fashioned revenge. It hits such a fevered pitch that some scholars believe the story must have originated in the epic tradition of northern Europe, which might have traveled to Spain through thirteenth-century royal marriages. In spite of the differences between this epic and other Spanish stories, *Los siete infantes de Lara* displays a typically Spanish obsession with geography and treats Spanish themes such as *convivencia* (how Christians, Jews, and Muslims lived in the same space together), wars with the Islamic governors of Andalusia, and the supremacy of Castile as a kingdom rather than a county.

Although specific to the exotic world of medieval Spain, I knew the extraordinary events and down-to-earth characters would resonate with today's readers. In drafting the novel, I relied on Alfonso X's prose text and a romanticized rewrite found in the *Chronicle of 1344*.

History and Fiction

Whether the incident in the histories ever took place has always been up for debate. Its provenance from an epic poem doesn't argue for or against its historicity, as traveling minstrels or jongleurs would have been the main source of news at the time, and they could remember the facts more easily when it followed a familiar format and rhymed. Two fantastical elements argue against the historical nature of the tale, but they can also be interpreted as miracles—confirmations of God's glory in everyday life—which medieval people would have taken as factual. I decided to write both of these fantastical elements plausibly because of their importance to the essential magic of this tale.

In the medieval sources, Don Gonzalo goes blind with weeping. Years later, when Mudarra comes to avenge him, his sight is miraculously restored. In the novel, I give Don Gonzalo trauma-induced cataracts and include a scene in which Mudarra's physician extracts the cataracts using techniques still customary in some parts of Africa today.

Don Gonzalo breaks a ring in two as a folkloric means of identifying Mudarra years in the future. In the sources, when they meet again, the ring halves miraculously fuse together. In my version, the characters have the ring reforged.

Fray Justo Pérez de Urbel pinpointed when the events could have happened if they ever did, extrapolating the names of some of the characters from historical documentation such as Latin land grants, and arriving at 990 for the wedding and thrown cucumber. I moved the date back fifteen years to match the estimates given in the thirteenth-century source material. Doing so allowed me to develop the storyline of Mudarra and Count García into a sequel. Almanzor came into power after much maneuvering following Al-Hakam's death in 976. For the sake of continuity over the fifteen years of the story, I have Don Gonzalo find Almanzor already in full control in late 974.

Although there is an important General Ghalib in the history of al-Andalus, my General Ghalib isn't based on his actions. The Spanish poets must have assigned whatever Arabic-sounding names they had at their disposal. In some sources, the other general is called Alicante instead of Viara.

I added many supporting characters to fill out the plot, including long-suffering Justa and faithful Yusuf, who take on first-tier importance. Giving Mudarra a love interest isn't a new idea, but I created Blanca Flor before I realized she had many literary precedents. She is a central factor in developing Mudarra's character beyond the automaton of revenge we find in the historical sources.

The Bloody Cucumber

The strangest passage in this novel deserves special consideration. I recently stumbled across Regulation 30 in a twelfth-century law book:

> Whoever injures someone with an egg, with a *butello*, or with a *cucumere* [two kinds of cucumber], or with any other thing that can dirty him should pay ten *aurei* if the plaintiff can prove it; but if not, he should clear himself with two of four named from his parish and he should be believed. [*The Code of Cuenca*, translated by James F. Powers]

Cuenca is a city in eastern Spain, a significant distance away from the area of Lara. Apparently, cucumbers were threatening enough to merit legal rules on them in the far-flung reaches of medieval Hispanic Christendom.

Aurei were the most valuable coins of the realm, cast in gold and with legislated weights, so ten of them is not an insignificant fine. It would cover the cost of a donkey or a few goats, or in this case, the cost of a new wardrobe. The key here seems to be the dirtiness and the difficulty of getting clothes clean in the twelfth century. The same penalty and means of acquittal are prescribed for anyone who creates a slanderous ballad about someone else. Here the soil falls upon the subject's reputation, and that is even harder to clean than a twelfth-century shirt.

The seriousness of the cucumber crime in the law books could make the uproar in *Seven Noble Knights* seem well earned. But let's compare the ten *aurei* to some other fines for offenses in the same section of *The Code of Cuenca*.

Anyone who breaks someone's arm or leg should pay fifty *aurei*, and if the limb comes all the way off, one hundred. A lost limb is worth ten times a ruined shirt. Acquittal for the limb requires twelve witnesses or trial by combat, a much bigger burden than the two of four witnesses required for cucumber throwing.

Scalping someone's beard will incur a two hundred *aurei* fine, a penalty that could buy five or more horses or a small house. It also costs two hundred *aurei* (and exile) to force a stick into someone else's anus. Loss of beards and violations with foreign objects are exponentially more serious than throwing a cucumber.

In *Seven Noble Knights*, the cucumber incident results in the life-and-death situations that propel the story forward. As we see in the law books, it's an impotent gesture to merit such a response. Perhaps in the tenth century, when *Seven Noble Knights* takes place, it was that much harder to get a shirt clean. Or is there more going on here? I provided character-driven context—lust and revenge—I hope you've enjoyed as a reader.

Historical Context

The following paragraphs give a minimal introduction to the historical events referred to in *Seven Noble Knights*. The curious reader can't go wrong with any of the works listed afterward, especially those by Américo Castro and Joseph F. O'Callaghan.

One of the earliest provinces to join the Roman Empire was the Iberian Peninsula, or Hispania. At the fall of Rome, the Germanic tribe that eventually held sway in Hispania adopted Roman culture as their own. The Visigoths enjoyed success for nearly three hundred years, speaking Latin and contributing to the subtleties of the early Christian Church. One of the Visigoths' deep-seated political flaws was their manner of succession to the throne. Choosing a new ruler when one died often led to civil war, and during the last of these, one of the factions invited the Berbers from across the Strait of Gibraltar to help them in their cause.

Unequalled warriors, the newly Muslim Berbers defeated the last Visigothic king, Rodrigo, in 711, and then took the ripe land for themselves and their Arabic-speaking lords. Within seven years, Hispania was a Muslim outpost for all practical purposes.

The new rulers named the land al-Andalus or Andalusia and established one of the greatest civilizations history has ever known. At its apogee, Andalusia had no competition in luxury and learning. Modern scholars have emphasized the *convivencia* of this place and time, saying that the jewel of culture wouldn't have been possible without collaboration between the Muslim, Christian, and Jewish residents. It's important to remember that for all the cooperation, daily life would have been rife with racial and religious tension as the Christian kingdoms in the north of the peninsula expanded their territory and power at the cost of al-Andalus. The largest groups were made up of Arabs (people from Arabia or modern Syria or Iraq), Berbers, Jews, muladies (Visigoths converted to Islam), mozarabs (Christians in Muslim territory), and Slavic mercenaries or slaves from the Holy Roman Empire.

The Christian kingdoms marked the beginning of the *Reconquista* (Reconquest) in the year 722, when Pelayo won a skirmish against Moorish troops at Covadonga. Pelayo would become a powerful rallying point in future years. At the time of our story, the diminutive start in Covadonga had developed from a unified Asturias into the sizeable and separate kingdoms of León and Navarra, and the France-dependent County of Barcelona.

Castile, where much of *Seven Noble Knights* takes place, was in the tenth century a county on the eastern frontier of León. The quintessential borderland, its name refers to its abundance of castles and fortifications. A nobleman from this territory of uncultured upstarts, Fernán González, took advantage of the instability after the death of King Ramiro II of León in 951 to amass power for his county. Although it wasn't as independent as the historians of the time would have us believe, Castile became the most important county in the Kingdom of León and the count at its head enjoyed a certain level of autonomy. Upon his death, Fernán González passed the government to his son, García Fernández, who is the presiding count in *Seven Noble Knights*. Later, Castile took over as the dominant kingdom in the peninsula and in modern times its culture has became synonymous with Spanish.

Meanwhile, in the Caliphate of Córdoba, Caliph Abderramán III made Andalusia its strongest even while planting the seeds of its destruction. He unified Muslim Spain with military prowess and political savvy his heirs would find impossible to maintain. He also began the construction of Medina Azahara in 936 and transferred the court to the palace city in 945. Al-Hakam succeeded him as caliph in 961. During this time of relative peace, Andalusia reached its highest point of culture, science, and art. Córdoba had such creature comforts as pavement, illumination at night, sewage systems, and a library with as many as 400,000 volumes. Although it's unlikely everyone in the caliphate knew how to read, a high proportion of Cordobese residents would have, giving Ruy Blásquez no doubt in making such an assertion to his brother-in-law in this novel.

Al-Hakam's successor in 976 was technically Hisham II, but through court intrigue and probably a few murders, the vizier, then *hayib* (personal guard or chamberlain), later known as Almanzor took control of the military and government within a few years. Such was the impression he made that the people in the rest of the peninsula referred to him as the caliph. Gonzalo Gustioz and many Christian visitors in the time of Mudarra make this mistake in *Seven Noble Knights*. They couldn't fathom a mere chamberlain as the director of so much force and terror.

In Andalusia: prosperity and political unity. Nonetheless, after the time of *Seven Noble Knights*, upon Almanzor's death, Andalusia quickly dissolved into multiple petty kingdoms at war with each other as well as with the northern kingdoms.

In Christian Spain: a hardscrabble existence and a multitude of governments serving their own purposes. Yet the end of united Andalusia marks the beginning of a centuries-long process of unification of the Christian kingdoms and their eventual consolidation into modern Spain.

This is one reason the story of *Seven Noble Knights* is so compelling: because it takes place during Spain's baptism by fire.

Sources and Further Reading

Álvar, Carlos, and Manuel Álvar, eds. *Épica medieval española*. 2nd ed. Madrid: Ediciones Cátedra, 1997.

Barkai, Ron. "Between East and West: A Jewish Doctor from Spain." In *Intercultural Contacts in the Medieval Mediterranean: Studies in Honour of David Jacoby*, edited by Benjamin Arbel, 49–63. New York: Routledge, 2012.

Castro, Américo. *The Spaniards: An Introduction to Their History*. Translated by Willard F. King and Selma Margaretten. Berkeley: University of California Press, 1971.

The Code of Cuenca: Municipal Law on the Twelfth-Century Castilian Frontier. Translated by James F. Powers. Philadelphia: University of Pennsylvania Press, 2000.

Escolar, Arsenio, and Ignacio Escolar. *La nación inventada. Una historia diferente de Castilla*. Barcelona: Ediciones Península, 2010.

Gerber, Jane. *The Jews of Spain: A History of the Sephardic Experience*. New York: Free Press, 1992.

Lowney, Chris. *A Vanished World: Medieval Spain's Golden Age of Enlightenment*. New York: Free Press, 2005.

Medville, Charles, and Ahmad Ubaydli, eds. *Christians and Moors in Spain*. Vol. 3, *Arabic Sources (711–1501)*. Charles and Warminster: Aris & Phillips Ltd., 1992.

Menocal, Maria Rosa. *The Ornament of the World: How Muslims, Jews, and Christians Created a Culture of Tolerance in Medieval Spain*. Boston: Back Bay Books, 2002.

O'Callaghan, Joseph F. *A History of Medieval Spain*. Ithaca: Cornell University Press, 1975.

Pérez de Urbel, Fray Justo. *El condado de Castilla: Los 300 años en que se hizo Castilla, II*. Madrid: Editorial Siglo Ilustrado (n.d.).

Ruggles, D. Fairchild. *Gardens, Landscape and Vision in the Palaces of Islamic Spain.* University Park: Penn State University Press, 2003.

——. *Islamic Gardens and Landscapes.* Philadelphia: University of Pennsylvania Press, 2007.

Sánchez-Albornoz, Claudio. *Spain, A Historical Enigma.* Translated by Colette Joly Dees and David Sven Reher. Madrid: Fundación Universitaria Española, 1975.

Vaquero, Mercedes. "El episodio del cohombro de los *Siete Infantes de Lara* en el marco de la épica española." In *Actas del VI Congreso Internacional de la Asociación Hispánica de Literatura Medieval (Alcalá de Henares, 12-16 de septiembre de 1995),* coordinated by José Manuel Lucía Mejías, vol. 2, 1543–1554. Alcalá de Henares: Universidad de Alcalá, 1997.

——. *La mujer en la épica castellano-leonesa en su contexto histórico.* México, D.F.: Dirección General de Publicaciones y Fomento Editorial, 2005.

Watt, W. Montgomery. *Historia de la España islámica.* Barcelona: Alianza Editorial, 1997.

Acknowledgments

Thanks to my dissertation advisor, Mercedes Vaquero, who shared with me an essay she'd written about the baffling nature of the bloody cucumber. That misappropriated vegetable led to my reading the medieval histories of the *siete infantes* and being so impressed that I could do no less than write a novel about them.

Thank you to the Low Writers critique group of Tucson, who waded through and enjoyed the epic first draft of this book, even though they "don't normally read historical fiction." The one who stuck with me through it all, cofounder and excellent prosodist Reneé Bibby, is destined to be a more famous writer than me.

Kim Rendfeld, author of *The Cross and the Dragon* and *The Ashes of Heaven's Pillar*, read through the first draft of this book and excised redundancies and historical gaffes too embarrassing to list here. The usefulness of some vital outside critiques of the beginning of the novel was lost on me until she illuminated them. Any problems that remain are my own, but I can never thank her enough for such generosity.

With a gratitude that comes late because it took time to mature, I also give my thanks to the members of the judging panel at the "Literary Idol" session of Grub Street's The Muse & The Marketplace conference in 2014 for the tough love that transformed the beginning of *Seven Noble Knights* from a turnoff into a compelling, publishable Chapter I at long last.

My Mudarra, my hero, is my beloved and loving husband. He may not be an avid reader, but he let me read some ten versions of the first chapter and two drafts of the whole book to him. For this, and for everything else he does, he deserves more than my gratitude.

Reading Group Guide

Author Jessica Knauss is happy to visit your book club in person or via Skype. Please visit her website, www.JessicaKnauss.com, to arrange it.

How did you experience *Seven Noble Knights*? Were you engaged immediately, or did it take you a while to get into it?

Which character did you feel the most empathy towards?

What major emotional response did the story evoke in you?

Did *Seven Noble Knights* take you outside your comfort zone?

Did you like the characters and, if not, was that important?

Were there any characters you loved to hate?

Did any character remind you of someone you know?

Did the main characters change by the end of the book? If so, how?

Why does Doña Lambra take such offense at her wedding, even after the count resolves the issue legally? Are her later actions justified?

Why does Gonzalico lash out at Little Page?

When Don Gonzalo rides to Córdoba, he imagines how the Christians can take over the land he's in, which has been under Muslim control for close to three hundred years. Does he feel at home when he arrives at Medina Azahara? What makes for a good claim to land?

If you were Almanzor, what would you do with Don Gonzalo?

Should Justa have escaped with Adalberto? Does Justa deserve to be happy? What would happiness look like for someone in Justa's position?

What would you have done if you were Mudarra?

Why do the ghosts appear to Mudarra and Doña Sancha?

If you were Doña Sancha, would you have forgiven Ruy Blásquez? Do you agree with her decisions about about her brother's and sister-in-law's fates?

Why do you think Justa and Blanca Flor flee near the end of the novel? What would you have done in their position?

Do you think Blanca Flor will ever see Mudarra again? Would she want to, after what he did to her mother and father?

What do you think the use of multiple points of view contributed to the story? Could the story have been told from a single character's point of view?

How might the events of Part One be different if they had taken place in the twenty-first century? Part Two?

Which location was your favorite? Why?

How did the environment affect the story? Do you think this story could happen anywhere other than medieval Spain?

Was the revenge satisfying? Do you think Doña Sancha and Don Gonzalo got it right, or do you sympathize with Mudarra's confusion?

Do you think the title *Seven Noble Knights* does justice to the novel?

Were you satisfied with the ending? What do you think the future holds for Mudarra, Doña Sancha, Justa, and Blanca Flor?

Did *Seven Noble Knights* leave any questions open-ended that you would like to know the answer to?

In Barbadillo today, there's a statue of Doña Lambra, and the crest of Salas de los Infantes shows Mudarra and Don Gonzalo holding a ring with the seven brothers around the border. Which town's memorial seems most appropriate? If you were the mayor of one of these towns, what kind of memorial would you create for visitors?

Had you read reviews before reading *Seven Noble Knights*? If so, did you agree with the reviewers?

If you could ask the author a question, what would it be?

About the Author

Jessica Knauss grew up in Northern California and lives in Arizona. In between, she's resided in Massachusetts, Oregon, Iowa, Yorkshire (England), Rhode Island, Pennsylvania, Georgia, Illinois, North Carolina, and Granada, Córdoba, Sevilla, and Salamanca, Spain. She's worked as a librarian and a Spanish teacher as well as an editor at small presses. She helped found Loose Leaves Publishing as well as Açedrex Publishing, and now does freelance bilingual editing. No matter where she's been, she's had two abiding loves: books and Spain. They culminated in her PhD in medieval Spanish literature and now, in *Seven Noble Knights*.

Jessica is also the author of the "quirky, intriguing," novella *Tree/House* (2008), "exuberant, never cloying" *Dusk Before Dawn: Poems* (2010), and the contemporary paranormal *Awash in Talent* (Kindle Press, 2016). Many of her contemporary short stories and flash fiction have been published in literary magazines. She collected these short works in *Unpredictable Worlds: Stories* (2015), which has been compared to the works of Bradbury, Kipling, Saki, and O. Henry, and received a Reader's Favorite Five-Star review. Her translation of Lidia Falcón's *Camino sin retorno* was published in 2013 by Loose Leaves Publishing as *No Turning Back*. Back on the medieval side of things, Jessica's 2012 translation of *The Abencerraje* has been adopted as a college textbook, she has adapted stories from the thirteenth-century songbook *Cantigas de Santa María* into short historical fiction, and is working on the thrilling sequel to *Seven Noble Knights*. Visit her website, www.JessicaKnauss.com.

CPSIA information can be obtained
at www.ICGtesting.com
Printed in the USA
FSOW03n1742301116
27927FS